DELANCEY'S WAY

DELANCEY'S WAY

James McCourt

Alfred A. Knopf

New York

2000

THIS IS A BORZOI BOOK
PUBLISHED BY ALFRED A. KNOPF

Grateful acknowledgment is made to the following for permission to reprint
previously published material:

Farrar, Straus and Giroux, LLC: Excerpt from "Hymn to Life" and excerpt from "In
Wiry Winter" from *Collected Poems* by James Schuyler, copyright © 1993 by the Estate
of James Schuyler. Reprinted by permission of Farrar, Straus and Giroux, LLC.

Grove/Atlantic, Inc.: Excerpt from *Imagination Dead Imagine* from *Samuel Beckett:
The Complete Short Prose, 1929–1989,* edited by S. E. Gontarski. Reprinted
by permission of Grove/Atlantic, Inc.

Music Sales Corporation: Excerpt from "Lush Life" by Billy Strayhorn, copyright ©
1949 (copyright renewed) by Music Sales Corporation (ASCAP) and Tempo Music,
Inc. All rights administered by Music Sales Corporation. International copyright
secured. All rights reserved. Reprinted by permission of Music Sales Corporation.

New Directions Publishing Corp.: Excerpt from "Canto LXXIV" by Ezra Pound from
The Cantos of Ezra Pound, copyright © 1948 by Ezra Pound. Reprinted by
permission of New Directions Publishing Corp.

Library of Congress Cataloging-in-Publication Data
McCourt, James.
Delancey's way / James McCourt. — 1st ed.
p.   cm.
ISBN 0-375-40311-6
I. Title
PS3563.C3448D45   2000
813'.54—dc21   98-51915
CIP

To Vincent Virga, a great American

I approached one of those who stood there and asked him the truth concerning all this. So he told me, and made known to me the interpretation of things.

DANIEL 7:16

For though, indeed, to the right-minded that doctrine was true, and of sufficient solace, yet with the perverse the polemic mention of it might but provoke the shallow, though mischievous conceit, that such a doctrine was but tantamount to the one which should affirm that Providence was not now, but was going to be.

HERMAN MELVILLE, *The Confidence Man*

DELANCEY'S WAY

A Debriefing

Contents

DELANCEY'S WAY

One / Aperture

I never went to bed early in my life.
Until a minute ago . . .
You might have known it would all start out that way.

The first sentence I heard in my own head on the Metro-liner to Washington. I'd put down *Democracy* (you know, the novel of Washington by "Anonymous" turned out to be writ-ten—depending on your politics, or your psychic—by either Henry or Clover Adams), gone to the back of the club car and from the window watched the tracks seeming to issue in two steel ribbons from underneath the train, then returned to my seat, a permeable signifier full of metaphoric dread, and suc-cumbed to a little nap, tired of others' voices and of my own plans.

No systematic chronicle, I told myself as I drifted off, but more a rambling disquisition, with copious historical discus-sion and many anecdotes.

I never went to bed early in my life. Until a minute ago. Two lies, a sentence and a phrase, in the forced conjunction (or dual emphasis) of which there arises a tensile ambiguity—between the stronger and the weaker force—that sparks nar-rative. Always a forced conjunction, a duality, since what is a true sequence (this/that) if not an uninterrupted flow of conscious-radical-unconscious ideation-pulsation, lasting from the moment of birth until the moment of insanity and/or death? Nothing.

Rearranging narrative, like dealing cards or holding on to a bunch of the dialogue balloons O'Maurigan and Patsy Southgate had said held the story's hot air (back then / back there, before the unspooling tracks, in the darkened offices of the *East Hampton Star* on the Sunday afternoon in early September when I'd decided to accept the assignment to go to Washington and report on the crucial environmental legislative battles in the 104th Congress), all of which—balloons—when pinpricked, would burst like Bazooka bubble gum, leaving a free mind (if maybe a funny-looking, Bazooka-bubble-gum-coated face . . . but then, why not?).

Until a minute ago. It's supposed to make you *nervous.* The climax of *Double Indemnity.* Who can forget Stanwyck's shattering intonation . . . *"until a minute ago"*? Enacting one of two things, maybe both: a sudden awakening and determination to say at least one true thing before dying—the wicked woman's last-minute conversion, the perfect act of contrition that would save her from the maw of hell by the skin of her teeth; and/or a born hellion's last desperate (and, as it turns out, useless) ploy.

(The narrative shuttle: it jerks back and forth, until it winds down, and then it winds up again and unwinds in crazy spools of dream life, as at the back of the train clacking along to Washington—me out on the imaginary observation platform asking myself: Will my story wind up like Fred MacMurray's, scraping its guts up off the floor and pouring them into the ear of the Dictaphone, while the older man who loves me—and still smokes cigars—waits to deliver the tag line?

It didn't: it ended up less than a year later back in the offices of the *East Hampton Star,* again on a sunny Sunday, with the shades drawn, at the debriefing that even as I speak you are reading. This is called interactive—the Vice President is all for it.)

"Every education is a kind of inward journey," he (the Vice President) had written in *Earth in the Balance*. "My study of the global environment has required a searching re-examination of the ways in which political motives and government policies have helped to create the crisis and now frustrate the solutions we need."

(That I should have wanted to listen to him any further at all struck me as entirely improbable, but that in itself might well have been the reason.)

So, to Washington—and to politics. ("Show business for ugly people," the late-night-television clown had called it. Did he ever so much as *glance* at the Vice President?) Politics done with smoke and mirrors. Smoky backrooms in which the President—POTUS—may never have inhaled—as the trick he's mastered of holding his breath until *others* turn blue seems to have ensured his survival.

And the mirrors? Something like: Hamlet tells the Player King to hold the mirror up to nature, but the Player King remembers what Jackson Pollock snapped when similarly advised: "I *am* nature." POTUS has done the same, saying, "Think I'll just hold the mirror up to me, and you can look over my shoulder."

"It seems to me" (Patsy S.) "you want to get as close as you can to the feeling the motion picture creates—not that a story is about to be told, but that it has been told already—that the readers have stumbled into a story they well know."

O'Maurigan said, "All right then, let's start with the telephone call."

September 1995, later that first Sunday afternoon. I was alone in Sagaponack. Phil, packing his circa-1957 Ceccone evening wear, had gone off a week earlier with Concha, the sister, in a black limo to the airport—and from there to Sicily to investigate the possibility of opening the old homestead as a hotel. (I wanted Phil to sell out to her: we have more than enough, and Concha has always hated me—wants to get Phil to go back to the old country for good.) I was about to turn the house over for the duration of my Washington stay to Concha's grandson Vinny (estranged from his father, Phil's nephew, a jerk, who also hates me, the rich uncle's faggot enchanter) and Vinny's boyfriend, Matt.

I'd started writing Phil once a day, getting as many responses, which could be another book, besides the one in progress I was amazed he wrote every day. I love him more than I can say, as Judy sang.

He wrote, for example, of the baroness Teresa Cordopatri dei Capece, in Calabria, whose brother was blown away for refusing to sell the last of their olive groves, and who is now a crusader. The Mafia in Sicily is more interested in tourism, according to Concha, who is a realist, I give her that. Nevertheless I worried; I said, "Why don't we go out and get you a cellular phone and I can call you once a day and tell you what's going on?"

Phil said, "That's crazy." I said, "It's what everybody's doing now." He said, "In the first place I'll be talking Sicilian all day long, which puts me in what the kids today call 'a different head.'" I said, "The day the kids who said that said it in is not today, it was the sixties. Today those kids have kids: *they* all use the cellular."

He said, "Look, Odette and the Mick will be with you, and this way I'll be sure everything's OK." I said, "He's an O', not a Mc." He said, "To me they're all micks; you know what I mean."

(Well, there's the feeling of manly freedom-in-action; then there's the feeling you're being looked after. I prefer it.)

Back to the telephone—me picking it up.

"Delancey, darling! A voice from out of the past."

"*Out of the Past* is a movie," I remarked.

"Would you ever guess who?"

(From out of the storied past.) "I don't have to; there's only one voice—"

"Anastasia."

"I was coming to that part."

The voice of Anastasia Harrington, beautiful eighties New York party girl (I'd first encountered walking stark naked out of the surf at Sagaponack one fabulous summer afternoon looking like a dark-auburn version of the Botticelli Venus-on-the-half-shell) whose fortunes, due to a truly stunning talent for rubbing up against the nether parts of Gotham's markdown-Eurovagrant glitterati, had often turned on a dime.

Exiled, it was said, after a spat with Brooke Astor over the financing of nothing less than her wedding . . . *not* of course to a Eurorat, but to Max Harrington (of the *copper* Harringtons, as Truman C. would have put it had he lived to bark out loud over it). Max was the kind of Harrington Gertrude Slescynski had in mind when she took the name (and Anastasia was a girl who wouldn't be caught dead in anything by Clovis Ruffin, and *into money:* "Money isn't everything—it just *goes* with everything!") and had been described as "a strange amalgam of Armand Hammer, George Soros, and Steve Forbes." He was—importantly, suddenly to somebody in my new role—a supporter of the Ethics and Public Policy Center, a conservative think tank. I would have to be entertained by him while opposing him, for the Harrington family had branched out from copper into leaching gold, polluting Western rivers with cyanide, and hoarding the helium reserves, whatever they were. (Pay attention, they become significant.) How handy, in the nicest possible way, to have been a friend of his wife's—on the Christmas card list, all that.

Anastasia Harrington, Washington wife, had herself taken to the television airwaves, while hubby had stayed closeted (and that word, in another connection, had been circulating about him for years too, more frenetically since his marriage). I found her as camp as Hedda Lettuce—that big-boned woman in the land of New York make-believe—but others she made nervous. These were they with some experience of the instinctual internal combustion of her impressively primed hereditary Greek revenge engine, which, consequence of intensely vindictive file-keeping startling even to Gotham touts—though not to those who recalled her late-sixties incarnation as a fascist kitten's paw in her native Athens—had already earned her the nickname Stasi. (They didn't like her any better on television than in life.)

"A voice," the voice continued, "from out of the past, but not a voice from the dead, thank God."

"Good, I don't think I could handle one of those just at the moment."

"This movie—there's a woman in it, of course, who dies."

"In *Out of the Past* they all die."

"Darling, I woke you. You went to bed early."

"I never went to bed early in my life."

"Until a minute ago—remember that? So, you are coming down to lobby? You are going to save the wetlands and your—what's he called?"

"The piping plover."

"Ah, yes. I was quite put out at first, I confess it, to learn I could no longer get plovers' eggs, except on the black market."

"The *East Hampton Star* is sending me—to report on the defense of the Wetlands Act, and the environmental lobby."

"I'm not surprised at all. What was that gay place you took me dancing—when all the boys went gaga over my jewels, and refused to believe they were real? And you said, 'With Bam-Bam *both* the jewels and the orgasms are real?' It was called the Swamp, no?"

"You have a good memory; that was a long time ago."

"Yes it was—before I was even a wife. And now you must let that very fact assist you as you once assisted me."

(I was interested. Max's senator, the only independent in the Senate, was a rabid western wildlife conservationist, champion of Indian rights and advocate of DOE reparations for the Wind River Shoshone.)

"You have Indians near you, too, do you not?"

"The Shinnecock."

"I remember them: *divine* name."

(As I said to O'Maurigan, the head was in the hand.)

"Never mind," he'd counseled. "On the plus side, the neo-Georgian Waddy Wood Harrington pile in Kalorama is worth a detour if not the trip itself, and you could hardly find a longer, more operative D.C. pedigree these days. The Harringtons have been Washingtonian presences for over a century. And Max put a lot of the family's resources into the helium reserves and Bahamanian dollar Laundromats."

In that Harrington D.C., Anastasia had become a favorite subject for the newspaper once owned by the daughter of her new husband's grandfather's poker partner—who herself used to own, and wear, the Hope Diamond—in the style pages of which references abounded to her decked out in jewelry by Ann Hand: things like the American eagle in diamonds clutching in its talon a pearl.

Which had made me laugh out loud alone. In my time with her in New York, she'd tended to trample that fine line between sizzling allure and good-heavens-where-is-the-rest-of-your-dress? Old Money was particularly severe with her. Let one ogress's summation suffice: "Rubens *indeed*! My dear, I don't care where she went to school, or who dresses her—stripped of those silks, she is pure Eilshemius on the hoof. And that entourage of hers! I can never *quite* understand *how* such people imagine that sexual intercourse in the balcony at Studio 54 can *possibly* be grounds for a social introduction at the *Waltzers*!"

It was the jewelry that did it. Making a shrewd wear-for-promo deal, she'd festooned herself with the Byzantine parure of a Florentine known as Adriana—to whom Vana Sprezza, tempestuous diva and controversial wife of Italy's condom kingpin (pay attention again: she's on her way into the story), also gave her custom—and so was a good dress match for Max, in his dark Savile Row suits, Hermès ties, and gold Audemars Piguet watch.

("From Ayn Rand to Ann Hand," Odette quipped.)

"We have nothing to do with the House, of course," Bam-Bam was assuring me. "Max can't even talk about Gingrich without comparing him—unfavorably—with Benny Hill. Although we agree with him when he tells the poor that they must learn new habits, that the habit of being poor no longer works. But I will introduce you to our senator—we call him Senator Shoshone, but of course you know his real name is Galt."

(I'd heard the legend. Elected as an independent from a western state to the House in '58 entirely on the strength of his name: identical to that of the hero of Ayn Rand's *Atlas Shrugged*, John Galt. Wooed by Democrats, he entered the Senate in '60 on New Frontier rhetoric, and progressed therein until edged out by Sam Nunn for majority whip, which turned him into a bazooka Reaganite. Hating Bush—as did Reagan—he went Clinton, but might switch to Dole. Keen on creating self-sufficient Indian communities by means other than gambling franchises.)

"And also to the Vice President, who is the president of the Senate, you know."

(I did.)

"And passionate."

"Don't you mean *com*passionate?"

"That too, of course—although he is perhaps not quite so compassionate as we are planning on becoming after the socialist welfare state is dismantled in this Congress. Tough love, you know."

"Are you offering trial subscriptions to *Policy Review*?"

"Oh, darling, you and I are *not* going to argue politics. But besides being terribly handsome and personable—the Vice President, I mean—*and*—well, he *is* passionate about the environment. You knew he was—you must. You would, no?"

(I would; I did.) "What about the President?"

"POTUS? Oh, darling, he is *ridiculous.*"

(I said to myself, This woman is nervous.)

"Anyway, we are becoming more and more disenchanted with the government, and more interested in the bubble-up theory and in the National Commission for Philanthropy and Civic Renewal."

"Does that mean less jewelry at parties?"

"No, darling—*different* jewelry. Are you bringing the cat with you?"

"I am, although Sylvester's environmental concerns are distinctly Republican."

"Well, darling, you will be in the middle of a revolution, you know. The Republican revolution. I must ring off now, darling. Till soon!"

"A revolution!" Odette snorted. "I hardly think so. Not with that little twerp from Georgia in charge. Hardly a Danton, Marat, or Robespierre—except the Robespierre who was on *Baby Snooks.* And no guillotine—not that one wants one; one doesn't. All one wants—metaphorically speaking—is a nice Italian stiletto, to serve, as it were, as a paper knife for your book."

"My book" (I sighed), "do you envision a nonfiction roman à clef?, or something like what O'Maurigan has given me to read on the train?"

"As I recall" (Odette), "you were always losing your keys—in the old days that was."

(That *were,* I thought.)

"There's a movie house," O'Maurigan mused, "called the Key—in Georgetown."

"I see," Patsy S. declared, "an article more along the lines of a nonfiction roman à keyhole."

I liked it—and asked her what she had in mind.

"Well, a roman à clef pretends to show the whole picture of figment-people—*whereas* the roman à keyhole, nonfiction variety, lets you picture the nonfictional flashing verifiable credentials while proceeding along the very same skid-risk course: lets you frame it all more from the point of view of the peeping servants, crouched at the keyhole watching characters in the library move to and fro—left to right, right to left. We did a lot of that as children."

(Patsy's father had been chief of protocol at the Roosevelt White House—which made it like knowing somebody who'd been at Versailles, talking of the time before guillotines and terrible *little* people in Washington.)

"In the moments in which the characters stand still talking," she offered, "the resultant configuration leads to greater depth of focus. The trouble with most young writers these days is they're too timid to thrust themselves into the world, pitching instead wan trips through their own tetchy-tortured egos. Not true of you."

(Because unlike most young writers, I'm not young.)

"Don't," O'Maurigan advised me, "let focus groups, smart-bomb surveys, or wedge issues stop you either. That you are the intimate of the fabulous cannot be held against you if you never substitute milieu for matter. Don't try to write a Washington book. *Democracy* is one thing, but today's Washington book—whether the crap tell-alls or the crap fictions that garner proxy votes in off-years—are no more contributions to literature than diet books, self-help books, or those tetchy memoirs of Patsy's."

"*I* never wrote tetchy memoirs!" Patsy gibed.

"You *know* what I mean," O'Maurigan rejoined.

"Why not," Odette challenged, "a *Delancey Goes to Washington*?"

"I'm not," I protested, "that asshole in the Capra movie!"

"No," the O' agreed, "I don't see you walking in a stupefied access of patriotic elation out of Union Station right onto a bus, or socking it in the jaw to every reporter in D.C. who tries to make a fool of you—but wrath comes into it. Anger is not always ignoble. It inspired the oldest epic in the canon, the *Iliad*."

"I dislike the *Iliad*," I protested.

"I know, so did Valéry. And of course the Greeks of the *Iliad* heard commanding voices, while those of the *Odyssey* made their own plans. But Achilles' fury makes him appear larger than life, and comes close to being a prophetic attribute."

"But," I objected, "by the time I'm finished, I'll only be retailing the stories behind yesterday's headlines."

"It seems people find them a relief; no one knows exactly why. You will," O'Maurigan declared, "take notes in Washington, imbedding motive taggants in situational raw material."

"Notes on the way politicians take us for a ride?"

"Oh, I never minded that," Patsy chimed in. "The more they did it, the more they at least seemed to be *driving*, rather than *driven*—the Incumbent's big problem. He may *occasionally* seem to be in the driver's seat, but the situation turns out to be bumper cars, or one of those driving games they had before computers. You sat at the wheel and nothing but zany obstacles were flung at you and you had all you could do to keep your eye on the road divider. What would Proust," she added, "have done with D.C., one wonders?"

"Oddly," O'Maurigan remarked, "there is a Swann Street in Northwest—it lies between S and T."

"Actually," Odette declared with finality, "the whole problem of politics is an exaggerated version of the problem of show business."

"For ugly people?" I put in.

"For *everyone*," Odette declared gravely. "And yet it may be harder on the ugly. Nothing is more universal than love and

the submission of another's will—over which show business
and politics are in relentless and unceasing competition."

"I never minded," Patsy continued, "them taking us for
long rides, not even in the days when the road was pretty
evenly divided between scenery and billboards. But now there's
something else going on. They've taken the billboards away."

"There are fewer and fewer, certainly," O'Maurigan
agreed, "and none of the anecdotal resonance of yesteryear.
And somewhere over there *behind* the utility roads and the rest
stops are the hills and dales—but nearly all you see are the
malls and the marts, the filling stations and the generic rest
areas of politics. No wonder people have taken to flying over
the issues, such as they are.

"No," he continued, returning his gaze to me, "you are
not like the moron in *Mr. Smith Goes to Washington*, but you are
something like the heroine of *Democracy*. She is a Magdalen—
Maud to her sister—who never goes to church, although she's
given to reading things like the last symposium on the sympa-
thies of Eternal Punishment."

"What I remember about that character," Patsy offered,
"is that she arrives in D.C. unable, in Philadelphia, Boston, or
New York, she avows, to have found anything bigger than six
inches."

"*What?*"

"Something sizable—casting a long shadow."

"She's also," O'Maurigan put in, "a nice woman who visits
prisons and workhouses, without a *thought* of hosing any of the
inmates down and taking them home."

"That's me?"

"It is not unlike your AIDS work—something you have in
common with Anastasia, although her style is not yours."

"I find it hard," Odette interrupted, "to believe she—"

"It's true," O'Maurigan sighed. "She glides through the
AIDS wards and the rehab centers of Washington in the manner perfected by her new role model, the Princess of Wales,

hoping to touch and cure—not as the English kings did scrofula, by the actual laying-on of gloved hands, but by a kind of radiant *social influence*."

"Any Washington book," Odette suddenly declared, "must wrestle with the big issues: passion, power, love, death, et cetera."

"Wrestle?" I protested.

"Well, *hand*-wrestle, anyway—and so far as psychology is concerned, *esprit de finesse* rather than *esprit de système*. It must make—and be—its own set of plans. Something, I've just realized, as we sit here, I must set about doing myself."

(Plotline.)

"Rather than only listen to voices," Patsy-the-newspaper-woman advised, "just plug *in* to the first thing you hear—you are yourself the blank page—and understand that Washington is for people who look upon life as a rumor."

Thus was the notion formed, there in the darkened offices of the *East Hampton Star*, that I was going to D.C. to fight the Congress that wanted to gut the Endangered Species Act, destroy government, *and* take all poor children and put them into orphanages (like they did me).

"Your perspective will be unique," Patsy declared.

"Yes," O'Maurigan declared. "Rather like that production of *The Flying Dutchman* presented as the Steersman's dream."

(To me it seemed more likely to turn into a production of *Aida* in which the whole show—"Guerra" chorus, temple boudoir, triumphal, Nile, judgment, and tomb scenes—was imagined in response to il Messaggero coming in and announcing the battle successes of the Ethiopians over the Egyptians, and all as if followed at a score desk: seeing the performers only when they came to the apron and stood wailing over the prompter's box.)

"When I told Phil I might turn out to be the Ernie Pyle of the congressional budget wars, he said, 'That's not so good; Ernie Pyle never came back.'"

"You will come back," O'Maurigan insisted, "in your chariot of Hermes, and with your calendar full of incident: your revolutionary calendar, organized around certain *concepts*."

"Concepts?"

"Yes. Let us begin with Aperture—and proceed until that telling moment when the hourglass is turned, dexterously upside down as in jiujitsu. The odd thing is that in the second telling the grains of sand slip through at something like twice the speed—rather like the way they do in the second half of life itself."

"Ain't it the truth," Patsy chipped in, as the sun passed over the roof and the shadows faded on the window shades and on the calendar on the wall.

So I was off, in Aperture, on my Chariot of Hermes, the Metroliner. On it I met no stranger, and I took Sylvester along—as in *Dick Whittington and His Cat*. ("Dick Whittington" could almost be the generic WASP name of every undergraduate—they were all Dicks to me—I used to seduce out of his brogues at the Astor Bar, and sometimes kept on calling up long after . . . their lusts eroding year after year with meaningless jobs and four-martini lunches. Thoroughbreds in pointless races: as surely the performing chattel of their overseers in advertising and public relations as Nashua was of Billy Woodward or in the boys of the New York City Ballet—both the dancers and the touts—were of Lincoln Kirstein. Lots of them—the undergrads, not the balletomanes—went into politics.)

The Metroliner. Trains. I never had a set, but trains were a part of my life; the trains I took—the IRT, BMT, and IND, then the New York Central to Lincoln Hall, then the LIRR, and finally smart European expresses. I never had toy trains, but I had train dreams: the Train to Hell with the boys from Lincoln Hall, dreams of the trains to and from Auschwitz after viewing *Shoah*, dreams of troop trains loaded with American soldiers going to Bosnia by way of Prague and Hungary (all Mawrdew Czgowchwz territory from a half-century ago and more) mixed with World War II screen dreams of GIs handing out chocolate to urchins in bombed-out places—urchins who would grow up to be major movie stars. Europe wasn't supposed to be like that anymore . . . then Bosnia.

The exurban landscape I was passing by—having cleared Newark—was between Linden and Rahway, a vast wasteland my friend Richard Rouilard, a castaway like me, had been adopted into and brought up in, before escaping to the glamour worlds of New York, Houston, San Francisco, and Los Angeles (where he'd spent the early nineties transforming the *Advocate* from a gay dish rag to an instrument of real political clout on the national scene, and where he was now getting ready to die after "just one more fucking Oscar ceremony").

Newark, Philadelphia, Wilmington, and Baltimore: seen across the marshlands and rivers of the Eastern Seaboard we were trying to save from the developers. (Did I care as much about the Public Rangelands Management Act? All I could think of in terms of that landscape was Richard Locke and the ranger having sex in a canyon in Joe Gage's *El Paso Wrecking Corp.*: as presumably Billy the Kid, Butch Cassidy, and Sundance, all known fag sociopaths who made Black Canyon, New Mexico, their open-air fuckpit a century ago.)

Newark meant the Mosque Theater; Philadelphia, besides *Philadelphia*, meant Tuesday-night performances there with the old Metropolitan Opera Company; Wilmington meant one family and its chemicals; Baltimore meant the catechism, Rosa Ponselle, Billie Holiday, the fabulous John Waters, and our own Hildegarde Dorsay, Black Pearl of the Chesapeake, long gone home to God and Lady Day.

I was reading Daniel Hall. "Over the past twenty years or so, there has been a catastrophic decline in American songbird populations due to environmental degradation, here and in their wintering grounds in Central and South America. I cannot explain, or even imagine, why this disaster goes virtually unremarked."

It was all that (and the Vice President's *Earth in the Balance*) that had made me want to go to Washington. Now, looking out the train window on a gray, overcast fall day, it came to me that Washington, like Venice, had been built on a swamp and was renowned for intrigue. (Not to say for women in red high-heeled shoes; but before long—I'll get to it—it came to exactly that.)

I remembered my paranoid reaction on the LIRR one drunken night—of crashing into the wall at Penn Station . . . and that there was no wall at Penn Station—but there was a wall at Union Station, and in January of the year after I first went down there—on the train—a train crashed through to the concourse.

Also before I got there, they had already begun to talk in D.C. of the government and train wreck. If government is any kind of train, I asked myself, how much sway does the fact of the absolute control of the engineer, the conductor, the redcaps, and the food-car person actually have over one's mental life or its landscape?

I put down Daniel Hall and picked up *Democracy*, remembering the earlier conversation at the *Star*.

"*Democracy*" (Patsy S.). "A fiction written by a notorious party animal: she did it in the wee hours, after those fêtes on Lafayette Square." (In the bygone fifties locus of the biggest outdoor nocturnal gay fuckpit in the U.S., in the very shadow of the Eisenhower White House. Which made me remember I was en route to what Odette called the Hallucination's Capital.)

"You'll enjoy it" (O'M). "One of the exemplary characters is called Gore—high-minded, if a little dull."

I looked at my image in the window again. I had never had a problem conceiving of myself as in a movie. But suddenly came this deconstructionist vogue for the comic book, and I was more and more experiencing stop-frame and panel memory rather than flow-through.

I plowed into *Democracy*. I guess I'd thought Patsy had been kidding about Maud and the six inches. (And as for Maud, well, the name Maud was for our generation an automatic giggle, because of Bea Lillie's "'Maud, Maud,' they said to me, 'you're rotten to the core,' and I, of course, agreed.") Then I got to the point where, apropos improving youth, this Maud asks, "Do you want me to go out into the streets and waylay boys?" I thought, I might like you.

She calls herself a woman possessed of the mind of a passenger on an ocean liner (Leo Lerman always said Manhattan was like a great ocean liner) "whose mind will not give him rest until he has been to the engine room and talked with the engineer." Who "wanted to see with her own eyes the action of primary forces; to touch with her own hand the massive machinery of society; to measure with her own mind the capacity of the motive power."

Well, bent I may have been, but never yet "bent upon getting to the heart of the great American mystery of democracy and government." (Maybe because I was born—or dropped—*in* the engine room, so to speak.) Nevertheless I was held—rolling downhill through Delaware toward the Chesapeake—by a passage which stated, "Society in America means all the honest, kindly, pleasant-voiced women, all the good, brave, unassuming men, between the Atlantic and the Pacific. Each of these has a free pass in every city and village, *good for this generation only*, and it depends on each to make use of this pass or not as it may happen to suit his or her fancy. To this rule there are *no* exceptions."

Uh-oh, I thought, I've *gone past my time*. This is not my generation: POTUS is younger than I am. (Bea Lillie would not charm him.) I should've stayed in Sagaponack and had

Vinny and Matt in for company, or just been content to play solitaire on the computer until Phil got back, and maybe read *A Man Without Qualities*.

Instead I was between Wilmington and Baltimore—just beyond Elkton, Maryland—on the Metroliner to Washington, D.C., reading *Democracy*. Keeping at it, past Baltimore (wondering who had climbed the trestle to write "Eat Shit and Die" on the wall), BWI, and New Carrollton, nearly finished by the time we pulled into Union Station, I must say it fairly bored the ass off me (I remembered *Advise and Consent* as riveting by comparison) and was I surprised to hear it so often referred to in the coming weeks as something one advertised to newcomers as a must-read for understanding—but then there *is* no understanding Washington; Washington is not *about* the faculty of understanding. I'll let O'Maurigan explain.

"It's all in Dilthey. *Verstehen* and *Bedeutung* are linked concepts. *Verstehen* is what we mean by understanding and *Bedeutung* does for meaning. Together they form a kind of tonic-dominant configuration of particular formal consequence. *Verstehen* holds we are given a cognitive purchase on the world, *Bedeutung* that we can learn to run it—*all* that Washington is about, except that Washington is finally about nothing but *Washington*, as Hollywood is about nothing but Hollywood. The rest of the country—the rest of the world (State Department or no)—can go fuck itself."

But read on anyway, OK?

I did enjoy one scene toward the end of *Democracy:* Europeans at a ball. Strange, because although I couldn't call *this* account a novel (in fact it occurs to me that the imagination in it, rather than stretching, *contracts*, as if held in the vise of the minutes from the *Congressional Record*), it too climaxes at a ball.

Time and again I put *Democracy* down and caught my reflection and remembered the first phrase of instruction at the reform school: *custos oculorum*, custody of the eyes.

Eyes of course were the high windows of the soul. And I remembered thinking, They have all of me in custody, and they want me to follow suit and put my eyes under arrest? They can go fuck themselves. Windows. When I began going to committee meetings and trying to collar staffers and congressmen, I would be told they would get back to me when they could find "a window of time."

Eyes . . . windows . . . train windows with ghosts (as it grew darker). With orphans looking in and with things going on in them people see from the street. The windows at Lincoln Hall: a saga.

But could I write? In high school, in addition to my expertise at mathematics (a natural bookie's kid, they used to say on the Lower East Side), I took up English, became "well spoken," and won a prize for an essay on the Constitution and the Bill of Rights (a map of the world, thick, flat, two-sided, Eastern Hemisphere on one side, Western on the other, with a central window where the date changed by turning the pole back so that a different hemisphere would appear each day). I was sent down from Lincoln Hall for a short "retreat" at the Christian Brothers novitiate in the nation's capital. Harry Truman was President. Arthur Vandenberg led the Senate. *Call Me Madam* was on Broadway. The McCarthy scare hadn't yet happened, and I was all caught up in the reading of Kenneth Roberts's Revolutionary War novels and Chuck White comics (of which an *undercurrent* study ought to be done now that comics are in such high vogue) and madly ambitious to make an impression: maybe become a Senate page.

Fade out/fade in. Back for the spring term all full of the state of the nation, dreaming I already dwelled in marble halls and rode the gilded elevators of the Senate, entrusted with handwritten peer communication, dropping off bills, reports, and legislation . . . like that, while in waking life preparing for Confirmation by no less than prelate, author (of *The Foundling*, published by his buddy Bennett Cerf at Random House), and even-then-notorious pedophile Francis Cardinal Spellman himself, and making more progress in math—calculus, in a class of one—I actually one day overheard myself being talked about by two of the monks.

"Some of these kids think they want to run away and join the circus; some think they can go over the wall right into the mob; this one thinks he wants to go to Washington." "Not so very different, is it?" "No, but it's the mob's loss—he's a cute little Irish redhead, like Owney Madden."

I was shocked. (I should also mention I hadn't yet had an orgasm.) And so for the first time I thought of the Big Top and the dome of the Capitol in the same way. (Odette said later, "Yes, and now we see Columbia as Lola Montez, on display in the menagerie on the Midway." O'Maurigan said, "You weren't Owney Madden; you were a Ganymede, carried away by the American eagle." "I never heard that, not there." "No, it's not the kind of thing the Christian Brothers would say. It's the kind of thing the Jesuits would have said." "To have their way with me, you mean." "In a way yes, but that wouldn't have meant at that time exactly what you mean now." "Spoken like a Jesuit," Odette remarked.)

Apropos D.C., the Religion monk let me know the government was like the Trinity (it comes up a lot in anything written by a Catholic) complete with the Second Person (Congress) partaking in the hypostatic union between the godlike Senate and the all-too-human House. The Supreme Court was the Holy Ghost (and like the dove, all white). The problem came with me imagining God the Father not in a white beard, but in the funny little hat Harry Truman wore on his morning constitutional (not to mention what to make of Bess and Margaret). But as I was needy, I went along with the analogy—and when Harry Truman gave the televised tour of the refurbished White House and we were shown the kinescope of it at assembly, I acted as if I knew the place as well as Lincoln Hall itself.

My fall from grace and the McCarthy commie/fag witch hunt occurred nearly simultaneously. It happened with the speed of summer lightning—only in spring. His name was (I swear to God) Amerigo Vespucci—called Rick—but in bed I called him America, sang "America, I Love You" for him alone, and when I reached "and there's a hundred million others like me" felt the true rage of—as I later heard Mawrdew Czgow-chwz as Amneris sing it—"atroce gelosia."

Anyway, one of the other "good boys" in Confirmation class (a dismal little nellie fag, a captain in the Legion of Mary: I'm sorry, but you couldn't make any of this up) uncovered evidence of an "affair" (a merrily uninhibited pornographic version of Chuck White: my first literary effort) and blackmailed Rick into confessing. He meant in the sacramental sense—to save his soul for Mary—but the poor little wop, conditioned by the down-on-your-knees-and-kiss-my-pinkie-ring discipline of Cosa Nostra, went all the way, throwing himself out loud on the mercy of *them*.

You want to talk about the end? And no slow curtain—the asbestos came down with a very nearly decapitating thud. All talk of my going back to D.C. stopped, and I began to hear instead that *I* was DC, as in not AC. Older boys trashed my locker—ripping the Washington pictures and pennants to shreds and writing "queer" in lipstick on the inside door. (Where did they get the lipstick, from the town whore? I never saw any on the school nurse.)

I got very sick—actually developed the symptoms of polio, which scared the shit out of everybody—was sent to St. Vincent's in New York, and kept in isolation, in the dark, for a month. (St. Augustine says, "All diseases of Christians are to be ascribed to demons.") Then, back in Lincoln Hall, quarantined in the infirmary, I completely fell apart. I got better in Holy Week, in time for Tenebrae, which had always been my favorite devotion, but this time I went through it with a stony heart. I also realized with absolute conviction and for all time that to enjoy being famous is utterly dim-witted. The only thing fame is really about is—well, when they want to smooth it over they call it "emulation." Hah. Anyone who knows the least thing about human nature knows that what they call emulation is only the desire to overtake, kill, and replace the object. There may be many reasons for wanting to do so, and much to be gained from the position, but to actually *enjoy* finally being in the *exposed* position oneself is simply dim-witted.

The cardinal came, but I was not confirmed: further preparation was deemed indicated before I would become (in the Tennessee Williams phrase I came to adopt later by way not of changing my nature, but of assuming it) firm and sufficient.

("You had a narrow escape, dear," Odette said the first time I told her the story. "But *not* being slapped by that odious fairy was the greatest confirmation of all, and is more than likely the reason for your extraordinary grace.")

I became the perennially *guilty party*—two words that have reverberated down the corridors of my life. (I mean, on the evidence, and in spite of the recent vogue of AIDS compassion, what do *they know* we were up to all those years, if not a *guilty party?*)

From Lincoln Hall I was sent to public school in Far Rockaway—just long enough to make an impression—and from there to the projects in Long Island City, a fascinating chapter. Another time.

Then came *The Day the Earth Stood Still:* the benevolent space alien and the adolescent D.C. boy who together attempt to save the world, and then *This Island Earth.* Then, in the late fifties, after Gore Vidal's *Visit to a Small Planet* (I remember the cat), D.C. faded away. I went down for the March in '63, but that was like going on a picnic. (You know that joke? It's a favorite of Phil's—and Vana Sprezza's too. Bold girl goes into the drugstore and says she wants to buy some condoms. "Small, medium, or large?" the clerk asks. "Mix 'em up, I'm goin' on a picnic.")

I'd reached the point in *Democracy* where the President and his wife (the Rutherford B. Hayeses) are raked over the coals as a pair of yokels from up Shit's Creek at the head of what was supposed to be a Great Republic. Sounded familiar. I tried to fix what I did think of the Clintons, going back to '92 and the conversations of that summer, when he stormed the Cuomo citadel and hit the tabloids as the Luv Guv.

One table-talk scene from the Sagaponack file:

O'MAURIGAN (to Odette): You observe he wore overalls at home in Shit's Creek—

"Hot Springs. I did. When others were wearing dunga-rees."

"And tell me this. Do you suspect him of having had in—"

"Hot Springs—"

"Hot Springs—homosexual experience?"

"I suspect him, alas, of not having had sufficiently exten-sive same."

"For his own good."

"Yes, dear, that too. You know, I've always maintained—in fact you could fairly accuse me of making it my motto: 'A good laundry does not starch a handkerchief.' That *said*, however, I must say I like his voice. If you lay FDR's faintly operatic deliv-ery on top of Harry Truman's twang you get something like it. It particularly appeals to rented strangers."

"Rented strangers?"

"Political consultants, dear."

"My first two Presidents," I offered, "were Roosevelt and Truman."

"Caesar, Pompey," Phil interjected, "what difference? They're all crooks. You might just as well just vote for the numbers."

"That *is* Delancey's method," somebody jibed. "Very big on number theory."

"Hot Springs," O'Maurigan announced, "is where Owney

Madden finally ended up. They gave it to him to run; it was—all things considered—thought to be a booby prize."

"They all say," Odette pressed on, "admirers and detractors alike, that Clinton is a virtuoso politician, to which one can only add that if politics is an art, it aspires to the condition of a strange music. I remember saying so to DeVors in '88. 'Oh?' she demanded. 'What's so strange, I'd like to know, about "Stand By Your Man"? Stand by him no matter how sneaky bad he can be—for he will always, always come back to you begging for forgiveness. Indeed politics is an art—and so is pornography, and they are not at all dissimilar. And that one there is right from Joe Gage.'"

(I thought to myself, *Little Rock Keep On Trucking Company? El Asshole Wrecking Corp.? D.C. Fool and Lie?*)

"Owney Madden was a redhead, like Delancey."

I woke with a start. Looking out the window at the evening landscape, thought in a panic: *Venice!* (As it happens, to the left as southbound trains enter Union Station, a distinctly Italianate red-tiled structure alongside the sidetracks creates this uncanny impression. You might well be entering Venezia Santa Lucia.)

And there they all were on the platform—as if I'd get lost or something, but it was gratifying all the same.

As I reached the end of the platform to greet them, I couldn't help noticing a Pullman car, at least forty years out of date, right up at the top of the track, close to the gate. "What's *that*?" I asked O'Maurigan, before greeting any of the others.

"*That*," Barb Vesteralen—Doug Vesteralen's wife, a kind of Patsy Southgate who'd stayed in (or returned to) D.C.—let me know, "*that* is the senatorial Pullman. It gets hitched on the end of the Amtrak train whenever required. Isn't it a camp?"

Is the lobby of Union Station more impressive than

Grand Central? The zodiac does not present itself on the ceiling, and no New Yorker can possibly acquire associations there fit to replace waiting at the clock by Information, but it is an impressive foyer, its cornice ringed with power paladins holding shields. Out the automatic doors, flags waving atop every building in view and the statue of Freedom hovering over an illuminated canopy of still lush green treetops: the Capitol dome obscured. (At Lincoln Hall the city boys would climb the trees along the Hudson, their doings thus obscured; so in this D.C. story the foliage was a mesh of everybody's turned-over new leaves—but they'd soon drop.)

Forcing the white dome into the picture, I summoned two things: first, the memory of coming out the same door on that first trip, when in bright cold daylight I'd walked out with the Christian Brothers to behold (it's what you do with it) the Capitol gleaming white, and second, out front a row of trolley cars, one of which we'd boarded and taken all the way up to some remote location near the national basilica, then under construction.

In fact my whole trip to D.C. that first time was mainly vehicular, including the famous "ride" on the subway from the House to the Senate. (I always called anything exciting a ride. In old Irish New York, as in Dublin, a whore was a "right ride.")

"The original sandstone columns," Doug Vesteralen was saying, "with their great Corinthian capitals, were removed from the East Front in 1958 and replaced with the more majestic white marble. They have been recently re-erected in the National Arboretum."

As we drove down First Street for a look at the Supreme Court on the left, I thought, Congress's high-wire act gives them the idea they are the center ring, but the Supremes and all their aides think *they* are—like the great circus act of the innumerable clowns popping out of the car. POTUS with his red nose is Bozo—or the guy who gets shot out of the cannon every four years and pretends to be Superman, cape flying, protecting America.

In this mood, I decided the Mall needed a Ferris wheel, powered like a mill wheel, by the Potomac, onto which, like into a chariot, I'd be invited for a spin, to check the overview from the high places of power.

I looked at the Capitol dome, revealed in its floodlit majesty, and thought: *to lift the lid.*

"'Till all white in the whiteness,'" O'Maurigan exclaimed, "'the rotunda. . . . Lying on the ground two white bodies, each in its semicircle. . . . White too the vault—the light that makes all so white no visible source, all shines with the same white shine.'"

"That has got to be Beckett you're intoning."

"It is. *Imagination Dead Imagine.*"

I looked west toward the facade of the House of Representatives and imagined the seventy-three freshman Republicans and their little white revolution, lit by no visible source.

"Usually," he continued, "the dome reminds me of the great white humpbacked whale, with Uncle Sam as roaring Ahab astride. And on your left, the Library of Congress Jefferson Building." (Where I was supposed to have gone to page school.)

"Libraries were always sacristies for books, librarians book sacristans. The Bible was chained to some altar, and the umbilicus between the library and the book is indissoluble. The New Age is a profoundly Low Church—or no-church—Protestant world: no sacristans need apply. Its capital, not only no lasting city, is no city at all, only public monuments atop a warren of sacristies.

"The facades of official Washington," he persevered, "are unlike Rome's, not done up in all the marble colors of the empire: Lacedaemonian green porphyry, sapphire and yellow

Nubian, translucent Thracian chalcedony, obsidian, but all pure white."

"The facades of official Washington," Odette echoed, "are like the facades of Hollywood studios compared to the sound-studio clutter and the back-lot debris which is the real factory."

Doug Vesteralen nodded. "Things written everywhere in stone, as in Rome, where inscriptions served as marmoreal archives: vehicles of perdurable publicity—the capital city thus becoming the center of the social mind."

"In Washington," Barb Vesteralen snapped, "nothing is true, nothing happens, and—apart from gossip value, which, however, is radically normative—nobody gives a rat's ass. Not only is there no here here, there isn't any now, either. Nothing said or done is in or about the present tense—everything is either an alibi for what either did or didn't happen, or it's a lie about what will or won't."

"Actually," Doug countered, "Washington is *the* essentialist city—and as a result the petri dish of American transcendentalist ambition. Every other American city from Boston to Los Angeles can be called existentialist to a degree, because each makes a deal with reality. You *cannot* say that of D.C., which was founded *specifically* to *house* a deal with the *unreal*—

"The Celestial City come to earth—a concrete instance of a limit case of language forever reaching after mystery and absence, in which anything at all may be appended sequentially to anything else without ever being anything you could call a result."

"New York," O'M said, "is well off without the capital. Of course, we'd likely have put the whole circus over on Staten Island, into a single building complex, and what is known today as the Beltway mentality would be called the Narrows mentality."

"The facades of official Washington," Barb Vesteralen cut in, "*all* look like Albert Randolph Ross's Carnegie libraries: sanctuaries of the so-called national mind. That mind is schizoid; what it says and what it does are nearly never congruent."

"D.C.," Doug continued, "like Indianapolis, traded in a distinguished Victorian American cityscape for a uniform and mediocre glass-box modernism, and now tries sporadically to tart that up with Pomo glaze. And the study of it by journalists and tank thinkers is mired in forties behaviorism. Stimulus strengths and response patterns, period. Attending, thinking, understanding, imagining, remembering, feeling, and knowing, like the Irish a century ago, need not apply."

(I didn't mention—though I thought to—that he, Doug, had indeed applied; but then he wasn't Irish.)

"That said," the O' (who was, and is) pronounced, "we are about to whisk you not to fashionable Ruppert's in unreconstructed downtown NW but to upper Sixteenth Street to Fio's, a fifties *mangeria* in the Woodner Apartments. You will find it surreal."

I studied Doug and Barb Vesteralen. Doug, described in reviews as "the brilliant sociolinguistic microanalyst," had just published *The State, Economics, and Self-Organized Criticality* and won the main prize of the International Society for the Study of Dissociation. It concerned the Wittgensteinian language games of contemporary American politics in relation to the theories of Freud and of Per Bak. He was with the Brookings Institution—as what was known everywhere in D.C. as a policy wonk—studying the language structure of the Constitution (and combatting the Ethics and Public Policy Center) and liaising with—some would say cruising—the Progressive Policy Institute and the Gore government-reinvention circles too.

Barb was, like Patsy back in East Hampton, whom she recalled with great affection, the daughter of a State Department factotum in the Roosevelt-Truman years. According to her their song (hers and Doug's, married for twenty-five years, with two kids of voting age) was "Just One of Those Things."

"Washington," Barb continued (peering out the window), "is to Nowhere exactly what New York is to Everywhere."

"City of domes," Doug said. "And double-domes. Domes, rational geometries, and axial vistas—whose highway system, according to the conspiratorialists, is laid out in the form of Satan's skull."

BARB: Besides being the nation's facelift capital, the epitome of every squalid lamebrain tank town in the Republic for which it stands. The squalid lamebrain tank town the Big World's circus train has come to. A city of children's toy-block letter-number streets for the cataloging of regulations. A city of vestibules, where every hat is tried on, thrown off, lost, refound.

DOUG: Along with one of the world's greatest caravansaries of art and science riches.

BARB: All held hostage as if by barbarians suddenly appearing out of a cloud somewhere along the Great Silk Route. Also has-been heaven. Lose an election, or get dismissed in disgrace, and go back home, you're not likely to have much of a life. Stay here with those very credentials, you'll never be hungry again. Henry Kissinger is a regular contributor to the *Washington Post*.

"A city of charlatans," she concluded, "playing shell games with the hollow concavities of their former selves. The first time I came back I thought everybody was on Stelazine. I've since recognized it as a vast realm of organisms previously unknown to me—extremophiles who manage to thrive in environments I had always considered hostile, if not impossible for sustaining life."

I liked the Vesteralens; they were truthful without being at all like what Odette calls "the New York white middle-class heterosexual liberal couples from hell who populate East Hampton on weekends."

"I'm advised it takes getting accustomed to, for a New Yorker."

Doug nodded. "New York has an engine at its center sending out energy, centrifugally: those who participate in its life are replenished. Washington's center holds only by virtue of absorbing, like a black hole, all the energies of those who seek to inhabit it, creating proactive synergy restructuring teams: a centripetal, sucking in. It can only take, never give."

"You won't find in Washington," Barb advised, "as you do in New York on any single block, such shameless displays of power and innocence, of beauty and cruelty all mixed together. 'Angry' and 'ashen' are two words you hear a lot describing D.C. contestants."

"It is perhaps worth noting," Doug said, "that the New York delegation to the Continental Congress abstained from voting."

We drove up to the Woodner Apartments, walked through a time warp and into the most amazing (and heartening) restaurant, Fio's.

"Nothing—but *nothing*," the O' declared, "has changed here in ages. A trifle *Night of the Living Dead*, perhaps, but then you'll find out, if you're impolite enough to look, that nine-tenths of the population of the District is walking around with little X's branded on the backs of their necks, there at the base of the brain stem. You get used to it: they begin to look like mosquito bites."

"I wonder if Vana would be happy here?" I asked Odette.

"Well, the lighting is kind, and the ambience that of her first visit to the States. Likely she'd feign ignorance rather than risk nostalgia. She's gotten very *today* since joining Italian AA."

"*What?*"

"Yes, dear, but it's not the *what* you think it is. Our diva is in fact nearly teetotal—a little wine with dinner—but is now a member of Arcigay, Arcilesbia. 'We are becoming very powerful and are against the Vatican,' she told me, 'which has turned vicious on us since we have begun to champion the work of the great *seicento* Venetian feminist Moderata Fonte. This is why I am determined to get Christo to wrap the Washington Monument in a gigantic condom.'"

"*What?*" Doug and Barb Vesteralen gasped, in perfect unison.

"You'll hear the rest at the Harringtons'," O'M interjected. "We're all invited as ourselves on Halloween to the Socially Committed American Materialists—say SCAM—in Kalorama. Vana too, bearing news of all the latest Roman scandals."

"Berlusconi?" Doug asked.

"More about Ruggiero—the poor crippled husband, who to hear Vana tell it is on the Secret Council of Europe."

"The Illuminati?" cracked Barb.

(Vana's condom-king husband had become known throughout Italy as "il barone Fuferito," with his picture—"uncannily resembling," Odette declared, "Bronzino's Cosimo de Medici"—on the cover of *Oggi*, *Stern*, *Paris-Match*, etc. Who shot him was not known; perhaps disgruntled Albanians. The incident had been virtually ignored under the Murano glass lighting fixtures at the Villa Firenze—that's the Italian embassy in Washington—but the assailant was at least no lover of Vana's, lately all young girls. Ruggiero was on the slow mend while Vana had gone on the road to market Scudamor, the newest in his line. Having failed to convince the French to let Christo wrap the Eiffel Tower in a giant condom to promote World AIDS Day, she was out to form a committee to do the Washington Monument. "It's only fair," she had announced on RAI television, "since the CIA introduced AIDS to America—through their own sodomite kamikazes in the baths in San Francisco.")

"Invited as ourselves?" Odette mused. Clearly her statement about having to make *plans* was already kicking in.

What *would* she do? I asked myself. Why would she *not*? came back, as if from a Quiz Kid, the ready answer.

"You are not, I hope," Doug chanced, "thinking of reviving Dagmar Vesteralen for the occasion? Because, you see, although mother is away on a world cruise, she's due back Stateside in February, and may well pay me a call."

ODETTE: I see. Maybe she'd like to try on my New York life?

DOUG: I don't think so.

BARB: Don't be a spoilsport, darling—you got behind it in Scandinavia, and the Dowager might get off on it.

DOUG (a little testily): In Scandinavia in summer. This is not only getting behind it, it's asking me to push it out of the snow.

BARB: It seldom snows in Washington in winter. (Then to Odette:) Perhaps you could be the maiden schoolteacher aunt, Hedwig? A Lorine Niedecker type. I seem to remember reading Lorine Niedecker mopped floors. You could address her as Aunt Eddie, darling.

DOUG: No! God knows *what* family secrets Aunt Eddie might divulge.

BARB: A point. Anyway, not an old maid. A widow—a relict of—what? A war hero? No—too Eve Harrington. A diplomat.

ODETTE: Practitioner of enlightened hemispheric diplomacy?

BARB: Let's say he joined the Foreign Service in, say, '46. She was a government girl—had come in from some place like Reliance, South Dakota, in about '43 to work on the War Production Board. After VJ Day, became a reference specialist in the Office of Operations' Records and Service Division in Arlington.

"They met," she continued, "and married. He was posted to the Far East, later Paris, and went on to become deputy chief in, say, Kinshasa, then Mali. She's known in the corps for enlivening diplomatic society with her imaginative picnics and parties."

"Yes, I see her," Odette declared. "A woman called . . . Maud MacGown, recently rearrived and installed at the

Watergate. An ageless bluestocking interested in promoting women's interests on subjects other than bulimia, depression, cold husbands, and careerism."

o'm: The *Watergate*! Maud doesn't stint, does she?

"One's had one's eye on the Watergate since the hearings. I remember watching them out in Sagaponack with Delancey and Phil. When that bozo revealed the code words 'The laundry's in the icebox,' Phil shouted, 'That's what Marilyn said in *The Seven Year Itch*!'"

"That was Anthony Ulasewicz," Doug announced.

"Was it? Well, what with so many people loitering about . . . In any case, Maud won't much care for her neighbor's dog Leader—or for Leader's mistress—although she can take the master in small doses. 'Seems an honest man,' she allows, 'although the smile is all wrong; seems a ghastly breach of decorum, like those welcome mats put down in funeral parlors.' What does she wear?"

"She wears," Barb offered, "pink St. John's knit suits— long jackets adorned with little camellias and pearls—and agrees that phallocentric ambition codes are an impediment to what women can do: proposes they emulate homosexual Episcopal clergy instead. Remember 'throwaway swank'? That's Maud."

(Actually, I thought, that's Barb.)

"What does she think of Clinton?" Doug asked.

"No worse than Warren Harding," Odette responded (authoritatively, as if to a press conference). "And *he* was much maligned—but he's on the way back, especially among the black population: he was an octoroon, you know. Yes, a decent Presbyterian Taft Republican is Maud MacGown."

doug: But not from South Dakota. Too close to Galt's domain. From Wisconsin—nobody in Washington has known a thing about Wisconsin since Proxmire.

"I am not an enthusiast of Wisconsin," Odette objected. "Not only did Eve Harrington come from Milwaukee, but in

Joseph McCarthy the state spawned one of the vilest specimens of unholy Roman Catholic Irish scum—talking of the
Know-Nothings' somewhat justified fears—ever to infect public life." She drew a breath. "Still, if one thought of it as a
redemptive gesture . . . Yes, all right, I'm warming to it. I see a
Coya Knutson type—sans drunken husband. Deploring the
Republican Party's slant on women while wafting Jean Patou
scents. I've a complete array: Adieu Sagesse; Amour Amour;
L'Heure Attendue; Chaldée; Cocktail; Vacances; Que sais-je?;
and Divine Folie."

"By the way," Doug said, turning to me, "apropos scenarios and Paris, you should know the senator has a staffer with
the kind of hold over him Pamela Harriman says Chirac's
daughter has over him. Also that the senator in his cups is apt
to suddenly turn mean and, like the Bible freaks, to quote
Deuteronomy 12:2 against eco-terrorists: 'Thou shalt utterly
destroy all the places wherein the nations which ye shall pos-
sess served their gods, upon the high mountains and upon the
hills and under every green tree.'"

I must have looked apprehensive. "Every *great* city,"
Odette had observed, "is the invention of *necessity*, truest of all
in the One World City, our own. There was, strictly speaking,
in terms of culture, commerce, civility, no *necessity* for Washington at all. It was founded on a *conceit*—that of a democratic,
republican Versailles for a democracy founded by merchants,
divines, and plantation owners. But take heart from de Tocqueville, dear: 'Among democratic nations, each new generation is
a new people.'"

"But do I want to meet any new people?"

"You might want them pointed out to you."

"I think we're both pretty ancien régime."

"Well, dear, I've certainly never gotten over Merman and
Bert Lahr in *DuBarry Was a Lady*."

From Fio's straight to the prewar building near the Villa

Firenze, overlooking Rock Creek Park: lobby and elevators full of those relics (or has-beens) of Barb's, all chatting away just as they do on the beach at Sagaponack, though it was nearly midnight.

They'd given me an early map of Washington: a thick-trunked tree with two main branches, the Potomac and the Anacostia, forming a Y, on which a web of city streets criss-cross and avenues are like dropped pickup sticks. Also calling to mind an outline of the brain: the stem the lower Potomac, forking into the upper Potomac and the Anacostia, forming a V that cradles the sponge that is the brain mass. In this scheme, at the base—around the Navy Yard—is the pineal gland, where Descartes put the soul. Then the hippocampus (memory) along the Mall, with all the archival buildings and agencies. Georgetown is the frontal lobe.

At the high window overlooking Rock Creek Park, a canopy of lush green soon to turn to flame, while down below mansions peeked through treetop waves. (In winter these would emerge, as from Atlantis.)

Thus began my sojourn. Mornings, keyed into digerati Internet blab and armed with the *Washington Post* and such tributary streams of local journalistic industry as the *City Paper,* the *Washington Blade* (the gay wipe), the *Rock Creek Current, Georgetown & Country, The Hill,* and *Roll Call.* ("*The New Republic, The Nation,* the *National Review, Commentary, Bottom Line / Personal,* and the World Wide Web's aptly named Drudge Report," O'M declared, "you may omit. Like the chapter on the fall of the rupee, they are somewhat too sensational.") I set to work.

With a flick of the switch, Legi-Slate's expensive and elit-ist (it was worth it) twenty-four-hour Federal News Service. Quick Member Menu: Committee assignments . . . abstracts of bills sponsored . . . amendments sponsored . . . remarks on bills . . . *Almanac* profile . . . ratings by interest groups . . .

attendance this Congress . . . staff director. Also my enviro-manual, the Toxics Release Inventory from the EPA, and America Online's Bird Chat.

"Washington is such a *forensic* town," Doug Vesteralen said, "so given to the concentrated halation of highlights, all deeply coded in phrasal verbs. All kinds of stuff will be coming in to you from sysops of Infotech bulletin boards—communications and environmental systems—stuff from the Mitre Corporation (a Pentagon think tank co-opted from the MIT) and undoubtedly both the American Prospect and the Evangelical Environmental Network."

"I can't wait," I said, a little inanely. And then, "Do you think the Tarot would be useful?"

"I can't think why not," Doug replied. "Suitably adapted."

In a card game of Washington, I thought, there would be three suits for the actual District of Columbia: hearts (sex), diamonds (money), and spades (power). The other black, wands, most esoteric in Tarot, could only represent in the abstract the black municipality of Civil War swimmers across the Anacostia. Similarly, the reader will notice, I do a three-card monte in time frames: past, present, and future only *seeming* to swivel under my hand—so to avoid the back-bend pluperfect (as Yogi Berra said, "It ain't over till it's over"). Of that fourth dark suit of wands that Time waves, the future perfect, only science fiction can handle it, and though I did feel like the Void Captain, I'm no Norman Spinrad.

Day and night the radio tower signaled over the treetops from Takoma Park, while raptors rode the wind as Sylvester sat at the long window (his television) lusting. (At intervals the raptors swooped. I wondered at my lazy looking preparatory to swooping down into D.C. for career carrion. Method of infinite descent. Quoth the raven: "Nevermore." Today the raven undoubtedly quotes, "Whatever.")

Often, instead of reading the paper with my morning coffee, I'd click in. Article after article about the woes of the District. "Some of Washington's troubles are its own fault. But after pols are blamed and racists have made their untenable assertions . . ."

Around and around any number of D.C. circles. Kalorama, Dupont, Logan, Thomas; White House circles, Hill circles, and all the bubbles blown by all the bubble pipes in them, and all the lives lived in the bubbles, spent running around in circles trying to square them into the Washington Square Dance.

Two / Ambuscade

I stood outside the National Gallery, looking toward the Mall at the remainder of the Million Man March the day before, and at the groups of white lobbyist stand-ins, of whose services I had no need. (I'd never really needed to stand on the opera line either, with the claques and the diva passes; I did it for the experience.)

Odette and O'Maurigan arrived for the Vermeer show. In front of the *Portrait of the Geographer*, a docent's discussion of Vermeer's symbols: acknowledgment of the darkness of human nature implicit in light bouncing off everything, et cetera. Vermeer's window. The earrings: not a silver ball but a black pearl. ("You can bet one thing," Odette whispered: "the earrings were his.")

". . . Decline in interest in a transcendent other world. Increasing preoccupation with material world; explosion of subjective self-absorption. What was once seen as the common sense of emotionally resonant subjects in the visual forms that re-elicit them and in the principles from which meaning can conceivably be constructed if there is any, and mounted if there is not."

Ain't it the truth.

What a day. We next took in the French culture show at the LC. There under glass was the sample Proust page: every addition folded out, like the AIDS quilt. (O'M said that the scant turnout proved the Proustians are dead, and all that are left are proustitutes. Thirty years ago there would have been lines around the block: the same crowds that went to see Mawrdew Czgowchwz and Maria Callas.)

O'Maurigan introduced two of our luncheon-companions-to-be, his colleague Blaine Marshall and her rather gorgeous husband Eliot (subsequently dubbed by Yours Truly, affectionately, Connie and Legs). Eliot, apart from being in his own right a gentleman and a scholar, just happens to have been a classmate (both at St. Albans, the National Cathedral school, and at Harvard) of the Vice President. ("I have to ask you right away," I said. "What was he like?" "Oh, I'm afraid he was perfect." I'd thought as much.) I was then introduced by the O' to LC staffers (both African-American) Ms. Delmarva Fly and Mr. Ornette James ("O.J.") Crow. We went to Ms. Fly's office in the Madison Building for morning coffee and were served madeleines, half-dipped in chocolate. "I learned that from your friend Hildegarde Dorsay," she acknowledged, "who I believe introduced the practice to the rue Pigalle in the sixties."

She turned to me. "We have been told you got yourself adopted, till you finally adopted yourself; I got myself *adapted*, ditto. Trouble with *my* family tree, see, is the people *hangin'* from it."

(I had no family tree at all. In place of the ones you see in some people's alcoves, libraries, and johns, I had a map of the New York subway system with a circle around Delancey Street.)

I admitted, looking out an oriel window, to being captivated by the Capitol, and from there remarking on America's obsession with ETs and angels. "Oh, do you go for *angels*?" Delmarva exclaimed. "Me too! I see bright angel wings in every pair of McDonald's golden arches—which puts me in the path of the pity of the liberals' patronizing relativism—poor nigger shaped by outside forces that preclude acknowledgment of social pathology."

(I was an angel once in a Christmas pageant. When Odette asked what kind, I said, "A Throne." We'd memorized the orders in the catechism, and I'd gotten fixated on Thrones. "Ah, yes," she cracked, "the order charged with the protection of infants abandoned in public toilets.")

Ms. Fly then nodded to her silent companion. I thought he looked like Bobby McFerrin, minus dreads: the same frameless glasses.

"Yes, this Pharaoh's army shavehead, wearing the black silk bandanna of the once-incarcerated black male, augmented with the pink triangle, surveying you with the Mack-daddy stare saying he can take you or leave you, is my dearest friend and boon companion, Ornette James Crow. In O.J. you see the *real* 'Jimmy's World' boy."

O.J.: Least I was never Hawaiian in Harlem.

DELMARVA: *'Cause* you were never in Harlem to be so.

O.J. (nodding): It's true, I never have strut in that darktown. Actually my great hero in life is Billy Strayhorn, who got into his oppression in a unique way.

DELMARVA: You're more of a horny stray than a stray horn.

O.J.: Now if that ain't the pot callin' . . . *Anyway*, just call us Grin and Flash. Sister Delmarva be *fly*—could be the coolest black vaudevillian since Sissieretta Jones, but she done *flipped the script* and got herself a *serious* position. And me? I get by. Welcome to the dis-*aggravation* mosh pit.

("Ornette," O'Maurigan had already let me know, "works in the copyright division of the LC. He will not own a car because black inmates of prisons are slave labor making license plates. He says if they put them to work processing garbage he may have to give up his Insinkerator. Also, he never wears or carries anything zippered, protesting the long stitched scars young blacks proudly call their 'zippers.'")

"Welcome to D.C., Boss," O.J. barked in the most perfect Rochester imitation I'd ever heard. "That stand, some say, for 'Dada Caca,' others for 'Demo-Crassity.' Others say for 'Dumb City': one angry, self-absorbed, and politically rudderless—or was that 'rubberless'?—metropolis *ab urbe condita*. Still more say everybody here is D.C. in the sense they *all* take it up the ass on behalf of the populace from the studfucker Powers That Be. Powers, of course, since you are Catholic, will be to you some angel choir."

(The angel orders: we were already on some kind of wavelength.)

"Listen up and nobody gets hurt . . . that bad. But you are here to lobby, yes? Now lobbyin' is difficult with this Congress, for they are rough trade with *'tude* and this is their summer night, so as with *cruisin'*—not that you go in for *cruisin'*, but you will seize the *metaphor*—like cruisin' rough trade with an attitude on a summer night. It don't do no good to come on *horny*—no matter you is—the result will be *zee-ro*, or as they say in hockey, *doughnut*. 'Cause the *easier* it *ain't*, the *harder* it does get to be.

"Because these boys, they miss the time a politician could stand on any street corner down here and the pockets would *silt up* with Ben Franklins. These boys like *new* Ben Franklins they just put out. *Whereas* to get the *boys* to put out, you need to stand on the corners of *K Street*, until your ears silt up with *stories*, at the rate of *zoom*, nearly all of them worthless, but *any one* of which could *turn into* an advantage worth a lotta Bens, dig? Problem is you could get to be *old*, or worse, *known* for standin' on the corner. Bad.

"So you need friends in the *Hilly* place—for as the old Greek proverb goes, though the ankle may not know so, the knee is nearer than the shin. And sometimes when you are out *makin'* or *makin' it with* said friends, the good idea, like a star in Hollywood, is to have a *stand*-in. Like they are there on the Mall for the hiring.

"We start off here," he continued, "in the Lie-berry of *Congress*—as in the *opposite* of '*pro*-gress'—in which place everybody has taken the *bureaucratic oath*, which is 'Primum non cognoscere.' Corollary, 'I could find out . . . some time.' J. Edgar Hoover, who started his investigative career looking stuff up here in these very halls, is a powerful example of one such who did so."

"I would say," Delmarva Fly advised me, "that white slice that you are, you will require no stand-in in the lobbying lines or elsewhere on the Midway. Pale, and male, you are not I conjecture, stale—for I have heard you are no stranger to the vamp, the riff, and the break. Know then that in D.C. it is not cool to seek out what is happening in the world, only *who really knows* what is happening in and to the world."

"Perchance you did see," O.J. cut in, waving in the general direction of the Washington Monument, "on the Mall yesterday a conglomeration of *neegroes* enraptured under the spell cast by Reverend Louis Farra-*khan*? Seems Minister Farra-*khan* saw on the television that Montel brings us together, and he decided to give ole Montel a run for his money by putting out the call—in the *two words* neegroes universally recognize as such: '*quittin' time!*'

"Now Malcolm said once, 'You want to hide something from the Negro, put it between the pages of a book.' We have no association with such. Sister Delmarva has never wasted her time cryin' no boo-hoo-hoos for no badass Leroys wit' heavy 'tude—ain't spread no sheets for those boys' agendas. . . . And speakin' of Hollywood, where they made that movie *The Colored People*, ain't this whole enterprise in actual fact a setup for another Spike Lee Joint? If so, I do not inhale.

"But these D.C. Leroys dig off-camera action; they do not find the fact that O.J. likely done the deed or that Rodney King was on PCP comin' at those honky LAPDs like Mighty Joe

Young relevant in the Wider Scheme of Things, *truth* bein' wha's in yo' *heart*. Dig?

"I did hear one interesting speculation, from the knot of speculators. 'Brother say the lass goin' be foist and the foist goin' be lass. That leave everybody inna middle inna same place!' That man knows politics is like horseshoes: close is good enough.

"Remind me of my own use of 'foist.' Where I work in the great Library of Congress—called by white supremacists the Lie-berry uv de *Congo*—they put me in charge of a lotta *yams*. Yams say, 'Don't you be dictatin' to me like no Simon Dee-*gree*! Ah *yam* what Ah *yam*—and gova-mint certificated wid-all. Ah *yam* mah own domain of validity—you ain't gonna difficul-tate my life wit' no woik ethics derived from people whose white Puritan ancestors inhabitated cold climates.' I say, 'That is one 'tude gonna get you 'xac'ly *nowhere* in life without you plan on makin' your life turn on *diss*-position and on the con-struction of those little coffee-stirrer-stick-and-bond-paper airplanes you turn out all day at your desk like a one-man Lockheed factory. The only one *evuh* got away with "I am what I am" was De Lawd's Big Daddy. You must *forge* yourself an *identity* and *foist* in on the *world*.'

"'Like *you* done. Uh-*uh*. We got a political action com-mittee in dis lie-berry. We won that discrimination lawsuit, and I don't have to formate no unwitty alliances wit' no jive turkey Uncle Toms such as you out to inferiorate me. I listen to Minister Farrakhan.'

"'You listen to Farra-khan? With his dumb-down mix of calypso jive and refried Sun Ra wa-wa? Old pharaohs whose names he can't spell? With his assumed "khan" name—Islam for "king"?' 'See?' they sass me back, 'already you castro-gate'n him like a white man.'

"I tell them they need to spend more time among the *collections* where we work, and less Web-crawlin' along the MelaNet and its Watoto World rumpus rooms and the World

African Network Online, diggin' what they *already* know, viz. the uncut black D.C. experience—which consists mainly of life on welfare (and *that* ain't gonna last much longer), women spreadin' money-and-house-blessing voodoo oil on the cheap linoleum and sittin' down to pray in front of the television, countin' up the black faces as *All My Children* turns into *Another World* turns into *General Hospital*."

"'All My Children,'" Delmarva added, "being the story entire of that life—all my children by different fathers."

"I tell them," Ornette continued, "to adapt their sets to the new technology—tune into such sites as NetNoir, learnin' some French. But it is their notion, derived from their hero Minister F-Khan, of political sabotage—one French word they have learned—to dismiss such programs as part of the New World Order Intel conspiracy to bleach the black mind, dig.

"Consequently it has been observed that, for example, given a choice between buying ice from a black man or a white man, most black people will buy from the latter because they actually believe his ice is colder. And they are *right*—it *is*.

"Now what these black people need is to break the isolation of the hypno-screen and *bond together and chill in twos*—much like Miss Fly and I—I, in the hierarchy of the LC, a lowly 7, but Miss Fly is an 11, a number known in esoteric dice-rollin' circles as 'boxcars with one side door slid open a crack to let in the next passenger.' That which is *you*."

"And you are welcome," Delmarva assured me, "long as you don't persist in thinkin' like white people, of white as light in shafts, straight, and of black as *spread out* and *chaotic*."

o.j.: That, I fear, is in the language; *intrinsic*.

"In the white view," Delmarva continued, "we are blind to the light that underlies the play of phenomena they miscall reality. So they must be kindly *led*, but in our hearing they are deaf and cannot *listen*. And in reality, baby, *sound* comes *before* vision."

o.j.: You just keep list'nin' to Sister Delmarva.

"I'll listen to you both, if I may," I said.

"Yo, but to Sis first—for she is the Sojourner Truth of the New Covenant . . . or Coventry . . . sump'n. Kinda a cross 'tween Barbara Jordan and Damita Jo off *Soul Train.* Between us we get you to the truth *as the crow flies*—'cause we reckon wuz you innerested in the *jive scenic route*, you'd've be wid a diff'runt travel agency.

"As to the political effect of the Mill-yun Man March—" he made the O sign, then extended three fingers—"you put Sister Delmarva's wings on it you get *flying asshole.* All them assholes flyin' back to Muthuh Afri-cuh. I want to *quiz* them, 'Who was it you think *sold* all them slaves to the traders— Ayeesha, White Empress of the Hottentots, She Who Must Be Obeyed? I do *not* think so!' And that completes our tour of the nation's brain box. Next stop—maybe you are interested?—is the National Arboretum, up back of the Anacostia River, off New York Avenue, to which place even as we speak are rushing in a covered car a certain senator in whom I believe you have expressed an interest, together with his aide, whom you could do worse than, as they say where you come from, check out. The senator is set to give a speech at the reflecting pool up there—reflecting upon the erection there of a mess of old *columns* from the original Capitol, recently uncrated and set up there for the edification chiefly of obscurantists."

We took a cab.

"Talking of scenic routes and jive," Delmarva commenced, as we drove up Second Street into Northeast, "the senatorial gatekeeper in question is a map unto himself. He is *placed*—or to *euphemize* in the D.C. way, it ain't he is *used* but *preowned.*"

"But you wanna be careful," Ornette interposed, "because it is no angel. Not of the McDonald's gold-wing type or of the type in the oil picture that used to hang near the Budweiser sign near the cash register in the Chesapeake House—"

"Legendary temple," Delmarva cut in, "of smoke, shadow, and miasma—'the Peake,' as it was called by those over and under who frequented it."

(Over forty, under twenty: also, in the flip order, top and bottom.)

"Calls himself Rain," O.J. offered, "and well named, for he is what the CIA calls a 'wet boy,' i.e., a *trained killer.*"

"Word *is*" (Delmarva), "Angel broke in dancin' naked on the top of the bar at the Peake. A bad-boy version of the Shulamite woman . . . a kind of Shulamite catamite—rattlin' those juicy chicken drumsticks—one of which already had a *bite* taken out of it—on the tabletops too."

"True, true" (O.J.), "that boy was an *ecdysiast*, and extremely callipygean too, in spite of the fact he does *limp* somewhat—from what he calls a *service* wound of the cruciate ligament. The Greeks had a word for such dancin'. They called it *gymnopaidia*, dance of naked boys, or *oreibasia*, wild nighttime dancing in the mountains—but as this is basically Flatland, the top of the bar sufficed."

"And this what you might call 'Rain dance'" (Delmarva) "was apt to drive the onlookers and other dancers *crazy*. Nevertheless, at the very same time he was—or *had been*—a model student, first here at the *Capitol Page School* in the LC, enrolled by the senator, and subsequently at St. Albans—the cathedral-school alma mater of the Vice President—from whence he went on to Georgetown for a spell, to learn the skills of diplomacy, power point presentation . . . whatever."

"But there" (O.J.) "the boy was not entirely happy, and so was allowed a leave of absence. Somethin' 'bout an *ambassador* who'd just reached the shore, a man of many loves, who forgot *them all* after *one look* at Angel, limp and all."

"And you should mention" (Delmarva) "that the ambassador wore funny clothes and was representin' a country that is mostly desert—just like the Western State Angel was supposed to have come from—but under all that sand is a *lotta oil.*"

"Anyway" (O.J.), "after a thorough and exhaustive investigation the charges were dropped, a motion for expungency passed, and what hadda-oughta never happened never did—except Angel was grounded—sent for a rest at St. Elizabeth's. That being the *spa* in southeast D.C. famous for its curative Anacostia waters and for the sometime residence there of the dee-ranged poet Ezra Pound."

"Ex-*pungency*" (Delmarva) "is very important in a swampy locale, and the power that can effect it can do much else."

"*His* story" (O.J.) "is *they*—that would be the AEIOU—put him *undercover* into St. Elizabeths to make the acquaintance of one John W. Hinckley, of attempted-assassination fame. Much is unspecified in the report, but Hinckley claimed psychic communication with Charles Manson and Sirhan Soforth—*pointin'* to a sinister and powerful *conspiracy* beyond *theory*, perhaps initiated by Ezra Pound *his*-self."

"Likely all rumor" (Delmarva), "as must be the contention that since it is the property of the boy's being that when he collides in complicated interactions, he has always preserved the *exact amount* of *strangeness charge* as existed before—"

"As it is said" (O.J.) "that when Krishna dances with the multitude, each believes he has danced with Krishna alone."

"That 'that'" (Delmarva) "would indicate that he is in fact an *autistic boy* with a programmed *voice chip* to *simulate* his behaviors."

"Up, down, and strange" (O.J.). "Thing they can't yet simulate is *sideways*—dig?"

"Is he an Indian?" I asked (thinking of Phil's favorite joke).

"The story goes," Delmarva advised, "the senator had found him as a Shoshone half-breed gimp out in canyon country—although I know an LC phonologist who, listening to him speak, declares that can't be so."

"Anyway," O.J. added, "when, after the spell at St. Elizabeth's, he returned to his old haunts, needless to say that Injun had all the appeal of a bad prom dress—wanted by nobody red, white, or blue."

"Nobody *believes* he *is* a *real* Injun," Delmarva declared, "but only a Washington Redskin—a *linebacker,* in the PC scrimmage—'Rain' bein' more in the nature of a cult moniker than a bestowed name."

"Nevertheless" (O.J.), "he does his *homework*. There was one afternoon he came into the library, to Prints and Photographs, and spent a *long time* looking hypnotized-like at portraits of two Shoshone men called James A. Garfield and William Shakespeare."

"Be that whatever" (Delmarva), "he was a lively little thing—known for somewhat exceedin' his instructions and also for little boyish pranks such as dressin' up the statue of George Washington in the Capitol Rotunda in drag, and emptyin' boxes of Tide into the Poseidon fountain just outside."

"Then later" (O.J.), "down at the Peake, known for the fact that you put a maraschino *cherry* in his mouth—from the Old Fashioned cocktail he liked to order at that tender age—he liked to swallow it, then tie the stem into a bow with his tongue and present you with it on the tip of same. Now is *that* not a metaphor? Not to mention what Krishna tricks he could do up there—where his favorite number was, *paradoxically,* 'If All We're Gonna Do Is Dance, I'm Goin' Home'—were *beyond calypso:* a forerunner of both hard-core techno *and* ethereal trip-hop, making of bad tendencies such clear and present dangers as had seldom before been felt. Weren't no buffalo dance, thass *fo-sho',* and it more than made up for his little *disability*. In point of fact, the titillation of knowin' he was already *chomped on*—well, at the time it was somethin' new and delicious for Washington: the *promise broken before it is even made*. What that pimple-dick muh'fuh in the White House has made into *a way of life*.

"And that boy could do much else too up there on those surfaces—with his *butthole*. Do the same wid' *it* what Miss Billie Holiday could do with her pussy—called *snatchin'* up de *dues* wid' yo' *kooze*. Only that boy could make the face of Andrew Jackson *disappear* inside."

"So that" (Delmarva) "what with all that *solid growth* and *inflation under control*, he could do all the profit-taking he wanted and shrug off the *dips* like any bull-market enthusiast."

"And these here turns" (O.J.) "wuz a big feature that *differentiated* that boy from the rest of those skanky faggots hopped up on amyl, flauntin' their dog balls and overripe puckerbuds. Oh my yes, the word is that Shoshone wit' eyes the color of money is *even* crazier than Crazy Horse wid'*out* de firewater, and wid'out the protection of the high and mighty would long since have been enrolled in some fed'rul penitentiary where *fried chicken* is regarded as a choice item on Saturday night's supper menu. You dust him for prints, you find he is definitely *preowned*."

"Many predict a future for him," Delmarva added, "what with members of the Congress now appearing in public with their *boyfriends*. Some say there's gonna be a *weddin'*, but others say nonsense, for the senator is a *chaste* man, married to the Senate."

"So," O.J. concluded, "although the general consensus on the child is that he would do almost *anything* to get on the front page of the *Washington Post*—*above the fold*—there are limits to the batshit-making behavior he is nowadays willin' to undertake. Anyway, what with the Big Man himself such a sinner— and I am not talking about Senator Galt, *or* about the Mayor-for-Life of D.C., but about the resident of 1600 Pennsylvania Avenue—there is a *tone* here of don't-ask-don't-tell. And so have we come to the scene of the occasion."

Moments later I saw Senator Galt for the first time, an impressive figure, standing on a hill, among his beloved columns at the reflecting pool. We "spectated" (O.J.) from the bonsai house, near a magnolia literati ("This unconventional bonsai is most often displayed in a small, round, shallow container that serves as a pivotal point from which the trunk emerges. The literati bonsai is sufficiently light to be self-balancing, as the small, shallow container indicates. On containers of this type, the sides may be straight or round, with or without molding." I was already starting to wonder if my shallow container was schizo-ceramic.)

Talking about the Council Tree, he started in—with news cameras rolling from CNN and the local D.C. networks.

Chanting—it came out later—from Shoshone tribal laws. (Remember when that Texas environmentalist was found out to have forged Chief Seattle's speech about the railroads and the Great Mother's body? To me it could've been Sid Caesar doing Italian.)

I thought of Demosthenes on the Acropolis, St. Paul in Ephesus, Savonarola in Florence, and Robespierre on 8 Thermidor.

"In the flames stood and viewed the armies drawn out in the sky
Washington, Franklin, Paine, and Warren, Allen, Gates,
    and Lee:
And heard the voice of Albion's Angel give the thunderous
    command
His plagues obedient to his voice flew forth out of the clouds
Falling upon America. Fury! rage! madness! In a wind
    swept through America.
The citizens of New York close their books and lock their
    chests.
The mariners of Boston drop their anchors and unlade;
The scribe of Pennsylvania casts his pen upon the earth
The builder of Virginia throws his hammer down in fear.

Each leader skillful in the art of war,
For the dread conflict hastily prepare:
As the grim lion in the lonely den,
Turns furious round, beset by dogs and men;
His glaring opticks dart pernicious fire,

His rising mane denotes his bursting ire.
Deep throated cannon belched pernicious—"

("I knew a deep-throated canon, once," Delmarva whispered into my ear.)

"Large hollow ships, with tenfold fury pent
Hot their red thunders and thick lightnings sent.
Awful the scene! Fierce horror stalked around.
Six hundred men lay gasping on the ground.
Of Freedom's sons two hundred bravely slain
And fierce warriors o'er th'ensanguined plain.
Then dread despair black as the shades of night
Chas'd the poor vanquished from the dreadful fight.
Yet some there were, whole hearts yet firm and true
The brave defenders of their native land.
Fortune chang'd sides on that eventful day,
And from the victor stole the prize away:
The fickle goddess loves to shew her pranks
Regretful of entreaties—

Say Muse, when all had run their martial race
What chief supply'd the fallen heroes' place?
Who was the man, and who his name could tell
For much depends on knowing men full well."

(O'Maurigan had to tell me later that all that was from Joel Barlow's *Columbiad*. What wrapped the occasion up I thought I'd recognized—and had—as William Blake.)

"Do I sleep amidst danger to friends! O my cities and counties
Do you sleep? Rouse up, rouse up! Eternal death is abroad!
Air! Bright freedom's air that cannot be molded
Into any shape by work of human hand!"

Then to the Monocle to meet the senator officially. "Hill staffers," the O' informed me, "have taken to trotting up to Ruppert's Real, on Seventh, to do lunch, or to Le Mistral— they call it 'Mistrial'—but not our senator, who is a Monocle loyalist. He thinks it's D.C.'s '21'. Neither is he ever to be found—though Max Harrington often is—either at the Palm or the Jockey Club."

"Oh, there's one of those here too, huh?"

"Oh, sure—and I bet I know what you're thinking. A Jockey Club, a Swann Street . . ."

And so I was. I described the doings at the Arboretum.

"Galt is interesting," Doug Vesteralen allowed, "more interesting than the bizarre coincidence that put him in office. Although he voted Democrat, and joined the party in '60, he thought Kennedy a murderer's son—only he thought Nixon worse—and finally in Johnson he saw absolute power corrupt absolutely, and thus went over to Goldwater, the man he has most admired in public life. Then, utterly dismayed by the Nixon comeback, he turned Independent again and opted for Carter, by which time he had begun to go a little funny around *good man* ideas. He fell for Reagan completely, but thought Bush was dangerously unstable. Sympathetic to Clinton, he fears Hillary, who in his estimation doesn't know how to behave as a political wife."

It was Odette's first outing as Maud MacGown, and she played it very smart. Pleading luncheon calendar mixup—with ladies—she managed nevertheless to give the old goat, just then coming in with his aide, a courtly boner before exiting.

"I would never have expected less," O'Maurigan insisted.

"Washington," Doug remarked, over the Appalachian mineral water, "is total *character* in reaction to plot."

"Which is why the President might yet do well," the senator announced. (The power of the Senate: POTUS is seen by its members as their protégé.)

"Directed by Hillary?" Doug offered.

"*No*, sir! If she wants to be seen to run things, she's gonna have to go out and get herself elected. And don't talk to me about Eleanor Roosevelt. Eleanor Roosevelt was a highborn lady, blood of the line, so to speak. No, he is going to have to do it alone—and his chance is about to come. I think he'll beat them—the Republicans: he resembles an outstanding chess entertainer, triumphing in blindfold games and simultaneous exhibitions."

This sort of bag went on for an hour, after which, happily, duty called.

I noticed Rain's slight limp as we proceeded to the Senate, where Galt left us in the reception room. I walked over to look at the portrait of Daniel Webster and thought of the devil—also that I would like to see the portraits of the Shoshone James A. Garfield and William Shakespeare . . . meditations interrupted by Rain's sudden invitation to accompany him to the senator's hideaway office on the first floor, next to that of Claiborne Pell (of Rhode Island, a regional neighbor, fellow ecologist, and the former—and, most of Washington agreed, gentlemanly but ineffectual—chairman of the Foreign Relations Committee).

"Let me wrap a couple of hours of my time around a couple of hours of yours—without invading your privacy, of course."

There followed the excursion through the marble halls, up and down the staircases, in and out of the gilded elevators, and through the fabled railway tunnels. As we entered the Senate Chamber a floor debate was in progress, in which I heard, and transcribed, the following:

"The dilemma we have at the moment is the *regular order* is *not allowed* because we have a procedure on this bill *to fill the tree*, which prevents *a second-degree amendment* at some point *to get back into consideration of it*." I must have looked dumbfounded. "You get used to it," Rain said. "It gets to be relaxing—watching our august lawmakers and their staffers scurry around the Senate floor, the groups forming and reforming like amoebas in heat."

In the senator's hideaway, the first thing my eye went to was the black drape over a bulge on the wall. "It's the clock all senators have," Rain explained offhandedly, "with a signal system of little lights on its face. The senator believes he is under both CIA and Department of Justice surveillance: a camera lodged in the clock face. The Big Brother Movement is furious since their bugging expert Mary Lawton was murdered by the Conspiracy in Bethesda in October of 1993. Covered as a heart attack. We talk in Shoshone in here, the senator and I. He isn't going to have anything to do either with the Senate World Wide Web site. Of course—" his tone changed markedly— "when we *really* want to be alone, we go into the stacks in the LC to the private rooms."

(I thought of all the chaste and idealistic frescoes in the Great Hall—Minerva, etc.—but then there was the one of Ganymede carried off by Zeus. Clearly, the best Washington roman à keyhole would be set entirely in the LC.)

"The senator has declared he will have nothing to do with any group of letters that doesn't *spell out* a *word*. He believes—correctly—that the Conspiracy thrives on cabalistic codes."

We moved over to the window looking down the Mall at the Washington Monument. Rain started sketching it on an empty pad.

"The hardest thing to do in this town is walk with your head held high and still keep under the radar. Yesterday, watching the Million Man March from this window, under that framed quotation from Matthew ('I Bring Not Peace But the Sword'), I made him go down on me, while I looked out at the crowd. The radio was on, and the whole time Farrakhan was bawling, I thought, 'You dumbass nigger, I am a beautiful white boy getting his cock sucked by a senator of the Republic; *you* can go eat shit and die.'"

(Was this then the Baltimore trestle climber?)

"When people call governments a crap shoot they are right, and the thing to understand about dice is that the numbers on any two opposite faces must always add up to seven. Get it?"

(I didn't. Rain looked out the window with "a look both fathomless and aimless" in his impossibly green eyes.)

"You're here with a political operative. Do you know how to absorb the impact of a cross-check? That's hockey. But you know that; I can always tell a hockey fan: blood lust; hot men on ice; painted faces. White guys playing Indians. I keep a picture of Wayne Gretzky in my wallet. The senator gets us tickets and we go up on the shuttle. Wayne's Ranger number is 99."

"I'd heard you were that—Indian."

"My mother was a Shoshone."

(And your father was on the Oregon Trail.)

"And my father was a pilgrim, looking for . . ." (He trailed off, having finished sketching the monument. He had, I noticed, given it a single eye, like the one on the dollar bill.)

"You know the monument is 555 feet high? In *inches* 555 feet is 6,660 — 555 and 666 is 11/11/11. Hitler was sent by German Army Intelligence to Munich to prep the zone—infiltrate and report on the German Workers Party. Instead he enlisted in the ranks; his membership card was 555." (Flashback: Lincoln Hall, American history: the Know-Nothings, who managed to halt the construction of the monument for decades, claiming it reflected an attempt by the Pope to take over the U.S.—but you knew that. As Doug Vesteralen might as well have said, "What goes around . . .")

Rain's beeper phone rang. In a trice he was off, in new voice, looking out the window and doodling the monument.

"Yes, Congressman, I can talk. . . . Got one goin', huh? I must say you do feature that monorail. Listen, you remember Rex Chandler—what if it was just us? Well, it is . . . just us. Unless of course you believe that it really is just *you*. . . . No?

That's good, Congressman, because the more you believe that I'm here for you, the more likely your constituents will believe that you're there for them.

"Yes, I do understand you; now peep this. They're down in Monticello, in the Dome Room, Jefferson's favorite hang, and he's reading to Madison. Now, remember, Jefferson is the splitter—most of his process he considers private, nonbinding and *ultra vires*, re Congress—while Madison is the lumper. Yeah, it's like the attic: Jefferson's tricks' initials—mostly slave boys'—all over the walls—*exactly* like the Senate pages' under the Capitol dome. . . . What? *No*, I can't change it to the pages now. Different voices. . . . Yes, slave boys. Remember Sally Hemings's brother James, the *first* Jim Crow? And speaking of hang, they're *hung*. Then too, in those days the fuckers wore wigs, but they did *not* wear condoms; they *rode bareback*. And the fuckees quoted Scripture. 'Greater is he who is in me,' they would declare out loud, 'than he who is in the world!' . . . You like that, huh?" (He stretched out full-length on the senator's desk.) "What? Well, *yeah*, when they get hanged, that *does* happen, but Jefferson wasn't into lynching—James Callender never hung that one on him. You into that? You have a spider-web tattoo? If so, you are a nasty *man* and I can't be seen in public with you."

(I thought, This *is* nasty; how far will it go? Here in front of me was Tarot's Devil Boy. The Lord of the Gates of Matter. The Child of the Forces of Time. The fire in his groin symbolizes the raw sexual power of his path: he deals the dice.)

"Hey, Congressman, with all due respect, my advice to you in the lower house is *get over it*. Whatever turns your crank, long as it spins the wheels. It is my job here to exorcise your demons by deploring the exploitive, drugged-out aspects of power praxis capture, all the while still showing you a good dwell time. . . .

"Really? You know, with urban seroprevalence rates what they are, I fail to see how following the negotiated safety guidelines of the National Institutes of Health can besmirch your office. You may be whacking it like any slobbering loon in the lockup at St. Elizabeth's, but you are doing so in the privacy of your office, not at one of the phone tables of the old Pier 9—and you know at the equivalent places today, they don't stop there: they get rough special-investigator types to nail their dicks to the tables. You don't do that—and for that I commend you, and what you do do is responsible, politically correct action, but I'm not your priest.

"What you are up to will *not* grow hair on your palms— not make you unworthy of power dining at the Hay-Adams . . . one day. The worst it can do—you *do* puff and pant like a hog at a roping when you get worked up—is bring on postcombat stress syndrome amplified by mild oxygen debt.

"You want to confess, talk to your whip, or to Bob Flanagan—he has a Web site; when you turn to it, it plays 'You always hurt the one you love.' Meanwhile, why not think of all this not as personality disintegration but the way your dad thought of bowling? . . . What?" (He laughed.) "Yeah, in my case it *is* bowling for dollars, but how is a staffer to make ends meet without moonlighting? And we are fantasizing *great men* here. After all, '*Moribus antiquis res stat Americana virisque,*' right? And if sometimes I let you call me 'corporal' in that friendly-captain voice, it's because you've got such expressive eyes I can see them over the phone.

"If you feel you are *deeply* troubled I can send you a couple of back issues of *Stand Corrected* and a subscription form; plug you into the action of grace, and the concept of sexual metamorphosis and the hot blessing. Here's a snippet I recall. 'Let the miscreant be taken to the common whipping post, there to receive twenty lashes laid on his bare back, that he be rendered infamous.' That jiggle you? . . . No? Well, then my advice is *loosen up.* Plead attractive-nuisance susceptibility—and as you come, *come clean.*

"OK, so Jefferson is reading—from section 47 of his *Manual of Parliamentary Practice*, the rule on Messages.

"'In Senate the messengers are introduced in any state of business except

"'1. While a question is putting.

"'2. While the Yeas and Nays are calling.

"'3. While the ballots are calling.

"'The 1st case is short; the 2nd and 3rd are cases where any interruption might occasion errors difficult to be corrected. So arranged June 15, 1798.'"

(Angels, evangelists, the message. A recent declaration on communication which stated, "True to its genre, the press release omits information that is not *on message.*" In the old days Ralph would say of a young article walking *that way* up Greenwich Avenue of a balmy summer evening, "That one has not gotten his message." You heard it of some kid who held his schoolbooks in both arms—it went with the way you lit your cigarette, the way you looked at your nails: tests that began in the fourth grade, ones you couldn't find the Regents Guide answers to, that marked you for life. For what it's worth, I passed them all—which ought to have been its own message.)

"'A question is never asked by the one house of the other by way of message, but only at a conference; for this is an interrogatory, not a message. 3 Grey, 151, 181.'"

(Interrogation follows hard upon the message, that is true, by all the whips in Faggotry.)

"And then he skips to his favorite part, English Customs.

"'Where the subject of a message is of a nature that it can properly be communicated to both houses of parliament, it is expected that this communication should be made to both on the same day.

"'The King, having sent original letters to the Commons

et cetera, afterwards desires they may be returned. That he may communicate them to the Lords. 1 Chandler, 33.'

"Chandler? Sorry, Congressman. Can't answer that."

(English writer, in Los Angeles; connoisseur of degenerates, like Marcel Proust; worked in bed all day.)

"But I *told* you, Congressman, Madison is *always* the top; he was a *Presbyterian*—like James Hammond of South Carolina, to whom his bedfellow Thomas Withers wrote in 1826 inquiring has he lately had the 'extravagant delight of poking and punching a writhing bedfellow with your long fleshen pole, the exquisite touches of which I have often had the honor of feeling?' I recall your saying at the time it was small wonder South Carolina was the first to secede. We discussed the likelihood of the gentlemen of North Carolina, Georgia, and Virginia behaving in similar fraternal fashion, notwithstanding Jesse Helms and Lauch Faircloth. . . .

"Yes, Jefferson's hair was red. You want it white and cropped like Clinton's, we'll put him in a powdered wig. . . .

"I *know* his middle name is Jefferson, and I can't *imagine* what kind of headlocks manly bedfellows comparing their distinguishing characteristics get up to in Arkansas." (He rolled his green eyes at me.) "And *you* told *me* Madison called Jefferson 'Dolley.' . . .

"No, I'd put your case relatively low on the weirdometer— you *are* working on tort reform. I know Jefferson freaks whose careers have been ruined on the nickel slots. Look, you're a Republican whose experience so far has centered around the adventures of Leonard and Larry. You start playing pinochle with Madison, you're gonna get your knuckles rapped a little— if some blood spills over into your one-minutes—

"So, *look*, this is the deal. They're in the Dome Room playing *pinochle*. I *know* Clinton plays hearts. This is more symbolic—Jefferson in drag as the Queen of Spades and Madison as the Jack of Diamonds. They *talk a lot* and only *maybe* go further. Jefferson's into the Upanishads and body-dweller shit, the Republic of Virtue and global meliorism. Loses sleep over the wanton blocking of axial views and dose-response relationships—and collects Indian dialects and vocabularies, including, as a result of the journeys of Lewis and Clark, the Shoshone, who as I believe you know are my people. But, like his partial namesake in our time, he also has a dark side. . . .

"What? That depends on what you mean by 'bad.' He's a laudanum addict, for one thing—and a major circuit pig with a salivating jones for power pecs and granite buns. Today he'd have a private trainer four times a week at Washington Sports in the Circle and weekends at Monticello. He'd be downing Winstrol and snorting Special K and Ecstasy, and maybe a *little* crystal at Cobalt every night—leading the coolest retro disco buff-bod choo-choo-train orgies after candlelight power suppers, with the energy of death.

"Madison on the other hand is into the difficult and unyielding in this world, is not above bait-and-switch deals, likes to pore over negotiating texts adding wiggle words, and has a capacity for enjoyment of the recurrent element in things. Thinks broad price signals convey the right message, endorses oral hygiene, contraception, and, as protector of the federal fisc, cross-border trading for cheaper pollution offsets, and democracy as niche product for the self-made. Believes more in coveted demographics and the Virtual Republic than in the Republic of Virtue—of whose deficiencies, including blatant pressure for physical allure, mechanical sexuality, unending consumerism, and social fracture, he is only too painfully aware.

"Thinks love is as hard and unbending as hell—or as James Hammond's fleshen pole. Thus much less likely to be blindsided in working out his agendas. . . ."

He suddenly sat up. "Yeah? Well, listen, in the slipstream of history stubbornness makes more survival sense than happiness. And look, talking helps, especially if as in your case a guy is in a psychically sero-discordant relationship with his overidealized alter-ego, due to the oversecularization of sex in the body. You don't have to ask *twice*, just *nice*—like I said, ever since my grandpappy taught me how to tongue-rumba, I developed a real *broad* imagination. Despite my age in years, you could call me *old school*.

"Your problem, Congressman, is lack of *spontaneity*. If you nail down all the carpets, you can't expect any one of them to take you on a magic ride, now can you? You like legislation crafted in committees and a floor schedule that builds to a crescendo of progress . . . *party-line gang bangs*.

"Learn to leap for the horizon—be more like Jefferson and more like Jeff Clinton—without the 'roid rage. Both those boys are into *toys . . .* and *visions . . .* and *readily achievable retro-fits*. Yeah, real *symbolic*. Work it up and call me back. The meter goes on when I pick up and clicks off as soon as your fist goos up. Only please, *no* Masonic shit; I told you, it draws New World Order flies. And no Klingons or Vulcans; *that's* pinochle for child molesters. And *please*, no New Age channeling of ancient warriors called Ram-whatsis, who sound like a cross between Yoda and Bagwan Rashneesh, and I assure you that yes indeed, they *did* suck cock in Atlantis. And *next time*, we can talk about going under the dome—

". . . The Dome—you know, the Rotunda. I have the keys to the lower level. We can talk about doing it in the catafalque chamber—*yes*, one day maybe even *do it on top*. . . . Ten-*four*, Congressman."

Folding the phone up, he said, "Jefferson is Clinton, Madison is that Whitewater bank that fucks him. They like allegory—I made him come with the catafalque stuff. It's the type I mostly get: PAC bottom feeders. Types that do the heavier lifting at work, dreaming of cresting with the big pinstripe kahunas and of one day scoring at interceptor sound-bite 'gotcha' with the media. Types that attend bipartisan J.O. parties in Cuddl Duds long underwear, Doc Martens, and white socks, rely on body-heat-activated deodorant. So dumb they pay you by personal check. They bite their nails over the latest rolling shakeout, trade newsfeed threads at lunch, harp on about comity and go crazy when you show them how to make a cock ring from a shoelace like they never learned in the Boy Scouts."

Here I am, I thought, at the Big Top—and how different *is* it from the old porn palace on Forty-seventh and Broadway?

As we walked to the Hart Building, Rain said, "I like to keep my hand in—bad pun. All my callers are on the Hill and know who I am, so it adds to the buzz, but phone sex is like eating a menu. What's ironic is, here I am turning tricks with my tongue and meanwhile the senator has started a campaign to do away with 900 numbers—the telephone bills in Congress are astronomical for sex lines and psychic lines. All my clients are congressmen.

"But the handwriting is on the wall; the country's turning *wholesome*. No more cutting lines to snort through the new Ben Franklins. Page-school graduates are now all insider *abs trainers*, running 'Predator' and 'Terminator' classes. All the ugly junior congressmen are now fasting and abstaining, doing laps at L'Enfant Plaza, sweating their asses off and hoping for a little action feel in the sauna in Washington Sports on D Street. When you go into the sauna those D.C. fags in the changing room don't steal your Jockey shorts off the bench, just your fucking *workout sheet*."

In the atrium of the Hart Building, I looked up at the Calder: a disaster—black clouds over a black pyramid. Pyramids are supposed to represent light. Maybe, I thought, the idea is black light for psychedelic visions.

I asked Rain about the billing.

"Billing records are a sensitive issue nowadays. We work on the honor system. He'll slip me an envelope in the hall. It's the only time I get to use a beeper phone. The senator became convinced they cause brain tumors, or if not that, then they are all bugged."

"What about people with cellular scanners?"

"We're not *stupid*. The way it's worked you'd believe he was talking to his dry cleaner."

On the Senate subway, likened in my mind to Odette's Metalunan go-cart from *This Island Earth*, I wondered as we rolled underground toward the Great Statuary Hall—the original House chamber—would I rather be hearing Rex Reason's speech about advanced civilization or this wild rant? I decided the latter.

In the Statuary Hall I had my big vision—more anon.

"Most politicians," Rain was saying, "are so like steroid shitheads whose dicks can never really get hard but stuff them into one another with fake moans and off-camera cum shots courtesy of Reddi-Whip. You see two *real* porn actors at it, *they* are the performance equivalent of *businessmen*, especially now that they're not going to die. What are Hill veterans but long-term nonprogressors, infected for years but showing no signs of immune depletion?"

"You seem to know something about the porn trade," already starting to work out the details of what the statues had prompted in my mind.

"I know this," he snapped, seemingly aware that he'd stopped being the focus of my attention, and determined to regain center stage. "I know you came down here as a lobbyist with an agenda—that's like a guy goes into the backroom in the video store to the buddy booths with the glass windows and the mechanical shades that go up and down."

(Not bad, I thought. I might use some of this stuff.)

"You feed quarters all day long just to watch the politicians fuck one another in short loops."

"Quarters anyway, and not the nickel slots."

"Quarters add up—but that Plexiglas wall separates you and your buddies, too thick for you to punch out glory holes like at the bus station, so you jack off on the floor and call that a contribution to the workings of democracy. It makes me laugh."

"No wonder."

"You know, I can make a difference to you in your work. I can get you into the picture. Pornography and politics are the *same*."

(Politicians: instant intimacy; pornography, ditto; check. Identical mass but opposite charge and spin.)

"The more you think about it the clearer it gets. Fuck power and political power are same-sourced: the ability to persuade. Not all that easy, what with regional customs and cuisines; you know the saying 'One man's meat is another man's—' "

"Poison." (I thought, Just what I've been warned you are.)

"Exactly. Look, when you hear some meaningless phrase like 'the great American people' you could just as easily be reading, like, 'my entire throbbing member.' They're the *same* thing—the same way of talking. And when you hear, 'After it was over, I sped down the Beltway, weary, aching, drained, and completely unsatisfied'—man, are you talking about politics or what?"

"You have a point."

"Definitely. They should be put together, in a video. Take some little faceless government wonk and star him in it—have him dream of making it with the President—or the Vice President. You know about *him*—or should I say *his*? It could be a billion-dollar industry."

("Politics-pornography, as theme and inversion, cannot be played for more than a measure," the O' declared. "Nevertheless the free, decorated form of the invention does render the initial subject more agitated and expressive.")

"The mantra is 'I have such a lot to give.' A laugh, when all they're doing is fucking one another's butts with a two-headed, two-party dildo and jacking off in the people's face. The Republican jacks off backhand; big difference. What you have to know is the tool's round and the hole you stick it in can be *made* round; that's the key."

He laughed. "Once in a while, the politician lets you play river bucker—lets you nuzzle your stiff prick in the fly of his boxer shorts and moan over an agenda—or for a special treat lets you stand behind while he leans back into you and moans what a great help you've been to the process, and you jack him off in the mirror.

"'I work damn hard,' the senator says, at least once a week, 'often all night long.' 'So does your Polident,' I told him, 'and so do the whores on the most lucrative shift. You can see them on Thomas Circle, outside the CVS.' The senator says a well-bred man may be desirous of, and even greedy after, the praise and esteem of others, but to be praised to his face offends his modesty."

"I was told you used to dance at the Chesapeake House."

"The *Peake*? How *old* you think I *am*? I *heard* about the place—and about Making Waves hot-tub parlor on Seventh, and the upstairs blackout room at the Class Reunion on I, and about Pier One, where they had phones on the tables and they snorted cocaine and drank Sazeracs and called one another across the room and had phone sex. Very D.C. I was going to show you D.C.—hop on."

We were by then outside, and Rain was referring to his sleek motorized mountain bike. (As I wrote Phil: "Me, silver-helmeted, on the back of a Trek two-wheeler—space-age white with black wheel gears, black handle bag with tools inside, and a mid-frame shock absorber for off-road pursuits [none].")

We zoomed across the Potomac on Memorial Bridge to the Pentagon, past a billboard proclaiming "Virginia Is for Lovers!" and a convoy of military Humvees headed south directly under the surveillance of a flock of black helicopters. Then back along the Potomac's west bank while Rain described Galt's hideaway downriver at someplace called Pohick, hidden in a cove above a palisade.

"It's where the senator and I first went all the way—after sex we swam against the swift current of the Potomac."

("I read a longer, more elegiac version of that sentence," O'Maurigan remarked much later, back in East Hampton, "in Gore Vidal's memoirs, concerning an adolescent idyll with the great love of his life, a blond called Jimmy."

"What else?" Patsy S. demanded at that same meeting. "Secret meetings no doubt, at which 'things' were discussed."

"Yes," I said, "there on the Potomac, at Galt's western ranch, and in a cabin hideaway in one of the thousand canyons near Four Corners."

"*Plus ça change,*" Patsy drawled, sipping her iced tea.)

"The twin parks along the Potomac" (Rain) "are named after the Johnsons. LBJ Park is where the boys go to cruise now. Out in the river is the Theodore Roosevelt Bird Preserve." (I made a note, as we sped back into the District over Key Bridge, to go sometime and check the nests.) Georgetown from that vantage looked like Heidelberg from the Rhine; the Potomac looked asleep: a few rowing sculls, but never a barge or a tugboat.

Through Georgetown over Dumbarton Bridge—the "buffalo" bridge with big bronze buffalo *zeppole*—and into Rock Creek Park. "I won't take you over P Street Bridge," Rain said. "P Street Beach is underneath, and you don't want to know about that." I kept my mouth shut. I'd find out later—obviously it was some suck-and-fuck ditch like the dunes of Two Mile Hollow. But, as I wrote Phil, the idea of a *beach* in this town was hilarious.

In Rock Creek Park (home to several endangered species, including the Hay's Spring Amphipod, which lives nowhere else on earth) Rain waxed poetic on the blazing crimson and copper foliage, calling it as it fell a recreation of the shredded field banners and the feathers torn off the wings of the fallen angels of the Great Defiance, and then broke into Milton's *Paradise Lost:*

"Long is the way and hard, that out of Hell
   Leads up to light; Our prison strong this huge
   Convex of fire Outrageous to devour,
   Immures us round Ninefold, and gates of burning
   Adamant Barr'd over us prohibit all egress."

I almost wasn't surprised.

He said the Intel Building on Connecticut Avenue was the Pentagon of the Conspiracy—the boys called it "the World Trade Center"—the core of the global boy-sex ring that sends them to Karachi, Katmandu, K Street, Kalorama. Then to Rock Creek Cemetery and one of Jefferson's surveyors' milestone markers: the District border, where "a brush fire broke out last summer, and in putting it out, the firemen found sixteen charred bodies bound in bungee cord and set out in a circle around an altar stone. Uncovered only to be covered up again. Not even *City Paper* told. Not racially motivated: victims were all white.

"I know the real reason. The birch trees have the story—see the bark script?" We dismounted. "I know about missing death certificates, boys murdered in Key West and people paid to say they died of AIDS." Was he simply playing at Halloween?

As I wrote Phil, *"I'm looking forward* to Halloween in Kalorama. 'Kalorama' *sounds* like Halloween."

THREE / CAROUSEL

Fade out/fade in. The Halloween dinner chez Harrington, as strange a night as ever I'd spent at the other, the original, Max's.

That Waddy Wood Kalorama house—with WW's bas-relief head, hair center-parted, looking down from a frieze over the front door. As to the decor, here's Odette:

"Basically an update on a McKinley stinker: high-seventies D.C. Bob Waldron. She tried to get our Gotham's Mark Hampton to redo it, but he was refashioning Pamela Harriman's Paris place. She next tried Stephen Miller Siegel, who was out to lunch. Rumors of consultations with D.C.'s own Mary Douglas Drysdale and Barry Darr Dixon followed."

Result: rugs, rugs, rugs, rows of leather-bound books, soft felt walls and overstuffed down-filled Bonaparte sofas, Janine, Faucon, and Chartard chairs, all covered in raw silk and hammered satin.

"Yes," Odette said, "Bam-Bam's nail-head leather sectional and lava-lamp phase is long over, but her taste has hardly risen above that of the Ralph Lauren home collection or the soutache-braid faggots who design *In This Our Life*."

Hundreds of porcelains, sterling boxes, and pictures in antique silver frames. Several Tiffany lamps from the original Victorian house. You might say that the place struck a balance either between deferential revivalism and eclectic insouciance or between the enhanced feelings of security and cozy familiarity, incorporating proven hegemonic cultural features in a characteristically decisive American world-power manner— like the Hay-Adams lobby. Or else you could just call it *ungepotchket*.

"When I look at places like this," Odette concluded, "I think, Whatever happened to the wit and wisdom of Elsie De Wolfe?"

Here, as elsewhere in D.C. on social occasions, the coat was hardly off the back before the conversation resumed. The first trick-or-treat was O'M's arrival with Delmarva and O.J. ("We have come as Buck and Bubble," the latter announced, "and *only* the devil could have made Miss Fly buy that dress—it ain't no way widout it.") Bam-Bam was stunned, but Max, waving his hand, wrist, and Audemars Piguet watch in a regal gesture, finessed the situation, declaring, "'Be not forgetful to entertain strangers,' Grandmother said, 'for thereby have some entertained angels unawares.' She was hoping for Moroni."

"An Irish angel?" Delmarva rejoined, eyes wide. "This gate crash is entirely Mr. O'Maurigan's fault—for we were actually on our way to the Gores', but got lost and were found by him tracing a counterclockwise ritual path around Dupont Circle. But the Harrington reputation for solicitude is such a watchword in Washington, we did not hesitate to join his entourage— reinforced by his insistence that our intrusion would be most unlikely to result in any 'family-hold-back' situation."

"I'm glad to hear it," Max rejoined genially. "The very thought of you munching GooGoo Clusters with the Goristas distresses me deeply."

The second *déguisement fantasque* was the arrival, with the Vesteralens, of Maud MacGown. I nearly didn't recognize her myself. (I'd said to O'Maurigan, "But surely Bam-Bam will read this Maud MacGown as Odette right off." "Yes." "And?" "Nothing—it wouldn't be at all wise of her." "Odette has information, then?" "Odette," he replied, very seriously, "is, as we all know, one of the best-informed, best-connected, most serious-minded and highly principled self-made women of our time. Bam-Bam has some inkling of that . . . and an even better one of the fundamental fact that you do not fuck with a drag queen unless you have a yen for big trouble.")

The third was the arrival—*sola*—of Vana Sprezza, in a knockout Versace that made Bam-Bam, at home in what Odette described as "a nonspecific Carolina Herrera," nuts from the start.

Cocktails in a long alcove given over to the history of political cartooning in the U.S.—and covered with exactly the same wallpaper as the Senate corridors: flags of the Republic. There was a whole wall of Whigs: Fillmore, from New York; Polk, from Tennessee . . . Harrison, Tyler, and Winfield Scott, pictured as a turkey opposite his opponent (the winner) Democrat Franklin Pierce (the wild drunken ex-army factotum who on his way home one night actually ran a woman down and killed her on Pennsylvania Avenue, and was allowed by the District police to go on to 1600 unmolested—no wonder most people think Clinton's peccadillos small-time).

"Anastasia hates this room," Max allowed. "She'd prefer something more along the lines of the long gallery at Fontaine-bleau—with its fourteen allegories of the triumph of the monarchy—but I reminded her we are living in democratic times."

"I've always been interested in the Whigs," I heard somebody declare. "I once thought of writing a book on them."

"Dick," Max addressed the speaker, "I want you to meet my environmentalist friend down from New York; he's been investigating Senate committees."

"I'm sure," the person next introduced to me as Dick Fauquier drawled, "it would be cumbersome to give a detailed,

consecutive account of your wanderings inside that cavernous
aeons-dead honeycomb—that mountain lair of elder secrets—
especially since so much of the horrid revelations come from a
mere study of the omnipresent mural daubs and carvings."

"What was *that*?" I asked O'Maurigan as Fauquier sauntered over to Barb Vesteralen. "If you mean the quotation," he
replied, "it's Lovecraft. If you mean the creature himself, with
the distinguished head of a Virginia failure, something like the
same source. Max probably laid him on to outdo the Gores,
who only get customers dressed up as the living dead, not the
specimens themselves."

"When I can't sleep," I heard Barb V. declare, "I count
Presidents, and I always get stuck in the Whigs." (I wondered,
Would the Whigs turn Rain's clients on, like Jefferson and
Madison did?)

Dick Fauquier now swung back in my direction. "She's
funny," he confided, "but of course ignorant. It was the demise
of Whiggery, the Wilmot Proviso, fire-eater appeals, and the
destruction of democracy by the psychotic Lincoln that led to
the War of Northern Aggression—from which this nation has
never recovered. Yes, she's funny, but *he's* brilliant."

"Doug? Yes, I'd say he was."

"Absolutely. His new thesis virtually equates the praxes of
politics and genetics. Like human DNA, of which over 95 percent does not code for genes at all—so political genetics, in the
vast onrush of the economic, religious, and social stream. Politics entire is like a lonely sperm fighting for a safe vantage in
the ovarian flux of civilization itself. Speaking of which, he's
been approached by the Repository for Germinal Choice—the
genius sperm bank in California. But you mustn't let on—it
embarrasses him—although *she* has been heard joking about
his being flown out there to jack off into an ice-cube tray. The
other day some Washington dame, hearing her do so, referred
to her as coarse-grained, only to have Doug, as if picking her
up on a scanner, sweep in to declare, 'If you mean by that the

averaging of dynamics over finite regions of phase space, then yes, she is.'"

"A very devoted husband," I offered.

"Fiercely. And they *are* refreshing—intellectual charisma offset, even enhanced, by vaudevillian strut. Nevertheless it's hard lines on him, as the English say. The smarter you are down here, the more terrible it is. Well, there are geniuses like Doug Vesteralen and then there are the likes of me, content to earn our keep by merely *observing* the merry-go-round, in which the issues, like the horses, get licks of fresh paint but never change, while ever-replenished hordes of avid children jostle to mount them.

"Of course there's study and there's study. Why, did you know that somebody was actually given a grant by the NEA to study the parallel lives of all the Presidents—six in number—whose Christian names were James, on the premise that 'Jacob' means 'the Supplanter'? Thus Madison supplants Jefferson, Monroe supplants . . . Anyway, it's entitled 'What's in a Name?'"

"Property, usually," Barb snapped, coming back within earshot to snag a second cocktail.

"How true," Dick Fauquier mewed, "but" (turning back to me) "I understand you, sir, are more interested in Prince Albert. He who must supplant the Incumbent."

"His environmental concerns, principally."

"Certainly. Well, I may say that at the very least your mentor is a gentleman and a statesman."

"Max darling," Anastasia cut in, fussing with a mum in a Khmer vase, "I want you to show Delancey the carousel horses in the ballroom, and all the rest of the house. Delancey does houses."

And Ferris wheel rides. At the top, looking out the attic window, I got a panorama of Washington history in one family.

Max opened the bidding with a quote. "'Washington, more than any other city in the world, swarms with simpleminded exhibitions of human nature, curiously out of place, cruel to ridicule but ridiculous to weep over. The sadder exhibitions are fortunately seldom seen by respectable people.'"

"*Democracy*," I replied. "By Clover Adams."

"So I hear. I keep telling my wife she could write the update. Give her something more interesting to do than this."

"Socially not very complex?"

"Try simpleminded. Before you arrived, Dick Fauquier was bending her ear about his *wildflowers* being *ticketed* by some District flunkies for being over *four inches* high. *That's* what they do down at One Ju-dish-u-ary Square!"

(Four inches. The Maud in *Democracy* came looking for something bigger than six inches, and was frustrated.)

"Dick can go on at length about the dereliction of the District's once-beautiful public drinking fountains, comfort stations, and monuments to Civic Virtue. For him ANC stands not for Advisory Neighborhood Commissions but African National Congress. (As *Democracy*'s heroine demands, 'Where did the public good enter at all into this maze of personal intrigue, this wilderness of stunted natures where no straight road was to be found, but only the tortuous and aimless tracks of beasts and things that crawl?')

"'You know,' he was moaning before, 'in the heat of last August, packs of rats in broad daylight were seen crawling all over the mayor's downtown bunker? I call that a signal.'

"By contrast, up here in Kalorama, we still like to play the games where the sternest purpose lurks under the highest frivolity—rather than the reverse. My grandmother was a great patron of Alice Pike Barney's allegorical tableaux vivants, often presented in the old ballroom here. You'll notice, however, that the board the game is played on resembles Byzantium rather than Cyber City."

(I'd had like thoughts at home at the high window.)

"We pay no attention at all to the polity at Ju-dish-u-ary Square. In Northwest MPD means Multiple Personality Disorder, not Metropolitan Police Department—its drug lab afloat with boxes of drugs and cash; its property warehouse, administered under an *honor system*, stacked with guns. Computers down; unsolved homicide cases in the hundreds; crime evidence destroyed and lost; cars missing. Did you know the police in order to get to the scene of a crime now take public transport? Television could make a *unique* cop show out of that: *D.C. Red, Blue, Green, Orange, and Yellow.*

"'What a strange and solemn spectacle it is,'" Max concluded. ("How," as Clover puts it, "its deadly fascination burns the images in upon the mind." It sure killed her.)

"Do you mean," I asked, "now, in our time—the spectacle of government itself, or the impasse between Congress and the President, or between Congress and the District—"

"The District of Chaos, or Corruption. I seldom discuss it, there being nothing to *cite* but a cross between *Amos 'n Andy*, *Umabatha*, *The Zulu Macbeth*, and the carpetbagger farce sequence D.W. Griffith put in *Birth of a Nation*—as Marion S. Barry pilots his crew of Lorton-alumni extortioners in the, I give you, Office of Offender Affairs, skimming the froth off every crap game and numbers racket stewpot in the dark metropolis.

"But speaking of colors of lines, lines of color, you've heard the mayor's own color mantra? 'Red and yellow, black and white, all are precious in my sight.' Trying his own squawk in the register of old Logan Circle's own Sweet Daddy Grace—but of course he's talking about *pills*, throwing in twelve-step-program orthodoxy as a red herring. What balls; they positively brush the floor along with the arms when he walks—when he can stand up to walk.

"Last summer, you know, he was *crowned* in Africa, and renamed, along with the *consort*, the fair Cora, late boxing commissioner, quondam president of the University of the District of Columbia, and I believe the fourth—or is it the fifth?—of Marion's legal wives. They are now styled King Yede and Queen Hypo of Sikensi. I'm surprised he didn't come back and pull a Mobuto Sese Seko: have a multimillion-dollar *bus station* erected in Anacostia on the model of all those African airports. 'Who does you *hair*?!' Queen Hypo asks reporters. 'Who put the bone in your nose?' is what they should ask *her*. I like Dick's line on her. He says she had a vision of herself center stage singing the big disco number 'Don't Cry for Me, Anacostia' in the musical *Corita*, until somebody told her the name was too close to that of a famously upstanding black woman.

"A pair destined for one another. A great love story; they take the cake in the cakewalk. Periodically, the *Post*, like a team of high-school-dropout cheerleaders, publishes the twelve steps of Alcoholics Anonymous. They must expect to hear Hizzoner one day declare that as a result of his spiritual awakening—assisted by meditation on the vanity of human wishes—he is ready to accept the diagnosis of Attainment Deficit Disorder, knuckle under, medicate carefully—a moderate Ritalin dose—and practice these principles in all his affairs. Step twelve, I believe.

"The twelve steps indeed. Unless Marion Barry had been born with six fingers on each hand, he could never *count* to twelve. But then Cora is said to wield a whip with twelve flails. 'What does he actually *do*?' I once asked one of his supporters. 'Well . . . he's very good at *tasking out*.' I give you—but whether Kingfish Marion and his flailmate chat on the long distance to Idi Amin or to Hizzoner's dress-code mentor, the exiled Emperor Bokassa—Marion doodling on his scroll of the twelve steps and the emperor fingering the crucifix given him by Pope Paul VI—is no concern of ours. This is a question not of intent, but blasted morale: a society particularistic, communal, and ascriptive, imbedded in a world that demands universalism, individualism, and achievement. A corporation with bonds rated by Moody's in the junk category.

"To which tyranny I respond, recalling the order of the proclamation secretly disseminated in France fifty-five years ago this month: '*Résister! C'est déjà garder son coeur et son cerveau. Mais c'est surtout agir, faire quelque chose qui se traduise en faits positifs, en actes raisonées et utiles.*' So have I appropriately advised the chairman of the oversight committee, Mr. Davis— who clearly aspires to the Senate, and might indeed do well for us there. I might go so far as to propose another Boston Tea Party—at the Anacostia River . . . but responsible citizens whose brains haven't fallen out of their heads don't dare go *near* the Anacostia River. Should *faction fighting* break out, as seems likely now that Kingfish Barry appears to be a badly wounded shark, a replay of the bloody melodramas of Central Africa—countless machete-hacked bodies floating down the Anacostia, then bottlenecking the Washington Channel and backing up into the Tidal Basin like shit into a white marble bathtub, like those that floated down the Congo into Lake Victoria—seems not out of the question.

"Ultimately, it should be closed down by the Congress with the backing of the Capitol Police and the National Guard. Nobody civilized who lives under the jurisdiction of the District of Columbia in this home-rule travesty can be anything but an anarchist—rather an extreme task, even for us dedicated to free enterprise. As Montesquieu points out, the process of building self-esteem in individuals, of harnessing creating energies, and assuring domestic tranquillity are not all that different, *mutatis mutandis*, vis-à-vis monarchy, republican institutions, et cetera—in different epochs, but they *all* depend on the spirit of the *law*.

"And they should throw Louis Farrakhan in jail—if for no other reason than for consorting with Muammar Gadhafi. Are they going to wait until the Capitol itself blows up? It very easily could, you know, with all these deluded and disgruntled exiles in six-hundred-dollar Hickey-Freeman suits swarming over the Hill like cockroaches fomenting . . . an atomic device on the Metro Blue and Orange moving between Capitol South and Federal Triangle would. . . . As one sentimental old acquaintance put it to me, 'It's been a long way down from Marian Anderson to Marion Barry.' What hath Polly Shackleton and company wrought. I prefer my mother's bandage rolling and conga lines. Come, I'll show you."

The tour continued. Chippendale everywhere, and lamps with silk Empire box pleated shades in ecru and dark green illuminating Cézannes, Renoirs, Sérusiers, and Braques, and sending random shadows cast by two Brancusis and a Rodin across the old walls. A proliferation of bronze Buddhas (not a piece of Greek or Roman anything) and Khmer vases Max was "thinking of giving to the Sackler, before I trip over something and break one. I'm sure they're all cursed; things you pick up in jungles usually are." And in the upstairs hall, John Marin's Woolworth watercolor series.

It was in the disused ballroom (in which the mirrored walls were all smoky and enough old folded-up Chinese screens were stacked along the walls for a whole Congress to hide behind—and maybe they were on Halloween: a very political room, I thought) that I found the Greek-and-Roman-American Hiram Powers stuff (along with a cigar-store Indian—which reminded me again of Phil's favorite joke) and eight fantastic carousel horses, which made me then liken the place to the Statuary Hall in the House of Representatives. A huge chandelier lay on the floor in the center of the room, covered in a dust cloth. "I won a prize once," Max told me, "at St. Albans, with a story about that chandelier. I'll tell it to you sometime." Also, a very large collection of the Ashcan school. "Grandfather's," Max said. "Banished here after his death by his widow, along with several Alice Pike Barneys. Mother used to take me in here, show me the paintings, and tell me, 'Reginald Marsh said well-bred people were no fun to paint. They're not all that much fun to know, either, but we do . . . we do.'"

I liked the paintings: the same flow of American energy as Pollock, before it was ready to go transcendental.

"As a young wife," Max continued, "Mother rolled bandages up here, with the other nice women who volunteered. That was in the afternoon. In the evening she was another woman; it was said of her that she was the first in the quadrille and the last to depart. 'The ballroom in Kalorama is her temple of inspiration and worship.' 'Quadrille' of course is fanciful; I recall rumbas, sambas, and conga lines. It was her dream to have a skylight put in, but father said one did not want to give the impression of a hotel nightclub, and anyway Civil Defense would likely not have permitted it.

"Those were great days," Max said with evident nostalgia, looking out the round window at what he called the Palatine Hill. "Big Christmas receptions at homes like Marie Beale's Decatur House on Lafayette Square, where you'd be served bacon and peanut butter canapes and tumblers of whiskey." (Yes, I thought: the D.C. Max was born into was the one I'd first visited: segregation, servile Uncle Toms everywhere—including Harry Truman's valet—nice women who volunteered, and dancing parties reported in the papers every morning.)

"And now," my host and guide continued, "the place has become something of a battleground—or a demilitarized zone—in the battle Anastasia and I are currently having over our *place*, if you don't mind, in D.C. society. Anastasia thinks we ought to make the ballroom functional again—repaint the walls, resilver the mirrors, for tango parties. I said I might consider it if she allowed me to hang the Ashcans—but I know she won't give in on that, and I'm relieved. People who want to dance should go to the Cosmos Club, is my feeling. You must join us there next month for the Yuletide Ball, or the Winter Cotillion, or whatever they call it, your whole gang; we need fresh blood—including the darkies.

"You know, it occurs to me your crowd might think that for our crowd an entirely dysfunctional government is actually something to be desired. But it's not so. We believe in a govern-ment that is largely *fictive;* but one that is entirely *delusional*? Well, the trumpeted and ideological divide between the major parties wasn't always, as you like to say in New York, a crock of shit.

"Formerly we thrilled to the spectacle of Strom Thur-mond and Russell Yarborough thrashing around in the Senate corridor over civil rights and the drunken imperial Johnson. Well, this lot have mastered the *form* of the enterprise, but not its *content.* Clinton, having been with the Jesuits, is rather good at the distinction—at exploiting the anxiety in the gap between. He is of course no good at all at closing it—but then zippers are not his forte.

"Today there are merely crucial *temperamental* differ-ences, *personality profile* differences between the typical Repub-lican and the typical Democrat—which we, the senator and I, have had to take into consideration over the years in repackag-ing him.

"Partisans on both sides are equally corrupt—but it is only the Democrat you can shame and artfully manipulate with the threat of a retributive investigation. Nixon, Kissinger, Gin-grich—that temperament don't—*can't*—give a shit, and the Dole temperament you can't really nail. But a Clinton or a Gore can be throttled by their party's vaunted principles— chief of which is that to be exposed, badly, is a sign of weakness that leads to elimination."

"Do you work hard?"

"Like a—sled dog. Do you? And *please* don't mention the travails of the Internet. All that bandwidth *window dressing.*"

(I had a weird nervous sense—looking out a window at the Washington Monument lit up—of *déjà entendu.*)

"Your approach, however, interests me. You have all the charisma of a motivational speaker, but inverted into that of a motivational *listener.* You're such an empath, you ought to go on television—do a political show while you're down here in D.C. *The Delancey Report.* Not some old piece of paleoliberal shit—something *camp.*"

("What's an empath?" I asked the O' later.

"As such? I don't know," he replied, turning to Odette. "Do you?"

"Yes, dear, as it happens, I do. It's from *Star Trek.* Touching, isn't it?—that Max is a Trekkie."

"I think," I said, "the expression is 'far out.'")

Just then, standing at the window at the top of that house in Kalorama, I remembered once standing in Michael Kahn's glass-floored townhouse on Beekman Place, feeling the worst vertigo of my life.

As Max expatiated on Washington, money, and why the really powerful rich take care to *never* get in the papers, I saw a frustrated performance artist, who belonged on the Agnelli party circuit but *wasn't permitted to.* (By the World Conspiracy?)

"O'Maurigan thinks I ought to do a television show here. He wants to call it *The Delancey Retort.*"

"I like it. Perhaps I'll look into putting you on. My lovely wife would, I feel certain, be interested in appearing with you. But you're not here as an AIDS activist, are you, but as an environmentalist—positioned rather like a cargo handler on a gun-running flight. What's that little guy you want to protect?"

"The piping plover—actually, wetland fowl in general."

"Right. That guy's in trouble even down here—or in North Carolina, on the outer banks, where the wild mustang horse is stomping all over him. *Buzzards* are protected down here, you know—and not just the Marion Barry variety. Just ask the citizens of Leesburg, where they roost from Halloween—today—until Easter, shitting all over everything and everybody. And do beware of any protonotary warbler on the banks of the Potomac."

("Is he talking about Rain being a canary?" I asked the O'.

"No, in fact he's talking about Alger Hiss. Halloween reminds him of pumpkin patches. As Herrick wrote apropos, 'Can I not sin but thou will be my private protonotary?'")

"And I'll bet you want to bring back the beaver too, and the prairie dog. Ever seen one of either? And there's a little guy out in Orange County who's got problems too, like your little guy. The California gnat-catcher—heard of him? Or of the brown pelican—or of the blue sandbill crane up in the Rockies?"

I hadn't—and felt a little provincial. But I'd never heard of bluebirds either, until Judy sang "Somewhere over the rainbow. . . ."

"The brown pelican is prone to botulism. The effluvium in Santa Monica Bay—garbage overflow . . . Insinkerators. Another endangered species in Malibu is the entire Owl clan of the Chumash.

"While down in New Mexico, talking of owls, they want to protect the Mexican spotted owl by restricting the cutting of firewood, but poverty-line New Mexicans like their firewood rights as much as do the timber boys of the Pacific Northwest, callous to the fate of the marbled murrelet. Turns out the poor share some of the ideas of the rich after all. You use firewood up on Long Island?"

"We buy it, yes."

"I see. Anybody there hanging you in effigy?"

"People who'd like the wetlands drained for development don't look too kindly—"

"Like Walden Pond."

"Yes. They aren't smiling on our efforts—but as yet, no hangings."

"Well, they saved Walden Pond. Of course in your state the Mafia is I believe represented in the Senate?"

"We don't go so far as to claim—"

"Wise. I wouldn't fuck with those boys either: the stool pigeon is hardly a protected species. Best let them do their own kind of waste disposal in the desert. The Harringtons, you know, have for seventy years been sentimentally attached to the California condor—making his comeback out at Four Corners."

Going into dinner, Max announced, "You won't be getting anything like the meatloaf Mary McGrory makes taste like something scared up on food stamps, nor iceberg lettuce with Thousand Island dressing, but we hope not to send you home hungry."

"I am confident you will not," Delmarva replied coolly, "and I and my companion thank you for not indulging in downscale chic by condescending to our taste for chitlins and other nasty fats—as much the result of the disincentives of federal assistance programs as inherent crippling cognitive disabilities."

As I wrote Phil, "Then the dinner theater: essentially the cartoon gallery updated, switched from one long room into another, and the cartoons come to life—all dialogue in balloons floating over the talking heads of real (enough) people set against the background of the eighteenth-century French Arcadian-scene wallpaper.

"More like D.C.'s most expensive restaurant than anybody's home, much with quilt-covered ribbon-laced dining room chairs, faux wood paneling, and elaborately hand-stenciled wood beams. (Bam-Bam is a great admirer, Odette reminded me, of Diane de Poitiers, whose Château d'Anet at Rambouillet she often speaks of dreamily.)

"The royal blue, red, and gold color scheme," I wrote, "is as Grand Street (minus the Capo di Monte) as the Limoges china and Riedel crystal is Europosh ('Were you expecting Roseville or Rookwood, darling?' Bam-Bam cooed), not to mention the contour and weight of the François Premier repoussé flatware that could give you calluses with daily use."

Delicious dinner. Bass with green papaya and baby bok choy, venison with pomegranates, salad, and passion fruit cannelais with coconut ice cream: burnt-sugar sauce. Coffee. (Barb swore later she'd seen the plum-colored van from Ridgewell's—D.C.'s Chasen's—parked at the curb.)

Fauquier, digging into the meal, declared, "As Sarah Booth Conroy might say, since Eve ate apples, much depends on dinner—though the business of there bein' no *pluvvuh's eggs* I find *offensive*." "Current thinking," the Food Writer declared, "favors pomegranates—like these."

I heard Doug Vesteralen say "Gibbon on religion," and listened. " 'The theologian may indulge the pleasing task of describing religion as she descends from heaven arrayed in native purity; a more melancholy duty is imposed upon the historian: he must discover the inevitable mixture of error and corruption which she contracted in a long residence upon earth among a weak and degenerate race of beings.' "

"In the District," Dick Fauquier declared, "church and state have become one in Marion Barry, whose pretense is *pharaonic*."

"Minister Farrakhan," Ornette replied, "speaking at a press conference from his bannered pavilion in Bengazi, would call *that* a white-male-instigated hegemonic insult. Marion Barry is simply the Alexander Robey—called 'Boss'—Shepherd of our time."

Fauquier looked brought up terribly short.

"Indeed," Ornette continued, "if D.C. is a swamp, then Marion S. Barry is the Swamp Fox—who sees himself as the Good Shepherd of all the black sheep entrusted to his special care. And as in Farrakhan's pharaohs, in every crock of shit there is a nugget of gold—like somebody swallowed a filling from one of his old rotted-black molars and *passed it*? For indeed there *was* some kind of black pharaoh, not in Cleopatra's time, but six hundred years before. The Twenty-fifth Dynasty, the Cushite, or the conquest of the pharaohdom by the Meroites—related to the Queen of Sheba who visited King Solomon—called 'Candace,' a very popular black name today."

"Johnson," Doug remarked, "famously touted his private taped memoirs as 'history with the bark off,' but"—turning to me—"as an environmentalist you know that a tree stripped of its bark dies. So does history. There is no way to dispense it without a coating."

"These pharaohs," Ornette continued unchecked, "ruled from 728 to 664 B.C.E.—that's Before the Confusion of Everybody. From their time of such common disciplinary matrix the Egyptians call themselves the black ones—'Kems'—after the color of their earth. And the *numerology* of it is, 25 is 7, 728 is 8, 664 is 7, and the *duration* is 64 is 1, which if you add to the rest makes 5, and if you multiply and/or divide, 4. Not a 9 in sight. So when I hear Pharaoh-Khan say, 'Were it not for welfare, I wouldn't be who and what I am,' I say let the muh-fuhs *starve*, or subsist on the *aphrodisiac chewin' gum* that the Israelis flood the Cairo market with to demoralize Islam's children."

"And," Delmarva added, "in terms of actual realpolitik, Marion is as good as Boss Shepherd ever was, and the people of the District know it. Marion and Cora say if all they can rule over is Lilliput, then they will torment the white folks long as they can."

"There are seven rather than five color lines on Metro," Ornette advised me, "if you add the *black* and the *white*—runnin' parallel the other lines and goin' to the same places. They are the public transportation of two different cities *coaxial* at Metro Center, symbolized by the route map in the shape of a *swastika* with some extra *attitude*. You take the black line some time, you end up in Simple City. In Simple City, in place of inscriptions etched on buildings, you got graffiti spray-painted guns and knives and shit and the names of all the children killed in the crew wars.

"Now I have heard the white folks say that his S. stand for Sambo, and Marion be good at chasin' congressional tigers around the trees in the National Ar-bo-*re*-tum to get the *butter* fo' his *flapjacks*."

He looked around at a captive audience. "You *are* aware that my rhetoric is neither Christian nor Muslim. I did not part from the Baptist Confession, with its impressive musical heritage, either to audition for the chorus of the Missa Luba or to embrace a degenerate form of Islam—despite the incessant drumming in my infant ears of the poetry and percussion of Umar Bin Hassan, Abiodun Oyewole, and Babatunde.

"But possibly because my mama was Jewish, I have become attached to concepts such as *derekh eretz*—proper respect. You could call me matrifocal—jus' don't call me *sissified*—but be that as it may, I am more Christian—Black Baptist—than not. Otherwise I might go in for Kwanzaa or some such other jive. I thought of becomin' a Quaker, like Bayard Rustin was, but ended up fantasizin' myself framed on a box of Quaker oats—a peaceable credit to my race and a living symbol of industry—but lookin' like Aunt Jemima on the pancake box, dig?

"Which I do not, never mind my headgear—which my enemies declare I wear to cover the birthmark on my shaved head, in the shape of a big white 8. I may sympathize with Black Baptist and AME churches, and even with the Philadelphia Worldwide Church of God and with *Mystery of the Ages* by Herbert W. Armstrong, but bein' Jewish by birth, circumcised *and* political, I am cognizant of the term *titulum*—what Israelis do to recalcitrant Arabs. Called *shaking*. Causes brain damage and sometimes death, same as it does in infants when parents lose it, or to Holy Rollers and freshman Republicans—they get so shook up so often, their brains go soft. Now, Israel being a USA client state—and the American Israeli Public Affairs Committee being number two in *Fortune* magazine's list of the most powerful interest groups in the nation's capital, right behind the American Association of Retired Persons—" giving Fauquier a sidelong look—"nobody *we* know. There's no existential difference between Yigal Amir and Timothy McVeigh. They are both products of the deepest strains of their nations' culture.

"Of course I admire the Israelis' focus on the single target."

I saw Bam-Bam freeze, and even Max go stony at the mention of Herbert W. Armstrong. Topics spun. Doug wondered would the fight ring return to favor with intellectuals— would Hollywood put a Denzel Washington into a fight picture? Delmarva said Denzel would tank as badly in a fight picture as he would playing O. J. Simpson.

"Or as he is called in certain quarters," Ornette snarled, "O.J. *Thello.* And there's a Shakespeare play you could do as a fight picture—the black buck assigned his place in the fight ring by a society that lets him know where it likes him best, neutralizing his organizational ability, left to promoters."

Delmarva said Spike Lee and Whoopi Goldberg ought to make a picture together. Ornette snapped, "Yeah? Like what, *Rochester Meets Aunt Jemima?*"

"More than half the army," Anastasia said then, "is black."

"Not the officers, ma'am. You get to officer, you turn white. You start quotin' Alexander the Great, sayin', 'Let the sons of dreams outlive the sons of seed.' Your uniform comes from Brooks Brothers, same as what Teddy Roosevelt wore up San Juan Hill, and you get your pearl-handled revolver, like his, from Tiffany.

"You think Colin Powell is black? Colin Powell is black like Bobby Short is black—like Luther Vandross and Vanessa Williams are black. They are what you call 'black derivatives.' And Mr. LeRoi Jones, a.k.a. Amiri Baraka, did not, accordin' to his autobiography, do at *all* well in what he calls the Error Farce. *Black* is what General Sani Abacha, chairman of the Nigerian Joint Chiefs of Staff, on whom Colin Powell pinned the Legion of Merit in May of 1991, is."

"I *cannot* agree," Dick Fauquier snapped. "Nor are you, a

civilian youth of whatever tincture, in a position to declare such the case. The structure of advancement in the military is more rule-bound than in the private sector. You cannot apply the military's *necessarily* rigid structure to hundreds of thousands of private employers hiring tens of millions of people. *But,* the military has *also* created *highly* successful training and education programs designed to combine merit promotion with affirmative action. They could have wider application."

"Dick was in the Navy," Max proclaimed, "for three years, in the fifties. Aboard the *Intrepid.*" (The *Intrepid.* And why not? Still, I couldn't picture this number in sailor whites like Phil.)

"Excuse me?" Vana interrupted, throwing her amazing shoulders and the hair cascading onto them into the fray. "What does this term 'black derivative' mean?"

"They who have succeeded, ma'am," Ornette replied, "to positions unavailable or unattainable or *unfound* by the overwhelming majority of their brothers and sisters. Such a one as Billy Strayhorn. Strays succeeded in making that *hegemonic* transition from the *otherwise* to the *additional.*"

"Now, *now*," Delmarva rejoined, "let us remember the words of Ralph Ellison chastising the angry Richard Wright in that most reliable and trustworthy organ of American opinion, *Time* magazine. 'After all, our people have been here for a long time. It's a big, wonderful country, and you just can't turn away from it because some people decide it isn't your country.'" (Was she kidding?)

"Hallelujah!" Ornette rejoined. "Not until the man I now call Corn-row West joined Minister Pharaoh-khan on the Mall last month has such a *sensible* approach been witnessed."

The food writer tried honing in on truffles in North Carolina, plover's eggs, and other *bec fin* topics. Dick Fauquier asked what my little bird feeds on. Worms. "Well, the American eagle feeds on small rodents, and the numbers of the population of worms and small rodents here is as incalculable as the number of luminous bodies in the *universe*. I am sentimental; one of my great-grandmothers was a Duck who married a Fowler."

("Fauquier," O'Maurigan explained later, "was originally Max's private secretary, home-officed at the Watergate, from which he was forced to decamp, declaring, 'What *is* the Senate besides some anachronistic repository of brass spittoons?'

"This was just around the time the senator left the Philadelphian Worldwide Church of God, came under the shall we say thrall of Max, and, on a sailing trip with him still shrouded in mystery, adopted the boy."

"So Max provided the senator with Rain—or vice versa."

"Not certain—although *vice* comes into it. Fauquier's lived ever since then in a pathetic little town home in Mary Washington Square, adopting the airs and graces of old Richmond—he's never really gotten over Pickett's Charge: is firmly convinced that the damn Yankees fight *dirty*—and hinting darkly of untoward doings here, there, and everywhere. His neighbors now include a pair of alien abductees, who talk about the experience as incredibly benign.")

"And so why should Colin Powell run for President?" Ornette continued. "To reach the swing voters of the Great American Republic by going on *Oprah* and *Montel* and *Rolonda* and *Paula Jones* and carryin' on somehow, like his tires wuz whitewall, huh?"

"I think," Dick Fauquier interposed, "you mean *Jenny Jones*."

"Whatever. Apologizing for his military advancement and declaring out loud that that war against the yellow peril from which the veterans came home and started right in offing themselves in numbers that have long since exceeded the actual casualties was one useless enterprise. Or that if he did run and did get elected and had done a deal with those dwellers of palacious apartments up on Striver's Row and did agree to make Louis Farrakhan secretary of state, that maybe Maya Angelou, miffed at not bein' declared poet laureate, would decline to read another epic poem at his inaugural.

"I like what the *Post* said, that the general was the first viable candidate named after a body part since LBJ."

"Will you," the food writer suddenly inquired of me, "write more about society or about politics?"

"So far I'm just writing about committees—the worm's-eye view—and not getting very far. Lately I've thought of asking the statues for the inside dope."

"That is a very good point," Doug interposed, "so long as you don't invite them to supper."

"Ah," Anastasia interjected, "but Delancey is the very most faithful of men. Yet I suppose we all have a Don Juan in us."

"So to speak?" Barb jibed.

"Do you know," Anastasia continued, "what Maillol said about doing sculpture? He went to London to the fights in Whitechapel, and said that was the only way to do sculpture. You ought to do politics like that. Of course he was talking about the nude."

Maud MacGown spoke up. "'With a woman, one gesture and it's already a statue. With a man, a gesture is ridiculous.' A statement borne out when one examines the public sculpture of Washington."

"Opinion is so *variable*," Anastasia replied coolly. "It is said of Versace, for instance, that what is most compelling about him is that he embraces the sensuality and titillating bravado of the harlot's wardrobe. Maillol found men more beautiful—or interesting—than women to do. So you will find men, who *are* politics, more interesting than women, who *are* society."

Barb inquired of the British queen, "Did Shakespeare like women?" "Shakespeare," he replied, "appears to have objected to gratuitous cruelty, thought a strong monarch-governed state preferable to anarchy, and looked upon the French as a bit of a joke. The rest is silence."

"Le Corbusier," Dick Fauquier offered, "made the male body his architectural ideal—calling it the 'Modulor.' He also thought slave labor a very good idea when applied to high and noble works, since one could change one's mind without incurring great costs."

"In any case," Vana added, rather frantically, with a toss of the head, looking very beautiful, very much, as Fauquier put it, *la distinta forestiera*, like the Monica Vitti of *L'Avventura*, a female postmodern sumptuary of daring habits in her titillating black-and-vermillion high-harlot Versace, "these art comparisons are a little out of date, no? Modern politics ought to be expressed at least in terms of a Giacometti, if not of a Brancusi."

"Or," Doug Vesteralen replied, "in terms of a Friedensreich Hundertwasser, who has declared that the straight line is evil. And Egon Schiele says that for him the male is the self, a realm in essence immaterial, whereas the female is the other, whose material opacity awakens a sense of bulk."

"Then there's Canova," Odette mused idly. "Started out sculpting butter centerpieces for Venetian dinner parties, and ended up doing Pauline Borghese's fabulous naked torso."

"Perhaps," Anastasia fretted, I thought almost hysterically, "art metaphors *are* a bit stale or overripe. Let's hope nothing was either at dinner. But"—turning to me—"you will have to be very *empathetic*, and not so *elitist*." ("Imagine!" Odette whispered. "Lady Politick Would-Be, in *Volpone*.")

"Ah yes," O'M decreed, "creative empathy. George Eliot's work was accomplished with a volatile series of lenses, suggesting at this time empathy and at that time severe omniscience."

"Well," Anastasia laughed, "I *always* have found Delancey *plugged in*. And as to *lenses*, if ever *anyone* was a camera, it is he. I am only sorry we are not quite so decadent as thirties Berlin."

"Interesting you should say that," I remarked, "because when I first arrived in Washington, I was assured that politics and pornography were nearly identical."

"An offensive opinion, sir!" thundered the senator.

As I wrote Phil: I didn't mind being roared at by the old guy—it reminded me of *Allen's Alley* on the radio—but I was (unlike Ornette and Delmarva) uncomfortable being served by a black man—being served at all: too used to popping up from the table in Sagaponack to check the help. Then I misunderstood the cookbook writer: I thought she said she'd like to make me part of the food *chain*, instead of the food *circle* she cooks specialties for, and would call me for *feedback*. Ernie Pyle's worm's-eye view.

As Vana, all Versace epaulets and cerise fougère, pressed on, Galt became furtive. Soon enough came the Washington Monument scheme: the senator was, unsurprisingly, appalled. (Doug V. said later, "She'd've been better advised to form a committee to dredge the blocks of Carrara marble Pius IX contributed to the original construction—they were dumped into the Potomac in the middle of the night by an angry band of Know-Nothings, furious over Catholic immigration and convinced that the Pope—and the Illuminati or the Carbonari—would get their hooks into American politics. Which Galt thinks they all did.")

"A vile discourtesy," the senator thundered, "was perpetrated against Senator Helms, and such behavior, I declare, is on the rise till hell won't have it." Then he stood up and left the room. Bam-Bam beamed delight.

("*Quale?*" Vana implored O'Maurigan.

"In 1991," he answered, "AIDS activists covered Jesse Helms's house in Arlington with a giant condom. It looked like a mushroom cap after atomic radiation."

"*Dio mio!*"

"Yes, a pity really, because the Washington Monument would look like the real thing—and your scheme might refocus attention on the shocking state of the monument's disrepair and away from Betty Jane Johnson Gerber's fixation on its relation to the Masonic Order. But the senator cannot as a gentleman of the Old West bring himself to discuss such a thing with a lady—or to admit to a foreigner that such a thing as the Helms affair could happen in the environs of the nation's capital.")

"After all," Vana, recovered, told the room, "it is not as though Italy's is the only corrupt government in the world."

"While in America we may live with corruption, madam," Galt replied grandly, re-entering and resuming his seat, "and with questionable attempts at 'gaming the process,' we do not, as I fear the Europeans have tended to do, live *by* corruption— the reason, I believe, that no European has been able to understand that chain of circumstances we call Watergate."

"Ah, yes," Vana resumed, "where Signora *MacGown* is currently residing . . . and I believe Your Honor also."

A silence of a measurable length ensued.

"I admit," she continued, her forces entirely regrouped, "I do not understand the Watergate at all—although I have been to the charming restaurant on the ground floor—but then it is the kind of thing that happened *after* I was last in Washington—a very long time ago."

"If I may say so, madam, I find it hard to believe that a woman of your apparent years can possibly speak in such terms."

"Belli complimenti, signore" (suddenly assuming, as Odette noted, the attitude of Titian's Penitent Magdalen in the Pitti Palace). "In any case, I agree about this Watergate—because no European can imagine *men* breaking into a *hotel* to steal *secrets. Jewels*, yes; but in Europe, if you want secrets stolen, you go to a *woman*—or in some extraordinary cases, a *travesti*."

"A what?"

(I kicked Vana under the table so hard—)

"Excuse me, *signore*, the table has kicked me. I understand table kicking is a commonplace in Washington, *non è vero?*"

"I'm reminded," Anastasia offered, a little hysterically, "of a remark I heard in New York about designers—they do always look better in their creations than anyone else—and that," she trumped, eyeing Vana venomously, "includes the men who design for women."

"A *travesti*, Senator," Maud MacGown murmured, "is a transvestite. A man in woman's clothing—or vice versa."

"Well, which is it?"

"Oh, either—both."

"That strikes me as a European answer, Mrs. MacGown. You've been away from the States too long." Then to Vana, "Table *knocking* was at one time an occupation—in Warren Harding's time."

"So, I believe," Delmarva interjected, "was the occupation of knocking up ladies on tables. I believe that particular President—referred to in some quarters as our first black President—was both adept at the exercise and careless about *traces*."

Galt seemed flummoxed. ("It wasn't," Doug V. explained, "so much the content—a black woman speaking frankly is no longer unusual—but the *figure* employed. Venerables of the Senate are unused to having their words caricatured by such *rudimentary* means as punning. The accepted practice is to reverse the language's *angle*, not to stand the language on its head.")

"You must forgive me," Vana protested, "if I offend in my *proposito* for the Washington Monument—I am more used to the dressing room than to the committee room—but I got the idea from looking at one of these shows your television so smartly crafts for the *popolo minuto* in the afternoon, about transsexuals deceiving men into thinking they are getting . . . but that was not the point.

"The thought came to me about your country that just as you insist there are only two sexes, so you insist there are only two parties—although your intellectuals will admit that like men and women, your Republicans and your Democrats are not so very different in what they want under the skin, but only differ in method. *Allora*, it came to me that in Italy, you see, we no more believe in two rigid parties than we believe in two rigid genders. I express myself badly perhaps—but in Europe a woman must only *declare* herself and her intentions, whereas"—sidelong to Bam-Bam—"in America, as I now remember, she must *proclaim* them."

"Beverly La Haye," Anastasia countered, baring her teeth, "says women can be aggressive only if they have first proved their identity as true women—which cannot be adequately done in brazen masquerades of phallic femininity."

"Yes?" Vana countered. "But was it not your own Kinsey who demolished the myth of the vaginal orgasm and also famously declared that from the purely sexual point of view men and women were badly matched?"

Galt seemed deeply shocked. "Concerning your remarks, dear lady," he continued numbly, "laws have been passed in many states preventing discrimination against persons on the basis of their sexual orientation."

"Ah, yes," Vana cooed. "And your Supreme Court is at this very moment sitting on some like issue. But I still cannot escape the impression that you in this country consider pederasts criminal."

The senator choked visibly. "Homosexuals," Anastasia corrected, primly. "Pederasts are not in."

"*Come vuole.* Homosexuals and lesbians you are forever trying to tame, like wings of your parties, by sending out your whips—to bargain with them, offering one day *caramelle* and the next tongue lashings. In Italy, we accommodate them differently."

Dick Fauquier suddenly chirped up again:

"The Hermaphroditic Condensations are divided by the Knife
The obdurate Forms are cut asunder by Jealousy and Pity.

Rational Philosophy and Mathematic Demonstration
Is divided in the intoxications of pleasure & affection—"

"Yes, both," Vana cut in, unperturbed, "but it is the men who are really interesting. Why, this very night they are holding a foot race in high heels around Dupont Circle—not a stone's throw from here. Not that *anybody here* would throw the first stone, I think."

"Actually," Max calmly corrected, "the race is run down Seventeenth Street to, I believe, Q Street. I have heard the participants described in certain quarters as '*drag goons.*' One of them is quite famous for imitating Bette Davis while turning somersaults. Of course, homosexual men in Washington have never needed to be outré. Of all the cities in the country, they are here most valued for stepping in to offer wisdom, advice . . . and the last dance."

"In Venice," Vana continued, "during the Resistance, the woman dragged from the Orfano Canal, '*spia*' branded on her forehead, and wearing red shoes, may have been a man."

"Italy can do that," the O' added. "Why did Berlioz, jilted by letter from Paris, feel it necessary to flee Rome disguised as a servant girl before attempting suicide on the Riviera at Cannes?"

"In the Library of Congress," Ornette suddenly informed Vana, "in rare books, we have the diary of a Venetian sailor, Niccolò Stolfo, who was a mate on Columbus's first voyage. Perhaps you would care to come and have a look at it?"

Vana, startled, replied she would, very much.

"Ah, Europe," Dick Fauquier burbled. "The Germans control the money and the French have the bomb. And a good thing, too—imagine if it were the other way around. Have you made the acquaintance of our ambassadress in France, Mrs. MacGown?"

"I have—but I do believe the term *is* 'ambassador.'"

"I like trannies, myself," Delmarva allowed, "even if their fantasy is to clone only males, doing away with messy menstruation, parturition, and breast feeding, and then let those who choose to be women be *career women*."

"Europe!" the senator huffed. "After clucking on for years about the United States entering an era of decadence and decline in the twilight phase of empire, they've now changed their tune."

"Italians have *always* admired America," Vana insisted. "Only the other night at the French embassy residence I informed the tenants that the grand *maison* they inhabit was built by the man who invented the fluted bottle cap. *That* is America, no? *Gli Stati Uniti*—such beautiful words! Once, after I sang Tosca, I was tempted to try Butterfly just to be able to sing those words."

"You have collected, I can see," Max primed Vana, "many interesting impressions of our country in your travels among us."

"I adore America," Vana persisted. "The minute you sit down to dinner with an American, he will tell you his whole life story in the frankest terms—although you might be sitting with a *travesti* and not know it. My psychic—the same man consulted by Mawrdew Czgowchwz, Victoria de los Angeles, and Sofia, the Queen of Spain—insists I am the reincarnation of Simonetta Vespucci, sister of Amerigo, who gave your country its name, who was Botticelli's model for Primavera and for Venus." (And, I thought, the ancestor of my adolescent *amor fatal*.) "And so I came here on a mission. Not the Washington Monument—that was a mere detail. I am here as a Green member—in my operatic career I was renowned both as a *verista* and as a *Verdiana*, and 'Verdi' in Italian is 'green,' you understand?"

"Is it not equally important," Anastasia chimed in, "that 'Verdi' spelled out 'Vittorio Emanuele, Rè dell'Italia'?"

The senator was confused. "Our charming hostess," Vana

cooed, "suggests I am a *monarchista*, as she was in her former homeland. Perhaps I am a little, but I know better than to— may I say, play that card, here where you have no kings or queens either, no matter"—shooting Bam-Bam a defiant glance—"how many expensive jewels a woman may put on."

"Did Bette Davis really turn somersaults?" Fauquier clucked.

"It is true, is it not," Vana rejoined, "that people hope vaguely, but dread precisely." ("Bearding her in her own lair," O'Maurigan whispered to me. "Although we must be careful of that word around here." "You mean 'lair.'" "Yes, of course.")

"If only," Anastasia continued, completely ignoring Vana, "people would allow us our appeal to the transcendent."

"Or to the irrational," the O' declared. "Sortilege by precious stones. 'Onyxes like the eyeballs of dead women.'"

He had her spanceled, and she seemed to know it.

Maud said something I didn't get about soldiers and I feared a gaffe, but Barb covered her by announcing she'd been an army nurse and getting on to the valiant show all the gay men put on. To my surprise Galt concurred, with stories about British camp queens on tour in the Far East and the bravery of the comrades on Iwo.

"Nobody ever asked were they or weren't they, you know, and now it turns out that one of them was Gore Vidal's ideal friend."

"What I would like to know," Vana declared, "is this: exactly what was Mother Teresa doing mingling with the Haitian oligarchy, a class justly renowned for its greed and pitiless use of force to keep the poor and the dispossessed under heel? But in any case, as an eminent theologian put it to me recently in Rome, 'The whole missionary-zealot movement, *signora*, is theologically suspect. It is one thing to console the dying—we are all that every day of our sad lives—but we have no right to interfere with God's plan for the purification of the human soul through suffering. None.'"

"Both Kennedys," Dick Fauquier told the food writer, "were killed by the mob. Jack for dishonoring a woman and Bobby because he was out for vengeance. As senator from New York he should've known better and copied the Westies. The mob had to get him before he was elected, as he certainly would've been, and not even the mob could pull off two presidential assassinations within seven years."

"I view Europe cynically, perhaps," Max declared, "abandoning all pretensions to world superpower, fretting about being eclipsed by a reinvigorated America in partnership with an ascendent Asia."

"An *emerging* Asia, sir," the senator insisted, "which desperately needs the support of a *permanent* United States."

Maud MacGown admitted a predilection for Europe, but an even stronger one for Egypt—which is why, she avowed, she was so very fond of Washington, with the Senate modeled on the ancient library of Alexandria and the Washington Monument an obelisk.

Galt railed against Ted Kennedy and Alan Simpson on *Face-off*.

"That two individuals of their attainments and character, who have mutually labored in sustaining an institution of the highest edification in the land, should so forget the dignity of their situation and the well-being of the common object of their solicitude as to fall into a *media trap* is a source of deep and sincere regret to those whose good opinion neither should forgo."

(I began thinking up *The Delancey Retort*. I saw the set: the Great Statuary Hall—what else to put in it besides old statues?)

Vana, pleading ignorance of how the American Congress works, invited the senator to expatiate.

"A bill originating in one house is passed by the other with an amendment. A motion in the originating house to agree to the amendment is negatived. Does there result from this a disagreement, or must the question on disagreement be expressly voted?

"The questions respecting amendments from another house are, first, to agree; second, disagree; third, recede; fourth, insist; fifth, adhere. First, to agree; second, to disagree: either of these concludes the other necessity, for the positive of either is exactly the equivalent of the negative of the other, and no other alternative remains.

"On either motion amendments to the amendments may be proposed. If it be moved to disagree, those who are for the amendment have a right to propose, and to make it as perfect as they can, before the disagreement is put. Third, to recede. You may then either insist or adhere. Fourth, to insist. You may then either recede or adhere. Fifth, to adhere. You may then either recede or insist.

"Consequently the negative of these is not equivalent to a positive vote the other way, does not raise so necessary an implication as may authorize the secretary by inference to enter another vote.

"Section, Committees. Standing committees, as of Privileges and etc., are usually appointed at the first meeting to continue through the session."

"What," asked Vana, "exactly, is meant by 'usually'?"

(Maud/Odette leaned over. "Can you believe it? She's doing Dorothy Malone in *Written on the Wind*, cruising the humpy gas-station attendant. 'I close in about ten minutes.' 'You mean usually.'")

"The person first named is generally permitted to act as chairman. But this is a matter of courtesy."

"*Cortesia*," Vana warbled, "is the lubricating oil of diplomacy, *eccelenza*, and the petrol—you say gasoline—is *sprezzatura!*"

"Eh?"

"*Sprezzatura*," Vana repeated. "It is the chief element of the courtier, according to our great Castiglione. It is the ability to, how do you say it, toss it off."

"I beg your pardon?" choked the British queen.

"Nowadays," Anastasia quipped brightly, "perhaps more the ability of the couturier. 'Castiglione' sounds like the name of an Italian couturier, does it not?"

"I was always told," Barb Vesteralen said, "that *sprezzatura* meant *verve*."

"'At these committees,'" Fauquier interjected, "Mr. Jefferson wrote, 'the members are to speak standing and not sitting: though there is reason to conjecture it was formerly otherwise.'"

Pointedly ignoring this digression, Vana sallied forth.

"Could not the *onorévoli* of your Senate resolve themselves into a committee of the whole in a worthy cause? If they have these *secret holds* to *keep* things *off* the floor—the language is so *colorful*, no?—then surely there must be an *opposite maneuver?*"

"Dear lady, I understand well that secrecy gains females' loud applause, but we are not living in the former Soviet Union."

"Neither is anyone else, *eccelenza*."

Dick Fauquier then asked Ornette about the black D.C. poet Essex Hemphill, recently deceased.

"Well, now, Essex was both negative and ironic *and* deeply sincere, balancing the paratactic and the hypotactic so *The Waste Land* met Beulah Land for pink tea. But being the Gaston Neal of his time did not protect him from gettin' pretty dizzy-fied by the notice bestowed on him, and before the kliegs went out he'd been runnin' his own jive Murphy on the white folks for a *long* time.

"His spin on the Mapplethorpe circus at the Corcoran finally put the cork in the jug of those liberals who thought they could make white America swallow anything. Saying Robert cut the heads off the naked black man with the foot-long Johnson as an act of symbolic castration and enslavement, testifying that a massive world wound did weigh oppressively on his own heart and immune system. Practically accused him of remaking *Mandingo—whereas* the fact of the matter is Robert assured his subject's anonymity by cropping him because that subject was his *boyfriend.*

"And when he did photograph his whole self, that Johnson was stuck in that *boyfriend's* expensive pants. Robert had spent a long week one time with B.F.'s *family*, and B.F. said his momma would *die* if she saw his head—the one with the eyes and the mouth and all the teeth—grinning on top of that Johnson. Strange of him to imagine his momma sashayin' into the Corcoran Gallery on any pretext, but if she *did* she would remember his *Johnson*. Unlikely—a black mother has a lot to keep track of, dig, like the *accounts*—you snooze, you *lose*—while Johnson and Johnson is out marching with nine hundred thousand nine hundred and ninety-nine other anonymous J-J's, none of whom has ever been photographed by Robert Mapplethorpe—who anyway, as decent white America knows in its heart, to its satisfaction, got his, world wound and all.

"Yes, time was of the Essex, but time ran out."

The silence was deafening, until the senator muttered, "*'Odi profanum vulgus et arceo.'*"

"*Concedo hoc,*" O.J. responded, startling everyone. "But do you know Robert isn't even *named* where he lies? Gravestones are a camp. Take Leonard Matlovich's over there in the Congressional Cemetery along with J. Edgar Hoover and the only signer of the Declaration of Independence buried in the District, whose name I disremember."

"Elbridge Gerry," Doug responded. "Of Massachusetts. Madison's Vice President. From whose name we get the term 'gerrymandered.'"

"Thank you. I shall ponder that. Meanwhile, Leonard's epitaph is: 'When I was in the military they gave me a medal for killing two men. And a discharge for loving one.'"

"The rumor *is*," Dick Fauquier giggled nervously, "that Al Gore is Johnson *City*."

"Actually," Max parlayed, "he hails from Carthage."

"Oh, like Dido."

"No, like his Gore forebears. Carthage is a town near Nashville."

"What I hear about him," Anastasia interjected, "is that he has disciplined himself to control a once fiery temper."

"And if I may be permitted to say so," the senator huffed, "that is indicative of what's gone wrong with Washington. That a man of character and spunk should feel required to snuff . . ." He trailed off, leaving a sense of foreboding.

"However," Ornette persisted, "I give Essex his gift for *diss*-ertation: the specialty of the nee-gro speculator for findin' the *black marks* with which the Republic had blotted its copy book.

" 'I live in a town where pretense and bone structure prevail as credentials of status and beauty, a town bewitched by mirrors, horoscopes and corruption.' Hand-jive rhythm—ebonic scansion."

" 'Pretense and bone structure,' " Maud mused. "A woman is beautiful if she gets eight hours' sleep every night and goes to the beauty parlor every day—and bone structure has a lot to do with it too."

"I take it," Ornette returned, "you are imitating Bette Davis. James Baldwin said Bette Davis walked like a nigger. She is the only white actress that black people admire—do you know why?"

(Not, I thought, because she put on blackface for her all-black seventieth birthday party at the Colonial House in Hollywood.)

"Because she wore that red dress to the Olympus Ball in *Jezebel*. Black people have definite ideas about defiance. My grandma told how my daddy used to comb his Brylcream hair in the mirror singin' 'Time Is on My Side' till came the day he started twistin' it into dreads, realizin' the only way time is on the black man's side is when he be lookin' out from the other side of the bars from what the white guards be lookin' in.

"I also like even more Cornelius Eady's *The Gathering of My Name* and the poetry of Malik Waleed, who read last week at the LC. Malik says fear is like tight underpants. How true. Now Malik is only six—but Rimbaud was only seven. They're going to put Malik's poem up in the Metro. I say bravo, because Malik is *clearly* a formalist—and I say formalism has been too long associated with white highbrows such as the late T. S. Eliot, whom Professor Gates does not consider what they call *analogous* enough to be included in the canon of planetary literature, but *who*—irregardless—wrote some pretty deep shit.

"Such as that mankind cannot stand too much reality, preferring as a rule various *fabulae faciles* of the Romulus–Remus–Aeneas–Horatius–Georgius Washingtonius–Father Abraham. Probably as T. S. came up in St. Louis, and hated to see that evenin' sun go down . . . 'cause it must follow as the night the day that you can't then be false to any man . . . a problem for T. S., who line for line wrote more horseshit—and is looked aside at more and more anymore, as he deserted his country. But many Americans have had to do the same, such as Paul Robeson, Josephine Baker, and Jean Seberg, from Iowa, who played Joan of Arc and was murdered by the CIA."

Galt, recharged, was thundering that the new Republicans have no notion of the *progression* of office, and describing for the edification of the assembly the Roman system, the *cursus honororum*—praetor, quaestor, rhetor, lictor, consul, etc.

"I believe," Anastasia interjected, "the senator is talking about pecking order, or dominance hierarchies. Pecking calls to mind chickens, and 'chicken' describes both the dealings of the present Incumbent of the White House back in Little Rock *and* the tone of his presidency."

"But," Vana dared, "'dominance hierarchies' sounds, *eccellenza*, like one of your secret societies rather than that august body the Senate. And *strong* Presidents make a pecking order irrelevant, no?"

"Strong Presidents," he answered, "are both desirable and not."

"Surely" (Anastasia) "strength of *character* is the important thing."

"Yes, in a way" (Maud), "and yet I can't help thinking that if you go on and on about *character*, what you'll get in the *role* is a *character actor* instead of a leading man." (Galt was definitely intrigued: what a pleasure watching Odette at work.)

"Clinton may improve," Doug V. proposed, "like Wilson."

"Wilson!" Galt snorted. "Wilson lived in an ivory tower. When he wrote his book on the Congress, he never left Johns Hopkins to come down to Washington to see either house in session. And his legacy to the nation? That bunch of freeloaders over at the Smithsonian—scholars indeed!" He turned to Doug. "I am glad to know, sir, that your efforts are more *directed*. After all my years in public life," he declared, "there are two questions for which I daily seek the answers: Why do the nations rage so furiously together? Why do the people imagine all vain things? Hypocrisy, greed, and corruption ride the globe. In every land, on every sea, the good and the well-intentioned struggle endlessly against the forces of dissolution and chaos, till hell won't have it! Is there nowhere in all the vast expanse of humanity's degenerate turbulation any vestige of hope?

"Those who labor in the earth are the chosen people of God. Corruption of morals in the mass of cultivators is a phenomenon of which no age or nation has furnished an example. It is the mark set upon those who, not looking up to heaven, to their own soil and industry, as does the husbandman, for their subsistence, depend for it on causalities and caprice of customers.

"Dependence begets subservience and venality suffocates the germ of virtue and prepares fit tools for the designs of ambition!

"It is not because angels are holier than men or devils that makes them angels, but because they do not expect holiness from one another but from God only."

("I've been hearing a lot of talk along those lines of late," Ornette said quietly to me, "much of it in pamphlets passed out at the Library advertising one Tony Alamo, World Pastor of the Holy Alamo Christian Church of Alma, Arkansas, 72921.")

Galt's security entered with a cellular phone. He refused it, asking to go into the library for a cord phone, raging now against environmentalists cleaning the soil with bacteria and invoking the specter of biological warfare as in Desert Storm.

"Both dignified and wise," Delmarva remarked, as he left the room. "Cellular scanners abound—just ask those Windsors. No need to make a booboo on a talk show anymore, like Wendell Ford saying 'nigger rich' on a call-in."

Returning, the guest of honor started right in on Satan, referring to him as "confounded but immortal," then on his own mission to confound his own "very mortal enemies."

"In the last days scoffers will come," he mumbled.

"Would you," Dick Fauquier inquired, "consider Islam and Buddhism worthy opponents, sir?"

"I would consider Islam an opponent, certainly, sir, and a worthy one at that. So does the Lord, in my honest opinion. The dark religions are not departed."

ORNETTE: Many consider the Shoshone the Palestinians of the American West.

DICK FAUQUIER (suddenly): *Ala ka barika di n'ma, n'ka dinye to lahan ni here ye.*

"Meaning, sir?"

"Roughly, 'God give me the strength to live another day in this world'—a slogan of the Save the Children Foundation. But I worry less about nuclear mischief in the Middle East than I do about the result of the bomb falling into the hands of those lunatics in New Delhi. It would do well, in my opinion, to remember what Oppenheimer blurted out at Trinity. 'I am Shiva, destroyer of worlds!' *That*, if you will, was prophecy. Armageddon, *when* it comes—and come it *will*—will come on the plains of Kashmir."

"Oh, *dear*," Anastasia declared in mock horror, "that will be the end of the rug trade!"

The senator stood:

"I care not! the swing of my Hammer shall measure the
    starry round
When in Eternity Man converses with Man they enter
Into each others Bosom (Which are Universes of Delight)
In mutual interchange, and first their Emanations meet
Surrounded by their children.

I will arise, explore these dens and find that deep pulsation
    that shakes my caverns with strong shudders.
Thus saith the Lord, the Lord of Hosts—

"Yet once a little while, and I will shake the heavens and the earth, the sea and the dry land. For behold darkness shall cover the earth . . . and the strength of sin is the law!'" Galt roared, standing to his full height, and tottering.

Then, storming out of the room into the vestibule:

"He who walks righteously and speaks uprightly,
And who shakes his hands free lest they hold a bribe.
Who stops his ears from the hearing of bloodshed
And shuts his eyes from looking upon evil—"

We heard a crash. I followed Rain into the hall. Galt stood in the open front door, holding a piece of something ceramic. Indicating Rain, he whispered, "'Take his yoke upon you, and learn of him!'" Rain came over with the senator's overcoat, taking the car keys out of the pocket. "Firewater to the Navajo," he cracked.

As the two walked down the red brick path and stood under the streetlight, I thought, Like an accomplished pool player, the kid has dead aim, a soft touch, and a plan.

In the taxi to the Villa Firenze, Vana was congratulated by Barb V. on her performance.

"*Grazie.* You know, *signora*, each time before I leave for America, I always light a candle to the Virgin of Antipolo—*not* St. Christopher, who is really Dionysus carrying the infant Eros on his shoulder to the mysteries, which were all-male orgies such as take place in the backrooms of homosexual video bars in every metropolis in the world—or so I'm told. Hardly the correct devotion for an Italian lesbian of the *alta borghese*, eh? What," she then asked O'M, "was that the senator was reciting?"

"William Blake—a visionary."

"There is," she countered, "an Italian poet who calls himself a visionary and is crazy about me and has a libretto."

("The life of Cicciolina?" Odette whispered.)

"He wants to premiere it in English, under the title *Mortal Woman.* I am to portray three women, Jackie Onassis, Maria, and Marilyn Monroe. More challenging than *Makropoulos.* I would like to get Berio to compose, but I fear he is, after *Un rè in ascolto*, how do you say, composed out."

After Vana had been dropped off, Odette remarked, "She might go into the bars to pass out samples of the product. You know the slogan? 'In Scudamor's world of the temple of Venus, a variety of love's little sportive joys . . . and no babies.'"

Barb V. said, "I think she's a spy—trying to get help set-ting up a fake company in Albania."

"The Defense Department," Doug nodded, "has merged the covert intelligence operations to expand espionage abroad, establishing phony businesses. A new civilian army living in high style."

Anastasia had referred to Rain as a climber. I asked Barb's opinion. "*Climber?* That little injun could scoot up the sheer face of a canyon wall in the time it takes *her* to stick on one eye-lash. Anyway, what is *she*? And that *Faux-queer*! I can't figure why Max goes along with all that. Still, I suppose in the end one prefers climbers to *rutters*, which is the common type of Washington."

"What is that perfume she wears?" Doug asked.

"Ma Griffe," O'M replied. "She's worn it since Cam-bridge, where her cynical detractors declared she'd taken a first in Mod Cons."

"She wants her husband's respect," Barb observed, "and all she can get is his obedience. He's like some apparatus tasked with receiving reports and appeasing the grievances of the harassed. Without him she'd be in some situation utterly re-actionary to bourgeois self-esteem—some tattoo and body-piercing colony near Santa Barbara, wearing Yohi Yamamoto rayon pants and a halter. *But*," she continued, turning to Odette, "I want to talk about another woman. Maud Mac-Gown—a triumph, especially the skin and hair. Very Harriet Hubbard Ayer."

"Max Harrington," Doug continued, "has core beliefs, but they succeed only in multiplying the frustrations of his life into more grievances than fewer. The one topic he seems terrified of is vice—vice and the revealing of *real secrets*. Tonight he went white when your black friend referred to Armstrong's *Mystery of the Ages* and to that evangelical church in Arkansas."

"The Church of Tony Alamo," I recalled.

"Yes. The senator, you see, adheres to them both. Really," he murmured, looking, I thought, a little worried himself, "the *names* supposedly rational animals give themselves in the American Eden!"

Four / Grandiose

At the High Window. It had begun to snow. The view had morphed from the lush green treetops of October through the full palette of autumn, as the trees seemed like upended paintbrushes, to this—the winterscape revealed through webbed bare-branch veiling. Rock Creek Park decked for the hols like the little village of twinkling lights under the White House Christmas tree. Some story revealed in the landscaping of this rich enclave of the northern South.

It was going to be altogether a *Christmas in Connecticut* kind of Christmas in the press, what with the artfully begrimed and deep-blue-eyed face of the American GI once again peering out from under a helmet on the cover of *Newsweek*, captioned "Hell in a Cold Place" (Bosnia). And in all the papers the government shutdown referred to as a "train wreck." (There had been a real one of a MARC commuter train colliding with the Amtrak Chicago express just north of Union Station.) I decided all the view needed to complement the snow, and the kids trudging through Rock Creek Park with their sleds (I'd had one—the firemen got together and bought me a Flexible Flyer: stolen by older neighborhood toughs, it was retrieved by the cops before being tossed into an Xmas-tree bonfire), was a forties-vintage Lionel train going around and around it on a circular track, and on the observation platforms lots of little symbolic Walter Neffs—a whole House of Representatives—dropping off the observation platforms just outside symbolic Glendale after each symbolic circuit at regular symbolic intervals. Also freight trains: running on a parallel track, symbolizing both industry and hoboes. (At Lincoln Hall I'd often dreamed of hopping a freight, twentieth-century equivalent of sailing down the Mississippi on a raft. Also, *East of Eden* and the image of James Dean atop the freight car, with his sweater wrapped around his head against the wind, had become *the* symbol of me for me in 1954.)

As if on cue, Rain's voice on the intercom. Admitted, he brushed past me, boasting, "I didn't really need to ring downstairs; I can work the door code of any building in Washington, but why show off." Then he lay down on the couch and started in talking. Sylvester left the room: I was alone with him to contend with (as Odette later put it) "the likelihood of being called upon to perform the *unheimlich* maneuver."

"Politics is hard on the nerves," he commenced.

"However do you manage?"

"I let them come to me. I never went out to them."

"Except on the runway. Doesn't politics resemble a runway?"

"Politics *is* a catwalk, but I let them come to me. I go only so far. I *did* dance at the Peake, like you found out—also at the Gaiety in New York, in between movies. I had a favorite one I'd watch there—*Dads and Lads:* it was the story of my life."

"You could say that about most boys." (But not me, I might have added . . . not exactly, anyway.)

"No, I mean about me and my father—the true story. The first time I was abducted—with his full permission—I was forced to kneel down, bound in leather thongs in front of a group of hooded men, and recite, 'I am here to do your bidding, masters. I am your slave and you will reward me, for I shall be faithful. I have worshipped you long and afar off. Now you are near, I await your commands, and you will not pass me by in your distribution of good things.' Come to think of it, I should work it into my next conversation with the guy I put in the Dome Room with Jefferson and Madison. He really gets off on fantasies of sex with his kids."

(Later O'M asked me to repeat what Rain said to the masters. "You think he got it from Geraldo Rivera's special on devil worship, don't you," I said. "No, in point of fact it's Renfield's speech to the count in Bram Stoker's *Dracula*.

"These beliefs," he continued, "are, like Tibetan *tulpas* and the Canaanite Moloch, who demanded the bloody sacrifice of the firstborn, *egregore* constructs, created by the collective imagination infatuated with the thrill of fear, in a three-part process: the creation of a *tulpa* through concentrated, directed imagination, its romancing, and the freeing of consciousness from its hold by an act of knowledge which destroys it.

"Where rage of this intensity is directed outward, we find the sociopath; where inward, the suicide. Where it breaks out laterally into mythomania—Isaac on Mount Moriah transposed to Capitol Hill—we sometimes find an artistic vision.")

"You consider yourself one of an endangered species."

"Yes, even though my mother immersed me in the sacred river. Achilles' mother did that. I read that he didn't get his heel wet. My Achilles heel is my hair."

"That's not Achilles, that's Samson."

"Well, she plunged me deep into the sacred river, but I was infant bald and only later grew hair. What protects the hair is the headdress, made up of thousands of bright feathers—not from endangered species. I never got old enough in my tribe to get one."

"Don't you think you're being too hard on yourself?"

"I'm like my dick—hard soon as the air hits it."

"You could shave all your hair off."

"The senator loves my hair, says it's thick like his was once. Water is very cleansing, so I pray to the Potomac."

As he lay on the couch, his leg bent, I couldn't figure out what—and then it came to me: the kouros of Melanes, on Naxos. Poor boy, lying there in the clearing for millennia. It was as if this boy, this Rain, had been lying there in the clearing sixteen storeys over Rock Creek Park . . . like that. What was it Freud said—humans have a prebirth nostalgia for return to the mineral state. ("Of *course*," DeVors used to say. "Why *do* you think a fulfilled woman *always* wears a few bright rocks after sundown?")

He sat up and wrapped his arms around his legs.

"When the senator first made me his page, he told me of how he'd dreamed of being chief whip, which I started to laugh at, as I was ignorant of political terminology. He said he'd persisted in his single-mindedness, describing himself as a loose cannon and the last true believer on the Hill, which I didn't know what he meant by either: I just saw some sort of hilltop with a cannon on top, defending some position, consequence of the Wounded Knee dream. 'The last true believer in the miracle of democracy,' he said. So I started calling him Miracle Whip and cautioning him about things like date rape and the rights of children. He laughed heartily.

"Then I started telling him about myself up to a point where I saw him getting excited. 'I call that hard,' he said. I looked down at his pants. 'I call *that* hard,' I said back. He blushed scarlet, and there before very long that mouth which had grown accustomed to thundering out streams of rhetoric on the great and important issues of the day had collapsed into a single theme and was repeating in a hoarse whisper over and over only two words—names: my name and the name of God."

(The kid was good . . . or good at it . . . or something.)

"I said, 'I can't impersonate anything as important as your page,' and he told me something that he said he learned from the most successful black people—to be meek but not look humble. It took me a while to figure out what he was talking about; then I remembered the runway, and the most successful boys, who could look meek even sporting the biggest . . . you understand?

"Not to look humble, because if you do, they will think you are afraid, and there is nothing to be afraid of in them, because in the first place all most of them ever did was win dumb popularity contests, and did I know what people who win those were like? Secondly, that the Lord would send his angel to watch over me. I said, 'Will the Lord really do that, if we do this?' That excited him, and he said that as long as it was love the Lord wouldn't mind. You ever hear that?" I said I had.

"Remember Gerry Studds? Well, I was different. And now it's a lot of years later and, well, although I reckon I am the only page whose real name does not appear scrawled on the wall at the top of the Capitol dome, or whose chewing gum was never stuck under the seat of the President Pro-tem, I did my job. So well, in fact, that they convinced me to be an opera-tive—although they didn't tell me that I'd be treated the *same* as the way they treat their captives. I guess I should've figured that out, but I'm cursed with a trusting nature.

"Did you know Lenin fucked boys in Paris?"

(Count your change; mistakes will not be rectified. Lenin . . . boys . . . Paris.)

"You live with an Italian, they told me, and you've been in the theater. Right?"

"Right on both counts."

"Right—so maybe you know what the Italian equivalent of 'break a leg' is?"

I was startled. It was as if he'd read my mind: the kouros.

"As a matter of fact I do. It's 'in bocca di lupo.' It means, 'in the wolf's mouth.'"

"Well, I was there. As the john told the hustler, 'I advise, you consent.' I was there, and now I am here. In a correctional facility. That's what D.C. *means*, you know, Department of Correction. You don't have to go to Lorton, it's all around you.

"The Shoshone say mother's milk keeps you a baby boy, whereas father's milk turns you into a man. My father was a Vietnam war hero. MIA. Unless he's turned up on the wall; I never go."

Crying now, he continued for some time on the number 9, the Mother Wheel, Louis Farrakhan, why blacks are lethal to Indians, how "they" put him into a trance and introduced them to Satan, ending up finally with the mortal curse delivered upon the white nation by Geronimo held in chains. The whole thing needs a Bernard Herrmann score, I thought, like *The Day the Earth Stood Still*. I took *Specimen Days* off the shelf and started reading a passage at random, to soothe myself.

> It is useless to talk to him with his sad hurt, and the stimulants they gave him and the utter strangeness of every object, face, furniture, etc, the poor fellow even when awake is like some frightened, shy animal. Poor youth, so handsome, athletic, with profuse, beautiful, shining hair. One time as I sat looking at him while he lay asleep, he suddenly, without the least start, awakened, opened his eyes, gave me a long, steady look—a slight sigh—then turned back and went into his doze again. Little he knew, poor death-stricken boy, the heart of the stranger that hovered near.

(What would Walt's take be, I speculated—his *response*, not his *profit share*—on homo porn?)

"You know," Rain suddenly said, jumping up as one sometimes does after a session, "the only way to send secret information is through the junk mails, marked 'occupant'—or by carrier pigeon."

(I remembered pigeons on the roof kept by older boys,

Brando in *On the Waterfront*, and how the monks made fun of his "I gotcha pigeon, Joey." They wouldn't permit pigeons at Lincoln Hall.)

He left as suddenly as he'd arrived, for the Cosmos Club, to make sure of the senator. He said he didn't trust Maud Mac-Gown: called her a spy. Sylvester, reentering the room, arched his back as the boy walked past.

Leaving the computer on for modem messages from cyberspace, I'd started dressing for the Cosmos Club when Sylvester put up such a stink (do we harbor such determinedly self-involved, rapacious creatures as totems of similar instincts?) that I called the O', who advised the kitchen there, arranging for the little bastard to have his dinner and skulk about to whatever corners of the place he might. ("After all," he reasoned, "if the senator's protector can gain admission, then your protector needs must too.")

As I wrote Phil: "At the Cosmos Club. At dinner, I sat with him and Max Harrington, while Anastasia danced with everybody and the orchestral music drifted in through one door, while through the other, Ornette's piano as he sat alone in the long mirrored gallery, in his evening clothes and the black silk bandanna with the pink triangle centered on it, playing Billy Strayhorn tunes."

After dinner I got up and went in to him. The snow had begun to fall faster outside. "Are you going to stay in here all night, Ornette?" I asked, as he sat looking at a half-drunk twist martini.

"That I don't know. Despite the visual startle of my presence here, I have not been asked to dance—not even whereas I am one of the only two men, our host being the other, properly shod in patent-leather pumps with black grosgrain ribbons.

"And it's manners to wait—so in the meantime I will just sit here impersonatin' one of Strays's E-flat-minor chords augmented with a major seventh, like when I play over at Madam's

Organ on Eighteenth off Florida Avenue. Nanna always said, 'There's always one, ain't it; I reckon that's you.' So I shall do what Strays used to do with *his* martinis—take one sip at a time . . . one sip at a time to amplify my glow of cultivated vitality, while I noodle Czerny exercises at the piano.''

I rejoined Max in the library—Anastasia had come in and commandeered the O' for the dance floor.

"I don't need," Max remarked, standing over a book laid open on the reading table, "to hire Bobby Short, do I, with your talented young friend inside." (Ornette was, as the saying goes, playing the shit out of the Czerny exercises, and interpolating Gershwin riffs. I thought, If you meant the Bobby Short who forty years ago was the co-sensation, with Blossom Dearie, at the Club Mars in the Eighth Arrondissement off the Champs-Elysées, maybe; about today's black-on-white Bobby Short at New York's Carlyle, I'm not so sure.)

"I've been in here reading Paul Metcalf's *Waters of Potowmack.*"

"O'Maurigan is a big Paul Metcalf fan."

"Yes. A book in many disparate voices, 'the whole being writ and limned with scholarly grace and wisdom by the many who took pains to record—with pen, graver, brush, machines for typing and the making of photographs—their several journeys.' Like you."

"We were talking—that is, *you* were—about the poor."

"Yes. Well, now, lest I sound like that fat loudmouth who pretends to original radio thought, let me state that the poor conform to the general rule of masses in relation to elites. They *don't* look good, don't smell good, they're not on television, except when committing a crime or being victims of one, are even out of fashion, I'm told, in the movies. With everything to whine about, but nothing to say and nothing to contribute, they're never even featured on what's called Wretch Television.

"The television-exec crowd, thank God, which wishes merely to *reign*, not rule, produces tell-all shows in the afternoon, putting the true level of the people's aspirations and abilities right on eye level, and bleating on about *depoliticizing* things like the State of the Union message, as if it were a Movie of the Week.

"Nobody who knows what power is, is *for*, would *ever* trust it to the masses. In *Democracy* the mouthpiece Gore rattles off a strange but prescient contradiction. 'Democracy, which recognizes that the masses are now raised to a higher intelligence than formerly'—and that itself is a charming illusion of the progressive nineteenth century, perpetuated by the current apologists for continued IQ testing—'is the only direction society can take that is worth its taking; the only conception of its duty large enough to satisfy its instincts; the only result that is worth an effort or a risk.' A statement high-minded enough, but dystonic with inconsistencies—principally that in *satisfying* its *instincts*, society—man writ large—fulfills his *duty*. Republican oligarchy is more in line with the perennial wisdom that the way to goodness in man lies in *curbing* his instincts—which does *not*, however, translate into a welfare state, since one of the warring counterinstinctual impulses man does as well to curb as he does to curb his greed is his impulse to altruism, and altruism can only and ever work at all in terms of another of *one's own*."

"The Irish," I admitted, "have the habit of saying, 'You're with your own.'"

"Exactly. One's own as in Irish or French or German or Swedish or Japanese or Zulu—to cite the workable welfare states—or Christian, Jew, or Moslem, to cite the workable charities. The British welfare state has failed along class lines, and of course Buddhists are the most callous and uncaring people on earth, since they don't believe they *are* on earth. But surely you have read Oscar Wilde's *The Soul of Man Under Socialism*?"

I never had. Somehow the idea of the author of *Salome* and *The Importance of Being Earnest* writing about socialism seemed to be like Karl Marx starring opposite Margaret Dumont in *The Coconuts.*

"No."

"Frankly, I'm shocked. It's an important statement."

"Do you think," I countered, "that free men have never been equal and equal men have never been free?"

"Do you accuse me of affiliation with Identity?"

"I may have confused it with Integrity."

(Or for that matter, I thought, with Rain's being intrinsic.)

"You answer like someone about to take the Fifth Amendment."

"Or perhaps like Joan of Arc." (Where *that* came from I couldn't have told you . . . until later in the story when I came to understand that it was writing me. That's what happens in D.C.)

"In any event, there has never been a working definition of America that is not based on *diversity*—and so welfare can never, will never, be anything but a dole based on self-loathing, contempt, and hypocrisy—the three principal liberal traits.

"Of course, coming from New York, and an opera lover to boot, you've never seen anything *like* democracy at work. Later on this Gore, more chastened, laments, 'Not one politician living has the brains or the art to defend his own cause.' Enter real power."

"Corporate enterprise."

"In two words. Think of it this way. The government and the military are the two rails a train runs on. You can walk all over them when the train's not coming. We are the third rail, the power rail: walk on it unprotected, and you're dead. The citizens of cities and towns coast-to-coast have always shown far more loyalty to their marquee corporations than to their local governments."

"What of organized labor?"

"Organized labor is the shadow corporate America has thrown over the landscape in the light of experience. Like any shadow, it is unable to stand up—but it may be *seen* to walk with impunity along the third rail, and that is enough to satisfy the people.

"I had the Senate majority leader on the phone earlier today, in gales of laughter, if you can imagine such a thing. Apparently the Speaker of the House broke down sobbing last night, and there are rumors of a complete nervous breakdown. The leader ordered, 'Will somebody go out and get a gross of GooGoo candy clusters, please!'

"Actually, Washington likes him better than Clyde Barrow in the White House. The laconic elder statesman has a calming effect on the voluble Speaker—pockets full of GooGoo candy clusters. The country, I think, will go for Clinton's striped candy more—perhaps it reminds them of Reagan's jelly beans.

"The leader sees my point of view, and has decided upon consideration—in defense of his own case, and with more conviction that he's being artistic than that he's being brainy—to alter his wardrobe from Revolution to Thermidor—and I don't mean by that he has developed a sudden passion for lobster."

("Max is no fool," O'Maurigan said. "He owns just one senator, but that one senator has been in Washington since the 1950s."

"What *does* he mean by Thermidor—the Big Heat?"

"You could say that. Thermidor, you know, had a second name; it was also called Fervidor.")

"If the parties really are so close," I asked Max, "why—"

"*Ah*, the great question—the distinguished thing, as Henry James said of death. If you know your Freud, you know it's the Narcissism of Minor Difference. Serbia and Croatia, New York and New Jersey—or homosexuals, or figure skaters with AIDS—or figure skaters without AIDS."

"AIDS is not a homosexual figure skaters' disease."

"Then it is a true mystery—defying the rule *esse est percipi*, the principle that underlies all American thought."

"And if it turns out that AIDS is a CIA plot—if the virus

was introduced into the drinking water and steam in the baths in San Francisco?"

"Some version of that scenario fits—probabilities probabilize, they say—that or the World Health Organization's bad-blood blunder, which the Conspiracy loons call part of the Illuminati plot. But AIDS wasn't politically a disease till your gang caught it. Still, good things can come out of bad times. The viatical settlement industry for instance; there's the great American entrepreneurial spirit in action.

"Actually," Max gabbed on, "I've always imagined the Mafia into environmentalism. You know, the old don in his garden.

"Anyway, I was wondering about the Narcissism of Minor Difference as concerns the Mexican spotted owl and your—"

"Piping plover."

"I remember . . . I remember the eggs. It's the gourmets want to string you up."

"Right."

"Funny. Anyway, the Narcissism of Minor Difference. How odd that the Freud exhibit at the Library of Congress should have been snuffed. And I might add, in case the writer is a friend of yours—I know you hang out, or you used to, with the *New Yorker* crowd—that op-ed piece in the *Times* bawling about the closure of the Vermeer show in this goddamn government shutdown is too typical of the stupidity of New York's provincial liberal vis-à-vis political concerns. No self-respecting Frenchman—barring Bourbon royalists—would make such a complaint. They're out there expressing solidarity with truck drivers, and at the same time every café *propriétaire*, every motorbike boy sweeping up Paris would have an opinion—"

"On the helium reserves."

"For instance. As they do on that book program—"

"*Apostrophe.*"

"Yes. Politics, or statecraft—of which that vapid writer

from that inconsequential magazine is completely ignorant—has been rightly called the art of the possible. 'I will give you what you want,' says the politician. The statesman says, 'What you think you want is this. What is possible for you to get is this. What you really want, therefore, is the following.' Know who said that?"

"Lenin?"

"Walter Lippmann."

("Zip—")

"Possibilities are not solutions—something this generation simply cannot accept. All their smug assurances swinging around them in midair—my wife calls it 'boomerangst'—have them in a perpetual state of ill-disguised tantrum. But there are no assurances in politics; politicians broker possibilities, they have no business—unless like Julius Caesar and his nephew they are totalitarians with the backing of a loyal army—enforcing *solutions*. Of course people have different ideas about recourse these days. The editor of *The New Republic* has a private chapel in his home."

(I'd heard the same. It seemed the kind of thing satirists . . . but then I realized there *are* no real satirists in D.C. The *City Paper*, *Washington Wit*, and the *Blade* don't cut it: the only funny things in the *Blade* being the horoscopes and the cartoon strip called "The Mostly Unfabulous Social Life of Ethan Green.")

"Whether or not it is furnished with stained-glass windows and stations of the cross remains a mystery. I suppose you could say that in the cartoon gallery in Kalorama, I have my stations, the record in images of the follies of the Great Republic.

"So much for the future. For the present, new millionaires would rather join the Millionaires' Club on the Hill and blather on about what the Senator from Wyoming calls—with unconscious irony—'insolvency creep' than do the kind of hard work that requires, for instance, a twenty-four-hour surveillance of the world markets."

(I believed him; I could see him calculating in his sleep.)

"They talk about the new politics. Politics is what it always was; there is nothing new to say about it since the Congress of Vienna except perhaps to observe that it is to war roughly what methadone is to heroin. Where was I?"

"Vermeer."

"Ah, yes, Vermeer. *The* crisis of the winter. Some do-gooder will undoubtedly come to the aid of the irate art public. I thought of doing it myself, but I confess I'm not so enamored of all those shellacked visions as high-minded aesthetes are. I'd be more likely to endow the Ashcan school or Winslow Homer. Rough seas and romantic beaches in the one oeuvre, rough city stuff in the other. Or the swimming-hole man—what's his name?"

"Eakins."

"Yes, him."

(I hadn't thought of Eakins in years—since the days of boy-boy frolic in the underground pool at the Everard Baths.)

"I can tell the spectacle I think we'll be treated to. As winter lengthens, POTUS will call the haggling Pharisees into the palace courtyard—don't expect the daughter to dance: Clinton has a sense of humor, but who'd get it? There, day after day, wearing what one congressional-freshman Jacobin—a high-school-graduate cheeseburger and ex–used car salesman, who obviously thinks he's part of the Second New Mobe—calls his 'wonk policy' hat, having his liaison man order in everything-ons from the California Pizza Kitchen and shrimp toasts and lobster from the Happy Panda Sizzling Wok, all spread out on the Roosevelt Room conference table like his buddy Jesus did the loaves and the fishes."

"You seem to like him in a peculiar way."

"Clinton? I find him extremely interesting, for an outsider. They thought because he had round heels he'd be a pushover—but he slipped on a pair of square-heel boots, dug those heels in, and—"

"Still an outsider—really?"

"Absolutely. All posthumous children are. Virgil says, *'Sua cuique exorsa laborem fortunamque ferunt.'* Which in Clinton's case could be read in any number of—

"But never mind Virgil, there's a homegrown product coming out soon from Regnery, a house on Capitol Hill—"

("A house on Capitol Hill"; I liked the sound.)

"—written by an ex-FBI Bush type, stranded in the Clinton White House. Says they put condoms and drug paraphernalia on the White House Christmas tree—reminded me in a crazy way of your dago diva's plans for our revered Washington Monument, a year-round Christmas tree. And that he sneaks out at four a.m. to the *Marriott*—probably an unconscious slip, if you believe in Freudian slips."

"A slip covering what?"

"*Marion* Barry, of course—seen any night of the week crawling in the gutters of lower Adams Morgan. I told the Senate majority leader that if he intends to make this run, he might well consider the potential of Marion Barry as a second Willie Horton. No gales of laughter that time, merely an ominous calm." (Pause.) "But we were talking of POTUS, who seems to subscribe to the general American attitude: lower your standards and your performance will rise—which is a *kind* of logic. He likes to get into sweat clothes and play athlete, but he's really nothing but a *fan*. A Boys' Nation icon. And to both compensate for and reinforce the reality of being a *boy*, he talks big. 'I *challenge* Congress to blah-blah,' 'I *challenge* every American, blah-blah.' Head-of-the-class boy words, translated freely as 'I *double-dare* you to elect me again.' His enemies complain that he brings nothing to a conclusion, but if life, apart from *ending*, leads to no conclusion, why should politics? The *Washington Post* is my favorite; every time he does a flip-flop they say something like, 'though substantive damage may have been done to no purpose that mattered.' They're not quite sure what's substantive, what's not been done to what purpose, what matters or what doesn't. He's got fine-tuned antennae, though, just as Franklin Roosevelt, another mama's boy, had. He's running *as* a snake in the grass, counting on the collective memory of 'Don't Tread on Me!' As an environmentalist, which is in his interest; the snake lobby is one he badly needs. Boys *love* collecting snakes; they feed them rats. Way funny, as the kids say. A guy who sold off his home environment to the state's chicken kings until there wasn't a stream in Arkansas that wasn't a chickenshit sewer. He was anything *but* an environmentalist—"

"Until a minute ago?"

"Exactly—by the stopwatch. And speaking of snakes—and scumbags—I find it odd that he's *sentimental* about Yeltsin, the ten-billion-dollar scumbag, and that he finds that grotesque zeppelin Kohl inspiring. He's the first incumbent who seems to have gotten himself elected expressly *in order to meet important people*, and yet he doesn't grovel. His predecessor—to the manner born—did, often, learned how to in Skull and Bones, and found, as the second-rate son of a first-rate man, it came naturally. Especially when he was on that medication, which when they tried to advise him against he snapped, 'If you're so smart, why are you standing there, and why am I sitting here?' He really *never knew*.

"Clinton always looks as though he's about to grovel and then he fools you. He's like an adolescent, really—cagey, incoherent."

"I can see that."

"I can see you do. My wife admires you—and she admires very few. Her father was Spartan and they hate everybody, including all their neighbors on the Peloponnese."

"Leonidas."

"That was his name, yes. You're good at your calling—and *calling* is what it is, no?"

(Does he mean social queer, journalist, or what?)

"And of course one *knows* what was in the Foster diaries—

and more will come out yet. Clinton's enemies keep stock-piling the shit, *howling*, 'Wait till *this* hits the fan!' All Clinton has to do is at the right moment unplug the fan. And, as he promised the first time, he can talk until the last dog dies. Only he doesn't want them dead. He wants them scalded and yap-ping at his heels so he can appeal to the electorate to call them off. Still and all, I find him insipid."

"And the leader of the pack?"

"The Speaker? The four-year-old who knows there's gotta be a cookie? I think he's in love with white-trash POTUS, and just wants and needs to be around him, howling for one."

"A cookie—or GooGoo Cluster—with a fortune inside."

"Exactly. His vision is of another term as Speaker and another term for Clinton. Clinton gets to call him 'Newt' and he must in protocol always answer 'Mr. President'—perfect for the servile little shit and all his bogus pretensions to learning. *Learning!* Do you know what happened when he went to the Library of Congress?"

"No."

"Well, I'll tell you. Piss ran down every leg in the joint. He is, with his Newt Deal, definitely Victor Hugo's *homme qui rit*. Know it? Sadistic fairground operators fasten a hideously grinning face on a hapless, ambitious little nobody—you get the picture."

"Pinocchio, Charlie McCarthy." (Or me a long time ago.)

"When that runty little suckass came around to us—"

"Looking like Benny Hill."

"*Exactly.* Fawning, 'You tell us what laws to make to make this country worth investing in,' our consensus was contempt and utter mistrust. The feeling was that he is bound to get caught and sell out terribly cheap—and if there's one thing we don't ever want more than to get caught, it's to be forced to sell out cheap."

"And POTUS of course is aware of—"

"Clinton is a masochistic hick out of Dogpatch turned high-toned sadist. The Jesuits said God writes straight with crooked lines, reinforcing his innate capacity for doubletalk, producing an infuriating combination of a first-rate mind with severely impaired goals who like Hugo's dupe asks to be loved for his imperfect soul. 'Love me for my human qualities; because I could at any minute be burnt toast. Because my sad story is I was looking for a white Sister Souljah and have wound up with Sister Frigidaire.'"

(I didn't care to express an opinion. I found I couldn't concentrate, having come to feel the way I did about the Vice President, on the President's appeal or lack of it—a fault in a voter, I realized, but I was more an advocate than a voter.)

"The Republican Party," Max continued, "wishes to be simultaneously a party of principle—an eastern conceit—and a party of power—which history has decreed has passed from the East and North to the South and West. In the South and West—look at American history, look at westerns—personality is *everything*. Principle is what—"

"Is what Clint Eastwood says it is."

"Now you understand perfectly. Clinton as Clint Eastwood—the quintessential Quantrill's Raiders personality. Dole is trying to be some kind of easterner. It won't play.

"There's something else you should know, though—or think about, if you're thinking."

(Was I? Jack Benny, when the robber—but you knew that.)

"It's better for them for this ugly mouthpiece to arrogate all the credit to himself—or as they say at the White House, 'aggregate it under himself.' God, *really*! I haven't been reading your dispatches to your town newspaper, but I hope you find space to wonder how these people, our governors' governors—and governesses—mangle language in their pursuit of the right spin.

"In any case it's better—even if it rankles in the hearts

of the others—Stephanopoulos, Rahm Emanuel, Bruce Reed, et cetera. If POTUS is *seen* to be governing by *committee*, indulging, on top of all his other promiscuities, in promiscuous *outsourcing*, then the *regal image*—and never mind what *kind* of monarch—greedy, vacillating, whatever, there *must* be a *regal image*—will be too compromised, especially when the contending opponent is, whatever else he isn't, a seeming principled loner."

("Whatever he is or isn't, a seeming . . .": a very Washington construction.)

"He seldom seems regal."

"He plays it down, but remember those years in England. Bound to have gone to the theater a lot—Shakespeare. Must've seen the one with the feckless prince who throws the fat old fuck—"

"Hal, who becomes Henry the Fifth—and Falstaff."

"Right. He throws him right back into the gutter."

"Who do you see as his Falstaff?"

"Oh, there must be one in his past somewhere—probably back in Arkansas, where everything else he doesn't want to look at anymore is. Probably some old kingmaker behind the scenes in whatever equivalent to an Elizabethan cathouse they have nowadays in Arkansas. One of those chicken magnates, perhaps, that he sold half the state to. Something along the lines of the fat old fuck in that Tennessee Williams play about the ex–football jock still in love with his dead buddy and won't service his wife, who's always raving about 'mendacity' and *poontang*."

(I didn't supply him with the title. "Good," O'Maurigan said later. "Max only pretends not to know titles—it's one of those things he indulges in, like the rich who used to never carry their wallets with them, before credit cards.")

"As to FLOTUS," I continued, "you find her cold."

"I don't find her at all. There are serious people who have referred to her as a kind of Helen of Troy. I find that incomprehensible—although the H is right—but for Hippolyta."

"But is he a Theseus?"

"Is life a dream? What was it Theseus did? Slew the Mino-taur for devouring the youth of Crete—the baby boomers. He promises neither they nor their spare parts will be devoured by—I suppose Leviathan rather than the Minotaur."

(Clever sonofabitch, I thought; draws you in. Meanwhile, I thought of "spare parts." In Lincoln Hall, we were lectured on "custody of the eyes" with respect to our own "parts"— in mirrors, showering—and particularly others', which led to jokes like "I yanked my *part* off—anybody got a *spare part*?")

"I think she's a woman who's taken to heart Adlai Steven-son's admonition to wives: to inspire in their homes a vision of life and freedom, to help their husbands find values that would give purpose to their specialized daily chores, and—if they were clever—to practice their saving arts on their unsuspecting men, particularly those suspected of—how does it go in the denials?—custom, habit, pattern, or practice of perpetrating indignities against womankind—while they were watching television.

"Apparently, though, the minute she gets a whiff of actual power, it affects her like a drink, or a whiff of cocaine—she goes absolutely out of control, leaving *him* wringing *his* hands like the battered wife. Which means he either learns to act like a man, or he slips Thorazine into her orange juice."

"What kind of man?"

"In his own mind obviously a White Southern Baptist Galahad. He must stop acting like—one can't say 'like a woman,' can one? Or that he's expressing his feminine side . . . except in the joke that *he's* a lesbian. Or Peter Pan. Peter Pan has always been played by a woman. I saw Jean Arthur—from *Mr. Smith Goes to Washington*."

(So did I, I thought, and I suddenly remembered her imploring Wendy to come back with him to Never-Never Land to teach all the Lost Boys *how to tell stories*. If they knew how to tell stories, they might be able to *grow up*. Far out.)

"She may in her rage break everything else in the White House before they will together break the bed, the way old Harry and Bess Truman did. At any rate, if he can continue to be seen to really *care*—convince himself he does—about what people *think* and that he is actually having a political *thought*, that what is really going on is a response to their current collective *mood swing*, he's got them. And then, when they change their so-called minds *again*, so will he, and as a consequence the press will continue screaming that he has no principles at all, no convictions whatever."

(This was where I came in, I thought—but that's all Washington was seeming to be to me: where I came in.)

"Well, they ought to realize that the very word 'conviction' can only mean one thing to him—*what must not happen in Arkansas*. Period.

"It's the Jesuits that warped him, I think. Jesuits are weak men with a strong case on a vanished past—a time when they were some kind of European CIA, and did things like murder Popes."

"You mean John Paul I?"

"Oh, I'd forgotten about him. The one from Venice. Pinocchio. No, I was thinking of Clement XIV. Horace Mann told Horace Walpole they murdered him with hot chocolate on Holy Thursday, in the late eighteenth century, before they'd begun to turn their serious attention toward our shores. Very Balzac, the Jesuits. Do you read Balzac?"

"I've read a few."

"You should read them all. David Souter, by any measure you care to use the most interesting man in Washington, reads *La Comédie humaine* through each year—and assigns it to his clerks as well.

"Anyway, Clinton fell for their vanity—the Jesuits—I think because he was a model boy from Shit's Creek during the Camelot charade. Also, they hold with Lincoln that you can fool all of the people some of the time. Two terms *is* stretching it, but time is elastic.

"I *almost* feel sorry for the bastard—body-surfing the electorate—and I refuse to descend to the levels of Richard Mellon Scaife or the Bradley Foundation, or Kenneth Starr, or this FBI scoundrel—I absolutely refuse. But you Clinton enthusiasts—"

"I don't know that I am that."

"Right. You're a Gore enthusiast. Quite different. But it is Clinton who'll be running, and in '92 the fundamentalists endorsed the sinner fifty-two to forty over the righteous Bush, and to risk a bad pun, he's sure to get the *swing* vote for how he plays the *sexaphone*."

"They say Ireland has had a profound effect on him."

"'Profound' has no meaning used in connection with a Clinton. I will allow 'dramatic'—or 'signal.' I understand, however, there is a political term in Ireland, the 'cute hoor.' Clinton is that. Smart."

"If he wins a second term. Not since Roosevelt—"

"Roosevelt was not smart, he was *sentimental. She* was smart—the smartest ugly woman in American history."

"Kennedy?"

"Kennedy was nearly all *neck*, as the Irish say, and the rest of him was cock. The father was smart, and so was the awful brother. I sometimes think Clinton—who does *not* have a smart brother—does the ghost dance to bring the Kennedys back to advise him. But what I enjoy most about having him in the White House is watching all the terrible Democrats squirm. They just don't *get* it that his loyalties are like a movie star's, with his fans, that his idea of 'party' is some low-down white female giving him what his wife won't in the backseat while another low-down white female sings over the car radio. And that his realization is the same as the *Washington Post*'s—particularly on your subject, the environment, *the* metaphorical sex issue of the age: that the differences between the major parties are, as they say, more practical than philosophical—how far to go, rather than in which theoretical direction. *How far to go*. You must remember *that*? Necking, petting, below the waist, all the way?"

(The guy could talk; I gave him that. I thought to myself, The chattering classes on Manhattan and the Hamptons, indeed.)

"Well," he talked, "Clinton is the one they will consider going all the way with—no doubt of that—even if he's still, after three years, only at the petting stage: busy fumbling over the complicated brassiere hooks while Liberty holds her smoking torch alight.

"Neither Bush nor Reagan—we called *him* Ronnie Ray-Gun—was in the least erotic, except to the deranged—the kind of people who profess to find Kissinger erotic, for example—and I maintain that Clinton's essential appeal is erotic, particularly to white trash who spend a lot of time exposed to the sun. He'll be getting them out next November from under their cardboard shelters and the trunks of their cars into the polling booths, as sure as—but then white trash is what puts the lot of them in office in this glorious republic. So, if you're planning a book, make it ironic—as befits a citizen of that unique state that can put into the Senate two such wildly disparate types as Daniel Patrick Moynihan and Alfonse D'Amato.

"As to our co-President, she is about as erotic as—my wife hates her. Calls her a sneaky frump who would make an Isaac Mizrahi look like Dress Barn."

"Your wife is dedicated to your interests."

"Indeed she is. She sometimes frightens people. Indeed she sometimes frightens me, so utterly does she—although I don't think she would immolate herself on my funeral pyre."

"Would you want her to?"

"Oh, yes. To imagine *that* much devotion!"

(Devotion? I began to think that maybe this guy was say-

ing *something*, but couldn't shake the feeling they really ought
to call in the snow-removal boys on him . . . an irony in itself, I
found out: there *are* no snow-removal boys in Washington.
Metaphor.)

"Actually, I find in Anastasia rather more of Shakespeare's
Desdemona. Without the slightest manifestation of intellectual power, but consecrated to harmony, grace, purity, tender-
ness, and truth. Exactly the kind of woman most onlookers
would find delight in seeing smothered. This appeals to the
Galahad in me. The anomaly is her abhorrence of black men—
but that's the Greek in her.

"But back to POTUS, the big white man. I recognize, as
the biography insists, he was first in his class—a fact that does
nothing whatever to erase the fact that the class itself just won't
do. You can campaign all you want to be president of the
class—but the class which so determines him to an absolute
degree is not one that *elects*, merely one that *acclaims*. Clinton
knows his own kind, and goes for acclaim, for the thrill of the
end run—or, I should say, the ten-pin strike.

"American ethnicity is still essentially white and Protestant. You Irish gave us no trouble: the first ones *were* Protestant
and the rest have had the good sense to behave much like us.
We may be—we are—through as a class, but so is the America
we invented. California will be the first to secede—in the
name of Ronald Reagan, whose legacy has been trashed and
name profaned in D.C.'s most hideous complex, that stable
juggernaut the Federal Triangle on Fourteenth Street—which
your Moynihan couldn't wait to wedge the Wilson Center
into. I can't help thinking it's his idea of subtle revenge—the
Irish think like that, when they can rouse themselves to think
at all."

(An advocate of Peconic County, a Pine Barrens activist,
and a secessionist at the county level, I wondered where this
might go.)

"Are you entirely serious—about secession, I mean?"

"Yes, completely. We let Orange County go bankrupt as a lesson in power distribution; unlikely to prove necessary again. There were also those crazy women who saw subliminal pornographic images in the children's books. All too pointlessly ugly.

"I do fear that Los Angeles may decide to re-form itself as a city-state like Singapore, holding California hostage to its tactical advantage as Eastern capital of the Pacific Rim. Sacramento could retaliate, of course, by cutting off Los Angeles's water. But I think as a preemptive measure we must seize Hawaii."

(I suddenly felt myself longing for California, a land, like Sicily, where the orange trees bloom.)

"And while you're at it, don't become the victim of that unavoidable lag between epiphany and publication that in our time produces in the Washington exposé a sorry collection of worn tales and obsolete notation."

(How I'd like, I thought, a little exposure myself right now. Phil's postcards from Sicily, one a day, had accumulated to the point where they were a small volume of lobby cards for one of those Warners pictures of yesteryear, prompting recall of long, happy days among the rose-tinted ruins of Agrigento.)

"I'd like to run off to the sun myself."

"You can run off to Inagua—that's an isolated island wildlife sanctuary in the Caribbean, loaded with endangered species—after which we're to call at Key West to be at Rex Vavasour's annual fish fry. You'd find him interesting, I think. Do you crew?"

"I can."

"Then why not do? We put out from Old Town Wharf."

(To Key West. Phil was in Navy signal school there. When people started going down in the sixties I asked him what it was like—supposedly romantic. "It's about as romantic as Canarsie.")

"In this weather?" (Outside the window snow fell.)

"Of course. We're running a three-masted schooner."

"I'll think about it. Congress is in recess."

"It might give you—I don't know how—a novel perspective. I know you ride motorbikes—with young staffers. You'd be well advised to remain pedestrian in future, or take taxis. They are value for money in the District."

"I was riding behind."

"Nowadays that is no guarantee of respectability. Are you getting bored with your dispatches?"

"Not with them, but with everything surrounding—it's the whole experience. Either they—I suppose I should say 'we'—are real characters in a fictional place or fictional characters in a real place, but not—just not—real characters in a real place. *I'm* being crazy."

"No, you're being a New Yorker—and you're right."

The guests were all reassembled in the long mirrored gallery with the gold trim. Someone was telling Maud Mac-Gown, "You, with your African background, know how things work, in a place like Zimbabwe." Ornette was telling an extremely uncomfortable woman he understood why minority police officers are racist, given crime statistics and the demography of the jails.

"The freedom of mind against which every government has waged war since the dawn of civilization has finally been assured, and anarchy is now the only way."

Bowing, he went and sat at the piano, playing and singing Billy Strayhorn's "Lush Life."

"The Shoshone," the senator broke in, "have hand-game songs sung with rhythmic drum accompaniments. They have been recorded by the Library of Congress."

"Mr. Jefferson, a decent man," Dick Fauquier announced, slurrily, "was woefully benighted, believing, as did many in the eighteenth century, in the inherent goodness of man, a grave error. Man is inherently wicked—one thing the D.C. police understand. Nevertheless, when they harassed me for trying to get to my own car in a *closed* street, on the night that the OAS states were giving a party for a group of Haitian so-called *dignitaries*—well, I did *not* say that I felt 'Haitian' and 'dignitaries' to be mutually exclusive terms, but I live in an historic district and am tired of having my streets taken away in this outrageous way!"

Sitting down next to Ornette on the piano stool, I asked why he was so eloquent privately and so shy publicly.

"You shouldn't confuse me with Dorothy Dean or with Bobby Short either, merely because I am into social climbing in B-flat.

"I am more like my idol. You know what is my favorite photograph of Strays? He is sittin' there—bombed out of his mind—looking at a *fish* in a *fishbowl*. And he ain't hummin' Schubert's 'Die Forelle,' neither. I, like Strays and like Miss Dean, am that fish in that fishbowl, but that don't mean I have to *comply*. The truth is, black dolls do not love their white handlers, the more those handlers find them startling and attractive. My momma's white Jewish friends would cuddle me, declaring, 'Oh, I could eat him *up*,' but I knew from my poppa there were little chocolate candies you could buy in Jewish candy stores called nigger babies . . . so I held myself, you might say, in reserve."

He began to sing, "I can't remember a worse December—just watch those icicles form—" and broke off. "Howsomever, preacher say the end is near; the gova-mint's re-arrangin' the deck chairs on the *Titanic*, and the people say it is colder outside than *evuh*, so they may be icebergs in the Anacostia—but preacher *also* say the gova-mint be fiddlin' while the planet burns inna microwave, and people say that sho' don't feel right. Preacher say the eleventh hour is nigh. Time to sing ''Round Midnight' and *fuck* tomorrow—course, 'round here 'round midnight is usually 'round ten-thirty."

(I thought how like the black preacher stock he came from

he looks—the same fire in his eyes I used to see in Jimmy Baldwin's, also inflamed by liquor, but in Ornette's case the inflamed eyes an amazing steely blue.)

"Did you know, there were two hundred thousand 'colored troops,' as they were known in those days, in the Grand Army of the Republic, and when that army marched in victory down Pennsylvania Avenue in what they called the Grand Review, none of the two hundred thousand colored troops were permitted to participate? Well, on September 8 of next year, that wrong is to be made right, in the African-American Civil War Memorial Freedom Foundation parade. If you want to see a black army of re-enactors—you might drop in for some watermelon. Make more sense than the Million Morons March, even if it *might remind* people of *civil war*—always a possibility."

He then rose and walked out into the hall between the mirrored gallery and the library to the photographic reproduction of the John Singer Sargent portrait of Mathilde Townsend Gerry Welles. He looked at the inscription.

"'Miss Townsend was the daughter of Richard and Mary Scott Townsend. In 1910 she married Senator Peter Gerry of Rhode Island in the ballroom. President Taft and his entire cabinet attended.'

"Hmm—it does not indicate here if this Gerry is related to the signer in the congressional cemetery—the Gerry of 'gerrymander.' Where is that handsome man who knows everything?

"'The Gerrys were divorced and in 1925, Mathilde married Sumner Welles. Mrs. Welles died in 1949, leaving most of her considerable estate, including this house, to her husband. Welles sold the house to the Cosmos Club in 1950.'

"I have something to say," he announced, raising his voice to be heard over the social hum, "relative to Mr. Harrington's observation that the black people do not have a language, they have a *patois*—one, moreover, that the *concerned* white citizens of this metropolis can make no more sense out of than the *cacaphony cries* of the District's ubiquitous crows. Many language theorists disagree, calling Black English—or as we in the trade prefer to call it, Ebonics—a separate tongue, as is Catalan."

The dancing seemed to have stopped and a group had formed—rather like a New York street crowd around a black busker.

"To wit, *patois* de *fwa-grah* is a thing I confess I dig to *ingest*—no reason a black man need limit hisse'f to peanut butter, jus' cawse George Washington Carver invented it at Tuskegee—and whenever I do, I drink vintage champagne wid' it—'steada *tambiko* from the *kikimbe cha umoja*—and *speshully* when I find myself in such a elegant nighttime lockdown facility as this, 'where one relaxes on the axis of the wheel of life to get the feel of life from jazz and cocktails'—

"Where white folks get all caked up to frolic and whereto black folks next to *nevuh*—'cept that they be *playin'* the jazz— or the *jive*.

"An' specially grateful at the White Christmas season— when the wind is howlin' and the snow is fallin' out the long windows, in which our like is normally invited only to office parties, Kwanzaa gatherings, and other holiday throwdowns in which are celebrated the spirits of all those who *supposably* kept the bright light of their faith burnin' despite obstacles that woulda drove lesser bein's to give up, give in, and give *ovuh*.

"And whenever I *do* imbibe that *dee*-luxe fizz, I make it a point to drink to the memory of every black brother of the Brotherhood of Sleeping Car Porters—*not* that the *porters* got sleep in *their* rollin' stock nighttime lockdown facility called Pullman. On the *counterclockwise*. I drink to every Pullman porter keeping his vigil through the lonely night as the Super Chief sped across the Great Plains or the Chattanooga Choo-choo snaked through the Shenandoah with trainloads of white folks dreamin' Blue Ridge dreams lully-byed in their berths by the mournful whistle and maybe the occasional improvised lonely tune the porter played on the little xylophone he carried to announce the mealtimes—*ding, dong, dell.*

"Every porter who ever laid his weary self back against the Pullman toilet wall—in a veritable *site of contestation,* dig—while them train wheels they went *clickety-clack, yakkety-yak, don't talk back* and them train whistles produced their Doppler effects on the more restless sleepers in the little river towns the choo-choo chewed through—while the porter got his *Johnson* spit-shined and shellacked—no lipstick, please, and I would be greatly obliged, if your teeth slip out, that you remove them, as the train is liable to take a notion to *swerve?*

"Yassuh, while they wuz Alabamy-bound, these customers they done swung them tootsies and what else outa the uppah *boyth,* havin' got they-selves *awl* spooned up, *moisturized,* and went *prowlin'* down the aisle of the rockin' choo-choo as if in chains of magic bound for the duration of a fast hot night into the sooty bosoms of such things as they—the *nee-gro* porters.

"Whereas the *porters* had to be *soo* careful in dem days wid' de *reactions* t' the ministrations of de honky bitches . . . had to be *cool* while bein' suppose-ably appreciative. *Cool,* dig? Reason bein' dat in dem days dere be severe punishment meted out in all states south of the Mason-Dixon line for what was term-inated 'reckless eyeballin''—dat always rings in mah ears, 'cause my daddy, in his endless quest for the method of rightly satisfyin' white ladies more accustomed to the delicate redolence of frangipani than to the bouquet of sweaty black armpits, came to be accused by a panel of *his* doctors of reckless *blue*-ballin', dig? So *no* rollin' of de eyeballs—and no callin' out '*Chris*'mas *gif!*'—was *condoned, nome sayn?,* no matter how *lubricious* the ministration.

"At any rate the members of a language community must proceed, on the performative assumption that speakers and hearers can understand a grammatical expression in identical ways: that like expressions retain like meaning. Dig?"

People had started gathering their oddments, an unmistakable prelude to hot flight.

"So anyway, dese *employees*—de *nee-gro porters*—brung de *proceeds* of dose hasty and after a while, lets's face it, *routine and lugubrious* transactions—spite of the fact there never was a black man didn't dream of fuckin' a white man up the ass, makin' him holler for Jesus' mercy—home to further dey *childrun's* educations."

I saw some people start running down the stairs.

"*Yowza.* Educations *not often* such as my own in the classics. That's Greek *and* Latin, baby—in the very Latin School of Boston attended by Minister Farrah-*khan*—where neither was the physical-education side of things neglected—for who was it said, 'The neglect of physical training favors far too early in youth the formation of sexual conceptions. *Whereas* the boy who, by sports and gymnastics, is brought to an ironlike inurement succumbs less to the need of sensual gratification than the stay-at-home who is fed exclusively on intellectual food.' Adolf Hitler, in *Mein Kampf*.

"Consequently, what wit' white Irish Boston ceasin' t'be a *kindly* place for nee-groes, even nee-groes well groomed as please-man stooges, I left that school, and its emphasis on muscular Christianity, in which far as I could make out, one muscle in particular always did lead the way—ungrateful maybe for the kindness bestowed upon a petted house nigger bein' groomed to turn hisself into the latest William Monroe Trotter, I dropped out—trottin' on down to the Duke Ellington High School right here in D.C., having developed by then, consequence of that muscular Christianity, a real taste for the male body well formed in all shades of flesh, hair, and ocularity, and would from the school in Georgetown frequently segue over to the fence protectin' the playin' fields of St. Albans there to observe the hard right in vigorous training for its many contests against the easy wrong—or on a rainy day down to the Corcoran Gallery for a contemplative half hour in front of *The*

Greek Slave by Hiram Powers, that ideal rendition of the bowed but unbeaten white male.

"But I digress. For from that school I *progressed* on to the very University of *Virginia* itself in *Charlottesville* where I *continued* in the dead languages of ancient Greece, home of both democracy and the slaves, and Rome, home of the gladiators and the *upstarts*—how come I know *Ebonics* and *et cetera* from *patois*. As when Horace says, '*Nunc et versus et cetera ludicra pono.*' Which mean, get down to the *seer*-y-us bidnizz of *life*, and stop fuckin' wid' *po*'try, and never you mind none o' that *epea pteroenta prosueda.*

"And in my *spare* time learned many Greek ways and Latin customs—and so in like fashion wuz I also busy storin' up data on the hegemonic social encryption codes of the white Anglo-Saxon majority—such as the *long pole* theory of moving the earth and the *praxis* male sexuality, by which, for example, all *fear* and *awe* of black men by white men is encoded in the fascination-detestation of the black penis. Dig? So dat my own penis being not more nor less den dat what it wuz, I did a little modeling and theatrics on the side—all due to af-*foim*-ative *action*. Thass the af-*foim*-ative action of *sassiety*—what the *Su*-preme Court member and black *role* model Mr. Justice Clarence Thomas, when he was *under* the *secretary*—s'cuse me, I mean the *under*secretary of *education*—done championed. Dat wuz *befo*' he read *Illiberal Education*, the woik of Mr. Die-nesh D'Souza—but Mr. J. C. Thomas, reckonin' he could be a *white* nee-gro, sho' nuff, and get *up the white steps* through them white *columns*, an' in duh *front doe*—and wid*out* ole B. T. Washington's counsels regardin' *adjustment and submission* too—he done gave up, gave in, and gave *ovuh*. Dig?"

Some guests in their coats had come halfway back up.

"Pity no education such as mine was theirs, those dentally compromised porters or the children who followed them into adult induration via *black normal school* for the girls and black *trade school* for the boys—'cawse white boss say nigger so dumb he have to go to *school* to learn *how* to be *trade*—thing *white boy* know how to do *instinctively*—jus' look at that *Prez-i-dent*—and *sometimes even* black doctor and lawyer school. Howsomever, so long as there was no longer any necessity you wasn't gonna get that kind of af-*foim*-ative *action* that the *porters* dished out back when—an' you traveled on Amtrak *lately*? No sir, no ma'am, no *way*.

"Fac' *is*, you can't hardly ride on a Amtrak train no *mo'* without gettin' yo' ticket punched by some other sassy-ass split tail—they are the *conductors* nowadays, *nome sayn? Despite* the fact that before you board the train you pass the bust of A. Philip Randolph there in Union Station. No, *no—lately* you be lucky you get up a game of *pinochle* wit' the *nee-gro* porter and that *only* on thuh overnight train to *N'awlins*, nome sayn?

"All dis *be-cawse* of the af-*foim*-ative *action* of *sassiety* on my behalf—which although *champeened* by Mr. Justice Thomas did *akshally* in a *spiritual* sense *originate* when Sumner Welles— who, while resident in this very house, commenced exacerbatin' the rhetorical strategy of his proclivities by goin' in for what you might call encoded enactment of multiple social transgressions—includin' that of both rigid class *mores* and behaviors and the received binary demarcation of gender . . . dig?

"And instead of he be keepin' *his* tootsies idle in a upper *boith* the length of the journey, he be *rousin' hisself* and goin' prowlin' and *goin' down* on as many of the attendant brothers of the United Sleeping Car Porters, A. Philip Randolph, founder. *Yowza*, as many as he was *able* to within the confines of reason and the train isself, an' callin' it by the *poetic* name of gettin' hisself a *Corona y Corona*, by which he meant a *big black cee-gar*, dig?

"Now as we *know* the professor in Vienna—*Austria*, not Virginia—say sometime a *cee-gar* is just a *cee-gar*. But only *sometime. Mos'time* it be somepin' else. And you can't beat dat wit' no bat, it require *adjustment and submission*.

"Now maybe you wonder *why* I be so hung up on this *train*

shit? Could it be be-cawse of my momma—my white Jewish momma—and my poppa—my black-ass Rasta poppa—dat dey usta liketa *fuck on duh subway?* In the wee small hours of mornin', and sometimes they got so carried away fuckin' they *rode all the way to the yards,* dig, where some years later the graffiti artists would cover the very cars with signs and symbols of the freer time they ushered in, along with Yours Truly, conceived, if truth was told, in the Uptown IRT yards at 238th Street after a jam session at the Village Vanguard down on Seventh Avenue, featurin' my namesake the great Ornette Coleman."

(I thought: Another New York subway native—must be the reason I've taken to him.)

"*Howsomever,* as you *know,* lib'rul sassiety's af-*foim*-ative *action* be gettin' isself *diluted* by duh *very Su*-preme *Court* on which Uncle Thomas, out from under that secretary, now sits studyin' the Ball-tee-more Catechism to bee-come *Cat'lick,* on account De Lawd made him to love Him and to *soive* Him and to *honuh* Him—dass by *adjustment and submission,* dig, in dis life and to be happy as a nigger in a watermelon patch wid' Him come de nex'. Ain't dat *sweet?*

"Yes, dis af-*foim*-ative action is bein' diluted—yes, *diluted* by the *Su*-preme Court—not to mention by the collective exacerbated patience of the *white majority?* 'Ooh,' they say, 'them darkies been pulling on our sensitive discretions *too long* with *rough hands,* and we are not just *conflicted,* we are *fucked up!*' And Uncle Thomas, *he* say, right along *wid'* dem: 'In my mind, government-sponsored racial discrimination based on benign prejudice is just as noxious as discrimination inspired by malicious prejudice.' Dat mean no *mo* set-asides, chillun, you just get in the line wit' the rest of the bruised *po'* people wit' dizzy-lexia an' attention-to-they-deficits disorder.

"Yowza. Meanwhile, *B-9,* dig, be the number of Uncle Justice's *parkin'* space.

"*Indeed*—so fucked up, they *drip.* The white majority plus Mr. Dinesh D'Souza, B. T. Washington, G. Washington

Peanut Butter, Justice Thomas, and every other *nee-gro* with a past *they* can *collect on*. They now say history have to *repeat itself*—like in *Birth of a Nation*, and like in the Tuskegee experiment when they scrambled the nee-gro's brain with injected *syphilis*—that generations of mutation later turned into AIDS what boomeranged into the white homosexual population mainly from honkies gettin' fucked up th'*ass* by infected black men. Then they done the same in the inner cities wit' *crack*—which they peddled as the inside track to the *groove-yard*, baby: you can feel as good as Miles, who dropped a fuckin' fortune, daily, fo' twenny bux a pop, daddy!

"And the *lib'rul*, he singin' again to the *nee-gro*, 'I Can't Give You Anything but Love'—love and *ptereonta prosueda*. And Thomas, flappin' the big black wings of his Negro-con judiciary robes, *he* tell the children, *'Remember that good manners will open doors that the best education will not and cannot. Even though you may have strong feelings about manners, that does not give you license to have bad manners.'*

"*'Cept*, O.J. say, when the fireman come to rescue you, he don't rely on *manners*, he *kick the door in. Yowza*. Or as Uncle Justice—'fore he did become such a *decisive significance*—did say ovuh an' ovuh on national television, 'Yowza, Mr. *Senator.*'

"He was bein', you see, *attendant*. Result of *which*, ever more *far-reachin'* multiple social transgressions in increasingly *contested areas*, far exceedin' W. E. B. Du Bois's contention that 'the way to truth and right lies in straightforward honesty, not in indiscriminate flattery.' 'Cause the fac' *is*, as Zora Neale Hurston did declare, 'Ain't everybody you can confidence—it ain't no use to try!' And as a more lately sister Ntozake Shange put it, invoking Garvey, Martí, Diop, Machel, Bearden, Barthes, and Micheaux, 'I have to scrape the bottoms of souls, dreams, nightmares and syllables to taste what justice might be.'

"'And I do *not*,' she might have added, 'have to wipe anybody's white ass.' For as O.J. say to the children, 'Children, *fuck* that Ebonic shit.' Never mind we use de dubble negative to aks-centuate the fac' we are in a double *bind*. Never mind Zora Neale Hurston's paean—tha's Greek fo' 'jive'—on the *rhythm of segments* in which all black folks do specialize. What *you* gotta do is get busy and acquire as I did not only a *distinctive interdental voiced fricative* but a *grand* vocabulary to go *with* it, and conscientious diction—so when anybody thinks it's *freaky* or *anomalous* that a *nee-gro* be speakin' *Latin*, he can be told Clarence Thomas's license plate reads 'Res Ispa,' though *some say* that he is havin' his own cock-snook, and that what it really *intends* to say is 'Re*zips* Her.'

"And Latin sometime be *necessary* for the nee-gro, 'cawse a black boy ain't no way gonna be paid no mind to in Ebonics *or* English should he—desperately cravin' a plutotropic hermeneutics—*aks* the likes of the senator, 'Old *man*, why do you not move your tired old ass *outa* that seat of power and let some new blood into the veins of discourse?' No way. *But*, if the black boy declare in a sober and judicious manner, '*Tempus abire tibi est, ne potum largius aequo rideat et pulset lasciva descentius aetas*'—well, it's the language of the *Republic* he be talkin'— tha's the Republic fo' which it stands—in where such talk is carved everywhere on the *walls* of the *halls* of justice—an' if you have to unnerstand what 'it' is, you just aks POTUS—'cawse every *time* he pledge allegiance it *stands out*. Not *far*—but ain't it the *thought* that counts?

"Now as to *Greek*, Homeric Greek culture, unlike today's diplomatic global enterprise, was sunlight direct— not unlike the gangsta rap of our inner cities, usually referred to by Negrocons as 'the darker reaches.' Darkness and lights: *chiaroscuro*—tha's Italian. Like Bayard Rustin and his white boyfriend and heir—only they wuz American. Some Italian shit is the same as American shit—like the Mafia and JFK.

"And now, speakin' of *direct*, dey done devised a *new type* of *ballot* for contestation in dese black districts that be so zigzag onna map. Dey gwan pass out *lottery cards* with *plastic chicken feet;* dat's how nigger gwan choose: straightforward and honest, and no mo' *flattery!* No otherwise Oreo-oriented individuals, under the direction of the Log Cabin Vice Chair Abner Mason—no respect to Mr. Lincoln, who freed us outa the goodness of his own big gay white heart—need *register.*

"*Speakin'* 'bout Mr. Lincoln, O.J. have *one question* to aks the children to aks they *teacher* 'bout him. How come he be lookin' *right profile* on thuh penny, when on *ev'ry othuh coin* the President in question, he be lookin' *left profile?*

"That to *one side,* me and Sister D we long since decided that 'gay pride' don't mean *nuthin'* no more, only a *gatherin'* of *dandy-lions*—some cocktails, some orchids, and a show or two—no more dedicated to *revolutionary change* than the DAR. We dig bell hooks, a co-gent woman tryin' t'discover *where* t'put the *fist* in 'paci-fist' and tendin' not to reify associations between women and thuh primitive, thuh uncivilized, and/*or* thuh instinctual. *Yowza.*

"And now, before havin' digressed, I egress—thankin' yew *awl* fo' duh *use* of duh *hawl*—a word of caution to the white man."

(I turned my head.)

"I see," Ornette declared, resuming the tone and diction proper to his achieved station, "I have succeeded in getting your attention—which I happen to count for something—but I must advise you in the strongest terms that if you are thinkin' of runnin' home and *transcribin'* any of thuh above, un-*uh.* Ain't no white man *allowed* to *characterize* no black man in any kind of article, book, recol-*lection,* or whatever by means of co-optin' his syncopated, epigrammatic language of vindication and self-defense, widout there be *serious repercussions* both to his machinery and likely to his *person.* Dig?"

He put his face up against mine. (I thought, The gin smells like my Hermès Equipage.) "You know what? I think you came down here thinkin' through your morally oriented cause or personality to force coercible limits on the external behavior of strategically oriented individuals—'cordin' to the lawful legitimacy theories of Immanuel Kant, the postmetaphysical concepts of reason and truth proposed by Jürgen Habermas, *or* Ronald Dworkin's theory of law as integrity. You hadda oughta stayed in New York and gone in for pissin' against the crosstown wind while standin' onna street corner readin' *out loud* like a Times Square street preacher 'bout the dismembered canon, the collapse of the Gutenberg Galaxy, the extinction of print media, and reception theory in the *New York Review of Books*."

He turned back to the assembled guests. "Therefore and in conclusion, in the best tradition of the Southern-gentleman after-dinner speaker at Kiwanis Club and Shriners Club and Ku Klux Klan of legend and yore, I lift my glass and *drink* to an imagined de-*piction* of an imagined encounter: the apotheosis and unfinished revolution of A. Philip Randolph and Franklin Delano Roosevelt's former page boy and world strategist Sumner Welles, blessed by the brotherly-love Quakerism of Bayard Rustin.

"Yowza, Sumner and J.P. locked in brotherly embrace behind lavatory doors on the *celestial* Chattanooga Choo-choo!

"And now, in the words of a song written by my tutelary genius and guardian angel in heaven, 'I'm checkin' out—goom-bye!' ' "

He threw his glass against the wall and stalked out, without stopping at the porter's for his coat.

Delmarva said, "*Shee-it!*" She then explained that O.J. had told in code the story of his grandfather, who put the father through school only to have him take up with the jazz set in NYC, knock up a white girl—how Ornette got his name and his cobalt-blue eyes—refuse to give his son his father's name, James (it was appended later), take up with the Black Panthers, do time, and get killed (why O.J. wears the black silk bandanna).

Sent by his white mother back to the black grandparents,

who then dispatched him to an aunt and uncle in Jamaica Plain, Boston—the uncle pastor of an African Methodist Episcopal church. He was tested and, due to affirmative action, sent to the Boston Latin School, where he became a teenage gay activist, playing champion baseball and setting a record of what he called "homo runs," making the white administration crazy. From there to the University of Virginia (by way of the Duke Ellington School) on scholarship.

He hated Farrakhan, not just as another Boston Latin School alumnus, but because he too is a singer, and he—Ornette—disdains "calypso ganja voodoo jive wailin'."

I went looking for Sylvester. He was in the library, on top of a bookshelf, and absolutely refused to come down. "Cats hate to go out in the snow," the night watchman said. "Don't worry, I'll look after him for you. You can come and pick him up tomorrow."

"Only American politics is fluid," Doug Vesteralen was telling somebody as the cars drew up. "South American, European, Russian, Asian are either adamant or combustible—never fluid—and the antipodes don't yet count in realpolitik terms."

On the short ride home, contraries swam in my mind. The duchesse de Guermantes vis-à-vis Pamela Harriman. The Faubourg-St.-Germain vs. Kalorama; the two Odettes; the baron de Charlus vis-à-vis any faggot senator. The hidden recesses of the Senate cloakroom vis-à-vis fuck bars and the male brothel in Proust. The pages vis-à-vis the proustitutes and all of it vis-à-vis Elizabethan England's Star Chamber, its necromancy, its boy actors . . . like that.

"That cat of yours is a pisser," Barb remarked. "How do you suppose he'd get along with Socks?"

"A cat may look at a king's cat," the O' quipped.

"I've had another thought about Clinton," Doug said.

"The rabbi Hillel says in a situation where there is no righteous person, try to be one. It's possible that was read to him, and he connected it with the oft-voiced canard about there being only scoundrels—"

BARB: Scumbags.

DOUG: Whatever—in politics. And then, with that passive temperament, he is just aching to have the office put an *imprint* on him—stamp him like a coin. He's looking for the right stamp.

"He wouldn't have got any of those notions from the Jesuits," O'Maurigan offered.

"No," Doug insisted, "it's the *elected* office."

"This rabbi," Vana cut in. "Surely he does not say 'person'; surely he says 'man.' You are just trying to be politically correct. There are no righteous or unrighteous women, after all; there are only practical and unpractical women."

O'MAURIGAN: Impractical.

VANA: Whatever.

"Judith was a righteous woman," Barb declared, "if a symbolic castrator . . . castratrix . . . whatever."

"And Signora Clinton," Vana asked, "is she righteous?"

BARB: Self-righteous.

VANA: Symbolic—

O'MAURIGAN: Self-castrator.

VANA: Self? I find American politics terribly confusing—much more than Italian.

"Surely, Vana," O'Maurigan jibed, "you can relate to Judith?"

"I can relate, *caro*, to Giuditta Pasta, the first Norma."

O'MAURIGAN: You were a memorable Adalgisa.

DOUG: Yes, well, in any event, that was my thought.

"Vana," I asked, "did the Jesuits murder the Venetian Pope?"

"Oh, poor Papa Giovanni Paolo! No—why?"

"It came up in the discussion."

(What I liked most about Vana is her histrionic ability. Doug Vesteralen is no rube, and he was absolutely convinced that she knew whether or not the Jesuits had done the Venetian Pope in.)

"*Listen*," Barb cut in, turning serious, "does anybody know why Lincoln is *right profile* on the penny? I won't sleep tonight."

Odette started in singing, "Penny candy, candy for a penny—I ask for more than a penny now; I grown very wise, you see."

BARB: Not wise enough, evidently, to answer my question.

ODETTE: I have an idea you could comb Washington and not get a satisfactory answer.

BARB: Who said anything about *satisfactory*? Is that it—all, I mean—about Bill Clinton?

DOUG: No. Seen as vacillating, or at best malleable, in his own mind he is likely willing to be hammered out on some new forge of freedom—and I think probably in his fantasies, when he sees himself on some future coin, he sees himself *full face* looking in that imploring way *right at the spender.*

BARB: Like a hooker.

"I haven't been here all that long," I said. "Washington's story hasn't—"

"Washington's story," Barb snapped, "is there is no story."

"Washington," Doug cut in, "hates plots but likes *agendas* and *disclosures* by aspirant politicos essentially stymied by unruly life, gunning for dictated fame more or less according—all unaware—to the Kuhnian model of theory building and defense. As Pliny the Elder said of those prior self-castrators the Essenes, 'Day by day the throng of refugees is recruited to number by numerous accessions of persons tired of life driven thither by the wave of fortune. Thus through thousands of ages a race in which no one is born lives on forever.'

"As for books, Washingtonians don't read them; they consider them things to *be in* but not to *read*—except, of course, for those—or those parts of those—they may be in."

At home I found the high window wide open and on the floor the "World's End" issue of *The Sandman*, open to the story "Edge City" with the balloon encircled in red "And who will be eaten when we run out of food?" On the computer screen:

A Left Right Top Bottom Center (Rel) (Abs) MRG: None Hit and run tactics ON OFF_OK to delete Hzone_Just Full All Dec Align___ JDef method of fighting.

(For pity's sake, fight dirty. This gibberish was an interception—and of course my files had been thoroughly trashed. I realized had Sylvester been left alone, he'd likely have been strangled.)

OBSIDIAN; YOUR RULES DO NOT APPLY.

^_s ^_' _ _ E/eaveto f _ _ documentation_t t _t' _ _ ^/Delaey p _ _ fpursuant_t _ ' _ _ Å/ _ _ scavenging compounds readily crossing blood brain barrier.com or discard dummy's last diamond _ _ngLogoplex_ jL_ ' _ Sag _ _ir ul Mark TOC List Index TOA None Follows ( ) Follows Flsh Rt Dot Ldr

Sovereignty destroy targets telephone relay centers, bridges, fuel Red White Red Green Blue Yellow Magenta Cyan Orange Gray Nxt Level - communication towers, radio stations, airports unfriendly websites current outline item to __Select Paragraph insertion point_! Select Family___Outline family at insertion point__2 Date Text Webmasters eradicate mediocre template HTML__ cause eliminate Columns Off - Bid four diamonds promise huge diamond fit. Oppose us (troops, police.) South ruffs club set off long club in dummy when _Gen Txt_Gen Txt politicos____ fatal ruff sluff you can't make the slam if East____@%&^!*)+? HSpace_Wid lead spade to dummy's king or finesse / Rgt an untamed Ultra mega-giga-speed cable modems____cash a club____Nabisco better crackers coming soon to your N=R*FpNeFlFcL wired world of killer app. West discards Orph_BOF Lft HZone.

It was the Orpheus code that got to me. I wondered if Ornette's warning against my reporting on him had been pre-emptively activated. I called O'Maurigan, not on his cellular, but through the front desk at the Hay-Adams.

"Hmm." (A silence.) "Listen to me. First thing, call down to the desk and order a cab to Union Station. Then take your black-and-white-attired, overcoated body down the back stairs to Connecticut Avenue. Then head for the Dupont Circle Metro."

"Why not over to Woodley Park? It's closer."

"No. Under no circumstances are you to cross over Rock Creek. You don't know *what's* down in that gully at this hour."

"You mean like a troll in the billy-goat tale?"

"Leave the President and his troubles out of it—they are scarcely greater than ours. Do not go into the Metro, but to Kramer Books. I will take a taxi back to the Cosmos Club, explain things to Sylvester, and hope he sees it my way. Bring nothing with you."

"I have to bring Phil's postcards from Sicily."

"Yes, of course; reading matter. From Kramer Books we will proceed to the Red Line to Metro Center, there changing to the Blue. We must not take the Orange, lest we wind up in Vienna."

"At the Café Sirk? They told me to take a streetcar—"

"Elysian Fields does come into it. The tower has been

struck by lightning and you sent, in the person of your work, to the Underworld to the *ghost files. Facilis descensis Averno.*"

"The hero in the Underworld—but I'm no hero, no champion."

"To me you are. The Blue Line, changing at L'Enfant Plaza for the Yellow Line to the airport. After a short phone call, I'm off."

"Where are we headed? Or can't you tell me, in case I'm abducted on Connecticut Avenue, detained, and tortured?"

"More will be revealed. Get moving."

"Well, at least I'm not stuck in bed like Stanwyck in *Sorry Wrong Number.*"

"The wrong number is what whoever's involved in this caper has played—as I hope to live to demonstrate come tidings."

FIVE / INTERVAL

I never went to bed early in my life.
Until a minute ago.

Together again on that December night, after fleeing
D.C. and flying down to Key West (free of all charge), regress-
ing in the warm Caribbean to the fish state (suspended, yet
under suspicion, in what the cops call a soft room) to the
womb.

Dropping like a rock off a cliff into sleep—like a sponge
into a pail of water (thought as a computational activity of the
wetware of the brain. The brain is a sponge, in shape and function—reading and listening is soaking things up; talking and
writing, squeezing them out; all the residual damp is memory).
I remembered something about Kant . . . and novels . . . and
poetry, together with this: if you put a live sponge through a
fine sieve into a pail of clear water, the myriad fragments at first
clouding up the water like shit will in some hours be so
attracted back together as to reconstitute entirely, leaving the
water clear again. That would happen, I told myself, both to
my shredded sponge of a brain and to the story it contained. I
made of it an environmental allegory . . . of some kind. What

if the voice card turned out to be like a chip in my brain, on which many echoes from the "year" resound?

I remembered two lines from O'Maurigan's *Magnetic Resonance Imaging Suite:*

> To visualize directly the living brain
> As if we were holding it in our hands.

Then I fell into a sleep beneath sleep that felt like a slug from behind (like in Raymond Chandler). More like a time-release mickey finessed at the bar—and I hadn't been at a bar in a long time. I was in a house in Key West (or was it only, after all, Canarsie?) tucked under the palmettos, among friends, put to bed early after a dramatic deliverance from the apparent clutches of sinister adepts of computer occultism, operating even around Christmas, as if to say, "All this *guilty partying* leads to being nailed right up there on the top of the hill of skulls."

Waking at dawn, I went out and down to Duval Street for coffee at an all-night stand, then to the southernmost point in the U.S. I sat on a bollard trying to work out the following question—one O'Maurigan had posed on the flight down, quoting an exchange between Hart Crane and one of his critics. Do the compass, the quadrant, and the sextant *contrive* tides, or do they merely record them? You can see why.

O'Maurigan had e-mailed a computer genius in New Haven. Almost immediately there arrived a rescue party of young, clear-headed cybernauts. (They looked, speaking of surfers, like surfers, jumping out of the taxi.) Operators of the Norton Retrieval System (I saw Ed down in the sewer retrieving Trixie's earring). Sysops keen to scrape my data—encrusted with, as they put it, "a shitload of random alien cookies and plates of refried spam" (computerese for *chazerei*, but to me another echo of Lincoln Hall: fried Spam and cookies: infirmary food)—off the back wall of the Mind of God, where it had been blasted.

I wondered if all the actual games of solitaire I'd played sitting at the high window overlooking Rock Creek Park would come back through this Norton guy's retrieval, along with all the advocacy info from Info Route 666. Then thinking of the Tarot: of myself as the Seeker—for although I wasn't after what the heroine of *Democracy* was after (quite enough extended shadows had fallen across my path since that first fireman to last any life), I was after something.

O'Maurigan then read to me from *Cyber-nooze*, a computer newsletter, the following elucidation:

"'Cookies allow a Web site to track where you have been in the Web. The info Web surfers use when they visit can be appropriated and analyzed by sysops and their administrators to build extensive personal profiles on visitors via their on-line transactions. Thus cookies account for a lot of visitors' lost control—over when where and to whom they reveal aspects of themselves.'

"You were beginning to compile a history, and history is what they are determined to discontinue, so they penetrated the rather insufficiently buttressed Web-site firewalls."

"It felt like that. What are they, Californians?"

"The last thing they left was in part a lyric by Zack de la Rocha, from Rage Against the Machine's *Evil Empire*. They're a Los Angeles rock band."

"Likely the attackers were Californian," Tim Young, the surfers' chief, declared, "followers of Master FWAP—before they were enslaved to FWAP they were enslaved to GWID."

(FWAP? GWID? So, listen, forty years ago it was John Galt. I knew about the commands "GWEP" and "AWK"—I'd been around K Street and on Massachusetts Avenue where Oracle and Sun Microsystems were in regular use, but the commanders FWAP and GWID were new to me.)

"They often start with Rage Against the Machine, and usually segue into messages from Salt and Einstürzende Neubauten."

So I'd been *hosed* by hackers out to *get* me (me!). Not only to undo all I'd done since my arrival in D.C. but to implicate me in something deeper and darker as well. (But what *had* I done—what did it amount to? I'd kept an impressionistic diary, copied disconnected items out of the *Washington Post*, gone on line. "All enough to rile them, apparently," was the answer.)

A day and a half later the O' came in to announce that they'd found more than they'd bargained for: top-secret classified info. "The feds are coming down. Somebody was trying to frame you as a hacker, which is worse than a flamer."

"As if," Tim Young declared gravely, "you'd been running a cybernet carrier-pigeon coop."

"Imagine. And all the while Sylvester was in the window eyeing the raptors. Some watch cat."

"Never mind," O'Maurigan said soothingly. "We're invited to Rex Vavasour's Christmas party. Rex is the local Lord of Misrule. Dresses entirely in black, like Lincoln Kirstein always did, and is given to improvising on the harmonium for his retainers—sometimes referred to as 'the barnacles'—on everything from the world stage to Dorothy Parker's life as a glorious cycle of song."

Fade out/fade in. Rex at his color-note harmonium, sitting in a high-backed chair in a design after Charles Rennie Mackintosh: surmounted by the oval *mon* of Japanese royalty, clad in a sheer silk moiré white caftan and white ballet shoes, size 14.

"Come in, come *in*!" our host boomed. "It's the special Yuletide edition of our regular meet-and-greet at Castle Grande. We are the local *Gulf Stream* chapter of the Universal Anacreon Society. Remember us? Our drinking song that gave the tune to 'The Star-Spangled Banner'?"

He played a few bars, as the harmonium lit up red, white, and blue, at which suspensory pause I was introduced.

"How *do*!" the host beamed. "*Attention*, everybody, we have with us a *valiant crusader*—a crusader for the rights of *endangered birds*. My dear, you have come to the *right* sky box —for we are all here endangered old birds. Old nightingales, hoot owls."

"Old *buzzards*!" a voice called out. "Buzzards are *protected*, you know!" (I did.)

"Even so," Rex cooed, "even *so*—anything but *parrots*. Parroting we do *not* abide. Beware the facts, they can wander you away from the truth!" He turned to me, flashing a wide, toothy smile. "I see you have remarked on my costume. Well, discarding in your honor for a while my inky cloak and customary suits of solemn black, I have decided to impersonate Walking Liberty on the silver dollar, striding the earth at sunrise. Quite a feat for a pegleg gimp, but it's my little gesture to the future of our beloved democracy. Also, I'm in white Chinese mourning for poor Lincoln K."

"Here in Key West," Rex continued, back at the harmonium, "and you *have* splashed down from your travels to the far galaxies in the *real* Key West, *not* in the *themed re-creation of Key West* franchised on five acres of Sea World in *Orlando*! Here in the *real* Key West, believing as devoutly as we do in the core sanctity of place, we have our own anthem" (and as lights flashed, he played and sang):

"Oh, it's a gift to be simple, it's a gift to be free
It's a gift to come right down here where yo'all oughta be!"

"Now you just get yourself a drink from Rob . . . or Roy, and don't *worry*, just *mix*. You won't know everybody, but that's part of my plan. It's years since I dispensed with an official nomenclator for these occasions, and left people free to *mingle*, anonymously if desired. Call it Beach Blanket Bingo . . . or gay bid whist."

(He played a few bars; colors: silver, green, and mauve.)

"Yes, 'life *is* a glorious cycle of song, a medley of extemporanea.' *Magnum miraculum est homo,* 'tis true. And 'tis of he . . . but *my* song, you know, was always 'I Want to Be Bad'—as introduced by Zelma O'Neal in *Follow Thru,* 1930, in color.

"Who says silence is the only perfect whole? The perfect *circle* perhaps—as is *zero*. Perfect for libraries, for cloisters, for totalitarian environments such as Washington, and for the tomb. We, on the other hand, while outdoors, alive, at liberty, and *numerous*—and before the dead zone of the Gulf of Mexico, whatever it is, but the size of New Jersey, *wouldn't it be* carries the drift of death to our island paradise—we favor freedom of expression—*trahit sua queremque voluptas*—"

"*Oh*, Rex Vavasour," a voice called out, "are you gonna talk that *Latin* again all night long and go on predictin' *disasters?*"

"All night long? No. But we *are* given to the recitation of maxims, in which trait we resemble the Sibyl of Cumae—save did we not make her blunder, putting in for immortality but forgetting to ask for youth. No, we are, idling at the lily pond, if mortal, at least human. Die we must, and be embalmed—and no 'grave uncertainties in old age,' as our young President says, whose reverence for the decrepit—as in his dealings with the majority leader—seems positively *Chinese*. We shall see if it lasts through the coming presidential campaign, whose Republican slogan, I safely predict, will be 'Bob Dole *is* 96.'

"Where was I? Oh, yes, death. *Nothing* is more certain, but we shall nonetheless rest serene in our coffin, like the divine Sarah catnapping between Phèdres. 'Oh, what a quenchless feud is this time has with the sons of men!' Anxious to forestall such at my passing, I have left my will, as the Romans did in the keeping of their Vestal Virgins, in that of my very own Maria Juana Bautista Milagro, my housekeeper.

"The grave yawns wide—a yawn mistaken by the unwary for ennui. Nothing could be less true, for the grave is an *avaricious consumer*, ravenous day and night, and that yawn is the howling mouth of time in full *roar*! However, there are neither caves on the island, nor graves that reach below ground, nor cellar doors through which to access the nether regions—without, as the darkies say, you listen to *stories*—only mausoleums and whole graveyards on built-up ground. Row upon row of whited sepulchers—you might think you were walking through the streets of D.C.—where Bahamanian mambos late held sway under the crepe myrtles, and where, *stories* tell, the restless spirits of the night—"

"*You*, Rex Vavasour, are a restless spirit of the night."

"How true—and like them too from time to time do fly free and frenzied in my mind as the debris in a hurricane or as the untamed youth on one of those infernal wet bikes. And yet, we must report we have ourselves even as we speak one foot— one whole *leg*—deposited as a kind of *down payment* in one's funerary *parterre*, and so much of what we are about to say will perhaps not seem so shocking as it otherwise might, for the less you have to lose—"

O'Maurigan leaned over and whispered, "Rex, in Washington, was one of the many suspected of what your friend Ornette would call 'transgressive contestation'; he was in fact in drag known as Vava Zubrovka, the Bert Savoy of the Garter Beltway."

("Not *only*, but *also*," Odette added later, back in D.C., "Rex could imitate *any* voice: Donald Duck, Bugs Bunny, both Roosevelts, and all three Trumans. The talent got him classified wartime assignments, disinformation broadcasts in German, French, Russian, and even, to hear him tell it, Japanese, as a payback to Tokyo Rose. It was how he came to the forefront of official attention.

"Rex was the only white man dressed by the legendary Thomasina Williams, couturier supreme to black drag D.C., whose emporium, a great Mecca of tassels, taffeta, and taste, is now a derelict site on L Street right off New York Avenue, in the immediate vicinity of the Rogue and the Exile. There was a dress parade one Fourth of July at the height of the McCarthy era, from Thomasina's down New York Avenue to the Treasury Building and on to Lafayette Park and the White House, led by Zubrovka herself.

"Falling afoul of McCarthy, he managed to save bits of his reputation and much of his accumulated loot through the combined good offices of 'Mary' Hoover and of Joe Alsop, a powerful if temperamental nance . . . but you knew that."

[It seemed to me I'd never known anything.]

"Rehabilitated during Camelot, employed by the CIA for the Bay of Pigs, after which debacle, admitted to Georgetown society, where he started in doing his satirical puppet shows, getting very bold indeed—hinting at the Marilyn connection and the Mafia stuff, all under the cover of Venetian carnival scenarios. He was hated by Bobby—and eventually after the assassination the CIA dumped him, intimating his drinking and swish ways made him a risk. He claims foreknowledge of the assassination through what he calls the New Orleans My-Oh-My Club and whacked-out lavender-conspiracy savants, all Clay Shaw connections. For years, Rex gave his version of Hoover and LBJ in on the plot.

"Then, in a bad drug deal, he fell afoul of the Marielitos, who literally crushed one of his legs—hence the Bernhardt allusion—which reposes in a mausoleum awaiting the rest of him.

"He started coming down here with Frankie Merlo and Tennessee—then after Miami, recuperating, he looked up one day and said, 'Well, darling Tenn, I do believe this is the end of the line for me. I have transferred off the streetcar named Desire and taken the one marked Elysian Fields.'"

What a story: everything but the bloodhounds.)

"Here in our rooftop flower-tub *finca*," Rex crooned, "on certain evenings under big white Floribbean moons that sail like ghostly Spanish galleons through the Sargasso of stars, under the red-light glow of Mars, whose orbit has the widest eccentricity—as Ptolemy pointed out in the *Almagest*—and with a practice known as *saving the appearances*—because unstructured reality does tend to be incoherent, digressive, and tedious—and whose dried canals bespeak an older, more tragic Venice in the heavens . . .

"Here, recoiling from the nihilistic assault on civilized life as manifested in the media-fueled degeneration of popular culture into a cult of violence and sheer filth, *hoi opoudoi* of flexible gender—polymaths and their secretaries—direct their awareness, through sacred rituals, conscious breathwork, and such *danses du ventre* as Mae West's daddy taught her as a moppet, into experiences of the most intricate recesses of the body: the thymus gland, the cerebrospinous fluids, peristalsis—to experience erotic energy as playful, sacred, and transformative. These are called Wet Shorts Video Nights.

"Because though we are not saints, we are *decidedly* high-toned—as befits the town that owns Harry Truman's summer White House. Why, do you *know* what *things* were discussed here back then? The atomic *bomb*, that's what, and everything in its aftermath.

"Why, between Stalin's satanic villainies on that side of the world and Senator Vandenberg's wicked wiles and those of the notorious Eightieth Congress on this, and under it *all*, talking of valor, young Margaret's no less valiant go at *portamento*, and what went into *it* as an earnest of her sincerity—oh, it was a longer voyage than any sailor ever sailed from May to December that our haberdashing Harry took from those Prendergast Kansas City cathouse parlors to the pinnacle of power and his dealings with the striped-pants boys and other fauna of Washington.

"And once there, he did, in his own immortal words, ride the tiger. Something to look at in a time when the 104th Congress has *ground government to a halt.* You know the big difference between then and now? It's this: ridin' tiger is *not* the same thing as straddlin' pussy. Not that Harry *relished* those meatless Tuesdays, or likely either the clatter of Bess and Margaret at Ping-Pong. You can nearly still hear him tinkling at the piano to the tune of 'Waiter, I'll Have Another Old-Fashioned, Please.'

"So eat and drink up. I've a great big bar and good caviar—yes, the *best* that can be found—earnests of *my* sincerity. Harry's old-fashioneds were bourbon; there's plenty of that and whatnot else—and that stuff in the other big bowl that looks like Cracker Jacks is a mess of *chapulines* fresh in from Oaxaca!"

("Deeply encoded," O'Maurigan whispered. "He does it to befuddle the unaware." "He's succeeding," I avowed.)

"They said to me, 'Rex Vavasour, whyever did you come down to this backwater, when you could be living in style in Palm Beach?' 'Oh, *honey,*' I replied, '*The Palm Beach Story* is an old *whorey* tale. Why, I'm told there was a painting—I collect, you know—in a gallery on Worth Avenue wearing a price tag of five thousand bucks—of George Washington as a *dog,* crossing the Delaware? Wearing a Santa Claus cap? *Need* I go *on?* No, this egocentric human Phaeton has found his garage here at the southernmost point, where up on blocks he awaits the coming of that chariot that cannot fail to take us where the sheep are separated from the goats, and speed *straight to hell* with the *goats.*

"Also we mull whether or not we should swim with dolphins to find ourselves, whether men in polygynous situations at risk for disease will tend to dress for maximum effect, and the news that *alligators* in the Everglades are being born with *shortened* penises and environmental *estrogen receptors*—and if *those last two* don't put the fear of God into you, you are no true endangered American!"

He then downed a glass of vodka in one gulp.

"*Literary.* Mr. Williams regaling us with stories of his time at the *Tradewinds Hotel*, before *settling down to business* here, and Mr. Merrill's world-and-otherworld travel anecdotes. Yes, we became a very Kit Kat Klub, and this place a second Upper Flash Inn—which it still is, most nights—just be careful who it is, darling, you flash it at.

"Can't say Mr. Hemingway ever did grace—preferring the *ground level* of Sloppy Joe's—nor was I sorry. And yet the older one gets, the more sympathy . . . *imagine*, having decided there must be one mess less in the corrida—you—the very last thing you see in it is your pitifully ugly old big toe—soon to sport the morgue tag—wound round the trigger of the shotgun you're using to blow your mind to disconnected syllables.

"As Maria Juana said to me last week, reporting a delay in the progress of the laundry, 'Señor Rex, that Speed Queen have unbalance load!' Out of the mouths!

"Oh, we have our little dramas too of course, and were one not given to reading philosophy—and religion—one might not be able to sustain the strain of them. But one is, and one has. *La bêtise n'est pas mon fort.* So stick around and live as I do in the enchanted and nearly unchanging present, with the Eternal Verities for company. The Great Chain of Being, the Music of the Spheres, the Enneads—"

"The Constitution and the Bill of Rights!" a voice cried.

"—and *you*," Rex concluded.

"And now, as the floor show comes to a close, get ready, you *all*, for the unencumbered self of Max Harrington, who almost never goes anywhere without his redoubtable and beautiful wife, Anastasia, making an *exception in our case*, promising to drop in—"

"*Alone?*" a voice cried.

"Oh, *indeed* no; in the company of one or more of his unencumbered, er, *bosuns*—energized throttlemen all—yet

tired as they must be of tacking in their ghostly vessel somewhere off the coast of Buggery Island—*soon* as they've finished,
er, *tying up* at the bottom of Duval Street. To somewhat amend
a famous *dictum* of the late lamented John Fitzgerald Kennedy,
not only does a risin' tide lift all boats, but it will do too to
lift a quantity of *bosuns*—especially those with *elastic* gender
behaviors."

"I declare, *they* are *all* right out of *William Higgins*, Rex
Vavasour!"

"Now, *now*, does anybody say that about the *President*
when he recreates himself with his all-male crew of Secret Service beefcake—and who knows, what with their secret code,
how *frayed* is the elastic on their Jockey-short behavior waist-
bands? Max is only like the President—a little—and the only
difference between the entourages is you will not see a *dark face*
hoppin' in here on *dark legs* accompanyin' Max. This is not
prejudice on Max's part, however, only that darkies—oh, *excuse
me*, men of color—tend *not* to be *nautical*. In any case, just as in
one's reading life one prefers Melville's sailors to Henry
James's dinner companions, so in reading *life*—and in addition,
I prefer to liken Max's crew to Joe Gage's men. I think of that
immortal phrase from *Heatstroke*, 'while all the wives are out
shopping.'"

"Where *is* the wife?"

"Anastasia is *not* an outdoor girl; indeed she most resembles those great beauties of the Edo period known as the
Ladies of the Great Interiors, and prefers on holiday the silken
charms of Bimini to the rugged ambience of Key West. Max
has been exploring for evidence of the western edge of
Atlantis—the northern edge was Ireland, and the temples of
the eastern shore at what is now Malta. Max of course is a
Knight of Malta—it is one of his most cherished *memberships*, if
you take my meanin'.

"Adventures! 'Make voyages,' Mr. Williams declared,

'attempt them. There's nothing else!' We ourselves are not for such dangerous seas and climes, preferrin' voyages of the *mental kind*. What with the resurgence of *piracy* on the high seas!"

I went to the bathroom and of course checked the medicine cabinet: a pharmacopeia: Prozac, Pozitron, amphetamines. Returning, I swerved into Rex's room. Dozens of photographs and paintings (two by Tennessee Williams: one of a lonely night street lined with houses with shuttered windows and lit by a single streetlight was particularly arresting), and hung on the wall dozens of puppets with faces from the fifties and sixties: Ike, Stevenson, the Dulleses, the Alsops, Joe McCarthy, Hoover and Clyde Tolson (unclothed, but with no "parts"), Cardinal Spellman, the Kennedys, Marilyn, Jackie, LBJ, Lee Harvey Oswald, etc. Also against one long wall a set of trains and an environment landscaped with a model of the Capitol and surrounding buildings—the Supreme Court, the Jefferson and Adams buildings (no Madison) of the Library of Congress, and the Folger Library, in white beeswax, with gardens: trees and flowers made of silk. Capitol Hill and Union Station: tracks shunting north and running underground, all trains stationary models of Chesapeake and Ohio, Baltimore and Ohio, Pennsylvania, Virginia and Western, Richmond, Fredericksburg and Potomac, Southern, Seaboard, etc.—all the lines that came into Union Station in the 1950s. And an old movie camera, made to shoot miniatures such as I'd once seen at Zoetrope Studios on Formosa, when Coppola was making *One from the Heart.*

Suddenly one of the waiters—Rob or Roy?—appeared.

"I'm Roy. All of Mr. Vavasour's boys are named for cocktails. There was a little blond especially good at making martinis; Mr. Vavasour called him Olive-or-Twist. Taught him to sing while mixing, 'Where Is Love?' Another he called 'My Man Hattan,' one 'Bronx,' and there was 'Ward 8'—Mr. Vavasour's favorite for a time; I guess I don't have to tell you what the 8 stood for."

Roy sat, lit up a joint, and continued. "Mr. Vavasour came down here in the 1960s to teach English and social studies in the high school and put on his puppet shows, telling everybody when he got drunk, which was every night, that he had been President Truman's aide de *camp* in the 1940s at the summer White House.

"Then one day in English class Mr. Vavasour was lecturing on *The Glass Menagerie*—how fine a thing it was, how everybody should be *honored* that Mr. Williams, a shy and reclusive man, had come among us—when a certain boy put up his hand and said, 'I *know* Mr. Williams . . . he gives me *money*.' And the very same afternoon, Mr. Vavasour began seeing to the intensification of that boy's social studies after school, calling the boy his protégé and himself the boy's tutor, and pretty soon after that boy and Mr. Vavasour were to be seen dining with Mr. Williams on Duncan Street very regularly. And that boy remained a legend until long after he up and left and went to New York City, because before he left he stole all the poker chips that Mr. Vavasour and Harry Truman used to play with, and from that day to this Mr. Vavasour has never played another game of poker. He and Mr. Harrington play pinochle."

(Pinochle!)

"Mr. Harrington," Roy continued, "will stay all night, to make sure Mr. Vavasour doesn't read his beads—for Mr. Vavasour as the evening progresses always carries on like he's the head of some patrician College of Augurs—that's ancient Roman, you know—but we all say more like an *ogre* than an augur. Do you know he keeps a *red telephone* in the bedroom? So Mr. Harrington must assert his authority—and leave a lot of laundered money for Mr. Vavasour to put away for him. Mr. Vavasour knows Mr. Harrington from the days before the epidemic, when he was on the *flip side*. If you ever hear Mr. Harrington say, 'I'm straight, but I'm not narrow,' remember that Mr. Vavasour once said right out loud, 'He's *straight*, all right, as in *Straight to Hell*.' Those are publications of Boyd McDonald."

(As the Speaker of the House would say, I knew that.)

"One day, Mr. V says, Max Harrington will have him murdered by Maria Juana Bautista Milagro. Everybody thinks she worships the ground he walks on, but she is Cuban, and Mr. V was in the Bay of Pigs. He refers to Key West as the Isle of Pigs and himself as Circe—that's from Homer's *Odyssey*— and to Mr. Harrington as Odysseus beached with his crew of sex pigs."

As Roy finished his toke, O'M came in and sat looking at the model and pointed out the building on D Street. "That's where you're going to live; it was once a convent: look at the great white towers. I opted for the House side; the Senate side is too murky. You'll enjoy all the frisky, self-important aides."

We returned to the patio, where the conversation was percolating still. A stranger approached. "Pardon me, but I couldn't help observe your evident strain, and I have heard you have recently suffered a contretemps in Washington and that when you return there you will be going to live on Capitol Hill. You will fall in love with it, I can tell from your demeanor. It will prove to you—I think you want proof—that your sojourn in Washington is a blessing in disguise. I *know* you love disguises—Venice and all that; I've seen your video—and I *bet* you just love surprises too, but may have relied too often on Jane to supply them."

(Who was *this* one?)

"I mean by that that Dick must certainly have ceased *surprising* you long ago, and that does leave only Jane, does it not? Does anything I'm saying strike you as at all true? Oh, you needn't *answer*—and never mind who I am. My name wouldn't mean anything to you—nor would it be to your great advantage to meet me for lunch. Rex calls me Margutta—I was once posted to Rome, to what he calls the 'Queers-in-the-alley' under Clare Boothe Luce.

"You know, the S.S. *Rex* was a great old battleship in its day. *Decommissioned* and *drydocked*, it is now badly in need of a cathodic protective system to shield it from *rust* and *mildew*. Instead of sitting up all hours eating rich food, swilling liquor, distorting reality, and reducing life to brutally pungent binaries, she should be in bed at ten o'clock, taking melatonin to adjust the phase shifts in her circadian cycle.

"Yes, Capitol Hill—once Jenkins Hill—is like living in the Plaka at the foot of the Acropolis. I lived there myself, well before the Rome days, in one of those all-bachelor apartment buildings that were a feature of those more civilized times, before all the inns of Washington were refitted with revolving doors."

(Remembering the reproductions of Greek statuary on the Plaka, I thought of all those political crew-cut *Stage Door* bachelors, wondering if they'd kept mantel busts of Jefferson and Madison.)

"A veritable cripple of high ground through which rustles the straggling wind of memory: a two-hundred-acre campus protected—I know you love good police—by the elite Capitol corps in bright white vehicles with smart blue stripes: circling all through the night to ensure the security of the many ancient revenants who live there in the most stark loblolly isolation, almost gathered to history.

"What Rex said of the above-ground tombs here is more than true of the byways of D.C. too, where living relicts and the corpses of their reputations, thousands of them—fobbed off, bought off, pensioned off, blown off—abide the passing of their days side by each with all the attractive young hopefuls who arrive—little roulette marbles in the Capitol dome's spinning game, little green veins in the *nervure*—much as their opposite numbers of another hopeful persuasion arrive in Hollywood. Mad they are to be discovered in some D.C. equivalent of Schwab's, and given new faces, new names, and new parts to play—and it's terribly sad to watch as the same old parts get stuck on those bright new faces and the boot-heel subjugation of the ideologues turns them dull and decrepit in a season. Do young hopefuls any longer arrive in New York? Tell me, is there room left for one single more?

"And, oh, the great magnolias in spring—and the cunning little saucer magnolias planted along the divide in that southeast stretch of Pennsylvania Avenue, a boulevard we much prefer to the northwest stretch—that melancholy *allée* from the two ends of which we in this great nation are governed by a bipartisan complex of incompetents locked in sordid, squalid conflict without the vaguest idea of what they are doing.

"Yes, the lovely souks along Pennsylvania Avenue Southeast—and the North Hall of Eastern Market, where the cultured gather for little lectures, slide shows, song recitals—just like here! You seem skeptical; I assure you it is the case."

(Reality: everything that is the case.)

"The one thing you must not seek is to *belong*. You may *partake* of D.C. life, but you will not be invited—indeed you will not be permitted—to participate in it, neither the genteel white life of Capitol Hill, whose boundary is the Eastern Market, nor the rugged, homespun black life that lies like a crazy quilt beyond Seventh Street. You will not likely ever venture much further than the Capitol Hill Natatorium—but you *must* dip in there, dear, to watch the young black men bathe, and bathe with them."

Max entered with crew. (I thought, They're not much like Melville's sailors—more like a chorus out of Gilbert and Sullivan's *Pirates of Penzance* or background characters in a Gordon Merrick novel.

"*Early* Gordon Merrick," the O' insisted. "*The Strumpet Wind.*"

"Does he ever take that watch off?"

"I don't know if he sleeps with it on or not.")

"I expect," Max declared, "Rex told you I've been off looking for Atlantis. He read it in the *National Enquirer* last week—planted there no doubt by the Bimini casino and tourist mafia—along with the fact that my wife is the reincarnation of a wife of a pharaoh—I forget which one. One learns to tolerate these fictions. Actually, if anyone pines for the lost Atlantis it is our host—the lost empire of the Atlantic Treaty."

He turned to me. "You and I have something in common, you know, since I pilot the skipjack—"

(And I cover the waterfront?)

"—the endangered-species boats. But shall we continue our conversation, so rudely interrupted by the outburst of your black friend? He certainly can clear a hall—even walking out of it. People probably thought he was about to *send friends back in*.

"Here's something else you can't write about. Why a decent young black boy, well educated—by white people—to a great love of books and disinterested learning, is so troubled. Because he knows just how many of his blue-collar coevals, loosely enfranchised by exactly so many white-collar whites, have for over a decade been systematically denuding the collections of rare items."

"Yes, I've heard that."

"It's a bald fact. The thieves don't give a shit about what they lift; it's urban guerrilla warfare—so when your black friend mentions burning churches, he's telling you *in code* about the LC *evaporations*. Consequently, apart from its charming architecture, one is apt to regard the Library of Congress the way one does Congress: scantily. There is no image I can invoke to convey exactly how little the problem weighs on the minds of our nation's legislators—or for that matter on the mandarinate that runs the library itself. I would leave the New York Public Library my entire fortune; I wouldn't leave the LC a dry-cleaning receipt. *That* is why your black friend is so torn up. He should find something else to do, before he commits suicide."

"So much for my black friend. What about your—or rather the senator's—Indian friend?"

"He is a boy."

"I got that part."

"Do you know about the phalarope at all?"

"A wading bird. There was a play on Broadway in the fifties—*Too Late the Phalarope*. It became a kind of joke."

"I must look it up. The phalarope, when there's too little food, spins around in the water at the rate of sixty times a minute." (I thought of Odette's Odile fouettés in *Swan Lake*.) "The spinning concentrates prey into the upwelling jet—a metaphor. But what was it we were talking about at the Cosmos Club? About Republicans and Democrats, wasn't it?"

"You were talking; I was listening."

"As befits a reporter. I believe I was about to say that the Republicans' most telling characteristic is the way they handle—or rather don't handle—proverbs."

"Proverbs? The word I remember was 'patois.'"

"Ah. Well, in any case, Republicans have a peculiar thought deficit. If you give them a proverb and ask for an explanation of it, they will simply repeat the proverb back in concrete terms. Their ratiocination is limited to the concrete."

"And what is it Democrats do with proverbs?"

"Democrats will tell you proverbial thought is a coercive, hegemonic device. If a Democrat sees a penny lying in the street, he bends over, turns it, and walks on. The Republican pockets it. But then the Republican—particularly the eastern Republican—has strange fears, which you may be hard put to understand. His idea of an endangered species is not the spotted owl or the piping plover so much as his daughters at Brearley and his sons at Choate."

"The Democrat is superstitious."

"The Democrat follows strange gods all his life. The Republican long has felt estranged from his God—like the blind man among blind men, each touching a part of the elephant but none able to define its shape. The whole point of being a Protestant and tramping under the lilies of the field to cultivate the land is that he has no need to break that God's very first commandment too.

"The *Washington Post* declares the Republicans have in the last generation proven themselves cynical and manipulative whereas the Democrats have been, and still are, self-indulgent and fatuous.

"Anyway, what has government yielded in the last two generations? A corporate military state decried after the fact by Ike and expanded to bursting by the Kennedys, the sine qua non in low cunning, pretension, and cruelty, and their captains of industry and American can-do-gooders in the ridiculous Peace Corps. That state did very well in effective competition in those areas of the world under the American heel—the army in Germany and Japan or the CIA in Africa—but as soon as that fool Johnson insisted on racial equality across the board, and liberals forced him into the no-win chicken game and America lost its first war and started falling to pieces, it was only natural that the original owners of the land and resources—I don't mean Indians: no ownership concepts—deemed it necessary to take back the reins in Washington. Fronting Nixon, a failed bet, but his appeal was irresistible. Even today he is among the low-down-lawless beloved.

"Then Reagan, a brilliant success: never has America's version of reality played so . . . Do you know what the Hanseatic League was?"

"No." (But Odette would.) "Something akin to the Wise Use movement?"

"Close. You see, the Republicans now pretend to think you can run government the way you run corporations—with flowcharts, baselines, hedge funds, and front-loading buyouts . . . all the paraphernalia of—"

"More peanuts, more satisfaction."

"That's it." (In a nutshell. And just think, before D.C. I'd have said baselines were chalked-on indicators that ran up from home plate and thought I was being butch and American.)

"And the cap on it all is the 1993 Government Performance and Results Act. If *that* doesn't make the piss run down your leg . . .

"Perhaps you're worried that in the corporate city-state world you are an artist. Plato's banishment of poets. But that world with merely virtual boundaries and nation states that function as year-round holiday display windows cannot be any *more* indifferent to what you have to say and to the way you say it than the United States of America has been over two centuries. We're more likely to give you a place at the table: as bards, celebrating our exploits."

"You have that already in advertising and public relations."

"Become so self-serving, they've forgotten who licensed them, and for what. They think plebiscite, forcing our representatives to pretend to care *what the people think* every two or four years."

"Particularly," I remarked, "people who, as Socrates says in *The Republic*, find justice useful when they've laid their money by. And how would you test us—to find us worthy?"

"All right, here's some homework. Consider the following eight entities in relation to the structure and function of that medium of exchange, or weaponry—money—particularly of that portion of the horde, or arsenal, people have given up exchanging for perishable goods and have laid by. Four constants, four variables: gold, oil, helium reserves, and superconductors; the national debt, credit balances, welfare, and the Sultan of Brunei.

"Scratch the balanced budget. The balanced budget is a scheme whose logic foundation is on the order of the Foundation for New Era Philanthropy—if you know what that was."

I didn't.

"The new possibility is the reinvention of money. Economics and politics are still understood in D.C. in the Newtonian terms Henry Adams—or Clover—depicted: a perception that works only in flat-earth terms: in terms of old bills—dollar and legislative—that must be turned in before they fray away in people's hands."

"Metaphorically."

"Metaphorically in Newtonian terms: understood that way in Gore Vidal's novels too. Whereas any true picture of them would have to be drawn in quantum mechanical terms . . . actually particle and wave theory. Money is generally seen as particles, but could just as easily be seen as waves—a two-party system, but not, of course, according to quantum mechanics, simultaneously."

"I thought politics was always thought of in quantum theory terms. Doesn't 'quantum' mean 'how much'?"

"That's very good. In fact, it makes me want to tell you the truth."

"You know the truth."

"Yes. Do you want to hear it?"

(I might.)

"Silence. Do you go sailing on Long Island?"

"I've been out; I don't go out very often."

"But in a boat with sails—and with a motor."

"Yes."

"Good. Then I will tell you exactly why corporations finance policy studies and institutes and put up with all this nonsense, this three-ringed circus. The American ship of state is a full-rigged schooner, beautifully designed to be sailed in all weathers by real navigators, which all the Founding Fathers were. The maritime metaphor—sea to shining sea—is our signal emblem.

"So the spotted owl gets guaranteed habitat—and the beaver and the prairie dog, although you haven't met them, and they want to give the sandhill crane his own lure crop fields—and logging companies get free quick kills, and you get breakfast with Al Gore. And the likes of Steve Forbes—a bozo among bozos. Of course, Steve never had a globe on his desk like the rest of us. He had a Fabergé egg, with a little window to look through at a little bejeweled universe."

(I thought back to the flat disk map with the date window.)

"Not that I have anything against Fabergé eggs. In fact, my wife—she's half Russian, you know."

(I knew. Odessa: jewels sewn into linings and the collection of Fabergé eggs rolled in molding clay, passing as bread.)

"Amazing people, the Russians. Ungovernable, but *elemental*. Rather like the residents of the District. My wife is a perfect example. I like my wife; she's rather like my mother. My mother read Ayn Rand too, and when I told my wife Alan Greenspan had told me Ayn Rand liked fucking in fur coats, she laughed, calling it simply overefficient. 'Most women separate the two—working hard at the one and luxuriating in the other. For her fucking in the coats was simply a celebration of work—entirely consistent with her view of self-interested capitalism. She supplied her own demand; many women do, darling.' Women's logic amazes me. And I like her sense of humor. Just last week I said, sincerely, 'You are very beautiful.' Do you know what her reply was? 'Just leave the money on the mirror, darling.' Amazing."

(O'M said later, "Max really is nervous about Steve Forbes. Talk about the narcissism of minor difference. Steve owns a lot of Colorado, Max a lot of Wyoming. Steve has a two-million-buck town house in New York, and Max's joint in Kalorama Circle is worth about that. Steve flies a Boeing 727, while Max flies the latest Lear. Steve inherited an island in the Pacific—"

"With," Odette asked, "sun to tan him, palms to fan him, and the occasional man?"

"I think not, not Steve," O'Maurigan replied. "Whereas," he continued, "Max owns that little parcel near Bimini."

"He certainly keeps them—men—at his beck and call. No lookers, though, you'll notice."

"I have never worked out Max's interest, but his strategies are broad brush. Men are in his world the ammunition; women are wives and secretaries. Then too, Max indulges in a degree of sentimentality concerning that class of American come to be known as white trash. The descendants of the monied often care deeply for the descendants of those who stood shoulder to shoulder with their grandfathers in flooded mine shafts and on grueling hot oil rigs."

"And the trophies?"

"There are none—men like Max don't seem to need them. Yet he carps on Steve's fortune in hot-air balloons."

"The helium reserves," I offered.

"A cover. Max is essentially a developer, replacing permeable ground with impervious surface. He would like to add that little parcel near Bimini called Cuba."

"*Cuba!*"

"Yes. Many think he'd be better invoking the 1856 Guano Islands Act, by which any American who discovers an uninhabited island covered in birdshit . . . But Max wants Cuba."

[I seemed to remember some American once ran Honduras, or Nicaragua.]

"Wants to run it?"

"It couldn't be done in the old way—in the way that French soldier of fortune Max admires took over an island in the Mozambique Channel and ran it in the eighties, but essentially, yes, that's what he'd like."

"For what reason? To install Anastasia as the queen of Havana society?" ["He ought to be wary of that idea," Odette said later. "There was a gringo called Max who took over Mexico once; he too had a wife with mystical leanings and a taste for jewelry and couture. When he was shot, she went mad. Bette Davis played the part."]

"Anything like that—rather than seeing it given to Jorge Mas Canosa. His ambition is to advance the day when the executive branch of the United States government is reduced essentially to the status of popular entertainment, like the royal family."

"He does seem smart."

"Max is a one-man Carlyle Group, with his grandfather's knack of using nobody or nothing to get in the door but the tip of an English-made shoe. He sees the principal function of our august lawmakers and their staffs as hopping on and off planes and trains and the odd yacht with their heads and briefcases full of the right *stories* to explain why they were. Government is to him a *service* industry, lower than product industry. For their part, the Harringtons have been in everything since the fall of silver through Teapot Dome to uranium, plutonium—"

"To the helium reserves."

"To the helium reserves—according to him the biggest yet, and maybe more than a cover after all. Helium in its liquid form is a coolant, and the world, they say, is heating up. Also, there's some controversy in the superconductivity race about the difference between liquid nitrogen and liquid helium—two schools—two parties. In any case, there languishes under the earth somewhere in Texas the world's most enormous and dis-used superconducting supercollider, inert, in danger of being submerged by effluvia from underground aquifers and septic tanks. The helium reserves are somewhere in the rescue sce-nario for that immense toy of science."

"Superconductivity has environmental applications. He wants to hold the environment *hostage*?"

"It's a scenario, no?")

"Well," Max continued, "this is what we talk about in the nineties, with no more commies and contras—that and Bosnia. *Imagine* what we'd have been talking about here in the eighties: invasion schemes, glass-in-Castro's-rice-and-beans schemes. Free-the-faggots-from-Fidel's-prisons schemes, and whether the CIA scheme to dissolve his beard with aerosol depilatory ever really came off and he's been living under horsehair ever

since. Instead, in the second half of the nineties, we sit here and
he sits there, and apart from a few crazies in Miami still dreaming of one last mambo in Havana, nobody gives a shit."

(I remembered Mercedes Benzedrine on Cuban politics.
"Honey, I *hate* Fidel, but *anybody* who thinks that the Cuban
people would be better off under those Miami Cuban fascists
is *fucking insane!* They are the same as Chiquita Banana, one
lying spic. Not only can you keep your bananas in the refrig-
erator, you can make a divine dessert out of them mashed
with vanilla, a little honey, and milk, in the freezer like ice
cream."

And now Chiquita Foods is a subsidiary of the Carlyle
Group and O'M said Max was a one-man Carlyle Group. I
pined for the days when "Carlyle" meant Bemelmans Bar and
the cabaret where Bobby Short sang and I would go with
Dorothy Dean to hear him.)

"It makes sense to send an army abroad, but not to send
development money."

"That leaves the field open for you. Rex doesn't seem—"

"Rex and issues have long since parted company—except
for the theming of Key West and the founding of Trans-
parency International. But speaking of issues, I want to produce your show."

"My show?"

"Yes, when you get back to D.C."

("You mustn't be afraid of Max," Anastasia advised when
indeed I was back in D.C. "In his official capacity he may seem
gruff and severe, but I can assure you he's just a little boy with a
dream. I'm afraid *I* shall not take part. Scruples." Get *you*, I
thought.)

The star finale turn was, even as we continued speaking,
upon us: Rex reappeared as Vava Zubrovka, in a strapless black
satin trimmed with jet passementerie, and enormous black
Reeboks—and bedecked in marquisette jewelry. Drunk, and,

as he put it, "lysergic," wheeled in on a slanting costume board, with the same Charles Rennie Mackintosh design—to keep him from falling.

"*Easy*, Beulah. The madame is sufferin' with her *subluxation*.

"She's back—in black—and feeling *bazooka*. Recharged, although *not* with any lithium ion batteries. Just a gay dose of doxazosin mesylate downed with a few stiff belts of her namesake nectar to ameliorate the Calvary of benign prostatic hyperplasia. Back in voltaic prime time! And black, you know, makes a face, any face, leaner, more purposeful, and individuated. A woman in black expresses a complex declaration of assertion and lament—so she reassumes her *ogre's* robes to read the auspices once more."

(Probably still has his seventies Marielito stash, I thought. No old bag of bones nailed up on the wall, yet, but . . .)

"Am I to regale you with tales of fifties D.C., of McCarthy, Hoover, Sherman Adams, and the Alsops, of the thoroughly *Florentine* State Department and how Adlai Stevenson lost the elections because Ike was so butch and Adlai would not fight dirty like Glenway Wescott admonished? On spies, and drag, and *Advise and Consent*? Or am I to talk to you about the Shining Prince of Camelot?"

"Oh, the Shining Prince of Camelot, Vava!"

"All right, though it beats me that merely because of the long shadows he cast on history, people impute to Jack Kennedy the radiance of a *sun*. Didn't anybody ever hear of rows of carefully positioned *footlights*? Unless of course you take the position that he singlehandedly saved this world of ours; in which case—

"Oh, he was something, all right. He had *it*, that thing first denoted by Elinor Glyn in the 1920s. Of course now that the question 'Has he got *it*?' has taken on a new meaning altogether . . .

"Witty, charming, devious, privately scornful of the Opti-
mates—the rhetors of the Republic—the Florries he knew
condescended to him even as they kissed his none-too-royal
Irish ass in public—as when on the day he stood up there at the
Brandenburg Gate and announced proudly in the Berlin ver-
nacular, 'I am a jelly doughnut,' they went *dizzy* with sup-
pressed laughter. Turned out to be horribly true in Dallas on
that latter day when the doughnut exploded all over Jackie's
pink Norman Norell.

"Possessed he was of that single-minded nature which in
politicians leads to either greatness or disaster, sometimes
both. But Mary Hoover had to have Jack done away with: little
brother had pictures of her going down on Clyde—like the
ones the KGB had of Joe Alsop in a Moscow hotel room—and
was going to *use* them.

"'For pity's sake, fight *dirty*,' Glenway said, and Mary
knew how to do *that*—never underestimate the capability of a
drag queen to wreak havoc. Somebody told her there was this
tape of the President *talking*, my dears, in his *sleep*, and repeating over and over again, 'Oh, *Angie*, that's *mahvelous* . . . keep
doing it,' and that although it was *presumed* he was moaning in
dreamland to that Mafia doll who was in the *movies*, they actually told old Mary he was in *fact* moaning to his *undersecretary of
state*, and get *this*: Mary *believed* it! That was on April 1, 1963.
Well, it may have been April Fool, but then it was that Mary
knew they knew she knew—and come November twenty-third
of that same year, it was no foolin'."

"That was *you* on the tape, Vava, imitating Jack Kennedy!"

"Well, now, *that* would be tellin' on one's own *self*. I am
savin' all my most intimate secrets for the first biographer of
Jack Kennedy who is serious about knowin' the *truth*. Not
likely to appear in my lifetime, I realize, but my papers—

"But Mary—who by the way recommended clemency for
Ethel Rosenberg, for she did—Mary—truly revere true strong

women, however wicked—Mary *was* the *biggest* camp in Washington—as big as Dillinger's dick, which she kept pickled in brine in a jar right next to the bottle of rye in the bottom right desk drawer."

"Is that *true*, Rex Vavasour?"

"True as I am sittin' here—kept it right in that drawer, and would *take it out and exhibit it* to any and all who expressed an interest—Thurgood Marshall, for example, who was *fascinated*! Those were the *times*—they *had* something."

"They had *une certaine je-ne-sais-quoi*, Rex Vavasour!"

"They did, Miss Regine, even if in your usual charmin' gender amnesia you have rendered it incorrectly. It is *un certain . . . although*, come to think of it, I *like* your version. Yes, they had *une certaine jeunesse . . . et quoi.*

"Of course people do not respect history. 'He's *history*,' they say, as if history were the worst—as if there were any escape or alternative. For instance, what have we now alternative to the resuscitated, *southpaw* corpse of Richard Milhous Nixon? *Permission* to go down on our knees a second time to a piece of *trade*—posing as some kind of Ptolemy. Hah! *Ptolemaios Philopator Philadelphos Neos Dionysos*. I mean, what *is* he? He doesn't inhale—doesn't even *smoke*, but likes to *chew on* fifty-dollar Havana *cigars*! What *is* that?

"As has been said, and wisely, 'The President has an unquestioned record of leaving in his wake much human debris.' I have my opinion—"

"*Tell*, Vava!"

"Must I? . . . I suppose I—well, to be quite candid, in my opinion, the President is a *bottom*—and we *all know* how true it is and in just what way that *the bottom rules.*

"Yet I *admit* that had I the choice of going down on him now, and *having gone down* on either of the Brothers K—well, *maybe* Bobby, a Bobby Madison with a snake's heart—but not Jack, with that head full of speed and pigshit Irish *contempt* for everybody who ever passed his exams and wrote his books for him—

"Such as his selfless *sebastocrator* Ted Sorensen—who's *back*, by the way. And *still* can't stop talking about him—it's like William H. Herndon on Lincoln, determined to the death to reveal to posterity the inner life—the passions, appetites, affections, and perceptions of the martyred President, just as he lived and breathed, ate, laughed, and fucked in this world.

"They called him a hero, that Jack-in-the-box; some called him something even more. Well, you know what Nietzsche said. I'm thinkin' of his brilliant dictum on heroes and other interlopers. 'Around the hero,' he said, 'everything turns into a tragedy; around the demigod, into a satyr play.' Well, what do *you* call the history—to which there is no alternative but the novels of Allen Drury—of the last thirty-five years? Does the charmed career of the present incumbent give you a clue as to which of Nietzsche's—oh, there are times when I really would like to see Billy Butt-head swinging at dawn from the yardarm of Max Harrington's yacht docked at the foot of Duval Street! And *oh*, can't you just see every queen in *America* gettin' hold of the video just to see that *little* bulge *rise* to the *occasion* in those—"

"Sailor pants like Guy Madison's, designed by Captain Guy Molyneaux?"

"Yes—yes, I believe we can fit him out in some of those. And watch the little *stain* spreading, just the way his bad-boy fibs did in people's minds! But as I was saying, *everybody knows* why Vince Foster blew his brains out. Promise them anything, but give them Arpège. Now do you call that *tragedy*? I call it a *satyr play*.

"It is all *right* for Hoot Niggerrich—of the Abraham Lincoln Opportunity Foundation—to say he melts, like the tiger in *Little Black Sambo*, in Clinton's presence—oh, *don't* get me *started!*"

"But it's too late, Vava!" somebody shouted. "You're *already* started. You're *roaring*!"

"So I am, Varina, roaring prior to takeoff—and just *try* and stop me now that I have mastered the forces of flight—lift, thrust, and *drag*—by which flyers slip the surly bonds of earth.

"Vince Foster wasn't the first boy-man to run away down *quelque chemin abîme et mal déroulé*, finally to excommunicate himself from the light of day over Butt-head Bill. The Oxford roommate—why won't people read Balzac, as David Souter insists? It's *all* there. Or if not Balzac, then John Rechy.

"I see that everywhere among the race of men it is the tongue that wins and not the deed. Vilification as a viable means of accomplishing the purposes and goals of a shared belief system. The American Centurions thought they had it all—professionals from many walks of life trained to cooperate unfailingly.

"Anyway, the jealous, wrangling, and addictive gods on the Greek *horse* side send *snakes* in vengeance and the snakes get Laocoön and his boys. It's the subject of a very great ancient statue unearthed in Michelangelo's presence from the ruins of the Capitoline Hill and ever since on display at the Vatican: miscalled by thousands of American tourists daily *Lay-a-coon*.

"The other thing about the story of the Trojan horse that may have escaped your attention is the presence of the enemy *in the belly of the beast*. Sound familiar? So do all prophecies converge. I did *not* make myself *queer*, but I do *try* to make myself *clear*. Have I *suck*-ceded?"

"You *have*, Vava, you *have*!"

"Good. I always said allegory should *succeed*. And *apropos* allegory, I was talking—"

"You *were*, Vava, you *were*!"

"Yes. As the great English visionary poet and repressed homosexual William Blake put it, 'Reasonings like vast serpents infold around my limbs, bruising my minute articulations.' Yes, and as you see I am like Laocoön in that I have incurred the wrath of the gods—or of the demigods—and powerful mambos and snake handlers like those in the Bible with their own snake lore have so far held me uncoiled . . . if an uncoiled prisoner of . . .

"Because I prefer to live on my own, like Santayana, before the blue nuns—associating with attractive, cultivated, curious, wealthy expatriate American men—and if you live in Key West you *are* an expatriate. And there's *more*. I will tell anybody who'll meet me in a safe place—I am monitored, you know, by *both* the Intel *and* the Iridium satellite—a thing I must endure if I am to enjoy the night stars. Yes, they may have me pent up here in my buzzard's perch, same as they have Gore in his swallow's nest overlooking the Mediterranean, but they permit us both periodic *lift-offs* to *circle* the truth!"

"*Tell* us what you'll tell us, Vava!"

"I will tell anybody the *true meaning* of the State Department's Republic of Z and a *lot more* about Foggy Bottom, if you can find a safe bottom cellar in Key West to take me to—*and* guarantee me a *safe way* back. And talking of safe cellars, I will tell *all about* what went on—and much still *does*—in the vast underworld complex called 'the Bunker' adjacent to the White Sulphur Springs, West Virginia, where so many took the waters.

"As Miss Flannery O'Connor said, 'I have seen the truth and the truth has made me odd.'"

("She was ever odd," I heard a voice whisper, "but whatever, or whoever, she's been seeing lately has made her just *freaky!*")

"Now, I do *not* go along with Eleanor Roosevelt: 'more profile than courage.' I do think Jack showed courage in the fall of '62, all the more because it sealed his fate, which he knew. But that Georgetown entourage! As fetishistic about the sides of Wisconsin Avenue as any neurotic in Beverly Hills about the sides of Wilshire. *Poncing* around for their thousand days, and when it was over—*bang-bang*—weeping and wailing, 'Oh, the bright Prince, oh, the young warrior, alas, the shattered glory. How it has all vanished in the night as if it had never been!'

"Whining that Civilization has gone down the drain— without a *notion* that the *drains*, like their *brains*, were so *clogged* that Civilization would soon *come right back up*—to torment us!

"Of course the opposition was even worse; they *hated* him so, because he *was*, after all, young, and rich, and gave off that reckless air of the sexually compulsive—the same air that could be seen on revue any night in Lafayette Park. Do you know that a week or so after he was buried, a group of Catholic school children arrived with their priest at Arlington, and in the course of aspersing the grave, the plastic bottle of holy water split open and drowned the eternal flame? 'God has spoken!' they murmured in their dark holes.

"Would that it never had *been*, that whorish time. Mind *you*, I absolve the *offspring*, for her sake. Beautiful children, both of them. As for the others . . . I *will not* turn Cobra Woman. The rarer action is in virtue than in vengeance. Many of them will find their niches, and others will perish. It is the way of the world. As for me, having proclaimed my own Act of Free and General Pardon, Indemnity, and Oblivion, *j'ai cultivé mon hystérie avec jouissance et terreur. Maintenant j'ai toujours le vertige.*

"Yes, for her sake—for the offspring and for the fact that she saved the houses on Lafayette Square—and that he saved the world by paying no mind to that rat pack of privileged American journalists, Soviet secret agents, and Washington bartenders favored by his big-dicked hothead little brother. Of course you are *never* going to get much thanks for saving the world, are you? And did you know how he did it, by the way— what tipped the balance of all those secret talks? He called the fat Pope on the red phone—oh, yes, he *did*, he called the fat Pope and the fat Pope said, 'You stand up to them, Johnny, but hold your *rosary* in your hand when you do.'

"You know, I have just been advised by insiders that

Jackie's *faux pearls* are to be reproduced by the Franklin Mint. Billed as 'a beloved treasure from Camelot, adorned with one hundred and thirty-nine European glass faux pearls, each nine millimeters in diameter and color-matched to the creamy originals. Each silken cord hand-knotted. Secured with a gleaming silver Art Deco style clasp, accented with nine period-style rhinestones, just like Jackie's!' My pearl fetish is as great as Pliny's and Aristotle's, and I must have Jackie's. I once tried on Mary Todd Lincoln's pearls-in-platinum—not reproductions, darling, the *real* ones. I can't tell you where—*security*, you realize—but I *did*, and did I ever *see* and *hear* things as a result—I'm that psychic!"

("'Psycho' is more like it," my Capitol Hill publicist "Margutta" whispered. "Silly bitch, if she tries to put a necklace that was crafted for Jackie around her ugly fat old neck, they'll find her all purple, choked to death.")

"Yes, my career was brilliant in that age of brilliantine careers. As brilliant as Eleanor Lansing Dulles's—or Kay Halle's—which it greatly resembled, except that unlike poor Kay, out to a long lunch up there in her old Georgetown pile, I have kept every one of my marbles in a little velvet bag—to cast before you, along with my complex melodrama of daring, regret, and placation—

"The Chinese old often talk of the poet Li Po, exiled to Yunan—an example of one of their favorite myths—that of those immortals who misbehaved in heaven and were sentenced to life on earth, where they would be encountered as wild, eccentric persons of extraordinary gifts. But I prefer the Japanese to the Chinese, and so to my own mind the man I most resemble is the tenth-century Japanese minister of the right, Sugawara No Michizane, who after his banishment and death returned to haunt the imperial palace."

"That's *you*, Vava! You haunt them—you *terrify* them."

"Yes, with what has been called in certain quarters 'the swivel eye of my promiscuous revulsion.'"

"It's *true*, Vava—that ought to be *you* advising the nation in *Parade* magazine every week."

"Thank you. You know they said at Foggy Bottom that I was too far out, and I replied, quoting Archimedes, 'Let me get far *enough* out, I can move the *world*!' I could have been one who, leaving his footprints in the sands of time, redistributes thousands and thousands of meiofauna—oligochaete, copepoda, sacromastigophoran, halacaroid, cladoceran, rotifer, gastrotrich, holothurian—all ablogate members of the food chain—but they went and *cut off my foot*, and now it is too late. *Solenopsis invicta*, vengeance of the Amazons, whose queens lay a million eggs a day each day, approach—

"Oh, let's lighten *up*, shall we? Let's live in the dizzy minute. This *is* Key *West*—*not* the Oberammergau *Passionspiel*."

"But you have always been passionate, Vava!"

"Yes, I have too. We are all *condamnés*, as Victor Hugo said. We have an interval, then our place knows us no more. Our one chance lies *in expanding that interval*, in getting as many pulsations as possible into the given time. Why waste a single *drop* that can be pressed out of this ripe, this melting, this too adorable world—as we dart through the sunlight of a summer afternoon in December?

"I do *not* see myself, finally, as a crucified old queen cast in a piece of uninspired porn with no money shots. Time *yet* for my appointment at the taxidermist and the one-car funeral—but rather as a living symbol, for did not Epictetus declare that it is difficulties that show what men are?

"I still see me sailing in a Victory Day float past the reviewing stand—am I a visionary, or am I *voluptuary*?—and like love and hatred, *are* they so very far apart? Well, these and many questions remain to be settled. In the meantime, like the lovely Loretta, I say 'See you next week.' Till then, keep these words of wisdom in mind. Life is too short, but *he* doesn't have to be."

Thinking of the trains and the model of fifties D.C., I wandered down to the point where the Atlantic, the Caribbean, and the Gulf of Mexico meet, and all the meiofauna infiltrate the sand. As I sat there till sunrise, I recalled Kennedy and Stewart Udall cooking up the first Clean Water Act. Then I went home to look up "subluxation." "Incomplete dislocation, as of one of the joints of a bone."

Six / Maquillage

Dulles Airport: snow-blanketed northern Virginia. As we entered D.C., the government's nonessential services shut down, O'M said it was as if all the major studios had stopped functioning at the same time. The LC Congressional Research Services were still open, but not much frequented. Delmarva had left a message: the Max Roach evening had been canceled.

The taxi, negotiating at a crawl through glassy streets edged with tall drifts, let us down at my new address on D Street SE, Capitol Hill, a cream-colored brick edifice that had once been a convent for the nursing nuns who staffed the old Providence Hospital a block away (Lincoln Hall, again, the infirmary). As we sat with Sylvester looking out the front bow window through the web of naked night cottonwoods at the Capitol glowing in the dusk—both houses of Congress in night session (windows alight in the two wings and in all the offices)—we were taken up for a spell, American disinclinations notwithstanding, with the metaphysics of the situation.

Being back was like sitting around all day in a bathrobe with the flu. I had a cat door cut into the window so Sylvester could go out into the magnolia, lunging across the divide like a flying squirrel into the sycamore and back through the window vent into the window seat. Well, I thought, that's two trees no birds will be coming home to nest in (emblematic of Washington in its entirety: the Capitol's magnolia dome and secrets stuck in holes). Good thing we moved in in the dead of winter; one could not suddenly hand Sylvester a decree declaring the birds off limits. Meanwhile, could I, a bird advocate, be seen in Washington to keep a cat, and still . . . ? What was political correctness here? Plus, would the raptors attack him?

Out the window when the shade went up: no traffic, no plows, no action. Just snowfall and stasis. The government was shut down, the District was shut down, and I was shut down.

> If a sparrow
> come before my window
> I take part in its existence
> and pick about the Gravel.

Keats. And from *Hymn to Life* by "our" Keats, James Schuyler:

> The bird goes
> quick as a wink
> to swim up
> and cast, like
> it, a shadow
> on the year.

A bird killing: and you could see the impressions in the snow: where the raptor hit when he grabbed the blue jay. Then you could see where the struggle had taken place, including a few loose feathers, a few drops of blood, and a lot of stirred-up snow. No tracks at all: the raptor had taken off with its prey.

The leaden sky seemed full of crows that morning, as many over Washington as the Blackhawk helicopters Conspiracy theorists see in their addled minds' eyes over America the

Beautiful's so spacious skies. Maybe it's no wonder, I thought, given the undeniably moronic level of much of the population, the story they tell down here is a bedtime story for narcissistic children. Maybe it's no wonder Eisenhower saw fit to betray Marshall and kiss McCarthy's ass right on television. (He should rot in political hell, said the firemen.)

A bedtime story before the sleep supported and secured on Capitol Hill by the elite Capitol Police cruising all hours of the day and night. Night whistles of the railroad coming over the Potomac from Virginia, and on the few mild days, when I opened the windows for fresh air, the steady drone of the freeway bypass.

In *Hymn to Life* the background city is Washington as an archetype of any place one has felt alien in. My early life in NYC was tribal, and the city has always been home to me, but all the while there's another city, where I am lost—like Tennessee Williams's picture hanging in Rex Vavasour's bedroom in Key West.

I turned to the poem.

> The wind rests its cheek upon the ground and feels the cool damp
> . . .
> And the winter weather here may hold. It is arbitrary, like the plan
> Of Washington, D.C. avenues and circles in asphalt web and no
> One gets younger: which is not for the young, true, discovering new
> Freedoms at twenty.

(Or nearly thirty, like Rain; where had he gone?)

> The turning of the globe is not so real to us
> As the seasons turning and the days that rise out of the
>   early gray
> —The world is all cut-outs then—and slip or step steadily
>   down

The slopes of our lives where the emotions and needs
    sprout.

    The Pentax was on the shelf—full of lots of pictures of the piping plover's environment to bring down to the committees. I started taking pictures for good luck. Soon I had enough of them for a picture section—also, my virtually wearing a Pentax around my neck seemed to give me a new kind of nervous appeal on Pennsylvania Avenue. But then finally that activity too seemed more nervous than appealing. Each picture seeming another of the

Odd jobs that stretch ahead, wide and mindless as
Pennsylvania Avenue or the bridge to Arlington,
    crossed and recrossed
And there the Lincoln Memorial crumbles. It looks so
    solid: it won't
Last. The impermanence of permanence, is that all there is?

    Maybe that was it—the temerity of feeling I ought to be doing only ever what *appealed* to me—what *called out to me.*
    But what else—follow the bridge across from the Lincoln Memorial, past Arlington Cemetery and down the Potomac's Virginia shore on the notorious Route 1? That way madness seemed to lie—even if, as the O' insists, Schuyler "lets us know the artist's madness, depressive rather than manic, is really the detachment of long perspective." (Pennsylvania Avenue, as photographed looking southeast from the Capitol, certainly long before it disappears in the picture at a point not even outside the District, not far beyond Eastern Market . . . down where the violence takes place at night. Or Route 1 as it wends its way south to Richmond and Palm Beach.) "And as such it is not an endpoint or a byproduct, it is a prerequisite." (He hadn't told me that in Sagaponack—but then Sagg Main Street, look-

ing southeast, disappears in dunes where there's nothing more violent than small birds scrapping over nesting territory or the odd beach-blanket spat.)

The way out may be the way in, all right, but the way down is certainly *not* the way *up*—even if it seems to be. Ask Virgil . . . ask any standee from the Family Circle at the old Metropolitan Opera House. No, as I early learned, singing Palestrina, and as Odette has always insisted, romantic chordal and chromatic writing is essentially Protestant—essentially Calvinistic, definitely keyed to predestination.

Whereas polyphony—well, look at this craze for Hildegard von Bingen (even Hildegarde Dorsay got into it). As O'M says, "Not even Schoenberg in Opus 7 or Alban Berg in the Violin Concerto could save us from the Romantics. It was Debussy and Messiaen, and Harry Partch, and finally Elliott Carter who has restored the truth of music.

Listening to the Carter string quartets, I could still hear the train whistle from two blocks away, next to the expressway, the boundary to No-Man's-Land, Southeast, where all the gay night sex, drugs, and some violence takes place. The train entered underground just on the other side of E Street (a plot point).

There was a plot, there were story boards, push-offs, pushovers, and action wipes—for long before there was reading, there were tellings, as long before the alphabet, pictures. And it may come to that again, I thought: let me go take some pictures.

The Pentax slung over my neck, I went out walking on New Jersey Avenue on the other side of the Southwest-Southeast Freeway, and soon, in the fleshpot district near the Navy Yard, came upon a video store, which I entered. Inquiring of the clerk after a vintage item called *Viet Man*, I drew a blank, but also the attention of a somewhat older man, who approached me.

"Excuse me, I *did* hear you inquire after *Viet Man*. I have a copy. I *would*, in the spirit of *fraternity*, offer you afternoon tea and a viewing, only that as it happens I am on my way to the marine barracks on Eighth Street and I. I troll after marines, and there are *eleven hundred* of them living there!"

"I see. Well, thanks anyway."

"Oh, I won't leave it at *that;* here's my card. Do you take an interest in local lore? I'm over on Duddington Place, on the site of the old estate of Daniel Carroll of Duddington, whose house L'Enfant had pulled down to put in New Jersey Avenue. It abuts the freeway, dear, with everything and everybody speeding by on their several ways to oblivion. I run a little reading group on Tuesday evenings. We read both serious things such as Steven Zeeland's *Barrack Buddies and Soldier Lovers, Sailors and Sexual Identity*, and *The Masculine Marine*, as well as the classics—*Teleny, Finisterre, Giovanni's Room, The Lord Won't Mind, Gaywyck* . . . that sort of thing.

"It's covered dish for the regulars, but no cover for new blood, if you take my neighborly meaning. I've never imagined, dear, that I had any great mission in life, or that life had any great mission in me either—and all these little people in this little town who imagine they do, or it does, bore me to death. 'Let me not seem to have lived in vain,' Tycho Brahe, on his deathbed, begged Kepler. Of the desire for truth and beauty in science and in art, art has the edge—for art, it is said, has come to you professing frankly to give nothing but the *highest quality* to your moments as they pass, and simply for those moments' sake—

"But for all that I am still an avid life student of military science—particularly marine biology, and of cookery—meat *marinades:* jarheads drenched in Yacht Club cologne from Woolworth's, whose idea of perfect freedom is to dress up in corporate-image civvies out of the J. C. Penney catalogue. A surprise a day—you might call it a bolt out of the blue. There's an old saying, dear, 'Tell it to the marines'—and I *do*!

"And the lovely thing is, I find them in the *neighborhood*!

No more treks to the Iwo Jima Memorial, which in any case always did cater to the overtly macho customer. Day lilies like yours truly never had much success there—and these days, dear, the place is *so* cluttered with workaholic soccer players getting together for what they call *pickup games* at twilight. Well, I find the participants for my pickup games out jogging here in the neighborhood. I take them home footsore and after asking them to strip down—

"I put it to them *jocularly*. 'Those Spandex running briefs are stunning,' I say, 'but they do clash with the drapes.' When I get them buck naked, I administer *reflexology* therapy, while running *The Sands of Iwo Jima* or the Battle Color Ceremony: forty-seven breathtaking streamers presenting every marine campaign since 1775. Then I talk a little about the Civil War— they all take great interest in it, if only because they've been told it's to come again—and I'm not above quoting Lincoln, dear—*not* the Gettysburg Address, but the far more heart- breaking, because unrealized, dream of the First Inaugural. 'We must not be enemies—though passion may have strained it must not break our bonds of affection. The mystic chords of memory, stretching from every battlefield, and patriot grave, to every living heart and hearthstone, all over this broad land, will yet swell the chorus of the Union, when again touched, as surely they will be, by the better angels of our nature.'

"Then, as they dry their eyes, the tape segues into *Com- rades in Arms*, and if they bolt at my less-than-better-angel touch, I ask them if they know of the brutal beating death of the gentle Allen Schindler by his vicious drunken homophobic U.S. Navy shipmates. All decent Americans want to atone; you only have to give them the proper opportunity. I tell these boys they have the opportunity of collaborating with me both in an act of restitutive grace *and* in the creation of beautiful memo- ries. They think it over; they are intelligent; generally they see I'm right. It's not just the Ben Franklin—the newly designed one—resting like a windfall leaf on their bare kneecaps. Then they nod, and as they peel off, whisper those magic words I never tire of hearing: *'Chow down.'*

"One of them—who calls his erection Corporal Lance—said, 'I like doing it here, indoors. Guy picked me up last week at sundown? We had a bar crawl until dark, then over to Congressional Cemetery and do it on J. Edgar Hoover's grave. Bizarre.'"

(Talk about Mithraic rites.)

"And you know, they can be terribly quick and clever—yes they *can*. One of my absolute favorites—called Travis—was telling me, in a casual way, of some touching intimacy, and I let out *'Do tell!'*—I say that, you know; it's my way of talking. And back came the reply, quick as the wink that went with it, 'Oh, no, sir, as a matter of fact, *don't* tell.' Isn't that *divine*? And of course I shan't—not that particular detail.

"There was once a whole *flock* of us khaki hawks, dear, circling, circling. One old hag has been at it for half a *century*—still never gotten over the days of Camp Simms, down south, as we used to say. 'You *Alabama* bound?' we used to call out as we saw sisters heading over the Anacostia bridges in the days before Metro. Sometimes one goes walking there in the debris. You mustn't pick anything *up* there—nothing *inanimate*—as there are sleeping grenades that might blow up in your face, and remnants of strange rites once held, and the temptation, like in an old junk shop, is great. Like all fairies, I am a great lover of bric-a-brac, both human and inanimate. And like another old queen, Victoria, I'd as soon have 'em dusky.

"We have a national club—rather like a church: we believe that God, with a little help from friends, will make His love known to us—and a newsletter out of Searchlight, Nevada, concerning pickup sites, photo sets of marines sitting pretty in the face of disaster—it's what they say about themselves, you know: it's their pride of work. And if you hesitate to either come and take tea with me, or to register your name for the newsletter—I would *quite* understand. Whoever you are, dear, you have the look of *serious purpose*, and serious purpose is so easily compromised in this nest of vipers—let me tell you *Viet Man* is probably also on sale in the back pages of the *Blade*. The same ad runs every week—another of our number peddles vintage porn—in *faded reproduction* copies, of course, but *who isn't* one of those?

"I tell you, dear, some of the numbers I take home are so high-strung, I'm afraid by the time I've finished with their feet and it's time for them to sit on my face that the minute they do *they'll* blow up in *it*! So many of them remind me of that poor boy out in Oklahoma—you know, he blew up that building? And they're going to *fry* him—or *hang* him high, until like Billy Budd he meets the full rose of the dawn—or *inject* him with *strychnine*, or whatever, or put him in front of the *firing squad*. It's too terrible to—

"Well, I feel I'm giving my boys a more socially acceptable don't-ask-don't-tell alternative. Yet when they come, with that marine cheer *'Ooo-rah!,'* I do hear the last trumpet call—and won't *that* be a relief, just to get away from *this city*! Bye."

Walking back under the freeway overpass, looking up at the fish-scale shingles of the turrets coated with ice and flashing like coins in the sun, I wondered if I had a mind at all. Now that the 104th Congress was effectively folding its tent, resorting to targeted appropriations strategies, and the officials I met were giving nothing but bland replies, and Washington was now gearing up for auditions for a new one, I could have joined the Clinton-Gore campaign, solving the question of which advocacy I was following, gay or environmental, by matching them: and hinting at the thesis that AIDS is an environmental (drug abuse) disease introduced as such to a drugged culture—quoting Vana, O.J., and Foucault on terrorist sexuality: how radical queers get unconscious revenge by *typifying*, if not actually transmitting—

Instead I went to the Capitol Hill Natatorium, to swim in companionable silence with the young black men—and then to the LC, where I called in at rare books and sat down with *Specimen Days* and with Walt's collection of calling cards from the boys he nursed. The bird hawk was right, of course, although "bric-a-brac" is a little brutal—and there was (wouldn't there be?) one photographic calling card that held the image of a boy who could absolutely have been Rain.

Then, feeling like a super at the opera of D.C. (or like the wardrobe woman who's got two things to do: pick up clothes and press 'em wrong), I went riding on the Metro (with its concrete honeycombed ceilings that reminded me of "You're in a beehive, pal," its flashing footlights, signaling incoming trains that might be beckoning to a suicide, and the woman's voice announcing "The doors are closing—please stand clear of the doors" that seemed to be the same bossy-schoolmarmy voice reciting the First Amendment prologue on porn videos). On the Orange Line that goes to Vienna—only the way the train man said it over the PA it sounded like "on line to Vienna." I imagined being on-line to Vienna, with somebody at the Bristol, with the gang at 19 Berggasse—and pondered in general the politics of psychoanalysis.

The "footlights" on the Metro made me think not only of suicide but of makeup, so I got off at Gallery Place/Chinatown, went walking amid the snowbanks up to Ruppert's Real, on Seventh off New York Avenue, and ate a quiet lunch, surrounded by staffers looking my way to see who'd be joining me (nobody).

Looking up at the melancholy spectacle of the derelict Carnegie Washington City Library, I retraced my steps in the direction of the Navy Memorial. Phil was in the navy, in the Pacific, on the *Intrepid*, in World War II, and I sat there missing him.

Then, turning in at Seventh and G, I found the theatrical makeup house Odette had alerted me to, formally known as Modern Wig & Beauty Supply, to which (in red-white-and-blue spangled stars) the prefix "Post" had been cleverly appended, went in and bought a full box of face paints. I came out and began to fantasize walking down a strange alley and coming out in another city altogether (that "Edge City" in the *Sandman* comic) until I found myself on K Street (K as in Kafka, or even more to the point, as in the still-most-popular homosexual power/dance drug, productive of the hallucination of capability: an impression reinforced by my reiteration that there is nothing to look at on this thoroughfare). A new Cesar Pelli building was nearing completion; it has a section of curved facade, but the gesture is really too short for the building. K also now means what G used to: the new computers have a 256 K pipeline burst cache, and K Street, D.C.'s Madison Avenue, is all about the number of K behind the plaque on the wall. (Odette said, "You don't knock on just any door in K Street.")

I was actually headed for the Names Project Workshop and Education Center at Sixteenth and K to confer on the next showing of the quilt, scheduled for October, before the election.

Quite
A few things are boring, like the broad avenues of
    Washington,
D.C., that seem to go from nowhere and back again.
    Civil servants
Wait at the crossing to cross to lunch at the Waffle
    House.

("Tied to counters, nailed to benches, clinched to desks.")
I was brought up short at Sixteenth Street by turning left at the southeast corner and seeing first the White House and then Doug Vesteralen with his actual mother—the fabled M.J.—walking across from the southwest corner, on their way

to tea at the Hay-Adams. Accepting their invitation to come along, I wondered how Odette's performance measured up to the real thing, and realized that somebody's *actual mother* is such a rarity in our circle as to merit serious consideration. This drove me back to the absence of one in my own life and to the substitutes Holy Mother Church and Mother Country.

M.J. Vesteralen discoursed on winter—and on America as a country working all through its history (because it was born in July?) to banish winter, culminating in the ascendancy of Sun Belt culture epitomized by the year-round amusement park. Amusement parks in the north are closed in winter and become in that season places of mystery: repositories of secrets to be revealed again each summer. All gone. Also about Washington and the people she saw in the streets.

In every other city and town there were, she remarked, *many games being played* with many different kinds of game-board pieces, but in Washington there was *one game*, a kind of chess, with black and white pieces, but all you can see walking around are the pawns and the rooks. *All the other pieces* are operating as if on another board, and so you get the feeling you are in an utterly unreal place, with missing pieces.

Doug said he wondered if at the level at which the game is played, it ought to be called checkers not chess. M.J. said, "No, these people have *checkered pasts*, but they are now playing chess all right." Doug said, "Mother always had a way with words."

"Your father," M.J. recalled, "used to say politics was like the high-school hop—the politicians and their wives were the ones who were good at fast dancing and the lobbyists and businessmen the ones good at slow. The judiciary and the Federal Reserve and that crowd were the monitors and the press were the wallflowers: too ugly or stupid or afflicted with b.o. to be asked to dance."

I liked this woman a lot, and was glad Odette hadn't decided to impersonate her.

"But," she added, "the most dangerously powerful, because they were the ones who could—and would for spite—get you kicked out for sneaking off to the locker rooms for heavy petting."

Doug blushed—which I thought sweet at his age—presumably out of habit in front of his mother. Must be something you just do, I concluded. I'd never—and never gone to a high-school hop, either. But surely "intimidated" was the operative word: intimidated and estranged. (Later Doug said, "You know, you mustn't fall into the error of thinking that this whole show can after all only *really* be explained by sensitive, liberal heterosexuals. Not so.")

That night I dreamed about the silver road from the *Sandman* comic (remembering, before I dropped off, the old number the Chordettes sang: "Mr. Sandman, bring me a dream: make him the cutest that I've ever seen!"). And because Metro is unlike any other underground—too clean, the ceilings white and vaulted—I traveled on a kind of Amtrak–Super Chief amalgam, to *Delirium City*, a place like in *Hymn to Life* remodeled like an amalgam of Rex Vavasour's little model village and Nero's Necropolis in *Quo Vadis*, and the phantasmagoria of my D.C. night walks.

When I got out, I saw the National Archives building dominating the surreal cityscape, and went in. Instead of office doors, row upon row of giant keyholes. I entered one and came out into a mirror corridor and from thence out into a mirror world. The facade was only that—and behind each door just inside was the egress to another time period. I was back in the winter of my birth—with FDR et al. in late-Depression D.C.

Then I was back home in bed on D Street, in the middle of the night, dreaming I was awake. There was a knock at the door. I got up and went to the peephole, looked through—the view distorted as in a convex funhouse mirror—and the face looking back seeking entry was my own. If that's me, I asked myself, why didn't I use my key? Clearly it's an imposter. I went back to bed. The knocking continued for a while, then silence. Moments passed and then the telephone started ringing. (The front door bell is, as in most apartment buildings in D.C., connected to the phone in each apartment.) The phone continued ringing; I decided not to answer.

I awoke to the sound of the telephone. A frantic call from Vana in Venice: the Fenice had just burned down. Raving about her triumph there in *Livia Serpieri* in the fifties, she announced she was on her way over to start a new campaign to raise the theater from its ashes. While talking, I made coffee, threw cold water in my face, and sat down at the window.

"Really, Vana? Your last little—"

"A fiasco, *caro*, I admit it, although I think my face did not entirely fall off with the senator, eh?"

"No—far from it."

"*Ero stato delusa dal Washington.* I confess it. But I have regrouped my forces. *La fede delle femmine è come la Fenice!*"

"That's the spirit. It's terrible about the—"

"It is *mortifying, caro*, the theater *burned*, with all that *water* everywhere! Some say the Mafia from Bari did it."

"From *Bari*?"

"*Sì, sì.* Don't you remember, *caro*, they burned down the Petruzelli." (I didn't.)

"For symbolic and trend reasons."

(Symbolic. Trend. Padania secessionists? The Mafia? Albania? Whatever.)

"The gossip here is that it is anti-Semitic, but that is a cover. They say people were in a rage that Woody Allen was coming to do a jazz concert—they saw it as another sixties *apertura sinistra*."

"Anti-Semitic. Well, the first ghetto was in Venice. But Tito Gobbi was Jewish. And Woody Allen is hardly left-wing."

"The other rumor is that the Islamic terrorists who

threatened to blow up Dante's tomb in Ravenna because he put Mohammed in hell—the Mobile Units of the Wrath of Allah—*they* did it."

"The rumor here is they threatened to blow up the Supreme Court because the frieze pictures Mohammed sword in hand."

"I almost believe . . . And as bad as the theater itself—Verdi's piano! But just between us, I hope it is not they; it would make me feel compromised about the enormous successes I had with Dorabella and with Isabella in *L'italiana in Algeri*."

"Could it have been the Padania zealots?"

"*I Pazzi?* No, I am sure it was the Mafia. They haven't allowed the Massimo in Palermo to open for twenty-five years—and *is* it a coincidence that the mayor of Venice is called Massimo Cacciari? People are saying they have torn the mask away from the face of the city—which will give the secessionists more publicity. Everybody is asking the same question: why was the canal in front of the theater *drained* on that very day? And the *irony*! The theater was supposedly being *rewired*. It is too much. And now there is this *inglese* going about saying Marco Polo never went to China! That he made the whole thing up in Constantinople!"

"Istanbul."

"Whatever."

("A book is a box full of words," the O' had said. "Some books are boxes full of boxes—Chinese boxes." "An effect resembling the circus clown car." "Yes, some books are just one big box with five sides that you put over a trapdoor in the floor of the world—and up comes everything until the box bursts." The story within the story within one of Marco Polo's Chinese boxes—and whether or not he ever went to China, I certainly went to Washington.

Or as in my favorite exhibit at the LC, Keith Smith's "string book"—instead of a written story, the reader follows strings shifting into suggestive patterns as they travel [like the ropes the Norns pass back and forth in *Götterdämmerung*] through the pages. Not knowing from page to page what form the strings will take creates numerous narrative yarns and multiple variations on the theme of loss.)

The voice of the diva was crackling on the satellite beam.

"Venice is demoralized. Everyone says '*Se l'honor è un premio della virtù, perchè un homo che viva virtuosamente—*'"

"'Un *homo*,' Vana?"

"*Sì, sì, caro*—the Venetian dialect. '—*perchè un homo che viva virtuosamente benche su mojer sia poco manco che puttana non halo da esser premia de honor?*'"

"Sounds like what Cio-Cio-San reads on the dagger."

"Something must be done—besides the chanting of '*come'era, dov'era.*' The Fenice is more important than the Campanile."

"The Campanile. Maybe you could get Christo to wrap the Campanile. . . ."

"No, I am finished with wrappings. *Basta.* When I return, with your help I will present a regatta on the Potomac."

"Really?"

"*Sì, sì*, with gondolas, and *gondolieri*. I have decided on a 'Venice is a *millennium-and-a-half*' celebration. I got the idea from our mutual friend the Irish *capo*."

"Chieftain."

"*Come vuole.* Remember when Dublin was a thousand years old in the eighties? Now the Austrians are cooking up the same farrago, a ball at Union Station next December. I will upstart them—and Laura Biagiotti's affair at the St. Regis Roof too, at which promises are made and nothing accomplished, although she perfumes the room with her scent Venezia—with fifteen hundred years of Venice."

"Up*stage* them, I think you mean. *Is* Venice that old, Vana?"

"*Più o meno.* Actually, the first doge was crowned thirteen centuries ago—but thirteen is an unlucky number, and fourteen hundred—well, who could get it up, as your vulgar American expression goes, for that?"

"I see. These *gondolieri*, will you bring them over with you?"

"What for? Are there no rugged Italian boys needing jobs in Little Italy where you live?"

"I live on Capitol Hill now."

"Nonsense. You will come up to New York and help me round them up, all the disadvantaged boys. We will take them to Washington and they will be inspired and their lives will be transformed."

"I don't think so—anyway, you could get cheap help down here, if not exactly, as our Halloween dinner companion put it, 'slave labor.' We could do *A Night in Venice* on the C&O Canal, a local waterway itself under reconstruction, and a pet project of the Vice President's."

"Ah, *sì*. Tell me, *caro*, is it true what they say about—"

"I wouldn't know."

"Well, I might get involved in that. It might help me out of my hot tub."

"You're in a hot tub? I hope you're holding a cordless phone."

"*Caro*—not literally. The *expression*."

"*Vana*, you mean you're in hot water?"

"That's what I said. And I *never* use a cordless *telefono*—they cause brain cancer! I do not need brain cancer—I am in enough of a mess already. I am booked to sing at the Kennedy Center twenty-fifth anniversary gala and *also* for the twenty-fifth-anniversary gala at the Metropolitan for that mafioso—that charlatan, that—"

"Venetian?"

"*Caro—please!* I thought I would have to check into the hospital in Rome with pneumonia."

"Caught while fighting the Fenice fire, eh? Beats brain

cancer anyway." (I surveyed my nearly completed Pierrot face in the mirror, deciding it needed Chinese red lips.)

"*Caro*, you're just *rimming* with political ideas since you went to Washington."

"I think you mean 'brimming.'"

"You spend much time correcting my English, *caro;* you will make me lose all my charms."

"Impossible. I think you should come to Washington and sing the Barcarolle—endear yourself to the local money. You know what they say about the Kennedy Center? A platform so popular both Democrats and Republicans are comfortable on the same ticket."

"*Come?*"

"It loses in translation." (Since "platform" is the same as "scaffold" in Italian: *palco*.) "Anyway, what do you care about the Met? You don't want to be in *Gatsby;* the word in the business is it already sounds like a cheap rewrite of *Blue Monday*."

"I have had too many of those in my life."

"Haven't we all."

"I *never* think of you as blue, *caro*. To me you are the—what is it—the cockeyed optimist."

"You flatter me. But *South Pacific* is a show we could *both* be in—in dinner theater. Come to Washington. Venice Day at the Smithsonian is the same day as the Kennedy Center gala. And we'll get local boys for *gondolieri*."

"Yes, I have been thinking, I must do the Kennedy gala. After all, I was there at the opening, twenty-five years ago. What a nightmare *that* was—that Bernstein *Mass*—*un'abo-minazione*, and that Nixon being brought in through the drainpipes because of security, they said, and sitting there like a completely mad thing. But *caro*, when you say local boys to be the *gondolieri*—are not all the local boys there—the kind you mean—black?"

"Indeed. I'm looking at them right now, shoveling snow

into mounds. Their skin shining in the sunlight. And they love outfits."

"*Caro*, please—*black gondolieri?* Be sensible. *Sicilians* are nearly black, yes, but Venetians are half-Austrian!"

(I heard Rex Vavasour saying, "This is not prejudice. Men of color simply are not *nautical*." Something told me that if the ancestors of the men I was looking at out the window swam the Anacostia and the Potomac to get free . . .)

"You do see my point, do you not?" she pleaded.

"I don't think so."

"You won't help resurrect the Fenice?"

"I always thought," I watched Pierrot say in the mirror, "the Phoenix's specialty was resurrecting itself."

"You are being perverted." (I thought, You should only know, and grinned into the mirror.)

"Old ways die hard. But the fact is, Vana, they are building their own opera house here—or renovating an old building into one, which is the same thing. Plácido Domingo is—"

"Yes, I know Plácido—preposterously self-centered. Singing Wagner now; very amusing. Perhaps I should sing the Liebestod—in Italian, of course—and not the Barcarolle."

"A thought. The amusing thing about the opera house is that the man they are going to name it after was a crook who practically singlehandedly destroyed the landscape of the state of Maryland."

"I don't understand. Most men who build opera houses are crooks, no?"

"Yes. It's nothing—it's just that there's a move afoot to give Washington back to Maryland, in toto."

"Well, in that case, we must make the cities—Venice and Washington—twins. To boost Washington's pride. This is a thing I know Americans are crazy for—to match with a European city and exchange delegations and all that. In this way I can also gain a jump over Consorzio Venezia Nuova, who only like to give parties. They protest me always, saying I am not truly Venetian—when it is on the scroll they gave me when I created *Livia Serpieri* in the Fenice and all of Italy was at my feet that I am justly so.

"You know, *caro*, I have never forgotten you in *Story of a Woman*, when you wore the Pierrot costume and sailed down the Canale Grande with that fat lady from New York. It was like seeing Valentino in the tango in *Four Horsemen of the Apocalypse*."

"Which I sometimes think I am in the middle of remaking down here. And I have never forgotten your Barcarolle, Vana, which is why I suggested it, but we are not on Joe Franklin's *Memory Lane*."

("Nice lipstick," I said to my mouth in the mirror.)

"You will help me, you and that drunken senator?"

"That brings up another difficulty. The fact is, although Congress pays for the city, it does not directly govern it."

"Who does, the Mafia?"

"No, it's called Home Rule, and is largely a black affair."

"*Sì, sì*, I know all about it. Bina Sella di Monteluce—she calls herself a *contessa*—is in constant contact with them from London, with her scheme to build an amusement park for black children in the middle of that other river."

"The Anacostia. I've just been watching the children making snow angels. The contrast of their black skin against the white snow is very beautiful. And their amusement and agitation—"

"Inspiring. You have always been a good person."

"Goodness has nothing to do with it, Vana."

"Of course it does—and there is no reason why I, having become a good person too—and your black friend who created the *scandolo* at Christmas is himself very beautiful, if perhaps a little dangerous. And he has in fact invited me into the Library rare book room. Now I have myself just had an inspired thought."

(Better than the backroom, I thought, deciding to with-
hold the information that Ornette was out for a spell on sick
leave.)

"They're coming thick and fast; I'd expect no less."

"You are sweet. As I remember, the black people are having a lot of *angoscia*, no, over their churches being burnt
down?"

"Well, yes, they are."

"And so they should—it is not *sopportabile*. But you see, it
is the same—the churches and the opera houses—for the
Fenice is not the only one. There was poor Montserrat standing weeping in the ashes of the Liceo and also, *caro*, as I
remember also, the black boy, before he threw the *scena*, was
singing something very sexy—a little like a *gondoliere*."

"That was Billy Strayhorn's 'Lush Life.' Billy Strayhorn
was the greatest jazz composer who ever lived—black and
homosexual."

"*Ah, sì—molto interessante.* So, you will help me to get to
know the black people, and I will make them see the similar-
ity—the *identity*—of the tragedies, and they will help me
rebuild the Fenice."

"We'll all help you, Vana—if for no other reason than to
be in a box seat when *you* reopen the theater in *Mortal Woman*."

"Which theater?"

"First at the Fenice, and then later—well, it could never
open at Kennedy Center, but might well have its American
premiere, after you've triumphed in it all over Europe, at the
new place—with lots of standing room for the *popolo minuto*."

(Odette said later, "Yes, I see it, darling; I almost *hear* it,
especially the part where Maria's ghost returns to the Fenice,
where her career took off. Perhaps there could be a scene like
in *One Touch of Venus*—everybody's stealing from the old
shows. Just right for the opera house which used to be a
department store. Just the right atmosphere for Vana, who
practically *lives* at Rinascente.

"Of course we must also work in Marco Polo. Well, Maria *did* do Turandot. And spaghetti. Marco Polo brought spaghetti back from China. Wasn't Meneghini in spaghetti? Anyway, one thing is certain; there will be no question of *replaying* the history of the Italian Republic a *second* time as farce.")

"I must ring off now, *caro*," Vana declared, sounding as if she'd done a day's work. "I feel myself becoming morbid, and in AA we are never morbid."

"God forbid, if you're fighting the Vatican."

"We fight, yes, but we are not militant—it is a program of attraction. And our chairman, Franco Grillini, is *very attractive*. I will get him to come to the regatta—and you will dress up again as Atys, the resurrected one, and be *very symbolic*."

"My specialty. Bye-bye."

Emboldened by my made-up face, and in spite of what I recalled Rex V. saying about black men not being nautical, I called up Ornette to ask him where he'd been and did he think black men could be taught to row gondolas.

"Very likely, boss. Yowza."

"Kindly don't 'yowza' me, Ornette, it is condescending and inversely hegemonic."

"Get you, white man." (Very white, at this particular moment.) "But you have a point. I do believe our relationship is emblematic of a wider pattern of trans-race needs and debts. What you been doin'—apart from swimmin' in the Capitol Hill Natatorium?"

(It's true you cannot make an undetected move in Washington.)

"Just now? Sitting here feeling clownish and humming 'Vesti la giubba.'"

"I know that boo-hoo song—'Laugh, clown, laugh.' I sang it once in high school off the record. You feelin' boo-hoo?"

"Maybe just a little around the edges."

"Been out Edge City way, like in *Sandman*, huh?"

"At the natatorium. I remembered your telling me about the *crews*—"

"Simple City."

"Yes, and I was wondering if they might consider turning themselves into crews of a different sort—rowing crews."

"For what—the Potomac Regatta? That's a *big* laugh, Mr. Clown."

"No, to row in Vana Sprezza's Venetian gala come summer."

"Now there is an idea. Maybe you should take a walk around the corner and talk to your neighbor Harold Brazil— on North Carolina Avenue, where very few black men are . . . indoors, that is."

"Who is Harold Brazil?"

"You have not troubled to scope out District politics. Councilman-at-Large Brazil may be the man to run against Marion Barry come '98. *Or*, you might try makin' a *devotional call* on the Reverend Archbishop George Augustus Stallings— *primate*, as Mr. Max Harrington would point out, of the African American Catholic Church, at his Imani Temple. He does a nice line in *altar boys*, and would I am sure do much to establish *relations* wit' Venice."

"I think you may be more the man to help me."

"I do believe you are correct, and not heretical, in your faith. As you may know, I have some time on my hands—having taken accumulated sick leave and accepted Sister Delmarva's kind and politic offer of further leave donation—which I had planned to use mainly growin' a new set of dreads."

"Really?"

"Yo. Actually, I have not decided yet whether to go for the dreads or for the Ellington *conk* look. Anything but a black *buzz*. But before I do cast my bandanna into the refiner's flames in favor of an altered image—for as Sister D says, the problem with expressin' yourself as I did at the Cosmos Club is *not* that you are ostracized and must walk around with your face behind a dashboard sun reflector but, contrarily, that the mail slot is *clogged* with invitations to *repeat* yourself at select venues around the city. Before I do so, I might make one last foray among the brothers. Properly attired, of course—feet first, in new sneaks with inflated soles and heels, because on the streets I must go down, penny loafers, a blazer, nicely pressed trousers, and a cheery 'Hi, guys!' could get me *hurt*."

"Dig. I'll spring for the costume; so can we talk?"

"Well, it's this way, boss. I figure that when you put rowboat-rowin' together wit' basketball—which all the brothers have in their sinews—you get gondola rowin'. The problem, I foresee—apart from convincin' the brothers to get onto *boats:* they not bein' exactly pleasure craft in our racial memory, dig?—will be what the brothers gonna *sing*."

"Ah."

"Dig. I have seen Gore Vidal's program on Venice, and there is no way the brothers goin' to want to learn those doofus dago songs."

"Are you telling me they're going to do rap?"

"Negative, boss. That I myself don't go for, nor trip-hop neither, although I have put in my time at the Capitol Ballroom on Half Street, near where your show is shapin' up."

"Oh, you know about the show."

"I do. And since we are coverin' the waterfront, I put it in longshoreman terms, you could call this an audition for the shape-up. And incidentally, I must say that De La Soul has *something*."

"I'd very much like to have you in the show, Ornette—and as to the regatta, you could row in it and sing too. Vana thought your voice was sexy that night at the Cosmos Club, and has not forgotten, either, your invitation to the rare book room."

"She is right there, boss—and more may be revealed."

"Ornette, your Rochester imitation is great, but doesn't it hurt your voice?"

"Yo, I am practicin' for to be a flamenco tenor, boss."

I decided on a dose of his own guff. "Now cut that *out!*"

Silence. It worked. Then, "Anyway, no rap—out of rhythm for rowing, but don't expect 'Ol' Man River' or any golden oldie like 'Dream Lover' or 'Summertime Blues' or Mungo Jerry's ode to that season, just because the crowd is likely to demand nostalgia—"

"Go easy on that word, Ornette," I said, pursing my Chinese red lips in the mirror, while reworking an eyebrow. "Your nostalgia is my life. What will you sing?"

"Hey, *whoa*—we ain't discussed the *bidnizz* part yet."

"On that I'll get back to you."

"I shall be here—growin' hair."

I next called Max.

"I would be delighted to finance the construction of the gondolas—in stage balsa. There's no need to get real—they have a lot of fun up in Columbia at the Lake Kittamaqundi Great Cardboard Boat Regatta."

"Cardboard—don't they sink?"

"Only those who want to sink. Yes, it will delight me to drive another nail into Marion Barry's coffin."

(I realized there was another way to render reality: the stereopticon. It depended, however, on two identical "takes" set side by side for the viewer to turn into a three-dimensional picture—related to reading the lines and also what's in between them, or to the object in the light and also its shadow. Dualities—like my columns from the *East Hampton Star* and this.

And as is well known, in any telling no two renditions or takes, even by the same writer, will ever be congruent, but always, as in *Rashomon*, merely versions from a vantage. Moreover, as in the predilection for culturally determined angle/reverse angle editing—a.k.a. *the male gaze*, a foresight/hindsight game of three-card monte, like politics.)

I then called O'Maurigan about *The Delancey Retort.*

"You want to depict the clown show."

"The clown show under the big top. Clinton as Holy Fool."

"Yes, the clowns were always the goods."

"Bulging out the seams of the taste envelope—like Al Carmines's *Home Movies* thirty-three years ago. I would like it to have luster, style, and moral seriousness."

"You don't half aim high, do you? Al Carmines at the Provincetown Playhouse with Sudie Bond—Father Shenanigan and Sister Thalia: double helix of the ridiculous and the sublime."

"'Now Mother Superior is playing on the same team.'"

"Well, pray hard. Some things you *can*, you know, pray over."

As I wrote Phil: "We modeled it more or less on the very successful, almost entirely black *D.C. Politics Hour*—a weekly dose of insight and insult on the city that isn't, but deliberately not touching more than very lightly the local scene—Marion Barry, etcetera—and decided to go out on Sundays, running open-ended, improv style: loose cable."

Anastasia, as she told the *Washington Post*, declined entreaties to participate.

Now let me take the reader backstage—at the Edge (in Nighttown, down New Jersey Avenue, beyond Duddington Place, under the Southeast Freeway)—to trip over that cable, hang out in the wings, view the menagerie, and watch the gang of midgets climb the ladder under the trapdoor to the little car in the old circus routine.

Picture a warehouse—or should I say a whorehouse? Resembles the Statuary Hall of the Capitol as transformed by Joe Gage in *Closed Set*, but with the men clothed. (Script form like Nighttown in *Ulysses*. Scope it. Xeroxed screenplays are all the selling rage as reading matter among New York street vendors these days. "Wouldn't they be," Odette snorted, "with all the ghastly fiction that's being turned out in the name of love and death.")

Logo: the Capitol dome—think of the Salute—and called by O'M "the nation's cranium": the brains and circuitry invisible. (Left wing = left brain capacities and thought; right wing = right brain capacities and plotting. Also remember my fantasies of space ships, circus tents, and D.C. as three-ring circus: executive, legislative, judicial.) Emphasis on *lifting the lid*—the Statue of Freedom atop the Capitol as the *handle* we grab to lift the dome off. "I'd like it to have luster, style, and moral seriousness," I repeated to Lynton Weeks of the *Washington Post* style page, on whom I was later accused of developing a serious crush. (Odette said "Oh, my!" Not to the crush, but to the dispatch.)

The Delancey Retort opened sponsored by O'M and Max Harrington. ("For those with a propensity for nostalgia, it's a kind of early *Saturday Night Live*," said Lynton Weeks.)

"And now, direct from the hysterical Frauds Theater in the Hallucination's Capital: *The Delancey Retort!*" Ornette on the "colortone" cocktail organ. The logo shows the Capitol dome and, standing atop it, Freedom, wearing the helmet with the eagle's head and wings; but the face (imperceptible but through opera glasses) is the face of Mae West, her eyes toward heaven. A tube leads from the dome to a retort, as in alchemy, and chemistry.

A pan up from the floor of the House of Representatives to the skylight, in the shape of the American eagle surrounded by the state and territorial shield: like the Holy Ghost on Pentecost—or, I thought, like the biggest raptor in the world. Then swoop down to the Chamber—not the Chamber of today, but the older, historical one, now the Statuary Hall. The statues gossiping about history, which has been decreed over, a thing of the past.

Under a sign, "Three Fates: No Waiting," three lady barbers, Clotho, Lachesis, and Atropos, grouped in the statuary masks and attitudes of Susan B. Anthony, Elizabeth Cady Stanton, and Lucretia Mott. They break ranks and one starts in strapping a razor, one plying a blow dryer, and one snipping away at a customer—with a great shock of white hair off which she snips a very few hairs.

"With regular special guest Maud MacGown—a fresh voice from the Plains, a woman of diverse interests and polymorphous concerns—or, as Will Rogers said of Grace Coolidge, 'chuck plumb full of magnetism.'" ("A gal with *buzz-zoom*, reminiscent of the legendary Rose Murphy," according to the *City Paper*, reviewing her singing "A Woman's Intuition" and calling her an asset on any Independent ticket.)

An admirer of Henry Clay, she's thinking of reviving the Whigs. Her work-in-progress, *The New Whole Duty of the Decent Woman*, seeks to strike a balance between utopian fantasies of overly complacent democracies and endangered-species paranoia, between "Nice women don't work, nice women volunteer" and "The feminine combination of intense imagination and unlimited patience can transform the whole concept of returning injury for injury into a thing of beauty and a joy forever" (Kate Saunders).

Maud declares, "In the immortal words of Mercy Otis Warren:

> A sister's hand may wrest a female pen
> From the bold outrage of imperious men!

"Our aim as women ought always be the same: to earn admiration extracting multiple interpretations for seemingly simple actions. Like that clever girl who took a piece of paper and batted her mascaraed eyelashes on it one hundred times. Now that *says* something. Nice women *still volunteer*, although we must aim a little higher in our avocations than dancing, cards, and travel."

Maud's party would be called the New Whigs: one of their

planks the Hatfield-Jackson U.S. Peace Tax Fund bill, which would provide legal protection for those who want their taxes diverted from the Pentagon. The Squeaker is terrified of a third party in the South, depriving the Republicans of their majority. "Render unto Caesar the things that are Caesar's!" he bellows. Maud replies, "Dorothy Day used to say that after you have rendered unto God, there ought to be very little left to render unto Caesar."

Delmarva appeared as D.C.'s Prophet Tess ("Don't go callin' me Motha Teresa. I'm nobody's momma. But I agree there are more tears shed over answered prayers and love is as hard and unbending as hell, honey, and if once ever you do *bend*, it is all *over*. Dig? And prophecy, chile, does not concern itself with what will be, but with *what will have been*").

Maud and the Prophet Tess became the stars of the most popular skit in the show, "Are You There?," in which they "visited" famous dames of American history: Dolley Madison, Mary Todd Lincoln (who go shopping together while the guns are heard booming from Manassas), Harriet Tubman, Emily Dickinson, Susan B. Anthony, Mary McLeod Bethune, Clover Adams (at her Saint-Gaudens monument), Mary Baker Eddy, Nancy Hanks (at the U.S. Post Office), Charlotte Perkins Gilman, Edith Galt Wilson, and Eleanor Roosevelt.

Two madcaps: Dame World (dishing the UN set) and Magnolia Jenkins Hill, the *Archetype* of the Capitol. These licensed fools say anything. DW wears a dress that is the map of the world, with New York prominent on the bodice. Magnolia wears a hat in the shape of the Capitol, covered with magnolia blossoms, and carries a mop and a pail, is black on one side and white on the other, and poses as the "inside dope peddler." Knows, inter alia, details of all the cocaine deals, prostitution, etc. that the black city bureaucrats and the hypocritical congressional staffers are involved in. "Not since Prohibition has there been such mendacity!" She sits down, lights up a cigarette, and says, "Do you believe I couldn't do this in the White House, not even if I promised not to inhale?"

Maud MacGown soberly avows the Vice President is by far the handsomest heir apparent for decades, and applauds rather than bemoans the fact that he's a little dull, taking the opportunity to inveigh against thirty years of liberal excess, including the NEA ("Lorine Niedecker never got a federal dime!"), and then, turning into the camera with "That *said*," commences chiding POTUS for his "slippery ways."

Then on Hillary:

"I am ambivalent about Hillary Rodham Clinton. She is not my idea of a thoroughly principled woman, but, Protestant that I am, the idea that she might, like the Virgin, crush the serpent's head of Republican male conceit fills me to the brim with forbidden pleasure." (That got to me. If anything I heard in D.C. seemed to sum up what I felt I was doing—to what end I still don't know—that did.)

(On March 6, the Senate Appropriations Committee, in what was billed as "a clean bill," restored 700 million dollars for the national service corps and safe drinking water controls.)

From Congress, "Vegetable House": All the freshmen Republicans are seen wearing Phrygian caps with little propellers on top, and all have trick arrows through their heads; they are corralled together under a sign "Grounded." The others sing:

> "Three cheers for Cap-i-tol High,
>   We're fucking off till elections are nigh.
>   Keep those freshmen down on their knees,
>   Then send the whips for takeout Chinese.
>   We'll drink the bars dry, we'll have a ball,
>   We'll never settle nothin' at all,
>   While our loyal staffers play croquet on the old green
>   Mall."

(On March 13 in the *Washington Post*: "Never before in American history has the Senate leader had to deal with a president of the opposite party for a protracted period of time, with both of them knowing they will be opponents in the coming race for the White House. It makes for unique campaign dynamics."

On March 28, the Farm Bill was passed, keeping funding for the Wetlands Reserve Agency.)

When POTUS says he is out of chicken and offers a congressman shrimp, a voice says: "Mr. President, don't *ever* confuse a chicken hawk with a shrimp queen—not even in Congress."

"And what does Zorro the Rooster say to that?"

Z: *Cock*-a-doodle-*doo!*

THE SQUEAKER: *Nobody* is hewing to the party line!

MAUD: Oh, I liked the party line; you could listen in.

CLOTHO: You can listen in now, dear. Everybody does—it's called cellular scanning.

MAUD: Everybody does?

CLOTHO: Everybody.

MAUD (to the Squeaker): You're mistaken—everybody is on the party line. Your trouble is, sonny, you don't know how to *listen.*

Suddenly, a scream is heard offstage (as in the end of *Cavalleria rusticana*, on "Hanno ammazzato compare Turiddu!"). Then freshman congresswoman Edie Walnuts rushes in.

"My *God*—my *God!*"

"What is it, dear?" (Maud).

"My *husband* . . . my *husband!*"

"What's he done, dear?" (the Archetype).

"He lied . . . he cheated . . . he stole . . . he *inhaled!*"

"Yes" (Maud), "the bold outrage of imperious men."

THE LOG CABIN REPUBLICANS: That is a homophobic statement!

"My career—my *career!*" (Edie). "It's gone up in *flames!*"

The Prophet Tess steps up. "Now one of the things I fore-see is a whole lotta *female* statues comin' in, executed in *black marble*. I see *whole monuments* of *black marble* comin' in, to such as Sally Hemings and Sojourner Truth and Harriet Tubman and Olive Risley Seward and Marian Anderson and Hattie McDaniel and Rosa Parks and Coretta King and—"

"And Cora Masters Barry?"

"No, I'm afraid I do not see one of those."

"In Committee." Dozens of portraits hang down from the flies to represent the portraits of the chairmen that festoon the walls of the committee rooms. (O'M decided it was like the portrait-gallery scene in *Ruddigore*. Controversy rages over which portraits ought to be retired, which cleaned up. Some have been slashed . . . etc.

A VOICE: We've cobbled together a compromise—but that it is *the last train out of the station!*

Rumors start that the plague is rampant in D.C.—the water, the viruses coming in from Africa in airplanes, Iraqi germ warfare. The rush is on to evacuate. The VIPs have the air routes all booked up and the roads are nearly impassable. They move to Union Station. The Newt, left alone (and acting like Benny Hill), screams, "I wanna *cookie*! I wanna *cookie*!"

Suddenly POTUS rushes in with orders of Chinese food. The Newt goes all gushy, but everybody has left for Union Station.

POTUS: Here, have a bite of this stimulus package.

The Newt starts ripping all the fortune cookies open, looking at fortune after fortune and screaming, as he eats all the cookies and POTUS pats his head, commiserating with him that whenever a real event in the world preempts the reporting on their shenanigans, they are bound to feel a little irrelevant. But not for long, "for mankind cannot bear very much reality."

THE NEWT: I'm *sick* of tactics—I want more *strategy*.

DAME WORLD (to the Archetype): What's the difference, dear?

THE ARCHETYPE: Between tactics and strategy? Oh, it's deep.

DW: Do you think POTUS strategic, or deep?

THE ARCHETYPE: *Deep?* Do *you?*

DW: Deeper than an ashtray, dear.

THE NEWT: This is all chickenshit! (He looks into the empty garbage pail.) I came here to see to the sweep of history!

ZORRO: *Cock*-a-doodle-*doo!* Thus spake Zorro the Rooster!

THE ARCHETYPE: From what I hear these days, you *are* history. (She tips him into the garbage pail and wheels it and him off-stage.)

As I wrote Phil: "People have started coming to me in secret—in the sauna at the gym, etc. Junior staffers, informants behind screens, etc. The spoof is getting serious. We're using as voice-overs historical recordings from the LC. For historic D.C. talking heads—busts from the city's parks, stations, and hallowed halls of science and learning."

Walking the snowdrifted, deserted streets at night, I thought I saw an opportunity for the same kind of "downtown" filming that film noir used to take in predawn Los Angeles. So many strange stories could be set against the "floating" back-drop of the Capitol, the Supreme Court, the White House, and the monuments: stories that had nothing immediate to do with the obsessive cant of Washington, but simply used the backdrop the way John Ford used Monument Valley. Even Rain's story, little by little, senator and all, I saw had less to do with Washington's self-regarding circular pavane, and it seemed to me that any city with so many empty nocturnal street corners just cries out to be used. Besides, as Gore Vidal had said, never turn down an opportunity to have sex or to be on television. If I'd not so much been doing the first outright as avoiding the proximate occasions of sin (not, for example, call-ing the marine hawk), then maybe the second, pursued relent-lessly, would—what?—balance the economy?

The statues in the Statuary Hall started talking in my head, and were joined by: FDR at the National Portrait Gallery, George Washington at GWU, Eisenhower at the Eisenhower Theater, Grant and Garfield from their stools on the Mall, A. Philip Randolph in Union Station (lamenting Amtrak, ashamed to welcome people to D.C.), Sumner Welles in the Cosmos Club, JFK in the Kennedy Center Prison of Culture when he'd rather be in a bordello (which the auditorium looks so much like, he ought to be quite as happy as he was fucking in communion with all those adoring cronies Rex Vavasour hated so, in a quasi-homosexual gang bang in Bing Crosby's pool).

FDR to JFK: The coming Republican convention could split apart on the issues of abortion and free trade.

JFK: I don't know about abortion, but they've paid through the nose for their pieces of trade for so long, it's unthinkable they should do otherwise.

Then the NRA controversy and repeal.

HOUSE FRESHMEN (rushing in firing cap pistols): Repeal! Repeal!

NRA: No repeal! No repeal! *We* are the National Recovery Associa—

FDR: No, National Recovery *Act*—that was *mine*. Sons of bitches tried to have it declared unconstitutional—I was trying to save the country. I *did* save the country! *They*, not content with going after me, then my wife, went after my dog Fala!

ELEANOR: Yes, Franklin.

JFK: Go back to sleep—this is about giving up drugs and alcohol and arming with machine guns.

HOUSE FRESHMEN: Repeal! Repeal! Bring back the pistols! Bring—

ENTER THE SEX PISTOLS: We're back!

FDR: We have nothing to fear but fear itself.

ELEANOR: Yes, Franklin.

FDR: How on earth did you get down here anyway, Eleanor? I thought they were going to put you up in Riverside Park.

ELEANOR: Why, the First Lady had sent for me, Franklin.

FDR: Well, now that you're here, maybe you can do something about this goddamn memorial they're talking about. They're going to put me in a goddamn *wheelchair*, Eleanor!

ELEANOR: But you *were*, Franklin—you *were* in a wheelchair.

SAMUEL GOMPERS (Mass Ave and Tenth, NW): May I say something pertinent? Labor is poised to come back to the Democratic Party.

POTUS says, "Ah need an advisor." Dick Morris walks right in. "Oh, not *you*, Dick. I need somebody who's *dead*—somebody who's dead to *come alive*. I need to *resurrect* a sage!"

Suddenly the statue of Frederick Douglass comes alive. (Et cetera.)

That night Rain was waiting "backstage"—at the closed bar of the Edge (in out of the rain, like Eve Harrington), dejected.

We went and sat in what Odette called my "loge" (remember Arletty's in *Les Enfants du paradis*? I remembered the one in the nabes of my youth: moderately expensive seats under the balcony). Rain had brought Monopoly with the D.C. board: "One of the things POTUS got for Christmas." As we played (and I thought about altering the cyc for the next show: fade out on the Capitol / fade in to the D.C. Monopoly logo), I asked Rain where he'd been.

"With them." (If I were writing fiction, at this point I could either inquire or decide for myself—and you, patient reader—who "they" were: aliens, ancestral ghost dancers, conspiracy bigwigs, escaped catamites. I did neither. Never intervene on a defense.)

"In an Underground Railway safe house on one of the little islands in the Potomac—offshore along the River Road near the Seneca Breaks. In this weather. It's not only the ambient temperature, you know, it's the wind-chill factor."

(Continually reacting, they remain imprisoned in states of retaliatory defensive aggression.)

"Do you know the chainman's oath? They make the boys memorize it for their ritual. 'I do solemnly swear that I will execute the duties of chainman; that I will level the chain upon even and uneven ground, and plumb the tally pins, that I will report the true distances to all notable objects and the true lengths of all the lines in accordance with the instructions given me.'

"Do you *understand* what that *means*?" (It sounded to me not unlike my brief from the *Star*, but I realized it might be anything from a catenary-frill goof by one of the more recherché New York Jacks to a nasty survivalist militia mantra.)

"The boys escape from their captors like the free blacks. . . ." He then unraveled a flag—fifty white stars on a blue field running across the top of the banner, each with the name of an Indian tribe, plus Esquimaux and Hawaiians, each with a bullet hole and running streaks of red blood on a white field beneath.

His cellular phone rang. He listened, then spoke, in a completely altered voice.

"Yes, well, as I was saying to one of your colleagues just yesterday, in the new politics, as in the new science, every dynamical problem can now be solved at the level of probability *amplitudes;* we no longer have to rely on certitudes determined by trajectory dynamics.

"But as to your direct question, we say this. Quote, 'The question is of course whether the political tide is only gone out for a spell with this thing or whether the entire Chesapeake, so to speak, is really drying up, leaving those long nourished by the currents and soil nutrients carried in on the tide marooned and fighting for their very lives on the primordial mud flats of a legislative meltdown.' No, wait, change 'meltdown' to 'quagmire.' The senator always called Proxmire Quagmire. That's off the record. . . . What? No, I have *not* been speaking *either* to Robert Novak *or* Richard Cohen; you're it. Let's get on the joystick, OK? Open quote. 'In this, as in everything always, my humble yet ardent confidence in the constant protection, preservation, and eventual redemption of the Constitution by our Almighty Originator has been so strong and unwavering as to sustain me, as it has done the Republic, in such storms as this winter would otherwise have overwhelmed the boldest spirit and the stoutest heart in the nation's capital or in the nation itself.' Close quote. That's it."

"You have a certain authority, don't you."

He preened a little—very like a warbler in mating season.

"I like to be a laser beam focused on pure expression, so there's no possibility of a 'so what' graph. It's why he sent me to Georgetown, to make me a scholar of governmental proce-dure and the ruling class. This I learned there. Politics is like Shakespeare."

"Is it more like Shakespeare than pornography?"

"About the same—in the same way. It too strip-mines popular culture and then coats it with a thick veneer of ex-ploitative sensationalism and overwritten script in approved hegemonic rhetoric for the sake of creating a big box-office entertainment—maybe you've noticed the white bogus-liberal so-called intellectual elite of Washington lapping it up in that converted department store on Sixth Street."

I said I'd lapped a little of it up myself.

"Yeah, well, they're about the same—Shakespeare and pornography. You know what campaign promises are? The Reddi-Whip cum shots of politics. Also, things *work* in both because they're *two*-dimensional. Like math. Math in two dimensions works. When they try putting it into three, it doesn't."

(Odette: "Diderot, dear, said men of geometry live with their eyes closed." "You're not suggesting the kid's read Diderot?" "Concerning that number, I'm not suggesting anything except that you rehearse giving him a wide berth." "I'm not planning on going anywhere with him on a train.")

"Because the really important thing that's going on today that they don't want anybody paying any mind to isn't this game of charades, it's what's going on in outer space. The shuttle *Atlantis,* with a Russian-built docking port towering out of its cargo bay, closed in on the *Mir* space lab after a three-day orbital chase, and the American skipper had to rely on data from police-style radar guns, TV cameras, laser range finders, and computers to perform an instrument approach. Understand?"

"Tell me something," I asked him. "What kind of underwear do Log Cabin Republicans wear?"

"Log Cabin Republicans wear boxer shorts, with Disney characters on them for when they *party.* The Democrats are into other getups—leather, denim, lingerie, toys, and rap. All the Republicans know how to do is take off their clothes—'It's *flex* time!'—and jump in the pool, get out, and sit around going 'Shoot it, man, shoot that load!' "

(I thought, Not all that unlike the Kennedys.)

"It's like they're goofing on *filibusters.* Very hard on the performer—seeming to stay naive and spontaneous." His voice changed again. "You know, I know why Boorda killed himself. He knew what high-ranking naval officer was killing all the Virginia fags."

I told him I'd take him back with me to Capitol Hill, where he could tell me the rest.

Seven / Cuspidor

cusp   *geom:* a point at which two branches of a curve meet and stop with a common tangent.

Wouldn't you know opera would come into it in earnest: at the turning point, no less, in song and dance and full panoply.

Vana decided to get up a Washington Opera theater party, Boito's *Mefistofele* the show. (She'd sung the roles of both Margherita and Helen of Troy, and was enamored of both Boitos: Camillo wrote *Senso,* from which *Livia Serpieri,* her Fenice debut triumph, was crafted; she had also sung Rubria in Arrigo's *Nerone,* and starred as his muse and great love, Eleonora Duse, on RAI-TV.)

As I wrote Phil, "It was a funny night, starting with my running into my doll-faced D Street neighbor John—the LC staffer famous for losing his keys and climbing up the wall into his own front window—on his way back from the Lustre Cleaners, also opera-bound, with all his white shirts wrapped in plastic bags fanning out over his shoulders like wings." (Angel motif: recurs later in Dollface's case—of which everything that is is the reality, but space is limited.)

Maud MacGown attended on O'Maurigan's arm. The

senator, hearing her on the subject of sobriety on *The Delancey Retort*, and obviously smitten, had gone on the wagon, and so for the first time in years at a musical-social function in D.C. was seen to stay awake. Moreover, bowled over by the allegory of *Mefistofele*, he promptly translated it into an American message.

(All of it—Faustian bargains, Ideal Society, the angels, the *beati*, and heaven—as Barb pointed out, rather Mormon, if you squint.)

The Kennedy Center Opera House is *so* hideous—red-walled like a whore's toilet—I spent much of the night zoned out in a vision of Carnegie Hall, imagining the gold trim on the cream walls beginning to glow as the whole of the audience lifts off (a cosmopolitan New York Sunday-afternoon Carnegie Hall audience such as, I realized, I could not live without being part of as I had been for forty years, since Mawrdew Czgowchwz sang Marietta's Lied from *Die tote Stadt* on my first visit there, and since Hank screamed, "Judy, sit on my faaace!"). Also, I had been dreaming of other halls again—the Everard, Lincoln Hall, the Harringtons' Kalorama ballroom—with smoky mirrors and red lights at the end. In those mind galleries I saw Ashcan-Vermeer panels hung like in the Kalorama cartoon gallery, like the stained-glass windows in a private chapel, like Tarot, or like the portraits of the performers along all the hallways at Carnegie, Phil's postcards from Sicily, the portraits hanging in the Capitol's committee rooms, or the "candids" in a book's picture section. *Mefistofele*'s opening sequence of heaven: the verismo cantillations of ecstatic *beati*, in gold crowns, white masks, and blue-lined white capes all ranged in opera boxes in the celestial theater, set the tone for a production of such monumental, *maniacal* vulgarity as to be visionary.

In scene upon scene the camp was augmented. Galt was riveted by the "journey" sequence: Mefistofele leading Faust on a long red velvet rope from a box stage right down a ladder, across, and up another ladder into a box stage left. (Max interpreted the first box as the House and the second as the Senate, "that other place," like the House of Lords—Galt sternly replying that in America, as in *Hamlet*, the "other place" is hell.)

By the final curtain, the sober statesman with the secret lock was seeing Maud MacG in Helen of Troy, and the Chorus of the Ordered Society in black formals as a reception at the White House, and in the people bowing to Helen—or Eternal Feminine—an indication of his future . . . and sharing the information! Vana (as we awaited our vehicles in the esplanade) said, "Ah, you are *responding, eccelenza*! You understand what so many do not, that the opera is a four-dimensional form. People when they do not understand it say it is two-dimensional, because they know it is not simply three-dimensional, but they are going in the wrong direction. Music is the measure of *time*; when the drama is sung, the fourth dimension is available to the soul in a way that it otherwise is not, except perhaps in the most elevated of poetic drama, such as Shakespeare and d'Annunzio." (*D'Annunzio*? That Vana, I thought, such loyalty to Duse—for d'Annunzio had been an even more famous conquest of that spiritual omnivore; such loyalty to Italy, to camp—as out of the corner of my eye I saw Ornette come out and turn left down toward New Hampshire Avenue. As if alerted, he stopped, turned, and grinned. I thought—inanely— You never see such white teeth as in a black face. Then, I thought, not so inanely: On the Old Met line, all those savvy, laughing black faces.)

Galt, as his limousine drew up to roll him and Maud Mac-Gown down the ramp to the Watergate, offered Vana its use to the Villa Firenze. As Vana swept in, continuing with the metaphysics, he very grandly let loose singing (*più o meno*) a thing I didn't recognize:

"Columbia's bright banner o'er the waves
Columbia, we pledge our souls to thee."

In the cab, O'Maurigan ID'd it as the finale of the Consul's aria from Victor Herbert's *Natoma*. Barb said Vana expounding on the opera had assumed the attitude of Beatrice addressing Dante from the car. "More like a *civetta*," O'M corrected, "from the rear saloon of a Hispano-Suiza. But since her Washington Monument scheme has proved *non avenu*, the Fenice will likely occupy, if not exhaust, her energies most profitably for all concerned. Let's go back to Fio's, shall we? I've made a reservation; that little voice I've learned to trust advised me nothing would do after an evening such as this but plates overflowing with spaghetti puttanesca and a rainbow jukebox that has Rosemary Clooney on it singing 'Mambo Italiano.' Good God at night! *Natoma*, how-are-ye?"

Next morning, Ornette called to ask a question. "You think I could become an opera singer?"

"What makes you think you'd want to be such a thing?"

"I was readin' in the newspaper 'bout this white boy of sixteen, already a big-money blues singer, and the writer says the following: 'The majority audience for any kind of music in the United States is white, whether the music started out black or not.'"

"Hmm."

"Continuin', 'The white audience can generally identify better with white performers. This is not racism, it is ethnicity.'"

"Uh-huh."

"Uh-*huh*. And concludin', 'There's no shortage of young black blues artists, but you probably won't know they're around until they get older. They tend to start out as sidemen in a band and work their way up to lead position.'"

"Hmm."

"You got it, boss. I have heard opera audiences are color blind. That true in your experience?"

"I can only tell you, Ornette, that if you—"

"Yes, I do believe you would assist me by introducin' me to many powerful and influential promoters—*but* I gotta furnish the goods. It was that I had in mind. I believe it is of even greater consequence than my hairstyle."

"In any place but Los Angeles it is."

"Dig. Now tell me somethin'—wasn't that diva of yours in a famous opera about Venice?"

"Yes, *Livia Serpieri*. She created the heroine."

"And there was presumably a tenor in that opera, who also had some'n to sing?"

"Indeed. Giuseppe di Stefano. The aria was called 'La vita è una cosa tremenda.'"

(That took me back. *Livia Serpieri*, "the first Italian existentialist opera," made Vana an international celebrity, and Pippo's recording of "La vita è una cosa tremenda"—we called it "Beh, Vito ha uno cazzo stupendo!"—played in every Italian restaurant in New York, Boston, Philadelphia, and Chicago; the piece was sung by every ship's tenor on every transatlantic crossing of the *Leonardo da Vinci*, the *Raffaelo*, the *Michelangelo* [the *Andrea Doria* had gone down] and became as big a popular hit as "Volare.")

"Much obliged, boss. Talk to you. And when you talk back, it will be to the tenor version of Todd Duncan. *Ciao*."

The Delancey Retort "Today in Congress" focused on April 1.

DAME WORLD: On this date, April first, in 1621, the first treaty between Native Americans and colonists was made.

CIGAR STORE INDIAN: And how!

THE ARCHETYPE: And on this date in 1789, the United States House of Representatives met officially for the first time and the first Speaker of the House was elected.

THE NEWT: On this date, in 1909, the first federal narcotics prohibitive legislation went into effect. (Screaming laughter.)

BLOB DULL: On this date in 1977, the U.S. Senate adopted an

ethical code requiring full financial disclosure and setting a limit on a senator's earnings in addition to salary.

Fade out/fade in. In Room H-227 Capitol Hill, the Archetype is mopping the floor. The Squeaker is reading the back ads in *Playpen*. He puts the magazine down and starts trying on a Wellington hat in the mirror, accompanied by a gaggle of Republican freshmen dressing up as Mighty Morphin Power Rangers and lathering up their faces with shaving cream.

THE NEWT: I am transformational; a Newt deal is on the table.

DAME WORLD: He'd never fake out a casting director.

NEWT: We are surfers on the wave of history.

THE ARCHETYPE (picks up *Playpen*): I've been wondering how he manages to wet his pants so much. (Starts mopping the floor under him.) *The President proposes . . . Congresses disposes!* (He giggles furiously as he tears up proposal after proposal.) Enfilade! *Enfilade!* Bring us the fascines to fill the ditch—bring the ladders to scale the *ramparts*!

DAME WORLD INTONES:

> Thus by contrivers' inadvertent jest,
> One fool exposed makes pastime for the rest.

The Freshmen, all lathered up, march off with the Newt.

Breakfast with Max Harrington and the O' at the Hay-Adams. I walked. Crossing Lafayette Park, I saw a poem written in black Magic Marker on a white wall. *Hana-Aware: Cold Spring*:

> Hayutake
> Snow falls on cherry blossoms;
> Were there world enough and time.

It made me think of Rex Vavasour as that ghostly Japanese minister of the right.

O'Maurigan was fidgety and distracted, as he generally is before an appearance—in this instance an appearance in his own past (photographed with Schuyler, Ashbery, and Frank O'Hara) at the "Rebel Poets and Painters" exhibit at the National Portrait Gallery. I was silent remembering the comics, the columns in the evening papers, and at the same time my first encounters with the poets—an audition—through whom I first met the O'. I was also fidgety myself, although loath to say why: I was due right after breakfast to be whisked away to Olmsted Island with the Vice President's entourage. There on the island I would meet POTUS, who with his veep would be moving a felled tree in a photo op. (Huck and Tom, as Gore Vidal called Clinton and "Cousin" Albert.)

"Two guys in a garage," Max called them, "out to remake the political psyche of the country via flashy Web-site motel and fast-food franchise construction along Info Highway. Of course they see their antics as the interface between manly Culture and manly Nature. Beavis is particularly fond of aligning himself with Teddy Roosevelt, another sufferer from allergies."

In the face of our polite silence, he augmented his argument. "Beavis and Butt-head is what I call the pair. Butch and Sundance is how they're billed by the Secret Service."

"Sundance," I thought, is also appropriate for a man so dedicated to environmentalism—and wondered idly what he would look like in Plains Indian ritual costume doing one—a sun dance, that is. I was by then being regularly invited to the Vice President's Thursday environmental breakfasts, finding the host relaxing, easy to look at and listen to (the drawl, the blue eyes), and he was, as they say, a heartbeat (mine?) away from the Oval Office.

I wondered, remembering what Dick Fauquier said, what the even-tempered and affable man I sat with would be like in a fit of Southern temper. ("You're beautiful when you're angry," the old line goes.) In all events, whatever Butch and the Kid were up to, I found myself preferring they got away with it, all told, and did not have to go jump off a cliff together in November, to be replaced by Dracula.

There I sat eating marmalade, realizing that while I got to go to breakfast next to the Naval Observatory, the O', Kaye Wayfaring, and her husband and twins had dropped into the White House for Chelsea's sixteenth-birthday party, and the O' had been invited twice besides in his official capacity of genuine Irish chieftain: on March 17, and to an upcoming dinner for Mary Robinson, the President of Ireland (his old neighbor in County Mayo). But then his elbow-rubbing history with the rich and powerful in New York and in Washington is a long one. On his account he was in Washington first dangled on the lap of Evalyn Walsh McLean, publisher of the *Washington Post*—in fact his nose was rubbed with the Hope Diamond—and later cruised by the supremely vulgar and sporting Perle Mesta, and taken by her as a teenager to the Truman White House, where he played duets with the President and accompanied Margaret (no tapes).

"*Everybody* seems to have been invited to the Robinson bash," Max drawled, "including us, Galt, *and* Maud MacGown. Anybody, it seems, with an Irish eyelid. On the *lawn*, the biggest state dinner of the administration, and the last before November. There are some who will cut me badly for descending to that level, but for the experience of seeing Maud MacGown flirting with Bill, or Hillary—

"You know what I think I like about him best? It's that he wants to be Robin Hood—and he's smart enough to know that you can't rob the rich in this country, so he *puts out* for them, and dreams of feeding the poor on the proceeds."

Vana too had been back to the White House, with Carlo and Sophia Ponti to the state dinner honoring the president of Italy.

"Did you like him?" I asked her the next morning.

"Scalifaro? No, not much—a boring old—"

"I was thinking of Clinton."

"Oh, *caro*, I *adored* him! He is so *needy*, and so *affectionate . . . molto sincero*. Any real woman would."

"Are you speaking as a lesbian, Vana?"

"*Mascalzone*. Yes, I am. He behaves like a *woman*. This is his mystery. He has an inner *glow* that you do not see on television."

(Must be the Claritin, I thought.)

"And I think I know what gives him this glow—it is—well, I put it to you in French: *il est célibataire*."

"*No.*"

"Yes. He is a sinner of the flesh doing strict penance; it is his appeal to the nation."

("I *love* it!" Ornette cackled, at rowing practice on the Anacostia. "See him at it wit' that picture of Dolly Parton he took from the john in Little Rock and brought up here wit' him to pin up in the little john off the Oval Office so for to contemplate while singin' some little song of the South and whackin' the First Dong raw—distinguishin' characteristic and all.")

"And there is something else, *caro*," Vana continued. "Do you remember that discussion about the *homo cromo*—something. From the red-blooded man all the way to the *violette*—the *travesti*?"

"Chromosomal spectrum."

"*Sì, sì*. We decided *you* were very much the *indigo*. Well, this man is in the middle. A kind of green, with a little yellow—very *spirituale*. I wonder if he may not be a multiple personality. That would account for all the flip-flops."

("Unless," O'Maurigan put in later, when he called to check on the Olmsted Island idyll, "it is simply Freudian. He was wedded to the Republic, and for that the Furies will put out his eyes. Indeed it may be that he never really wanted to be President. It was only what the mother wanted for him."

And Ornette: "I love it, but it just ain't true. I don't know much, Boss, but what I do know is POTUS has a secretary name of Betty, and well, Betty is a very tolerant black woman, and even so, she is *very upset*. Don't know why, but it ain't her salary.")

"In any case," Vana concluded, "I worry about him. He works too hard—gives too much."

"Ljuba Welitsch always said she gave too much."

"Welitsch . . . Maria . . . I myself. But so hard that he sometimes—I fear—leaves his voice in the rehearsal. And he is not *célibataire* the way you are—awaiting the return of the beloved."

"Vana, don't let any of this get out, eh?"

"Never. I am too much the politician—you know my good relations with the Quirinale have always contrasted with Maria's, never mind what I think of Scalifaro. Of course she was a Greek—and they are so politically naive—la Harrington, *per esempio*."

Max asked O'M about his work at the LC, while I ate marmalade.

"The library position is a type of on-line patriotism—we have declared the first-ever annual Poetry Month—cruelest April. We put a poetry anthology in the club cars on the Metroliner, next to the sugar and the peanuts, and pass out cards with simple little things on them like: 'The Spectre is Reasoning Power in Man & when separated From Imagination, and closing itself in as steel, in a Ratio Of the Things of Memory. It thence frames Laws & Moralities To destroy Imagination the Divine body, by Martyrdoms and Wars.'"

"Blake," Max drawled. "Apposite to the situation of the Republic in our time."

"We thought so too."

"Anything by that six-year-old who read at the LC?"

"Not just yet. We're keeping an eye on the boy."

(Meanwhile I, the *East Hampton Star*'s star reporter, had advanced socially to the point of a Gridiron Club dinner invite and one to the upcoming White House Correspondents Association fête at the Hilton. "No dreadful imposter lunches at the Capitol View Club atop the Hyatt Regency for you," O'M declared. "How grateful you must be not to be representative of that phony prep-school trust-fund liberalism suffusing the incestuously intertwined Ivy League cliques who run the corrupt East Coast media establishment."

"Very deeply. But I was asked the other day in the sauna why I'd bothered to become a reporter for a newspaper instead of a member of the Center for Public Integrity. I said it was probably because I'd have to come and live in Washington."

"Good. Next time they ask, tell them your vocation is to the Center for Private Integrity.")

"Because people," Max was saying now, "who write about the media are fixated on the big-city papers, they remain ignorant of what is going on with newspapers in most of the towns of America, not put out by rich editors or staffed by rich reporters—and the *Washington Post* and the *East Hampton Star are* in the same league: the small-town newspaper.

"Although I don't doubt the latter is more sophisticated—unlikely, by way of political analyses, to refer so pathetically to the Los Angeles Hadassah as 'certain wealthy Beverly Hills women.' Pathetic—but the *Post* is that: it whines for the old days and fairly begs either party to give it the whiff of a high crime or misdemeanor, by which it may again justify itself as necessary to the nation. Which it is not—for high crimes and misdemeanors are a thing of the past. Contemporary detection devices have rendered commission of great civic sins obsolete. It sounds like some small-town Yankee version of Sinclair's Lanny Budd in charge up there.

"The poor," Max continued, "know instinctively that there is a *great* distance between us and them, they hate one another's divisions more than they hate our ranks, and the mid-

dle class have no notion, for all their rattling on about it, of
either what money is or how it works. They think it's something to leave to their children—so to validate their lives."

"Your class thinks differently?" I asked.

"Yes. We don't leave our money to our children—nor do
we give a shit what they think about us; we leave our children
to the money, with the following words of advice: 'You have
only a life interest and not a fee simple in the things of this
world. Wealth is the product of industry, ambition, and untir-
ing effort.' I realize, of course, that for you, as for Anastasia, we
accumulators are only really laying down the gold brick road
along which you artists traipse in costume on your way to the
Emerald City.

"You might want to know also that each time—six in all—
in the nation's history that debt-reduction mania has surfaced,
a major depression has followed. The dates, to be utterly
pedantic, are 1819"—the year, I recalled, of the birth of
Herman Melville, whose father went famously bankrupt and
completely insane—"1837, 1857, 1873, 1893, and 1929. The
seventh, in 2002, will be a lulu of insolvency creep, but depressions are demagogues' delights, as Franklin Roosevelt, that
mediocrity with a clever wife, well understood. Depressions
followed by wars are even better.

"Of course, many people think I am a mediocrity with a
clever wife. Let them. My wife, you may have noticed, has a
deep feeling for things that have taken a long time to become
what they are."

("Yes," Odette remarked later, "diamonds in particular.")

"You know what Breton Woods was?"

"It wasn't a battle, was it?"

"Like the Ardennes? You're not far off. A battle on a wider
front, with weaponry of its time similar to the helium reserves
today. Breton Woods reinvented money—by institutionalizing
monetary *craving* and simultaneously cutting the fiduciary
appetite as if with amphetamine, the effect of which—after

much trade in and hypothecating of what we fancifully call 'futures'—has turned out to be more paradoxical than could ever have been imagined.

"You're going to like the world we're making," Max said, "more than you think. We will not ban abstract expressionism, and we will not allow plover's eggs to be eaten. Unless, of course—" he suddenly looked into the middle distance, which in that instance would have been the Hay-Adams lobby, with its hegemonic cultural features—"the whole shitload blows up in everybody's face—in which case it's *sauve qui peut*."

I reminded Max about the Internet.

"Do you think Dick Holbrooke used the Internet on Bosnia? The Information Highway is a *game* for the *populace*—like those Drive-'ems you used to find on the boardwalk. No, we use *words* and the telephone. The *tone of voice* is—but surely you *know this*. I've watched you; you work the room. The way you do it is the way I work the Senate, *none* of whose members is Infotech-ish.

"I am *not* in agreement with *the Rational Public*. Nor a big fan of the Court, which seems to *believe* the dictum that democracy aims to translate voters' desires into beneficial collective action. That is a scream—here, have some more hot coffee."

(I didn't want to drink any more coffee; all I wanted to do was scream. Peculiar. Trapped in a story that had started out being my own, but turned into—yes—some D.C. parody of *Hollywood Squares*. There I was: upper-left-corner box, making funny faces.)

"For example," Max expatiated, "in 1964 seventy-six percent of the American people expressed a clear confidence in the workings of their government. The figure this year is nineteen percent. We're getting there."

"Yet you persist in supporting the Senate."

"I revere the Senate. And so should you. For all the fools in it, the Senate is the closest thing to a *reasoning* body the

Constitution has spawned—entirely because it is the farthest, the Supreme Court aside, from the venal bawling of the electorate. You have little to thank the House for in terms of conservation. Do you know what 'Uncle Joe' Cannon of Illinois, Speaker of the House, famously declared in his time? *'Not one cent for scenery!'* And he wasn't talking about doing theater on the cheap.

"Yes, I revere the Senate. In it I toil not of course, neither do I spin; the image-control experts do that, the way POTUS uses Strobe Talbott. Imagine being called that. They were *lights*, weren't they, meant to enhance hallucinogenic experience?"

"I admire Strobe Talbott," O'Maurigan said, seriously. "If only because Kissinger is against him."

"You despise Kissinger," Max jibed, "not only as the very comely are uncontrollably revolted by the terribly ugly, but as only one to the manner born can despise a slimy climber who would betray the doorman for a nod from power—and because you are sentimental about Jews. I work with his ilk all the time—not Jews, slimy climbers—and I don't credit them with integrity any more than I credit broadcasting with substantive value, as for instance I do credit revelation—small *and* capital R. And now that Republicans have been instructed by Gingrich to be environmental—to counter Clinton's running up and down the Billy Goat Trail near Great Falls on the C&O Canal on a fine cold April day such as this—you (me).

"And though not perhaps yourself rich, you have admitted to a friend with a portfolio—which may become a serious object of your enemies' courtship ritual. Rather like birds at mating season."

"Do we," O'Maurigan queried, "detect a note of Big Sky sarcasm?"

"Not at all; it's true westerners nearly all started out as southerners, but we learned to dispense with the sarcasm, in favor of retribution. You are," he advised me, "terminally eastern. You will fight for your wetlands but ignore the Public Rangelands Management Act. I heard an eastern liberal proclaim recently that the American Republic lies right on the fault line between the past and the future. According to that analogy, in case of major seismic disturbance, the *future* will tumble into the Pacific Ocean.

"However, even as an easterner, you *must* know that Oklahoma City and the fastnesses of Montana have between them handed your Hill-Billy his second term."

"Really?"

"Really. The resurgence of shame started *the day after* that dickhead blew up the Federal Building. There is no way Clinton can lose the bleeding heart of America, unless Chelsea starts having recovered memories—not unless, that is, the feverishly demented fantasies of Ambrose Evans-Pritchard, who has been charting the eclipse of American democracy for the London *Daily Telegraph*, are somehow proved real."

"Let's talk," the O' interposed, "about the helium reserves."

"Ah," said Max, "the helium reserves. The helium reserves are of the greatest importance—for superconductors. Do you know about superconductors?" he asked me.

"Not much."

("I've always thought of the stuff," said Patsy, "in terms of balloons." We'd reached the point in the debriefing where she'd started doodling on a pad: outside, the violet light of evening suggested a cocktail break, but we soldiered on. "Kids' balloons, the Macy's parade, the *Hindenburg*, of course, and then again of the gas that makes the human voice go very high."

"Well, as a coolant, in liquid form, it's apparently terribly important."

"Far out.")

"Not an environmental subject" (Max). "Well, some years ago now—after the Senate hearings on the *Challenger* disaster, in which Richard Feynman showed the country how the reluctance of NASA to try Ronald Reagan's patience by sending the thing up in freezing weather—well, after all that, at a private coffee, Senator Galt became fascinated with Feynman's old hobbyhorse from the fifties, liquid helium, which, like gossip in Washington, can literally seep through airtight walls. Feynman, still rocking, was mystical about it—and about the fifties too. 'Everything that was *real* was found in the fifties,' he said, 'and not much real has been found since.'"

("Dorothy Dean," Patsy remembered, "used to assert the very same thing.")

"You're talking about all this as weaponry?"

"Money, the medium of exchange, is the only viable weaponry. Understood properly, in terms of the twenty-first century. Corporations can spare themselves unwanted entanglements in only one way, and that is to arrogate to themselves the ability to make war."

"The Constitution says only the Congress—"

"The old definition of war. An easy study, compared to . . . Let me put it this way: they will let us manage the helium reserves and we will allow them to keep all the gold in Fort Knox. A trade-off. Of course, gold isn't money anymore, only money's lipstick and mascara, but all the same. . . ."

("This guy's a trip," Patsy said, doodling balloons.)

"I really should," Max continued, "quit Washington, and move to California—California's gross national product would be seventh in the world were it to secede, and free itself of the autocracy of the Federal Reserve.

"Of course, they'd have to annex Baja Mexico, and close the Nevada, Arizona, and Oregon border stations."

(I thought, What the hell.) "And the helium reserves?"

"Part of the strategy. It would be a supreme irony, since the rest of the country has been saying for generations that California is full of hot air.

"You know, since the Court's decisions against the Semi-nole, the senator sees increasingly the possibility of devolution. Secession in such an atmosphere is far from unthinkable—even for certain wealthy Beverly Hills women."

"You might get Vana Sprezza interested," I suggested. "You could twin California with the Republic of Padania."

"D.C.'s moment in history will have been as capital of a fiction—that of a nation formed from rag ends and no history other than exploitation. Useful, however, as a dry run for the larger self-regulating planetary nexus of corporations."

"And democracy?"

"Something else out of Athens, like polychrome-painted white marble figurative sculpture—which didn't last, either."

"Is your wife," I asked, "keen on California?"

"*Very*. We're thinking of producing something. She's furi-ous, as you must know, that as a result of *The Delancey Retort*—not exactly what in her view she got you down here for—she has lost nearly all of her Log Cabin Republican retainers."

("Bam-Bam's a game girl," Odette remarked, "but she can hear the old wall clock too, and even in digital *tock* gets percep-tibly louder than *tick* with each passing year. She'll never divorce him; both here and in Los Angeles, when a woman like her divorces a man like him, it is seen not as shedding him, but as losing him—and as you well know, neither D.C. nor L.A. can long abide a loser.

"Also, she's conventional at heart. She read somewhere that in great souls the repercussive conventional, when cou-pled with grandiloquent ego abandonment, has an effect more cowering than personal indiscretion."

"Have you a vision of her—for the future?"

"I do. I see her becoming a kind of New Age Calafia driving through Topanga Canyon like Shanakdekhete in her chariot through the pass at Napata."

"'Di Napata . . . le gole'?"

"The very same. In the meantime, I *must* do something about Russell Feingold."

"Who?"

"Russell Feingold, dear. Senator from Wisconsin—where Maud's from, remember? The Senate sponsor of the legislation to terminate the federal helium program—a relic of the 1920s blimp warfare scheme that is $1.4 billion in debt.")

"Happiness itself is unachievable," Max was saying to O'Maurigan. "But you knew that." Then to me: "My wife told me you were an orphan."

"I was." (I no longer miss losing both my parents.)

"That explains your civic-mindedness. In 1992, nine out of ten orphans surveyed voted, compared to three out of four other adult Americans. Not only that: fifty-eight percent claimed to be happy about their lives—exactly twice as many as the twenty-nine percent of other adult Americans. I suppose it tells us something."

"It seems to me," O'M observed, "beneath their rhetorical faces at least, that for the first time in a century both parties are effectively committed to the proposition that major social and economic ills are beyond government's capacity to remedy."

"That's the situation in *Democracy*," I ventured.

"Ah, but Prince Charming—Bryan—lost. Clinton's going to win. What I shall relish most in the victory is the sight of all the feminists in America, having convinced their sisters that Republicans denigrate them, and on the pretext of endorsing the ambitions of a clever Amazon, promoting the cause and elevating for posterity a hard-core, down-and-dirty, tit-licking, snatch-crazed—"

("Max," O'Maurigan declared later, "when he's stopped his nutsoid yodeling and settled down to close reading, takes very seriously Jefferson's words to David Rittenhouse, stipulating 'an order of geniuses above the obligation of public service.'")

"You write well, as I've said," Max said to me, "rather like a sports writer. And that's as it should be, because, even if you can't say so, what we have done since Reagan is to make politics the national sport, replacing baseball. We've leveled Capitol Hill to the height of a pitcher's mound, flattened the White House to a stencil on home plate, and in Clinton found the very type of the player of the future: vocative, well paid, and compliant.

"And *you*," he declared, turning to O'Maurigan, "could be the most important poet in D.C. since Archibald MacLeish."

"Not since Ezra Pound?"

"I have never responded to Ezra Pound. To my mind a lot of haiku afflicted with goiter. Wouldn't you at least like to be poet laureate?"

"No."

I went home and wrote: "The Republicans agreed to restore $727 million worth of cuts in the Environmental Protection Agency's budget and to make scores of concessions on GOP-inspired provisions dealing with timber salvaging, desert and wetlands management, mining, and protecting endangered species." (I left out the $1.4 billion helium reserve debt; it didn't seem to fit in.)

Then, at the White House correspondents' dinner at the Hilton, an ecologist cornered me.

"I've been reading your wetlands pieces—and I think you should write one about the Mojave Desert, for contrast." (Max had twitted me about my eastern ecology prejudices.) "The Mojave Desert Protection Act was the last act of the 103rd Congress, only to fall afoul of the Republican majority in the 104th."

(I thought of the desert as the refuge of all the John the Baptists and Marys of Egypt and the cliff dwellers and the archaeologist who found the centuries-old pot imbedded in the clay. "You cannot set out to find such a pot," he wrote, "it must burst upon you by accident when you expect just another corner of the sandstone, hiking through the starkest badlands to reach the ledge where the pot awaits." It would be a contrast all right, I thought, to my New York canyon experience, where in my childhood Wild West canyon melos were replayed with the rooftops as the mesas, the dark sex and gambling cellars as the hidden valleys and caves, the shower rooms and the pool as the furtive cascade through which the heroine would spirit the hero to the bower of bliss, and finally, the trucks in the meat-packing district as the covered wagons.)

I called Odette to hear what was what. Seemed the senator had taped an interview on the Larry King show that had sped around the world. "Whenever a man reaches the top of the political ladder," he'd been quoted declaring to *Newsweek*, "his enemies unite to pull him down. His friends become critical and exacting."

"Tell me some more."

"Well, I was just sitting here reading Elinor Glyn's *Three Weeks*. I don't know exactly what I'm after, or what I'll do if I get it, but in the meantime Maud seems to have become for the senator something like la Glyn's Russian queen who mediates the forces of darkness and light: a sexual woman, but also a cultivated one, whose almost-masculinity manifests itself in worldly wisdom, learning, and ironic disdain for moral posturing.

"This morning we went to the archives—stayed the afternoon. Nothing but row on row of lined-up keyholes. It is the biggest, whitest sepulchre in Washington. I lamented not finding any V-discs from World War Two: the recordings had been given to the LC—so off Maud and her senator went, and were facilitated.

"Together we sat listening to Lana Turner frying a steak for the boys overseas and Judy singing them their favorite songs and, well, you might say, cemented our relationship. 'I'd like you to come out to College Park with me one day,' he said, 'to listen to the Nixon tapes.' 'That would be fascinating,' I said, 'but the sound of that steak frying has, I'm afraid, made me ravenous.' So it was off to lunch à deux in the Senate Dining Room. There, under the Bierstadt painting of the rainbow, he continued about College Park and the tapes out there. 'Absolutely crazy, the things he—I *knew* Deke DeLoach, and he *never* would have done such things.' I said I thought a body might *develop something*, such as madness itself, listening to that awful man in that awful time.

"Well, dear, tonight's the ball—see you there. I'm wearing the Mainbocher—a copy, you remember, of the one Merman wore to the Lichtenburg palace ball in *Call Me Madam*."

(I remembered the diplomatic nobs' ball toward the climax of *Democracy*, and wondered if indeed the end was in sight.)

At the Opera Ball at OAS: everybody (except Maud/Odette) in black and white, like the final scene of *Mefistofele*, or as Bam-Bam kept insisting, "like Truman's divine party at the Plaza!" (A foolish comparison—she herself hadn't been anywhere near New York in the year of that big bang—that thoroughly confused the entire collection of Beltway reptiles, who couldn't recall Harry and Bess ever presiding over such an event at any hotel so named.)

Highlights. Vana started the conga line with the wife of the Mexican ambassador (I wondered, Was Max thinking of his mother?) and was quite soon canvassing everybody for her Venice event.

The senator, fallen off the wagon, started in reconstructing *Mefistofele* as a four-dimensional experience, for all comers. Maud MacGown (in the Mainbocher that was the talk of the evening) got herself cornered by Rain, who blamed her for the senator's indisposition. ("It was a little like the third act of *Traviata*, dear, in form. In content of course it was more the second act inside out: boy threatens the whore about Father.

Whore turns the tables, pointing out how much more he had to lose—and wondering why wouldn't he like to be adopted and come first to the Naval Observatory and then eventually into the White House with the senator and herself? Stunned, the little strumpet actually said he'd think it over.")

"Yes," Max was drawling into a fat face, as the beat went on and voices honked like horns stuck in a gridlock box, "Habermas is dead wrong when he writes that the transition from stratified to functionally differentiated societies is complete. Simply more Teutonic wish fulfillment. Of course, what else could sociology ever be, no matter how stunningly phrased?"

Somebody said, "The difference between these affairs in New York and down here is, up there you don't have these Capitol Hill hacks and K Street flacks rubbing elbows with the diplo element."

"If you're talking about the UN," a voice answered, "the *dipso* element is more like it." "All the same, it's not fair—not when cunningly concealed *elbow patches* are dress code down here." "Look, there's an essential difference. Up there, the flack is epiphenomenal, down here it's definitive."

"Oh?"

"*Yes.* In D.C. the reality—political, whatever—is *only what the flack says it is.* In New York the existence of an elite *precedes* its publicity."

"Well," a policy wonk in rented drip-dry and clip-on tie whined, "*I* wish people up there would *stop* digging at the policy analysts down here as though we were simply *language game* players, when we actually are performing crucial probabilistic analyses on matters of national security."

"You mean such as which Air Force One, tail number 28000 or 29000, is more likely to be the target of terrorist attack?"

"We often," the fat face insisted, becoming exasperated, "spend days mulling over the arrangement, condition, and function of disparate sets, the role of procedures, or the correct interpretation of descriptive statements, in order to best assess each foreseeable possible sequence of events."

"I don't," Max eased out dismissively, "want to get into semantics—focus particles, discourse markers, and generalized transition net grammar. I leave that to morons like Safire and the sociolinguists over in Georgetown, who like telling us how we shape our identity by murmuring assent or by being rude, by agreeing, interrupting, gossiping, or trading barbs. I don't believe them."

"I don't either," a voice said. "After all, what would Doug Vesteralen *be* without Barb?"

"True enough," Max smirked. "What would *I* be for that matter without Anastasia?"

(Even more suspect, I said to myself, than you already are.)

"I believe Thomas Jefferson," Max continued. "It behooves every man who values liberty of conscience for himself to resist invasions of it in the case of others—or their case may, by change of circumstances, become his own."

"Life in Washington is ever interesting," a matron opined.

"It *is*—and people say we don't give a rat's ass—it's dispiriting."

"That 'nobody gives a rat's ass' is nihilism," the matron's mate declared. "It's Russian, and more of a religious idea than a philosophical one—but certainly not an *American* religious idea."

"It behooves him too," Max continued, I thought ironically, "in his own case to give no example of concession, betraying the common right of independent opinion by answering questions of faith which the laws have left between God and himself."

"Our religion is our country—a land of promise and fulfillment. Although it is true that the strong presence on the best-seller lists of mystical and self-help books attests to the hunger many still feel for a yet more significant life."

("Let me not seem to have lived in vain," Rex Vavasour had seemed to plead.)

"Well," Max declared, "it's been an interesting Congress anyway, for connoisseurs of virulent ineptitude. One that amusingly suffered its mortal procedural and interpretive Crisis of Thermidor in the dead of winter; I suppose we should call it the Crisis of Frigidaire.

"You know, there was a metaphor going around last year I thought pretty funny—that the 104th Congress was operating at that degree of fever pitch. I remember telling the majority leader that at that rate, in two more congresses the Republic must certainly expire."

"Right at the millennium," Dick Fauquier snapped, "proving them right after all—all those fat and sassy Christers cluttering up the Mall and the Metro. *Quelle galère!* I suppose they can't help being ugly, but they *could* stay *home!*"

"You know," Max declared, as the evening began to wind down, "you know Henry James was *dead right* calling Washington the city of conversation—only *not* because, as he thought, it is a place where the chatter is of such quality, such *import*, but rather because Washington is *summoned*, as it were, out of the *abyss* of *nonexistence* merely by *talking* about it—so wherever you are, if you're talking about Washington, that's Washington. It's a *concept*—like 'Hellas' or 'Christendom.' Another way it is summoned is by voting it in. Washington is Las Vegas in slow motion."

The ambassadorial matron approached. "I find what you environmental lobbyists do fascinating to read about. 'Conversion of terrestrial ecosystems to agricultural monocultures gallops apace, along with human-induced spread of exotic species.' I couldn't help thinking of you and your kind."

(Who was this bitch?)

"Piping plovers?"

"And spotted owls."

Anastasia, in her long silk coat, moving in the line for the hired cars, upbraided Max for saying that the last vestiges of the concept of government believed in by Franklin Roosevelt have been wiped away. "Really, darling, get with it—nowadays Franklin Roosevelt is considered camp!" "My wife," Max drawled, in an exaggeration of his western origins, "has a touching faith in the efficacy of mutual trust. A mistake, if a lovable one—no man ever trusts a woman, and surely no woman trusts another woman: all entirely to everyone's advantage. Men trust one another, precisely the root cause of war. If we could abolish trust, we might see an end to war."

A French ambassadorial weasel then praised Max as "a man of the Far West rather than a man of the far right."

"You are very prescient, monsieur, which does not surprise me—as you are French you are no doubt a cinéaste, and French cinéastes, I find, understand us better than the run of our countrymen east of the Mississippi. Yes, we Harringtons are from the Far West, out of the Deep South, and as such we did not join the Union whose Constitution cites the disestablishment of religion merely to turn around and cooperate, as the eastern establishment—following the lead of you French, who bequeathed the ideas out of which that Constitution was forged—in establishing the religion of the state. In that we are more *laïque* than you."

"Yes," the cinéaste purred, "I think your ambassadress has helped us understand you and your President even better than you do—in the same way we better understand Jerry Lewis."

"Indeed?"

"*Mais oui.* We believe that what we see is a master politician at work at last in America. When he was elected, he seemed to be promoting a romantic vehicle for two charismatic stars. We do not think what happened thereafter was an accident, but intentionally designed to show the American public for once what life *is*. Clinton has shaken Washington up not only with his plot switches, but he, as it were, shoots with multiple cameras throughout, hands out dialogue only at the last minute, and picks unforeseen, even inhospitable, locations. The results are powerful, and disorienting; we commend him—and hope for more."

"The French," Max allowed grandly, "hold ideas a matter of public discussion, and sex a private concern. Americans, whose evolved brain pans seem to secrete a universal solvent of ideas, hold the reverse."

"*C'est ça, monsieur,*" the Frenchman continued, "and as Tocqueville remarked, two streams flow from the *source* of Revolution—one allowing men to build free institutions, the other leading to absolute power."

"A truth," Max laughed, "amply illustrated in Washington, where the power flows as a driving force down the Potomac from Harper's Ferry, and freedom to build institutions—such as St. Elizabeth's—dribbles from a drainpipe in Maryland down the Anacostia."

"Of course, middle-class or no, the question of what money is *is* vexing. In German *Geltung* is the normative itself. Habermas is better than Freud on money. Freud says only that money is good shit—which is primitive; it leads to the assumption that the money process is roughly equivalent to the alimentary process. Primitive. Money works much more like the processes of mentality: it has a memory—stored in the monetary hippocampus." (There on the early map of Washington, I thought, on my wall back on D Street.)

"The Cultures of Guilt and Shame," Dick Fauquier assured the fragrant night air, "are both tyrannies. And in the Balkans people fight a war they've been fighting since Dracula was a lance corporal, and do you know over what? Over an alphabet."

"You are being terribly short-sighted," a policy analyst drooled, percolating with gravitas and mission mystique. "Bosnia has everything—instant nostalgia for the last real war we won, and for the ten or eleven years when the U.S. was tops in the world bar none, and the movies were like *A Foreign Affair* and *The Third Man* and Berlin and Vienna were ruined temples of modern cufflink intrigue with Freud and holiday waltzes and Sylvestersnacht."

"In my opinion," I heard Maud MacGown tell the French embassy type, "the world's problems entire would be much more effectively dealt with in bridge tournaments than either in the field of war *or* at the political bargaining table."

Then we were all in our cars. I wondered what the last couple on line could have to say—left alone with no audience.

("Nothing to one another," Patsy said, doodling a soft balloon, its air depleted. But each to the private self, about the life companion or the companion only of the evening, "Who *is* this—and *what* did he bring me *here* for?")

An e-mail came in from Kaye Wayfaring: would I escort her to the Mary Robinson state dinner at the White House? (From breakfast with the Vice President to dinner with the President!) Her twins had been invited, as it was Chelsea's first state dinner; the husband was escorting Mawrdew Czgowchwz; his twin was going with O'Maurigan—leaving her a single. I accepted—my first heterosexual date since that prom back in the fifties.

On Easter Saturday, We Three convened at the Watergate, in Maud MacGown's apartment—one that not one of us suspected for a moment would be bugged. (It was.)

"He seems so weak," I pleaded, talking of Rain.

"Nobody," Odette insisted, "is too weak to pull a trigger, dear. The willingness to be violent is a force multiplier."

"He told me his challenge was to register the dimensions of his crisis in self-consuming Indian-world circularity."

The O' jumped up suddenly, as if at a Quaker meeting:

"'Who dares!' this was L. Pitkin's cry,
As striding on the Bijou stage he came—

'Surge out with me in Shakpoke's name,
For him to live, for him to die!'
A million hands flung up reply
A million voices answered '*I!*'"

"Neither of you like him very much, do you?"

Odette peered out the window, across the Potomac at Rosslyn. "As the divine Diane DeVors once said, dear, some people are *so* awful, they seem to *deserve* their awful childhoods."

"We realize," O'Maurigan said, "you have a soft spot for him—perhaps because in some strange way you connect with the fact that, as Clover puts it, 'to tie a prominent statesman to his train and to lead him about like a trained bear, is for a young and vivacious boy a more certain amusement than to tie himself to him and be dragged about like an Indian scout.'"

"Prominent statesman?" I objected. "Hardly."

"Perennial figure, then," Odette insisted. "And I must say, darling, although he may be nothing, he looks everything."

"And that fascinates you," I jibed.

"Let's say it fascinates the actress in me."

"'He loved power, and he meant to be President.'" I remembered. "That can hardly be the case here."

"There are more things, Horatio Alger, in heaven," Odette intoned, "on earth, and in old fools' minds than are dreamed of even in your hot luck story. As the heroine of *Democracy* laments, confronted by *her* senator, 'I confess my sins; life is more complicated than I thought.'

"But to return to your protégé. There may be a point to his television ambitions. He will have found his proper audience. Have you ever seriously *looked*, dear, at afternoon television talk shows? The inmates of flight decks and fat farms out on day passes."

"That's called a cross-section of America."

"Of its *scar tissue*, perhaps."

"You can see that same crowd any afternoon walking along the Mall."

"Must I go there? I've just gotten comfortable at the Watergate."

"You might drive by and shoot them—with a camcorder."

"I might. I never did go on safari. In any case, to them he may appeal his case—that of the innocent, coveted, eroticized, seduced and abandoned—not to thrust aside inner and missing—commodified, label-on-the-outside sex toy that is American youth."

"As you know," I cautioned, "Rain fears Galt may be falling in love with Maud MacGown and if it goes on, she will have to be dealt with. I asked what he meant, and he said, 'There's something called ricin, derived from castor beans—people use it against coyotes in Los Angeles.'"

"I liken that," Odette snapped, unperturbed, "to Eve's scene with Karen in the ladies' shall-we-say lounge of the Stork Club. With this exception: you really would *not* personally empty the bean bag."

"Sometimes," I said, "I think I'm listening to a call boy motormouthing on cocaine and sometimes to an American Rimbaud. And I find him strangely *real*—can you tell me why that is?"

"It used to be said," Odette declared, "that nothing could come out of nothing. But quanta can be created out of it *for a very short time*. I find him more like that little tramp in *Lukas's Story*—the same impudent dark looks—and very nearly the same voice. He's very Bel Ami video indeed!"

"He reminds *me*," the O' put in, "of Denham Foutts. That part about the senator liking to go down on him at night on Kennedy's grave at Arlington reminded me of Denham's cavorts at Oscar's tomb in Père-Lachaise."

Odette concurred. "Absolutely—also of all those Victorian whores who worked the same line out of Highgate Cemetery. I see this Rain in his name play, standing downstage the

way Jeanne Eagels did, barking in that cheap whore's voice, 'I
have the right to stand here and say to you the hell with you,
and be damned!'"

(Taped: every word of it—can you guess by whom?)

Later, at home, while Sylvester climbed in and out from
the window to the magnolia to the sycamore and back, I continued to think Rain's freedom in jeopardy—and as it turned
out, that much was true. (Doug V. said, "I don't see why one
wouldn't believe his story—or why, doing so, be so unwise as
to provoke a denouement." Vana concurred. "Yes, there is
definitely something surrounding him—something *stiletto* . . .
something Venetian.")

EIGHT / ARPÈGE

In a way, it ought to have ended right there.

But it didn't.

Earth Day. When you're an earthling, and they're out to get your mother, you're supposed to do something about it—walk the talk. In preparation, I contemplated the Chariot and Death.

"Understanding acting upon Severity: Saturn acting through Cancer on Mars." (Cancer: the U.S.A.; Mars: the aggressive action of the male on the female environment—an investigation into Framers' Intent. *Framers'* intent? What was going on in the mind's eyes of Billy Bitzer, Gregg Toland, Russell Metty, Russell Ballard?)

Then I read my horoscope. "Harmonious lunar aspect coincides with philosophical concept relating to people and nations. You'll be called upon to articulate customs of unique individuals.

"Change your artwork—rotate your photos, pick up something new for over the sofa, something different for the bath. New towels in a vibrant color will change your life."

Ought to have been enough for anybody.

The biggest problem was the season—the campaign season, in which Washington is The World and the white-noise drone of the Washington-World Clock becomes so loud, so relentless, and so monotonous it drowns out nearly the sound and surely the sense of anything that might be called substantive. Then too the late spring: cool, and yet malarial—

"This filthy, pestilential air!" Odette moaned. "And this *sewage* they call water! Have you looked at the gardens, at the trees in the street? Fluorescent, all right, but the peonies didn't have a chance, the magnolias look like somebody flung shit all over thousands of white Limoges plates, and the *roses!*—they all look like photographs of malignant tumors!"

As a hedge against capitulation I remembered that it had always seemed, I don't know, *fair* that there was only one sin that you absolutely *must* not commit: the Sin Against the Holy Ghost, the sin for which there was no forgiveness, ontologically speaking, the sin of despair.

(Although "fair" and "ontological" don't exactly go together: "fair" goes with "existential.")

It always struck me as quite different from the Old Fuck saying in the Garden of Eden, "Look, there's *one tree . . .*" I mean, that is a patent setup. But Father Greg convinced me that the idea of committing the Sin Against the Holy Ghost —typically the Sin of Judas ("It was not betrayal, Daniel— betrayal was the *destiny* of Judas—but *despair* that led to his suicide")—

Then I remembered the hourglass. If I couldn't make the sands of time run backwards, I'd make them run upside down. Yes, the sand—of Sagaponack—now at the bottom of the heap would, when I flipped the hourglass, work its way back to the top, and the sand of Venice, now at the top, would . . . it would, I realized, bury Richard Rouilard . . . like Winnie in Beckett's *Happy Days.*

There's no way out: in order that anybody win anything, even a working metaphor, somebody loses something: an election, a life.

We were back at the Hay-Adams; Max was rattling on to O'Maurigan; it was as if we had never left. (The same might be said, I thought, of the table talk in Sagaponack, but in Sagaponack I could always disappear for half an hour to make the coffee.)

"The Stockman line—unfettered production of corporate wealth engineers the expansion of private welfare—was necessary horseshit. The country had lost a war, and the returning drug-addicted failures were offing themselves more effectively than a firing squad after a deserters' court-martial. We told the nation, 'OK we can't validate you as conquerors anymore, but this we can do to make you feel American: be too *proud* to *accept* assistance.' *And it worked.*

"The majority certainly does not yet again want mass assistance. Earning not enough, fearing for their economic future, they have no use for political parties that only want to tax away more of their uncertain incomes in order to assist those who do not work and to feed huge, inefficient bureaucracies. And if a segment of the political spectrum is left vacant in American politics—the unwaged, the wards of the state—fuck 'em. Depressives who neither think nor, unless overstimulated, vote. Morons across the length and breadth of the land going on ranting about everything they've ever read about they think will command attention—"

"You said as much earlier," the O' observed.

"More than once. Hardly a vast political spectrum. A political black hole is what they constitute, and nobody can run on that?"

"Not like the guy in the middle."

"No. Oh, that fabled guy in the middle. Makes the two parties a couple of whores with a bet on which one will he stick it to. And of course the American people's idea of democratic power is to say, 'We don't like you, but we're voting for you—so *watch* it.'

"Today's populism is bound to grow. A candidate dedicated to exploiting the economic insecurity of Americans threatened by efficiency and unemployment could have done better than Buchanan if unburdened by extremism. As you both know, the *linings* of each of the parties is the same *color* as the *outside* of the other, and so turncoats think they have only to walk out with their vesture reversed, but the fact is, the *fabric* of the linings is instantly recognizable for what it is, and shows its *seams*."

"We'd like to get rid of Gephardt, Bonior, and Obey, the Winken, Blinken, and Nod of anti-free-trade economic theorizing—especially Bonior, champion of the unwashed, with the preternaturally Clorox-clean hands of a failed priest."

"Why not run Galt—as a new independent?"

"I'd relish the spectacle; there really isn't a bloviator like him anywhere in the country. But it wouldn't work—he's far too clean. Too high-minded—Americans won't have him. The plain fact is, unless your linen is filthy, they're just not interested."

"Not interested?" O'Maurigan objected. "He's been on the cover of two national weeklies, on *Larry King*, on *Nightline*, on *Meet the Press*. We may have to start rewriting *The Delancey Retort* to keep up. Not that he's come out as a candidate."

"No," Max agreed, "and he won't. It's going to be Clinton—perhaps by as much as sixty percent—Johnson and Nixon territory—but he will have to restrain *her*. A reprise of that Michael Lerner horseshit about the politics of *meaning* will *not* play a second time."

"What Maud MacGown has been saying is the same."

"Maud MacGown can say what she likes. Maud Mac-Gown is a sideshow."

"He will win on his platform—loyalty to the electorate's inner needs. Kennan thinks loyalty is an absolute—that to be loyal to even the worst causes is better than being incapable of loyalty to any. I think loyalty does nothing but mask fake out-rage, true malice, secret laughter, ultimate indifference. All, loyally, take part in the same determination—or betray the same torpor, depending on your point of view. Reminds me of Jefferson's comment on Voltaire's evidence for shell remains of the Great Flood. Ignorance is preferable to error; and he is less remote from the truth who believes nothing than he who believes what is wrong. What"—he turned to O'Maurigan—"do you think of that?"

"I detest cheap sentiment."

"Spoken like a Jesuit."

"Especially in politicians. Promise them anything, but give them music on the harp strings. Voltaire reminds me—" turning my way—"Vana is doing the Old Lady in *Candide* at the Kennedy Center gala."

"You yourself," I tried Max, "would not run for public office?"

"Are you mad? Fling myself before the American people—fucked-out trash that they are—in an exhausting, potentially humiliating, expensive, and possibly futile effort at identity definition? I would accept an appointed post. I will not stoop to the *retro* tactic of *employing* the *mythos* of the poor and the criminal and the otherwise unfortunate in the same way plutocrats used to employ the masses in heavy industry. You may have heard that politicians *use* people? The truth is they *use* the *people* to get to the same parties the plutocrats used to have a corner on. Liberal politicians in particular do nothing—a lot of it—so as to foster the idea that it is possible to do noth-ing and be worthy, in some mystical sense.

"And in some mystical sense the captains of industry and the leaders of factions agree with that. Anyone who has ever *done* anything learns after a while the point is not to *manufac-ture*, or *provide*, or anything else; the point is to *make people do what you want*. Then comes the crunch. What do *they* want? They all want *stories told about them*, that's what.

"There's no point in doing anything, there never was, unless—and maybe *except*—to have someone tell a story about it, and preferably *one you can hear.* This used to be the point of bards, and then of the novel, and it is now the point, pitifully, of home movies and charity functions like opera balls—which, as we've been recently been shown, are increasingly *combined.*"

(O'Maurigan said later, "Poor sons of bitches, the Harringtons and their ilk ruled the West in their day—as we did the west of Ireland in ours. Washington could no more dictate to them than London could to us. They were the hidalgos of America's Estremadura until history hemmed them in. Now with every variety of rich industrial sonofabitch buying up vanity tracts of western land twice the size of the District of Columbia, and what with tracking satellites registering every coordinate on the planet, the old guard can no longer even retreat to their secret canyons to dance. Atlas doesn't shrug anymore; he's become a Chippendale in a bandanna, stirrups, and a jock strap from Reno, performing at awards dinners and fund-raisers in D.C."

Apropos *Atlas Shrugged*, the senator's sudden sharp rise out of nowhere into the popular mind did certainly re-enact the sensation caused by his fictional namesake. As for the Maud MacGown phenomenon, it was more like Judy Holliday in *It Should Happen to You:* the matter of a moment . . . but what a moment.)

"The market mentality has allegedly blocked progressive politics—inducing despair, cynicism, and feelings of powerlessness among the people. No *wonder* Marion Barry has taken the first step—again."

"David Boas," O'Maurigan declared, "of the Cato Institute, declares that in a free market, people achieve their own purposes by finding out what others want and trying to offer it."

"And," Max asked, looking at me, "what does the correspondent of the *East Hampton Star* make of those sentiments?"

(Not much.)

"I will," he continued, "read your silence as a positive sign, even if 'positive' has been defined as being wrong at the top of one's voice. I happen to *know*, as I'm sure you do too, that we are as much what we shut up about as we are what we *say*."

"Are you referring, for example," O'Maurigan asked, "to government restrictions on encryption techniques?"

"I'm referring to all this reclassification *cant* come about as the result of a study done of communication problems among different castes in India—appropriate to us here in New Calcutta. Are *we* simply having a *pleasant conversation*, shooting the breeze over elevenses in a Washington power alcove, or must we really consider this a *speech event* leading to a *preclose* prior to leavetaking?"

("I think you must," Patsy said, back in East Hampton, now doodling only the strings and not the balloons. "I hope you did."

I couldn't say. All I could say was that this—and that too—would pass.)

"I am sanguine, however," Max allowed. "Unionism is fashionable again, and I rather like thugs. Some thugs—not thugs like David Bonior."

"An intense and driven admirer," O'Maurigan remarked, "of liberation theology."

"In other words, a spoiled priest—like that wop who runs New York. A hoodlum priest.

"Government in the United States is *only* about *scenarios*, and that is what makes Washington fascinating to people in the theater of politics. They care no more about the *polity* of the place than actors do about any city they happen to be playing in."

" 'We open in Venice,' " O'Maurigan quipped.

"Exactly. You know, Europeans incorrectly score Americans for lack of imagination. Not true—it's just that they have to spend so much time imagining their nation, they have none left to—who was it said, 'The masses are indifferent to individual freedom.'"

"Herzen."

"Herzen? Really? I thought it was Gore Vidal. In any case, think of these two statements in conjunction—or disjunction, if you prefer, but linked. When, twenty-five years ago, the President of the United States ordered the break-in and/or firebombing of the Brookings Institution, he wasn't acting as a lonely paranoiac—that was the mood of the greater part of the Great American Public. 'Government is the greatest of all reflections on mankind.'"

"Madison," O'Maurigan said.

"Right, but government in a democracy is run by committee and compromise and corporate enterprise, by 'do as I say,' and if the bastard is wrong you fire him and he makes up some outrageous lie—fable—gets hired by some other outfit, and you keep screaming panic over shit like the directive on carcinogenic fluorocarbons."

"An elected official can be fired."

"Not easily, and for a very good reason. Ninety-nine out of a hundred of them couldn't get a job in lower-middle management in any industry with stock worth your portfolio's— you *do* keep one?"

"My friend owns stock."

"Glad to hear it. He's undoubtedly familiar with Fannie Mae and Freddie Mac, thus with the truth—that the Federal Reserve, the most utterly undemocratic institution in the country, is the final arbiter of policy, although I wouldn't harp on it if I were you. Why torment the voters of East Hampton with the knowledge that the country is in actual fact in the same receivership position as the District of Columbia, and has been for decades? Stick to your little bird fables instead. By the way, would you consider being staked in a Wild Bird Centers of America franchise when you're through here? The *Wall Street Journal* is very pleased with their performance, and so is *Success*."

"I don't think so—thanks just the same."

"You don't like money; that's odd." (Pause.) "In any case, the populace don't care whether things get better or get worse, only that they get different. Listen to this for moronic." He unfolded the *Washington Post*. "'You can't have a genuinely free market if one set of interests can buy themselves special privileges at the expense of other interests.' *Jesus!*"

"Corporations," O'Maurigan said, "will simply hire elsewhere, abandoning the nation to—"

"Fuck 'em. They're a nation of slobs, led by a prize slob.

"Clinton knows very well what the reverse of politics is—and in relation to the Republican Party has devised a strategy for which I'm sure he is only too happy to have this Dick Morris take the credit." Then, again, to me: "You do not love Washington."

(Love Washington? Who could? A place where at the end of the twentieth century, if not of history itself, the central thesis of Wagner's nineteenth-century *Ring of the Nibelung*, the renunciation of love in the pursuit of world power, is played out daily as a funhouse-mirror distortion of assorted French eighteenth-century illusions concerning the perfectibility of man? I recalled Odette's definition of love: the *unwilling* suspension of disbelief.)

"It's evident you do not," Max continued, "from the way you report it—which is, if I may compliment you, very intelligently—even if it is, as I believe, an exploded view in the manner more of a jigsaw tumbled out of the box than in the manner correctly aligned, you are still better than that dizzy broad *The New Yorker* used to have down here, whose in-depth reporting of players in the Washington game made Barbara Walters look like Madame de Scudéry.

"And now we must put up with the likes of Sidney Blumenthal, another JFK flame-keeper—from Chicago, you know. An envelope stuffer of 1960 who might well have done similar service with the ballot boxes—but don't quote me, he's litigious. Terrible anglophile to boot, with suspect *florid* taste in ties, who lives in *Takoma* and obviously chants over and over into the shaving mirror the mantra 'I am the new Walter Lippmann . . . I am the new Walter Lippmann.'"

(Walter Lippmann wasn't nearly as good-looking as Sidney Blumenthal, who I would have to say—and I've never gotten close enough to check out his ties—is a hot Jewish number.)

"You see, when Clinton wins his second term, he will be the first Democrat since FDR to do so, and for a mind like Blumenthal's *that* is a sufficient likeness. And in the meantime, he needs to feel needed: why he specializes in holding Hillary Clinton's dry hand long into the night . . . while the wife holds the damp one—demurely.

"Altogether I prefer the likes of Nancy Dickerson Whitehead and Nora Beloff. But no matter who reports Washington, they all fall eventually for the same crap. As Alfred de Vigny said, 'La presse est une bouche forcée d'être toujours ouverte et de parler toujours. De la vient qu'elle dit mille fois ce qu'elle n'a à dire, et quelle divague souvent et extravague.'"

(Something to do with waves, I gathered. I missed the ocean—both oceans, any ocean: surf. Not even surfers, just surf.)

"The only thing to add is that as a general rule, the liberal hacks are a lot better-looking than the conservative ones, who are nearly all trolls and grotesques—another of the many mysteries of life my wife finds maddening."

"Can it be true that one's looks have what to do with one's ability to assess the workings of the American government?"

"I can't imagine so, no—especially since if there's one thing I've learned after being here all these years, it's that American government *doesn't work*."

"Not at all?"

"Oh, once in a while, I suppose, when the sun rises behind the Supreme Court or sets behind the Lincoln Memorial, you get a *notion*—why they keep coming—though comparisons to the Sacred Way in Athens strike me as quite ridiculous when applied to these people lined up outside the Aeronautics and Space Museum, for whom the existence of an actual *government* in this city is something on the order of a vague rumor.

"These ideas of mine were in my youth routinely derogated at Georgetown dinner parties by arrogant specimens of the so-called meritocracy accompanied by overgrown-adolescent retinues in flag-bunting togas to wreak havoc on the nation—"

"Sebastocrators?" O'Maurigan interjected.

"And archimandrites. The Mac Bundys and McNamaras and the McNaughtons of whatever era, who every few years rear their empty heads. Having with their entourages worn paths paved with optimum intention and the investments of special interests to and from the Auguriculum of the Great Republic to solemnly assure the dumb sonofabitch in the White House—whoever he may be—that the time has come for *harder choices*, when the hardest choices they'd ever made, once they got through multiple choice in college, were listed on menus and wine lists—and who, some of them, survive a generation more in order to lament their hysterical judgments and cry crocodile tears under the bright light of renewed attention.

"And why do we let them, these losers—these Bobby Bakers and worse, with their old stories of the Quorum Club? Why do we have them back? Why, for the *stereoptic* view of history, of course—and because in spite of the fact that losing is the only American sin, the only thing that America likes better than sin itself is the groveling repentant sinner. We forgive ourselves our losers as we forgive our debtors.

"Athens. Why do they—and why do I—keep going on

about Athens and its archons? Plato of course was crazy: *he* argued in *The Republic* that representatives should be *drawn* from a *pool* and *required to serve*. Our application would have to include equal numbers of men and women and come from all classes, like *jury duty*! And you know how popular jury duty is! What a riot! You know what, I'm beginning to sound like Rex Vavasour."

("No you're not," Patsy said, in the sunset glow. "I *like* Rex Vavasour; I don't like you one bit."

O'Maurigan said, "I just want you all to know—not that it matters—that when Max raves on about Sidney Blumenthal, he is really sore about the fact that Sidney's play *This Town* is rumored to have been optioned by Fox, and that whether that is true or not, the wife with the swanky foot in the White House has rankled Bam-Bam to an intolerable degree: it is exactly the *position* she envisaged for herself.")

Back from the prayer breakfast, I called Odette, interrupting her studies.

"I have been reading the ancients, dear—Ptolemy and company."

"Then tell me, are writers and politicians trying to do the same thing in two different ways?"

"Quite the reverse; they are trying to do two absolutely different things in the same way."

"Which is?"

"The praxis? Duplicating the sound of one hand clapping. The Puritans gave it, it seems fair to say, the characteristic tone of moral urgency and the allegorical frame of mind that has proved so important to high-minded white Americans."

("You might," Patsy declared, as the clock in the white tower of the First Presbyterian Church across Main Street struck the hour, "have to use *Investigation into the Allegorical Nature of the American Republic* as a subtitle after all."

"The dual emphasis," O'Maurigan declared, "on the individual conscience and the communally signifying details persists. Sublimated power relations characterized by moral urgency and the allegorical frame of mind."

"Couldn't I just write a potboiler?"

"A *potboiler*?"

"You're not going to say unworthy of me."

"No, only a stupid lie, easy to detect, would be that, and even if art is a lie, smart art cannot be a stupid one.")

I picked up the *Washington Post* to find a picture of POTUS out jogging with his Secret Service palace guard, the lead man wearing a T-shirt with the clearly legible legend "Billy Goat" (with sketch of same). As usual in such pictures, POTUS was the least happy-looking athlete—and the only one wearing a (duck-billed) cap.

Vana landed in D.C. again after voting in the Italian elections on April 21, did Venice Day in New York on April 27, and then the Kennedy Center gala—the Old Lady from *Candide*, a knockout.

Then, on the afternoon of April 30 (Walpurgis Night in Europe), she met me at Constitution Hall to check out a born-again Christian rally on the Mall.

"*Brethren!*" a preacher was bawling to a small crowd gathered around the Garfield memorial, "even here in the belly of the Beast Jesus calls on you to walk tall—walk proud—and *not* with downcast eyes. These wicked representatives of Satan and the New World Order? They think we're *stupid*—they think we were born again yesterday—ha, ha! Well, we *weren't*, and it's up to us to *show 'em*. Pray, brethren. Pray all day in every way! Pray outside the bolted doors of their Temple of Mammon there before you on that evil hill. 'For surely this is the fast I choose: open the bonds of wickedness, dissolve the groups that pervert justice, let the oppressed go free, and annul all evil decrees'—Isaiah!

"We will get our bodies in condition for the race to salvation—keep up those Jesus laps, younguns. Strengthen those feet and legs—ain't no Scripture says you can *pogo* your way to Jesus!"

(And even as he spoke a squad of somewhat chunky boys lumbered past in white shorts, T-shirts, and caps imprinted with "Americans for Jesus"—looking, I thought, rather happier than POTUS.)

"Jog along with these other joggers—and particularly these military boys. Jog along beside them as members of Jesus's own God Squad, and yank their hardened hearts toward heaven. If you do that, the good Lord God Almighty will *bless your socks off*!"

Vana, appalled and terrified, protested she'd never seen the like of it—not Sicilians whipping the Madonna, not Mexican *penitentes*, not rabid Moslems, nothing.

"*Ma è uno manicomio, caro!*"

I tried in a knowing, almost offhand way to compare home-grown American Protestant religion—Mormonism, Armstrong's *Mystery of the Ages* (which she'd heard of chez Harrington as something the senator held with), California Orphism, Toronto Blessing Vineyardism, and UFO abduction fantasies from Roswell, New Mexico—to the visitations of the Virgin so popular in Europe in this century and the last. It placated her troubled soul.

"They have a friend, these born-agains, in one Supreme Court justice."

"This must be the judge out of the Venetian comedy."

"The very one."

"You don't suppose he'd come to the regatta—for charity—and tell fortunes?"

"You know, he might."

It began to rain, and Vana produced her Mantuan Palazzo Te umbrella; the inside reproduces the famous ceiling: Tiepolo's treatment of Phaëthon crossing the heavens in his chariot. When you look up, he's directly overhead, and naked, so you see the works.

"I got the idea for it, *caro*, after I visited Mantova last year. There in the Palazzo Te were all these Japanese lying on the floor taking pictures of the ceiling and giggling, and the guard was *outraged*, and *screamed* at them: 'Shut up, the whole lot of you: where do you think you are, in a *pagoda*?!'

"Now, to be serious, *caro*, I must in this setting outline the plot of *Mortal Woman*. The three women are one woman, you see."

(I thought, naturally, of the triple statue of Elizabeth Cady Stanton, Lucretia Mott, and Susan B. Anthony—herself the subject of an opera—on which we had based the Three Fates motif for *The Delancey Retort*.)

"I would like to show again what a fully committed *verista* can do with allegory, when veiled. Not that I am going to play an icon—or three of them. No, I am going to play a real woman, subject to real men's cruelties, as Maria and Jackie and Marilyn all were—by sexually abusive fathers, by political husbands, by Hollywood producers, by obscenely rich barbarian industrialists and pirates."

"You've known them all."

"I have, *caro*," she responded solemnly. "You know, after what happened to Ruggiero, I went to him at Montecatini and said to him, 'I have been in your situation always—humiliated, in a helpless and obscene position. When a woman is naked on the floor, she is the target for insults as no man ever since he was a boy can ever have been, unless he has fallen among abductors.' Do you know Tiepolo's Sant' Agata, *caro*?" (I could see it—exactly as Tiepolo painted it.)

"'Without blasphemy or exaggeration,' I said to him, 'I have felt no less mutilated.' And do you know, he broke down weeping right there in the *sedia a rotelle*, surrounded by his bodyguards caressing their Uzis—saying for the first time he understood what a crucifixion his mother's life had been."

"They say grave injuries make men reflective."

"I suddenly thought, Not for nothing did I take up Tosca

in the sixties. In any case, from that day to this, Ruggiero has been an angel, I tell you. I can have any girl I like . . . more or less.

"But now, *caro*, for this opera, not only must I sing in English but sound *American*, eh? I myself of course would much prefer it done in Italian—if only," she giggled, "to relish singing at one point 'in questo popoloso deserto che appellano Washington.' But it must premiere here—and I must accept the challenge of getting the President to come. He must dispel this frightful image of the overgrown fast-food-moron child with no culture at all. Surely he will come to hear a Kennedy opera?"

"Presuming he's re-elected."

"Oh, but he *must* be!"

"Fine, moving right along, then, if anyone can drag him into the opera house, Vana, you can. Especially with anything to do with the Kennedys. Actually, you might arrange a little scene in the opera set in the Rose Garden—where a sixteen-year-old boy . . . sort of like Galahad and Percival."

"Such *ideas* you have, *caro*, since you came to Washington!"

("As if Washington," Patsy Southgate snapped, "had anything to do with ideas!"

"'The deceit of mutual understanding,'" O'Maurigan said, "'irremediably founded on the empty abstraction of words, the multiple personality of everyone, and finally the inherent tragic conflict between life and form.'"

"All right," Patsy declared, breaking into the silence, "who said that?"

"Pirandello, as he sat alone in his *stanza* at eventide—as we sit here now together—sensing the presence of intruders—characters begging him to write them into a context, thus bestowing upon them orientation, broadcast adhibition and status.")

"It is absolutely terrible, I think," Vana continued, "the

way the press snaps at him, only because he is the boy with mud on his shoes who comes in to party in borrowed and ill-fitting dress clothes, reeking of cheap cologne to mask the barnyard odor or the odor of poverty from the trailer camp, charms the father, puts the mother into a delirium, and walks away with the daughter."

("Not neglecting," Patsy snapped, "to make a date with the maid.")

"But tell me," Vana was whispering, looking nervously around, "these people, they are completely crazy, no? I know Italians are by reputation—but after all, public displays of contempt for the Italian nation are a violation of the constitution and can carry a one-to-three-year jail term."

"Don't you think the Pope is as bad?"

"Ruggiero and I were at a dinner in Rome, just after the elections, with a priest who declared, 'We all resemble the Pope in this—we must all walk in the mysteries of pain and failure.' *'Failure, monsignore?'* Ruggiero declared, starting up only a little out of his seat. 'I do not think the victor in the Cold War can be called a failure. No *Italian* Pope could have accomplished the same!' It seems that since being elevated, Wojtyla has operated a secret espionage network in Eastern Europe that effected the collapse of communism—as promised in the letter at Fátima."

"Here in Washington," I offered, "that claim would be called mad."

"It does seem so often that he thinks of himself as really *in charge*—as in the outrageous wording of *Tertio millenniae adveniente*—and of the Santo Spirito as no more than an endangered species-of-one that he must protect—as you, *caro*, do your *ortolano*. But are not we all mad? I often feel I myself am a madwoman who has become convinced that she is Vana Sprezza.

"Still, I know what you mean—these pharaonic mad

reconquista schemes—*acromegalo*. His tyrannical rule over the Vatican is legendary. Hundreds of embittered clerics are only waiting for the sonofabitch to die before going public. Perhaps he can't help himself. If you *really* think you are fulfilling the will of the Holy Mother of God—towards whom he exhibits classically pathological Oedipal longings, which is another scandal, and the cause of much that is wrong."

"All depends on so much else, as Odette says."

"*Sì, sì*—including the fact that when they told him the Dalai Lama and the patriarch Bartolomeo are both also entitled to be addressed as 'Your Holiness,' he screamed as if the antipope had come back to Avignon! Did you know, *caro*, that the men's rooms in the Vatican are filled with fresh flowers every day, but that the women's rooms are like something in a detention camp?"

I did not—but speaking of Avignon, remarking that it was already Walpurgisnacht in Europe, I compared the orgiastic scene in *Mefistofele* to that on the Mall. The rain had let up as we came to the Tidal Basin, where the last of the cherry blossoms were blowing away into the Potomac, in a moment of, as the *Genji monogatari* has it, *"mono no aware" ("tristesse de la vie")*.

"Yes, we are all hypocrites! But tell me this." She looked straight ahead at a phalanx of jogging marines, approaching along the river walk in a somewhat more inspiring formation than either POTUS or the Jesus lappers. "I may be a lesbian convert, but I am not under sexual novocaine. These nearly naked boys one sees all over Washington, with their heads shaved like Buddhist priests. Marines, no?"

"Yes."

"Why can I not have *them* for my *gondolieri*?"

("That Vana!" Odette said later. "Can you see the headlines? 'Diva Fucks Jarheads Silly.'")

"I've already arranged the gondoliers."

"Yes, so you have—and I am very grateful. And I am going

to see your friend at the Library, to look at the Venetian sailor's diary. You know, *caro*," she said suddenly, her tone changing dramatically, "I am not a stupid woman—even though I may put myself in such company. The irony of my situation is not lost on me."

"It is on me—a little."

"*Think* of it, *caro*—married to a barbarian. I mean *I* am—*io stessa*. You are married to a saint. Yes, a barbarian—for all industrialists are that. And Filippo is dedicated to Culture. *They* are not—not there, and certainly not here, those dreadful men at the Kennedy Center; it is absolutely clear they would like nothing better than to see Culture—European, American—trampled underfoot once and for all.

"*Sì, sì*, here in this terrible city, with all these terrible cherry blossoms. As Butterfly says, in her third act, '*troppa luce è di fuor . . . e troppa primavera!*' And whether I like to admit it or not, *caro*, I am in my third act."

From our side of the Tidal Basin, once the beefcake had trundled out of the picture, she noticed that the Jefferson Memorial looks enough like the Palladian Redentore to do as backdrop for the regatta, which she thereupon commenced in earnest to envision held on the same day as Redentore and, inspired by the huge television screens on which the Christians on the Mall were viewing themselves, for the same to be positioned all along the waterfront to televise the "real" thing from Venice.

"Uplift, *caro*. I am told Americans must have this before they part with their money."

The Delancey Retort reached what I think of as its zenith at just this time, with "D.C. Circles" in the form of face-bubbles blown from pipes held by Madison and Jefferson—very Busby Berkeley. Also under the rubric of "The Wheel of Fortune" it had become a game show, where American eagles instead of ducks dropped down out of the flies and people dressed up funny.

O.J. made his talking debut as Minister Fabrication, "impresario of racial street theater," watching *The Delancey Retort* from his office, and announcing that Max Harrington was from a family of vague Middle European origins, whose name was Herringbone, allied to the Warburgs and the Rothschilds, and he read out loud verbatim from *The Protocols of the Elders of Zion*.

"We gonna *peep* his *game*, what de brothers say."

The Archetype reads to Dame World and Maud Mac-Gown commentary from the *Washington Post*. "'Republican politicians want their political efforts to take place underground out of public view. They complain only when the crazy aunt in the attic insists on making a public statement.'"

"Well, *sonny*," Maud huffs, "I am far from crazy and I don't come from any old attic, but I am an *aunt* and *am* making a public statement, and here it is. As James Madison declared in *The Federalist*, this body the House of Representatives must evince '*an immediate dependence on and an intimate sympathy with the people.*' The Senate, on the other hand, ought to '*consist in its proceedings with more coolness, with more system and with more wisdom than the popular branch.*'"

The Squeaker and POTUS resume their tête-à-tête.

NEWT: We can't take *anything* from you. You don't understand what we want *at all*. I'm going to the Pentagon, where they hate you; you want to fill the army full of sissies. I get them at the Pentagon and they get me. After-action reviews! Small unit cohesion! I am in combat every day!

A FRESHMAN: The Newt's *losing it*—he's gonna *cave*! It's the date-rape drug!

POTUS: You and me, Newt, we're the same kind—jes' two ole Southern boys who like to eat.

Newt undergoes a mood change.

NEWT: My hero!

POTUS: So, what do you think of this government stuff?

NEWT (scratching his head): Some of it is very funny, some of it is very sad, and the rest of it is very confusing.

POTUS: You got that right. You know, Newt, laws represent the failure of love.

NEWT (aside): Sigh! What is this thing called love?

Ornette re-enters.

"They told *POTUS* he wuz gonna *grow* in office, and he's *waitin'*, for if he *does*, he'll beat that ole Paula Jones's *evidence*. He is *Pinocchio*, but bein' he gets a second term, he gonna turn into a *real* boy—then *watch out!*"

Enter Blob Dull.

BLOB DULL: I've got a long history of experience.

A VOICE: Jeesus!

A SECOND VOICE: The question is, does Blob Dull want to *slam-dance* or does he want to *cakewalk*?

Scene shift to crowd in cowboy hats line-dancing. They try to teach Blob Dull to dance.

"Is he *dancin'* or is he *walkin'*?"

Enter Senator Sally Tomato.

SENATOR SALLY TOMATO: We gotta contract on *America*!

(A voice hisses off-camera: "*Sally*, that's *with*—with America!")

We gotta contract wid' America! And since when is it a crime to make money on Wall Street? I ain't no Hillary Rodham Clinton. Italian-Americans have been maligned! Read the report of the committee: it's a threat to democracy!

Maud MacGown introduces a campaign to save the Everglades and soon the Squeaker of the House makes a floor speech in favor of it:

"We must save this peninsula Florida . . . !"

May 20. The Supreme Court landmark decision against Colorado, in favor of Gay Liberation. We celebrated with the "Daddy Dearest" caper. A mad drag queen with the face and wig of George Washington goes down to the tidal basin at midnight, starts chopping down the cherry trees. Hauled into court, she demands a national Stonewall Memorial. (We couldn't, of course, let Odette attempt it: we got local talent from the Triangle Club on P—a man called Waldo.) The Christian Coalition TV critic had a field day with the stunt. "Sodomy *advocated* on the public airwaves!"

Meanwhile, interrupting again the long slow-motion High Noon pacing of Blob Dull and Hillbilly Goatboy toward their confrontation on the Mall—we restaged the Montana Militia standoff. The Militia, the FBI, ICM, C-SPAN, CNN negotiate a deal: viewing time on the National Agenda networks. Sponsors rush in: the NRA, the CIA, the Conspiracy-Coordination Corps (CCC), etc. Circus melee. O'Maurigan too to the microphone, on holding the mirror up to nature.

"Hamlet was naive about the mirror held up to nature. Nature, like the rest of us, is only too glad to get it backwards, the way the mirror shows it. Whether she could stand a mirror of the self-correcting variety is yet another matter."

Dame World rushes in, distracted.

THE ARCHETYPE: What now?

DAME WORLD: Some yahoo has won in Israel.

THE ARCHETYPE: A lesson to us to leave things as they are.

DAME WORLD: As an archetype you resist all change. You put aside all consideration of which candidate is the clearest example of presidential timber.

THE ARCHETYPE: I see no reason to change whores in mid-dream—even if he does seem to have more *suaviter in modo* than *fortiter in re*. (Picks up the newspaper.) Anyway, there *is* no more presidential timber. Like heart pine, it's been lumbered out. Says here there's a new set of ideas rapidly overtaking liberalism and conservatism.

DAME WORLD: About time, don't you think, Magnolia?

THE ARCHETYPE: I do and I don't. I *would* like something a little more stimulating than the political equivalent of the introduction of daylight savings time—just so the populace can stay out and play an hour longer after school, and they do say that Blob Dull would turn back the clock. Says here the new trend is called the politics of *sneering*. Sneerers don't take ideas seriously at all.

A VOICE: It's a free country—who *cares* who's President?

THE ARCHETYPE: That's what comes of sending all those people to *school* in all those *programs* on all those *loans*. Now they just sneer at the whole country and tell them in luscious detail what boobs they are.

(Magnolia looks down at her bazooms.)

"Luscious boobs." Where have I heard those words before?

DAME WORLD: From behind red velvet drapes in your Supreme Court.

Threats had started coming in, serious ones, we realized, and the reason no real show like this had ever been done in D.C. Conspiracy paranoia is an American constant, often erupting in real killing.

Maud decided to have an "American Women Round Table" and invited all the characters from "Are You There?" —Dolley M., Eleanor R., etc.

MAUD: To a woman of sense and spirit the admiration of even the noblest and most gifted man is esteemed as nothing so long as she remains conscious of possessing no directly influencing and practical sorcery over his soul. For when a man grows old they turn him into a sage, when a woman grows old they turn her into a hag.

THE ARCHETYPE (to Dame World): Who is this "they"?

DAME WORLD: The archons, dear.

MAUD: Yes, a true woman is nature's paragon, but more has to go on the application blank than "sex: female."

After the Memorial Day weekend, I filed the following report to the *East Hampton Star.*

ENVIRO-WAR: THE CEASE-FIRE

In what one official described as "a remarkable reversal of fortunes," the EPA has survived proposed cuts of between 20 percent and 35 percent, taking only a 1.5 percent reduction, from 6.6 billion to 6.5 billion. Less fortunate is the Department of the Interior, which faces an 8 percent cut for Native American programs, and a 40 percent cut in the program for continuing the further listing of endangered species.

Legislation whose effect would nullify various sections of the Clean Water Act remains on permanent hold—cynics and other adherents of politics as metaphor say perhaps depending on the final outcome of Whitewatergate.

The Prophet Tess declares, "Ain't but one way to determine the future in Washington and that is with 'The Tarot of Washington'!"

Together Tess, Magnolia, and Dame World play "The Tarot of Washington" (background music, the Card Scene from Bizet's *Carmen*, instrumental version):

Aker: Nixon
Fool: Kennedy
Emperor: Roosevelt
Old Man: Lincoln
High Priest: Washington
High Priestess: Eleanor Roosevelt
Lovers: Jefferson and Madison
Justice: Supreme Court
Chariot: The Pentagon
Sun: White House
Moon: House of Representatives
Star (Chamber): Senate

Death: Arlington Cemetery
The World: Monumental Washington
The Two Ways: Republican and Democratic Party
    Headquarters
Wheel of Fortune: The Ballot Box
Empress: Jacqueline Kennedy

Before "The Tarot," Dame World reads from Plato's *Republic*.

"In my opinion the true and healthy constitution of the state is the one we have described. But if you wish also to see a state at fever pitch, I have no objection. For I suspect that many will not be satisfied with the simple way of life. They will be for adding sofas and tables and other furniture—also dainties and perfumes and incense and courtesans, and cakes— let 'em eat 'em—all these not of one sort only, but of every variety."

On the scrim: girl and boy prostitutes, drag queens, models, perfume ads. The Archetype, turning the Wheel of Fortune card, proclaims that the hype has crested; the backlash is setting in. Tess cries out in anguish, "There can be no Equal Justice Under Law, as inscribed on the portico of the Supreme Court, as long as the building remains so relentlessly *white*! For a start, the sixteen columns should each be a color: black, red, pink, yellow, etc. And Court Television should be brought in. Justice Day-Glo Zoot-Suit—"

"Over my *dead body*!" a David Souter face barks. "The Supreme Court is not a political institution—and *therefore not part of* the entertainment industry of the United States!"
CHORUS OF HOLLYWOOD LIBERALS: *Fascist!*

Three *dum*s, pause, one more *dum*, as in the opening of Beethoven's Fifth, then lights out.

Nine / Découpage

At last the Mary Robinson state dinner: my White House debut.

"Dolley Madison's ghost (in yellow velvet Empire gown and dripping with pearls—not faux) sighted in the windows from the Rose Garden. Absolutely, but I was looking the other way. 'Oh, hello, Dolley,' I heard some old Washington bag say right past me, into the lantern-lit gloaming, nonchalantly, and that was it. Seems Mrs. Madison has been turning up for years in various parts of town: the Washington Arts Club, Blair House. 'Very like Dolley to check out a woman President,' was Max's comment. Anastasia's was, 'She must be disappointed, however, by the jewelry.' "

Bam-Bam, despite her declaration to the *Washington Post*, had approached to berate me for not creating a part for her on *The Delancey Retort*, after she was responsible for convincing her husband to produce it. I told her I had in fact been thinking of her for the part of Mammon. Dick Fauquier sauntered by, with Vana on his arm ("working the lawn," as the O' observed, trying not to glaze over). "The Whigs," he was saying, "were the pivotal American presidential dynasty. It is no accident that the great American epic was written at the crescendo of the Whig era."

("We will learn to realize crescendos in human affairs more easily," the Vice President had written.)

Time passed. I was introduced to the First Lady. "Your show is a riot, buster. Chelsea and I are big fans. I reminded Bill you were coming tonight *and* that we'd better watch our steps. He seems taken up just now with the charming unofficial lady ambassador from Italy—they're out on the South Lawn."

(Later I recalled these encounters in terms of, what else, *Democracy:*

> He himself took great pride in his homespun honesty. Owing nothing, as he conceived, to politicians, but sympathizing with every fiber of his unselfish nature with the impulses and aspirations of the people, he affirmed it to be his first duty to protect the people from those vultures, those wolves in sheep's clothing, those harpies, those hyenas, the politicians. He came to Washington determined to be the Father of his country; to gain proud immortality— and a re-election.
>
> But everyone conspired against him. His enemies gave him no peace—and ribald sheets, published on a Sunday, took delight in printing his sayings and doings, chronicled with outrageous humor. He was sensitive to ridicule, and it mortified him to the heart to find that remarks and acts, which to him seemed sensible enough, should be capable of such perversion.

The ribald sheets had not yet segued from remarks to acts, and concerning the code name "Mona Lisa" which began to circulate at just that time, I was dumb enough to imagine it referred to Vana. Don't send me to discover anything you badly need to know.)

Moments later, Dick Fauquier came up to me. It seemed

POTUS himself had indeed taken Vana off his arm and led her to the Solarium ("safer," Fauquier drawled, nearly hysterically, "than *public dalliance* on the South Lawn—Harry Truman called it the backyard, you know—under the tree planted by Andrew Jackson"), where he and Mary Robinson were receiving privately while Hillary busily worked the lantern-lit Rose Garden.

"Since neither of us," Fauquier continued, "is likely to be summoned into the Solarium for a midnight *sunbath*—known as *face* time, and ought to be called *sit-on-my-face* time—nor called into the Sun King's Presence Chamber to make obeisance before the Kundun of Little Rock on his Cowardly Lion's Throne in the Hall of Good Deeds, this is an ideal opportunity to tell you what I haven't as yet. Much as I enjoy—even get off on—watching your show, may I be candid about its value? I'm sure you wouldn't expect less. Essentially it fails because in a busy world already brutal and confusing it does nothing to alleviate the situation—but then here in the black hole, the antipivot of every collapsed libertarian ideal of the last two hundred years, how could it do otherwise, as produced by Max Harrington, but be itself drawn into the maelstrom of the very hypocrisy it purports to score—a concept in physics known as frame dragging?

"As for lifting the lid on the Capitol, a little parable. It isn't that the lid is screwed on so tight that no *terrestrial* force can lift it; if that were the case, an accumulation of outrage would force the issue to the point of eventual demolition. No, it has been necessary to create and maintain the illusion that the *contents* of that democracy are visible, but so *elevated* as to be in fact intangible, although absolutely real.

"This is how it is done. I have known about it for some time, but recently, on a visit home to Charlottesville, I was shocked—*shocked*—to discover that the secret has been *exposed* in the most *insidious* manner, in the design and promotion of a *new toy*—one I snapped up as soon as I saw it, to give to my godson. I shall explain its workings to you now, as I must do to him later—and let's see what *that* does to the distributive parallel processing of his global workspace, ha, *ha*."

(For the first time since coming to Washington I thought I'd rather be with POTUS.)

"A dish and a lid with a circular hole in the center. Because of the double concavities: the apexes of the focal points, the mirrored convergences of the elliptics." ("A city of charlatans," Barb Vesteralen had called D.C., "playing shell games with the hollow concavities of their former selves.") "Things put in the dish—a miniature of the Statue of Freedom, for example, represented as the *handle* on things—will be seen to *pop up* through the *hole* in the upper dish; but when one tries to *touch* it, it will be shown *not to be there*. It is, you see, a sublime trick of *optics*."

(I thought the toy a cynical gift for a boy—and wondered what it would be like having a cynical queen for a godfather. I likened the optics in the toy—and Dick Fauquier's story too—to the optics in Vermeer. The hole in the top of the covering mirror is the keyhole [or the glory hole] and the illusion that *pops up* [or is pushed through]—a bone of energy something like light so far as the libidinous psyche is concerned—reminding one of Jack-in-the-Box, *the* phallic toy that is this book.)

I thought of something. "Lincoln said, 'If you once forfeit the confidence of your fellow citizens—'"

"'—you can never regain their respect and esteem.' Lincoln was a depressive psychotic who suspended the Constitution."

"Which Republicans have wanted to do ever after."

"Not suspend—abrogate . . . or corset. I will admit Lincoln did say one thing that is pertinent in the present circumstance:

"'As our case is new, so we must think anew and act anew. We must disenthrall ourselves, and then we shall save the country.' But he was a depressive psychotic all the same—to whom history was generous in affording as theater the Great Psychotic Moment of the American Nineteenth Century. You make me suddenly wonder, though, if in the end Clinton—maximally exposed—might not be the one most like Lincoln. After all, trailer-park white trash is the approximate late-twentieth-century equivalent of the log cabin.

"But Clinton isn't interested in the people's respect or esteem; he's banking on their complicity. There is no honor among thieves, but there is certainly mutual interest.

"So go to him—better you than me, for 'as I detest the doorways of death, so I detest that man who hides one thing in the depths of his heart, and speaks forth another.' That's Achilles on Odysseus, in the *Iliad*—but don't take it personally."

("*Achilles* yet!" O'Maurigan howled later.

"He was in a fury" [Odette], "and all heel to boot.")

"Go to him," Fauquier hissed. "There he sits, the President of the United States, in his glory, maximally exposed."

("The President . . . maximally exposed." I got an erection. Whenever I'd hear "Clinton" or "POTUS," I'd think in an *idealized* way, closely identifying with the difficulties of having one's peccadillos turned damning evidence. When I'd hear "the President," I'd turn on. Was I an enthusiast? Is inconvenient sexual arousal the same as enthusiasm? I never turned on when innuendo concerning the Vice President circulated.)

"Maximally exposed, day after day, which neither of his predecessors could bear to do."

As I made for the Solarium, I heard Dick Fauquier attacking another guest. "There he is, in there, looking with interest upon the petitioners, as if there were anything in the world he could do for them. Have you heard the latest? They want to put a big white marble *couch* across Pennsylvania Avenue opposite the White House and enormous *television screens* on either side of the entrance gate, so the couch potato *canaille* can sit there and *watch POTUS and family*, eatin' dinner, or the chile doin' her homework—or the First Lady throwin' *lamps* across the *living room* while the cat runs and hides in the *cellar*. And here you are right on the set!"

Leaving them, he intercepted me again. "And soon *you* will be in the very same *room* with him—you have been summoned, you must go in. Being here, you know—in the White House—is being in the ellipse. It's what the ellipse means. An ellipse is the product of two foci. Do you know geometry?" (The double concavities again.)

"I passed the Regents exam back in high school."

"That's all you need; I'm reading Feynman's lost lecture on the planetary orbital ellipses. He came to Washington and made them all look exactly the fools they were—"

"The O-rings on the *Challenger*."

"He was a great man—a great American. One of the special properties of the ellipse is that if a light bulb is turned on at F_1, and you imagine the inner surface of the ellipse as a mirrored wall—if you like conspiracy theory, think of a two-way mirror, with the watchers on the other side. There's two of everything in Washington, you know—the so-called substantial and its often more substantial shadow, or stand-in, and the only way you can understand anything at all is getting them together *stereoptically*.

"Anyway, stand there, and as the light is turned on at F_1, all the reflected rays will come back together at F_2—which is you. Since it would do your eyes a damage to look straight into the sun—POTUS—you are concerned in the process of reflection from the tangent point with curve fitting, and with the principle of least effort—which ought to appeal to you as a writer."

"They appealed to Vermeer as a painter."

"I've been overhearing you, Dick," Max cut in, "and I agree. Now they are going to have to be really careful, because attempts on his life will intensify."

"Intensify?" I demanded.

"You didn't think, did you, really, that incident on Air Force One, over *Texas*, was *weather*? There was no—and never will be any—record on any weather chart of any turbulence at thirty-seven thousand feet on that afternoon's flight between California and Andrews Air Force Base. Do you think the Texas Civil Air Patrol—a volunteer search-and-rescue operation—is incapable of effecting private maneuvers?"

("Odd," Doug V. remarked in the car later. "After Dallas they told Johnson to get into the air, where they could protect him better . . . and he did.")

"At Cato the debate is whether to call him Catiline or Caligula. I opt for the latter. Really, how can he be a Catiline? Catiline was from a long line of Roman aristocrats, and Clinton is a glad girl's whelp from Dogpatch."

"He *is* Catiline," Fauquier whined. "Don't take *my* word—ask the ghosts of those who have suicided over him. Ask the families of those young men and women he has corrupted."

"And what families are those?" Max drawled, suddenly nervously—as if Fauquier might be about to give out information.

"More will be revealed," the little weasel whined.

"Well," Max, resuming his cool, pronounced, "Clinton, remember, did play Catiline's *defense attorney* in Latin class."

"I don't give a shit whom Clinton fucks, and it may be true that young men have come to grief because of him—as some members of his party have—but he is no party man at all—rather a force no party can count on—except one of a night's duration in a backroom—a confidence man on his own showboat.

"However, as to his being guilty of the murder of small children by those who call Oklahoma City the result of a sting operation gone wrong—well, I don't think so. But"—turning to me—"you have been summoned; you must go in."

(Of my face time with POTUS, I allowed, back in East Hampton, in the *Star* offices, he's of a type I feel I know.

"How so?" asked Patsy.

"I've seen a lot of male hustlers in my life."

"You have," she nodded appreciatively. "And were you not sitting right by me I'd say, 'Come over here and sit by me.'"

"And watched the way they operate, and I'm convinced that by whatever turn of events Clinton learned to get what he wanted more by behaving like a male hustler than anything else."

"Expatiate."

"The hustler doesn't—can't—dare *not*—care anything at all for you, only for what you can provide in the moment. He looks right through you: not even over your shoulder to see who else might be more interesting, but *through you*, as if you were glass."

"Don't most politicians?" she asked.

"Yes and no. Most politicians' behaviors are spins on this one, but in Clinton I see the behavior raw—I see him *come on* to the electorate."

"This is nothing new in the world" [O'Maurigan]. "There was Alcibiades in Athens, and there was, as was pointed out that night by the odious interloper Fauquier, Catiline in Rome—"

"And in America," Patsy interrupted, in that wonderfully seductive tone that challenges you to know is she kidding or is she serious, "there was John Fitzgerald Kennedy, who saved the world."

"The hitch is," I continued, "the hustler's pitch has nothing to do with *stability* of any kind—in fact it *absolutely depends* on the *nervous instability* of the john.")

Odette called for the report; when I mentioned Fauquier, she confided, "Oh, that awful woman! Approached me, you know—thinks it would be a fabulous idea to make a fool of the senator. *So like* the Virginia politician who approaches Madeleine in *Democracy*. Really, dear, one does *not want* to be at all like a character in a novel—particularly not one a *century old*! I wouldn't put it past the worm to have read me already as Odette O'Doyle."

"Hmm—and the latest on His Nibs?"

"His Nibs wants to take your mother to a place in the Blue Ridge called Swannanoa."

"Swannanoa."

"Dig it. The very name, dear, for obvious reasons, sets off alarm bells."

"Swannanoa."

"You do like the sound of it—I can just tell. It is some marble Renaissance pile that sits on a self-styled Christian Holy Mountain. There's said to be a statue of Christ in the garden that rivals Sugar Loaf's down in Rio—well, I've been to Rio twice, dear: once with Bette Davis and Paul Henreid in *Now, Voyager* and once with Mercedes Benzedrine and Diane DeVors in life, and I don't know, I have the idea that three strikes would be out."

As I wrote Phil: "The scene Fauquier had in mind to take place in the Blue Ridge took place instead in the Bishop's Garden at the National Cathedral next to the statue of the Prodigal Son. (Odette said, 'I kept hearing the Wurlitzer at Radio City, dear, playing "In a Monastery Garden"!') Rain and I scoping it all from the vestry in the chapel at St. Albans (with the altar-boy vestments hung up around us, reminding me again of being with Rico at Lincoln Hall), our wired gaze directed down into the garden."

Back at the suitor's Watergate apartment, curtains drawn, we played Rain's tape—the live-bait contents of which I give you now.

Galt began by telling Maud she resembled George Willoughby Maynard's portrait of Justice in the Great Hall of the LC. She warned him that it was a June with a blue moon in it. His response: that was a good augury—"Once in a Blue Moon," as sung by Marion Davies, was a tune that had always haunted him. In love with the star as a boy, he'd been as outraged as Hearst by *Citizen Kane*.

Maud countered with "Blue moon, you left me standing alone," appending a little lecture on the linguistic derivation of "blue moon" from "belew" or "belie": being the second full moon in a calendar month, it advises of deception.

("Miss O'Doyle," a guest in Sagaponack said later that summer, "did go out on one gay limb—nothing like it since the very young Hildegarde Dorsay duped Father Divine." "Almost." "What *almost*? She switched drinks; Father got the mickey, Hildy got the dickie, with nobody but Jesus the wiser.")

Galt, who'd always imagined himself alone in the garden with Jesus, suddenly found he preferred being alone in the garden with Maud. ("Come into the garden, Maud." I'd never read the poem, so asked O'M about it. His answer: "Some snowy night . . .")

In the garden, Maud had seemed properly grave about being preferred to the Lord, declaring that alone in the garden with Jesus implies Gethsemane and not the rose garden from T. S. Eliot. Then she took a minute to remark on the durability of the stock plant of her favorite bloom, the "black" peony. Whereupon—

GALT: You are a charming woman, Mrs. MacGown.

MAUD: You know, Senator, I don't much care for charm. Often I like people, and they like me—but I don't think I could set out in cold blood to fascinate a stranger.

GALT: You couldn't call us strangers, Mrs. MacGown.

MAUD: I suppose not—but if not, then call me Maud. I suppose I'm still a little disoriented in Washington, where no one talks of anything but politics—and revolution.

GALT: Oh, that. I wouldn't put too much stock in that, Maud: that revolution thing is just something the House cooked up after the fact when the Republicans got the majority after a lifetime of waiting. And now the Democrats have bamboozled them.

MAUD: There was a woman at the time of the French Revolution who said, "I cannot fully enough share the hopes of the democrats nor wring my hands like their adversaries." And if at dinner parties I talk music instead of politics, that seems unwelcome.

GALT: Not to me, Maud. That night at the opera gave me a whole new understanding of politics, and my place in it.

MAUD: Yes, I can talk politics with you, I think. Tell me this: you broke with your party, but never went over to the opposition. Why?

GALT: I discovered a thing greater than party allegiance—national allegiance.

"Tell me about your companion, Senator."

"Rain? We found him—Max Harrington and I—on Tangier Island, in the Chesapeake, his leg broken in a fall off the mast of his father's fishing boat. The leg had been improperly set, so he was useless to the drunken father—who had farmed him out."

"In the area?"

"No, in D.C.—as an . . . escort. Pernicious, Maud."

(Augustine on children and sex: "Their members are innocent, but not their wills." A modern on the same subject: "Children place an abstract constraint on what single nouns might mean and implicitly reject hypotheses about category membership as a result of having learned a label for the object.")

"Tangier Island is a wicked place, Maud."

"Very like its namesake. Tangier," Maud said.

("I thoroughly dislike Pound," O'Maurigan said, "but one can't help remembering him in this connection:

but in Tangier I saw from dead straw ignition
   From a snake bite
  fire came to the straw
  from the fakir blowing
  foul straw and an arm-long snake
  that bit the tongue of the fakir making small holes
   and from the blood of the holes
    came fire when he stuffed the straw into his mouth
dirty straw that he took from the roadway
     first smoke and then the dull flame . . .
  elemental he thought the souls of the children."

Maybe not. I remembered "Tangerine"—on the radio in *Double Indemnity*.)

Galt seemed shocked that Maud knew about such things, but she reminded him in that no-nonsense midwestern way that she was a diplomatic widow and had seen much of the world.

"I never have understood State's doings, Maud."

("I think," Odette said later, "that all along in this he had been in another world—and I don't mean abducted, at least not in any vulgar sense. I think he'd been living in a circular world, like the Shoshone. And of course, he and Rain never had anything you could call sex."

"No?"

"Absolutely. He's as chaste as Walt Whitman, I'd stake my reputation on it. It's funny how people think the only thing to unveil is fornication, whereas the seventh veil is, as Wilde knew of Salome, the veil of chastity."

"He fucked not, neither with the one sex, nor the other, nor the other?" "No." "He danced with wolves?" "Does anybody really believe in drivel like *Dances with Wolves*?" Odette complained. "*Dances with Wolves*," O'M said, "was the story of Delancey's life before he met Phil." "No, they really believe in *The Searchers*.")

Anyway, Galt took Rain away from Tangier and taught him to read the Bible; but once in a blue moon, he would have an episode.

"And go dancing naked on tabletops at the Chesapeake House," Maud offered.

"Oh, so you know about that, too."

"A woman in my position comes to hear a lot, Senator."

"There are women who have the power to remake whatever corner of the world they occupy to suit themselves; you are one. I do wish you'd call me Jack, Maud. Yes, a terrible place, Tangier. The whole island seems to be covered with graveyards, and the boy's father was of that penal-colony mentality found along the seaboard—fatalistic, opportunistic, disdainful of introspection, contemptuous of those they call do-gooders and God-botherers. He spoke a strange English. He used to beat Rain and his twin black and blue."

"Twin?"

"Yes, there was one. The boys had not keel nor rudder, Maud—I've tried to give the one boy something of both—something to steer the current with."

I heard Odette murmur, *"against the swift current of the Potomac"*—and then out loud: "And what became of him—the twin?"

"He disappeared—after the discovery, in the middle of all this that I've been telling you—off the Eastern Shore—of—something."

"Something," Odette rejoined, "that had been a man?"

"Yes—a disemboweled, throat-slit body with no teeth in the head nobody went to great lengths to identify."

(Rain, rudderless, had fallen ill with what they thought was meningitis. When he awoke in Walter Reed Hospital, talking about a past life in the Old West, the doctors seemed actually relieved.)

"I managed finally to get him as a page and put him into the Capitol Page School."

"Where he got into trouble, didn't he, Jack."

Galt eyed the statue of the Prodigal Son.

"You know, Maud, they called him a *prostitute* for the House of Representatives! I had never been so shocked in all my years—I just *know* he was hypnotized—and, well, you may remember the revelations surrounding the congressman from Maryland."

"And the rumors of the senator from Oklahoma."

"That is the Senate; I cannot discuss it." There was a long silence; and then, in a somewhat changed voice, the senator declared, "You know, Maud, there is a profound wisdom in the Old Testament prohibition against casting eyes on the uncovered loins of one's father. In this case the breaking of it led to unspeakable consequences. Well, I managed then to get him into St. Albans, with a little pull from the Gores, where he tested very high in IQ, and on weekends he went to the Library of Congress and learned Shoshone. Then he started at Georgetown, but—"

"Disappeared at the Christmas break, and was recovered in New York."

(Good old Sally Tomato, I thought at once.)

"I myself went up to bring him back. They'd found him on Forty-second Street and Eighth Avenue, recruiting for Covenant House."

("They put him in St. Elizabeth's," Odette testified, "which he returns to whenever he spins off; it's where he was in January. Some think he should be sent someplace more sophisticated, and some say he should be gotten rid of altogether.")

"And so, despite his work with me, you see, because of his past he can never run for office. He's been a great help to me, Maud; taught me the difference between dominion and stewardship."

(As we were looking down—here I was again peering out of schoolroom windows—Rain, fiddling with a mechanism, snorted, "That's *funny*. In Italy they had a prostitute in their parliament—prostitutes are a *constituency*. Anyway, who in his right mind would run for office? That isn't stewardship, it's *stupidship*.")

Galt then showed Maud a snapshot of Rain, his twin, and their father on the boat. ("I gasped. He's a dead ringer, dear, for Fred Halsted." *"Fred Halsted?"* "That's what I said, bub.")

"I have no reason," Galt suddenly blurted out, "to suppose that he who would take away my liberty—"

Maud interrupted him, singing, "'Perfect submission, perfect delight.'" Galt was surprised, and chastened.

"I'm an old coot, Maud."

"Nonsense, Jack."

"Black Jack. Yes, an old coot. The joke on the Hill is that I'm an arid canyon country parcel protected by the provisions of the Antiquities Act of 1906. 'Historic landmarks, historic and prehistoric structures, and other objects of historic or scientific interest that are situated upon the lands owned or controlled by the Government of the United States.' Others find the Wilderness Act responsible for my preservation. The plain fact is that at my age sex is a question entirely of gender—you understand that."

"Yes, Jack, I do."

"You're a white woman, Maud—white all the way through."

(May you live long to think so, Jack, I said to myself, but she's a white woman with a difference—as Barb V. quipped, "She's a guy who's been abroad in the world"—and one to boot who's sung the blues, won the Purple Heart, danced the Black Swan, and played both the Red Queen and the Green Hornet.)

"Not that I'm against sex, like some of the pro-lifers. Pro-life and against sex; makes no sense, does it? It's like these people who think brush fires ought to be put out, when it's the heat from them that makes the very seeds germinate."

"Black Jack seems odd. How did you come by that name?"

"Named after General Pershing. Then as a boy I used to

be very tanned—always out in the desert. But now I don't dare
the sun. I'm just an old white man with old white hair—just
another white-handed, starched-white-collar, white-handker-
chief monument in D.C."

"Nonsense, Jack. You are just hovering over the prime of
years, which in a man like yourself is the sweetest—and to a
mature woman by far the most attractive of manly life."

"Prime of years? No, Maud, I'm an old coot. An old shy
coot."

"In reserve and not in revelation do men build imposing
character."

"Thank you, Maud, for that sentiment. You are a true
woman."

But what really got him, it seemed, was that he was naive
for so long about what Advise and Consent really is. Max is
right to say that time and again idealists come into the Senate
deluded by Jeffersonian romance, when the truth of American
democracy was irrevocably turned 180 degrees by Andrew
Jackson and has sailed that way ever since. In a true democracy
money is the *only* reliable sign of practical ability and hence of
merit. Anything else is an aristocratic, theocratic, or otherwise
totalitarian ideal. If he were ever to run for the White House,
he thinks, it would be a McKinley-type campaign. Maud
would be First Lady and he would get the Hope Diamond for
her to wear. This was so far out, Odette told us—the image of
her as Dolley Madison, Eleanor Roosevelt, and Bella Darvi in
The Egyptian all in one—she *had* to listen as they walked up and
down the aisle of the National Cathedral.

"Which must," I offered, "have been in itself strange for
you—after Chartres."

"Yes, it is, of course, if not the very antithesis of Chartres,
then certainly its *slant*-ithesis. As the D.C. Metro is to the
Parisian rapid transit system—and the spiritual transit it pro-
vides is indeed rapid. Only so very lacking in destination.

"But you know, all that clean Indiana sandstone made Maud feel secure, the way a sable coat does a decent woman as she views with satisfaction the Bouguereau 'Pieta' or Edith Galt Wilson's tomb."

The Delancey Retort. Maud on a new tear, inveighing against the ornamental cabbages, the bane of public planting in Washington. The whole D.C. melos is a dialogue between them and the magnolias—the delicacy of the one and the utter vulgarity of the other.

"I ask you to imagine the Capitol dome as an ornamental cabbage!"

The Freshmen decamp and build their own Treehouse of Representatives, to which they retreat.

At one point the Archetype of the Capitol hears the Republican freshmen have been off at an *advance* (not retreat) being lectured to by the CEO of Scott Paper, who tells them Clinton is a jerk, the Senate is yesterday, etc. Delmarva cuts in with: "Appropriate that crowd should pay somebody who makes something you wipe your ass with to counsel them for dirtying their freshman diapers."

Aristophanic choruses of Frogs (from the Neptune Fountain and the lily ponds of Georgetown and all the swamps of the South). Birds from Audubon and Clouds from the National Weather Channel.

"Remember when the enviro-freaks thought we were all *disappearing*? We were all on our way to Washington!"

Sally Tomato flirts with Maud MacGown.

MAUD: Sorry, Senator, but there are certain shades of lime-light—

Zorro says that this Congress thought it was going to run circles around POTUS, but a rooster knows all about the power of the sun, and he begins to quote from Richard Feynman's lecture proving from high-school geometry that the planets orbiting the sun *must* do so in elliptical paths.

CLOTHO: The freshmen in Congress won't know that; geometry is a *sophomore* course.

DAME WORLD (to the Archetype, reading the *Washington Post*): You see, dear, it says so right there, talk shows are *out* and *game shows* are in.

THE ARCHETYPE: What shall we play?

DAME WORLD: Bridge.

THE ARCHETYPE: No, canasta.

DAME WORLD (witheringly): *Canasta?* Why not *hearts?*

THE ARCHETYPE (timidly): Monopoly?

They sit down to a board game of Washington, D.C. Suddenly, the Three Fates rush in with computers, which they begin setting up.

CLOTHO: No, no, no, *no*.

LACHESIS: *All* games these days are *computer games*. Boot *up!*

DAME WORLD: Oh, dear.

ATROPOS: It's the wave of the future.

THE ARCHETYPE: We don't hold with the future.

CLOTHO: No matter. In the future no opinion, only info.

LACHESIS: We are in a formative period of challenge in which the form is as yet unformed.

Enter Game Czar Al Pachinko. He outlines his scheme. *"The campaign effectively begins this week."*

"High Noon." Enormous clock and a wide-open Pennsylvania Avenue. At one end Blob Dull and at the other Billy the Kid Glove ("No Glove, No Love") Flintlock (dressed like Jefferson), who start walking toward one another slowly. Billy, stepping out to see to the business of state, replaced in the showdown by M2E2 (Medicaid/Medicare/Education/Environment), the issues robot.

THE PROPHET TESS: M2E2, star of the thirty-second short, will trump the character issue, rout the Republican Revolution, defend the ramparts of federal government, and win out over Soccer Mom.

BLOB DULL: I will go to San Quentin! I will go to Richard Nixon's grave!

NEWT (hisses): While you're there you might as well jump in with him. (He hisses again.) They have conspired together and used up their faculties in base and dirty tricks to thwart my progress in life! They are all turncoats! The Treaty of Ghent was a capitulation! We will not capitulate! We won that war fair and square in the Battle of Lake Erie. The Rush-Bagot Agreement was a sellout. We'll *never* sell out!

POTUS enters (sound cue: "Hail to the Chief").

Newt salutes. "Mr. President."

"Newt, it's gonna be you and me, in this thing together."

"It's destiny—it's kismet!"

"Nope—just dumb coincidence."

"*Golly!*" (The Newt, in tears, takes off the uniform and the Wellington hat.)

Enter Mammon, in her car driven by Life Stylist Plush DeLuxe.

PLUSH: I'm Plush DeLuxe. I drive this little baby.

Mammon addresses her constituency of campaign contributors (dozens and dozens all coming out from under the car). The Senator Galt mask upbraids her: "'Against whom do you make a wide mouth and a lolling tongue, O children of harlots!'—Isaiah."

Figures keep pouring out of the car. On TV monitor: montage of all the D.C. marches since 1963: peace, women, ACT-UP, American Legion and Vietnam vets, the Million Man March.

Cut to: Blob Dull and the Newt, both in their underwear, at a window overlooking the Mall.

BD: Have you faced the fact you're through?

NEWT: No, I don't believe in it.

Meanwhile, apropos girl nemeses, as I wrote Phil, "Odette has reached the status of Pandora—or of Gaby Rodgers in *Kiss Me Deadly*, who opened the Doomsday box as Ralph Meeker, with a belly full of lead, staggered helplessly into the Pacific in the embrace of a frantic brunette.

"Here's the breakdown—and it's the right word, all right. Call it the Column the *Star* Will Never Get.

"Galt, after the Memorial Day recess, proposed—a little trip to the West in his private railway car and there a 'secret' marriage. Odette started driving us crazy by *considering it*, allowing she liked the idea of a settled life in Virginia, and the odd Washington gala.

"The Fauquier, in panic, attacked Maud on two fronts. First he went to DACOR (Diplomatic and Consular Officers Retired) to check out Maud's dossier, finding it largely appropriated from records of some Lindstrom (from Minnesota). Secondly he obtained a print of *Wigstock* with a frame enlargement of Odette with the Lady Bunny, RuPaul, and Hedda Lettuce captioned, '"It's a common astrological event," declares veteran drag supernova Odette O'Doyle, "for three celestial bodies to be aligned in such a way that the body passing between the other two obscures the line of sight between them. An alignment of four prevents any such mishap—and is so much nicer, too, for a game of canasta. No, we never play bridge. How could we—*who* would ever agree to be dummy?"'

"On July 2, a massive power blackout in the West caused the BART to stop in San Francisco and all the casinos in Las Vegas to go dark. Tension mounted.

"On the night of the third, Dick Fauquier played the Watergate tape. Galt became completely unhinged, believing not that he'd been deceived all along, but that 'his' Maud had been murdered and this imposter sent to deceive him into revealing state secrets."

And so it came about that, distraught over the evil of men,

plagued by the idea that government had stopped working and the corporations edged further toward domination, advised by the *Washington Post* astrologer that the "blue moon" of June had indeed signaled betrayal, and, according to some reports, weakened by visions of the Tribulation brought on by compulsive Christian fasting at Easter—although others maintained it was a bad dose of jimson weed, administered in a fit of jealous rage by little agate-eyed, hophead familiar, he finally lost it.

As I wrote Phil: "It's now the 4th of July. Everybody is due to go out on the river with the Harringtons, but the O' and I have opted instead to spend it with Blaine and Eliot Marshall—you remember, Prince Albert's schoolfellow—at their place up in the lush wooded precincts of Upper Northwest, near the National Cathedral."

Phone call from Odette. "Position yourself, dear heart, for a set piece."

(And govern yourself accordingly.)

"Yes?"

"Yes. Come again, alone this time, to the garden of the National Cathedral. I can't tell you more—but come . . . on foot."

(What could she mean? The ascent to Gethsemane? How else arrive—in a goddamn *helicopter*, like W. C. Fields in *International House*?)

Herewith a synopsis. (As one of O'Maurigan's Dublin friends put it, "I have no time now, dear, to go into the whole syllabus—we'll be incommunicado in the morning—but here's the gist.")

The Retro-cognition Scene.

I arrived in the garden to find Odette with Galt and Fauquier, in the recess right by the statue of the Prodigal Son. Hovering in the background (not even decently out of sight), the Secret Service and Rain. Odette is in men's attire—Bill Blass—but from the neck up is still Maud MacGown.

GALT: What does this mean, Maud—coming here to this place dressed as a man?

MAUD: It means, Jack, that I am a transvestite.

"Like George Sand," cracked Fauquier.

"Who?"

"A French writer, Jack" (Odette). "Lover of Frédéric Chopin. You liked Chopin's music when I played it to you. Of course that is a European answer; I think you would prefer an American one."

He seemed to soften. "You like to dress as a man sometimes . . . I can understand that."

"No, Jack, I am *compelled* to dress as a man—most of the time . . . and more each day."

Galt asked Fauquier to show Maud the pictures. "Who is this person, Maud?" "That, Jack, is Odette O'Doyle, whose real name is Daniel—one of your favorite biblical personages. He is my twin brother. Transvestism tends to run in families, you see."

(As Garbo once said of mixed nuts, That's enough retrocognition.)

Galt, Fauquier, Rain, and the Secret Service left at once for Union Station (from where next day Galt and Maud were to have departed together for the western hideaway).

As O'Maurigan and I reached the Marshalls', CNN had just picked up the Galt entourage in the lobby of Union Station, making for the Special, but swamped by the audience coming out of *Independence Day*. The senator addressed them.

Telling them for openers that the picture they'd just come out from seeing was *not* fiction. (Meanwhile, Odette, wigless by now, had come back from the bathroom in an authentic one-piece twenties-mode men's Jantzen swimsuit— the last-ever vestiges of Maud MacGown flushed down the toilet—and dived into the pool, while the rest of us stayed glued to the box.)

As I wrote Phil, "By now Galt's got up a full head of steam

and is ranting, declaring corporations are hoarding the helium reserves for the coming War in Deep Space." (He seemed to have split in half—into Isaiah on the one hand and on the other into St. Paul talking about men becoming eunuchs for the Kingdom of God.)

About to board that Senate Pullman, he stopped and turned full into the cameras. In pretty execrable French, he started reciting.

"Adieu Sagesse . . . Vacances . . . Que sais-je? . . . Divine Folie . . ."

Midway through the litany, he disappeared into the carriage, leaving Rain behind, looking very much the captive, with the SS.

Odette, toweling off while noshing a little barbecue, made a phone call, then asked Eliot to drive her to a launch a little upriver. They departed—and an hour or so later, Eliot returned, reporting Odette picked up by an older gentleman with a certain military bearing.

I hadn't the slightest idea where she'd gone, nor did anybody else, but Odette is a cat who's landed on his feet more times than Deuteronomy could list, and I went home confident it wouldn't be all that long before I'd know . . . the more if not the rest.

TEN / ESCAPADE

Washington was abuzz—Maud MacGown had disappeared from the Watergate, leaving not so much as a hairpin behind. Then Vana called.

"Where have you been?" I inquired. "You've missed . . . things."

"I have been in Santa Fe, darling, investigating the new composers. I heard this *Evangeline*—musical *porcherria*, *caro*, but the libretto was divine! It is, I believe, an American classic?"

"Yes, reworked by a friend of O'Maurigan's."

"Well, *caro*, it was a *divine* story—and this *favolosa* young soprano in the name part! I tell you, I had to watch my—what do you call them?"

"P's and Q's."

"Yes, especially around the stage director—an Italian-American. By the way, *caro*, how is Filippo getting on back home?"

"He's decided that back home is Sagaponack."

"Of course. In any case, this *Evangeline* was a *scream*, musically. I am listening and suddenly I am hearing *Fanciulla*, and I whisper this to my companion, but he corrects me. 'That's not

Fanciulla, that's *Phantom of the Opera*. Lloyd Webber stole it from Puccini, and this is stolen from *that*. Really— these careerist Americans are an *open scandal*.' Well, I don't mind careerist Americans; Bernstein stole from everybody —Wagner, Strauss, Puccini, everybody—but this one *goes nowhere* with his contraband. Vocal lines that are nothing more than chromatic *scales*! Also, *caro*, I felt very badly for the Hispanics in Santa Fe—which is in any case a lesbian nightmare."

No sooner had the Revenant hung up when the Fugitive called.

"Where are you?"

"Spending a little time in Montgomery—hunt country— with an old army buddy."

"Not at the Gone Away Farm?"

"Not far from it. I first considered the Aged Women's Home on Wisconsin Avenue—Georgetown is the place to go, speaking of gone away, if you *don't* want to be looked for—but it turns out there is a required *inspection for drug paraphernalia*, and, well, Mother's set of works might just give them a turn they weren't looking for."

"I don't believe a word you're saying."

"Washington has made you very cynical. It's restful here—the air is spiked with dung and heavy perfume, the unmistakable scents of big money—and the people are *colorful*. All the women carry guns in their purses. I was offered one— pretended I wouldn't know how to use it anymore. On the other side of sensibility, some placid lunatic down the road is keeping tabs on a *seven-foot celery plant*. I mean, *really*—that such a thing should be *allowed*, much less brought up in *conversation*! I suppose it's what they mean by Southern Gothic; I'll never get used to it."

(Maryland, Southern Gothic? Well . . .)

Outside the window on D Street the magnolia was out of blooms; the stubs looked like artichoke hearts ("Remind me to tell you about the time . . ."). A crazy little tufted titmouse—a cartoon bird with a yellow crew-cut—was popping in and out of the branches. I began to feel the exhaustion, and finally the *aura*, from my childhood—when the blinds would come off the walls in a weird dance and there'd be voices in my head—of what they thought might be the onset of epilepsy. I was warned at that time not to overexert myself, a message that took, I nearly forgot the threat of the falling sickness, which it now turns out that drinking the way I did in later years may actually have *prevented*. So, on that glaringly hot day, the lens of my attention was pointed not at the keyhole, but straight into the sun, so that until the sun went down, the lens was spotted with light—it made me almost scream out the window in answer to the crows' "I want to go *home!*" Instead I called Gennaio, my aged and beloved analyst.

Gennaio credited the magnolias. Unlike Proust's outright worship of the hawthorn, my reaction to the magnolia was one of erotic mania followed by dread and collapse. In memory it had come to me that when I first returned from the magnolia-scented D.C. of the fifties (the Capitol Page School), seduced Rick at Lincoln Hall, and all the glory and all the troubles began, there was a saucer magnolia—like the ones in City Hall Park, the small variety, with purple and white cuplike blooms and the smell of vanilla—outside the infirmary window.

Regatta day dawned, August 10. A propitious day, according to Vana's numerologist. Day-month value (10 × 8) 8, the number of infinity; and day-month-year value when added (10 + 8 + 7) 7 and when multiplied (10 × 8 × 7) 11, the two luckiest numbers you can have.

Max had rented the *Spirit of Washington* Potomac cruise boat for the day, arranging for it to be tied up and hung with banners, which was kicky, but because Kay Shouse had gotten all the planes coming into National Airport redirected away from Wolf Trap for the summer, there were more than ever over Georgetown and the Potomac, and so "Venice" seemed to me more and more like Rockaway (Broad Channel–Howard Beach in the middle). Odette (checked into the Mayflower for two nights) wished it were more like the "Great South Gay" of the immense drag-queen regattas of the 1950s out to Cherry Grove that were all year in preparation, and for which the Long Island Mafia paid the Patchogue and Sayville police extra for protection against the mainly Irish thugs then newly moved out to suburbia.

I rose on that morning of Saturday, August 10, with the eerie foreknowledge that it was to be my last day in D.C. (I thought of it as a "symbolic" feeling, but found out otherwise.) My view of work done was that I'd succeeded in doing a set of story boards, not in making a moving picture. ("A faceless, arcane job, performed only on the run and always in the shadow of that media carnival, modern presidential politics.") I looked out the window and saw my story *written on the window-pane* by the accursed Hope Diamond.

I met the *Washington Post*'s crack Weekend reporter Kevin McManus—connoisseur of "singular events"—in front of the Watergate. Two Venetian facades had been erected on the esplanade: the Doge's Palace and, slightly upriver, in front of the boat club, St. Mark's Basilica—and between them the Bell Tower (not condomed).

"This disguise is entirely appropriate," one old mandarin in a summer seersucker suit and white shoes observed, as McManus interviewed him. "We must reject mall culture entirely—whether the mall is in Columbia, Maryland, or in Sherman Oaks, California—and that includes ultimately the Kennedy Center, Lincoln Center, Las Vegas . . . all of it *climate controlled*. Air conditioning has made every building in Washington sick—and in my opinion the *entire* population of Crystal City is psychotic. The only place to do business anymore is outdoors. Nothing of value can be purveyed in a climate-controlled environment. It is only—as in the original Rialto, in

Venice—in an environment subject to extremes of temperature, of precipitation, crowding, flooding, et cetera, that the
exchange of goods and services can be effected."

Lunch upriver in Potomac at a Venetian mansion Vana
had scouted for the RAI television crew (all flash lines on
comic smiles and people sitting around on rock formations
that looked like Central Park), followed by the regatta, in
which the Washington crew clubs' sculls and skiffs were
trimmed to look like gondolas (a few of the genuine articles
had been laid on as well) and the gondoliers were all fitted out
in straw hats with red, white, and blue ribbons running down
their backs.

Most of the D.C. drag queens were all het up over the
opening of *Stonewall* the day before, but a few had been to
Wolf Trap to see *The Passion of Joan of Arc* and were all agog
over Falconetti, who seems to have been a woman impersonat-
ing a man playing a woman. For me, at Wolf Trap with Vana (a
social obligation; the Wolf Trap crowd had promised to show
for the regatta), the screening turned out to be my penultimate
D.C. social outing.

At lunch, Ornette, sitting at the piano out on the terrace,
sang "Lazy Afternoon," attracting Vana's attention and making
me remember. "Don't you worry, boss," he whispered to me. "I
ain't plannin' no *reprise* of that chilly scene of winter—*no* way.
I have abandoned the crow's caw, and have been rehearsin' the
sweet and pretty warble of the *nightingale* . . . just so you
know."

Dick Fauquier was barking comments on the campaign in
relation to the regatta.

"They *should* be like a chariot race in ancient Rome or a
drag race or at least bumper cars—but this one is exactly mirrored in the regatta: gondolas bobbing up and down in the
water and people thumbing their noses at one another from
behind fans and masks."

"I've just heard," a voice called across the terrace, "of the most absolutely *divine* plan for renovating Washington. Each state *adopts* the *avenue* it's named after—or vice versa, you know—and remodels it in the *image of its own capital city in its own chosen period.* Just *think* of it. For instance, New York gets to put in the new subway on New York Avenue as a New York *subway*—you know, with *graffiti* and homeless people singing off-key and begging!"

"There are at least two things wrong with that," Fauquier snarled. "There is no more graffiti on the New York subway, and New York is not the state capital—Albany is. Do you *really* think New York Avenue ought to look like the Albany Mall?" He got up, came over to the piano, and stood over me.

"You must get out of Washington—you must."

"Why?"

"They're talking about getting you to *stay.*"

"I don't think so."

"Oh, yes they are, but you *mustn't listen* to them. You know, I came here like you did—although my case was different. I was one of those Southern boys who thought *this* was the *big city.* But I came to do good—and did *not* stay to do well, though I'll never go begging . . . but then I'll never go anywhere. And I don't after all this time know what it's all *for.* Oh, public service, advancement—but *it doesn't work.* Washington doesn't *work.*"

The Venetian Carnival had started off in two directions—from Mount Pleasant on Sixteenth Street and from Christ Church, Georgetown, converging at Foggy Bottom to proceed to the Mall and the Sylvan Theater on the grounds of the Washington Monument, where a Venetian puppet show was to be enacted. Washington's black-drag-queen elite, beaching from a second regatta—down the Anacostia from the Arboretum—showed particular interest in Harlequin's black mask while taking seats and commenting like church picnic goers on the weather.

"It ain't no clouds in the sky!"

Later the clouds drifted in—enormous cumuluses, creating the desired Tiepolo-Venetian effect—and that night, under a waning moon with the man in it making a moue, the drag queens were to come into glory in their Thomasina Williams originals and fantastic Venetian masks. (Delmarva came in a little black dress, a Dorothy Dean mask, and carrying a golliwog doll.)

"The masks," wrote the *Washington Post* correspondent, "were a great relief. By early August social Washington is sick to death of looking at its hydra-headed self, faces lasered into ageless, orthodonted rictus. Covering all that in clown face did the trick to relax people. And so they talked . . . and talked . . . and talked, of matters of state."

We left the lunch and sped down the Potomac in a Chris Craft to check the regatta. Passing the Kennedy Center, making for the Tidal Basin, I looked toward the Washington Monument, realized I'd never been up, and decided, as a farewell gesture, to make the ascent.

Docked at Waterside, I walked to the monument and took my second ride to the top on the Ferris wheel. There at the top, looking southeast through the telescope at one of the rooftop fleshpots at Half Street: all naked sunbathers in sexual frolic. (Interesting contrast to the puppet show, I thought. How many of them will be under masks later at the LC?)

Musing on the circularity of the Washington Merry-Go-Round, the radial energy going in spirals as opposed to the grid energy of NYC, and computer chips, I copped a vision of the Last Judgment (not Blake's or Revelation's or the senator's, but Michelangelo's, which I've not been to see since the Japanese cleaned it up). Clockwise motion like a clothes dryer. Scanning further, I zoomed in on my building.

Focusing in on the bay window, I saw Sylvester sitting in it with a crazed expression. Then he jumped out of the window and into the sycamore—and into the window frame came

Rain, who climbed out after him. Sylvester jumped over to the magnolia and hid his head behind a blossom. Then Rain reached into a "hiding place" in the sycamore and left something there.

I descended and took a cab to the apartment. As I got there I saw my neighbor John carrying two enormous white feather wings—for the LC party that night. I asked had he noticed another second-story man around, but it turned out Rain had come up the back way, from an alley off North Carolina Avenue.

I entered the apartment. Rain was there among all the boxes and packing crates for the move back to Sagaponack, having broken in easily, and was playing with the snow-scene paperweight the O' had given me as a souvenir of the Winter of Discontent.

"Your cat's mad at me; I saved a crazy-looking little bird from his clutches."

"That's the tufted titmouse. He's bold."

"He's crazy. He's an endangered species of one around that cat. He doesn't like my eyes either—the cat; they're too much like his, I think."

"What did you put into the sycamore tree?"

"*What*?"

"I saw you put something in the sycamore."

"Saw me do what?"

"From the top of the Washington Monument."

"You're going crazy, like the senator did. Did you pack your *Sandman* comic? The series has been decoded by the anticonspiratorialists and is being discontinued—it'll be a collector's item: something to show your grandchildren, in case you should ever adopt some."

I called out to Sylvester to come in from the tree. He retraced his way through the sycamore and entered through the window panel, hissing. I picked him up and tried to put him in his carrier, but he scooted under the bed. I started packing up my discs.

"Look," Rain said, "there's a train coming over the bridge from Virginia—with a shipment on it from Fort Riley, Kansas, of sarin. Do you know what sarin is?"

(Not Nabokov's pseudonym.) "I've heard of it."

"Unless I stop that train, both POTUS and your buddy—meeting together this afternoon in the Oval Office—are *toast*, and Gingrich will be President by tonight. Do you want that?"

(Patsy said, "Oh, that's not nearly good enough—what he should have told you was that the meeting at the White House was Clinton, Gore, *and* Gingrich. But who comes then? I forget."

"Strom Thurmond," O'Maurigan announced.

"Far out.")

Rain confessed to unintended complicity in the sarin plot—saying first he was enraged over Maud MacGown, then that he was under the threat of death from the Conspiracy, and that now after certain deaths—Casey, Boorda, David Schine—he was being closely watched. Claimed to know the whole story. "These guys are not interested in flying body parts—they are interested in having the guts melting out of their victims as they sit in the Oval Office."

Galt had been drugged and hypnotized. Fort Riley, Kansas, the center of the Conspiracy, was, handily, right on the route the train (with the senator's parlor car as caboose) took from the Far West (as was the place in Arkansas—Fort Mena—which had been the launching place of the missile that nearly downed Air Force One).

"Fort Mena, Fort Riley, Junction City, Geary Lake—*Harrington*, Kansas. Do you understand what these locations *mean*?"

"Should I?"

"Only if you're alive."

The plan: to detach the senator's car from the train at the

bridge over the Potomac, so that the train, rolling into the tunnel near the Smithsonian, would stall; hijackers would then release sarin into the tunnel that runs under the Mall to the White House.

("Not exactly fail-safe," Patsy announced, poking holes in doodled balloons. "Grace Slick's plan for Nixon was, when you look back on it, much more likely to come off.")

"Mid-Atlantic military installations," he was saying, "particularly those at Fort Detrick, Maryland, and Camp Lejeune, North Carolina, have special chem-bio response capabilities—"

(Did the marine barracks on Eighth Street as well?)

"—but the legal concerns of how to command the troops in a domestic incident still haven't been decided."

(Nonsense, I thought, crazily, all decent Americans want to atone: you only have to give them the opportunity.)

At that very moment a whistle sounded. Rain declared the next train the one.

"I think you'd better be on your way," I said. (As I imagined Rain shimmying up the bridge to stop the train, I remembered Barb Vesteralen: "*Climber? That little Injun could shimmy up the greased walls of a canyon!*")

(Flashing forward, when I caught up with Ornette at the LC ball, I quizzed him.

"You were out there in the regatta—what did you see?"

"The following. Two bodies—live ones—drop off the railway bridge into the Potomac only a few feet from one of the gondolas—almost immediately retrieved by a patrol boat, which cut across the wake of the *Potomac Star* on its way to the bird sanctuary. The backwash I thought would capsize the small craft, but as in Venice they held the water."

So, it seems two men really did jump into the Potomac and a boat did pick them up. That's all, folks—except that, as O'M pointed out later, that town in Kansas is called *Herington*, not Harrington.)

As the sun declined in the west and the spots cleared from

my lens, things got under way in the Great Hall of the Thomas Jefferson Building of the LC, air perfumed with Laura Biagiotti's Venezia. ("A bit oppressive, no?" a voice declared. Better, I thought, than sarin.)

A gibbous moon in and out of an overcast sky. The fireflies in evidence all over Capitol Hill: ideal emblems of gossip and also an indication of the progress of the environmental lobby—signaling to me: Go home.

A late bulletin (relayed over cellular phones, carried, it seemed, by everybody present). Senator Galt, approaching D.C. in his private railway car, had demanded an urgent meeting with POTUS.

"Interesting turn of events," one State Department mandarin remarked. "Did you catch the old bastard's turn on C-Span?"

"No," I replied, truthfully.

"That afternoon, delivered from the rear platform of the Senate Pullman. I understood how people must have felt at Vezeley, in Burgundy, on Palm Sunday 1146, when Bernard of Clairvaux preached the Second Crusade—although the king of France was at Vezeley, whereas I don't think Clinton was tempted to scoot down to Catlettsburg. Thank God, however, crusades are *out*—Desert Storm was iffy enough. Why, do you know what those boys and girls got *up to* out there? Gulf War S-I-N-drome is no *fiction*."

The orchestra was playing excerpts from *Le notte veneziani*, bringing me full circle from Jones Beach and *A Night in Venice*—I'd gone out from Far Rockaway with the graduating class—forty-odd years before. The audience in black tie and gowns reminded me again of the cartoon gallery at Kalorama with the Whigs—whatever the Whigs really were.

As I wrote Phil:

You'd have been proud of Odette's spectacular re-entry, as herself, into high society: in black mask in that backless

white silk with embroidered black carnations number that
Dior made and named for her in '53 to wear to the Ars et
Métiers ball. And Vana's gown—a silk damascene map of
eighteenth-century Venice with a deliberately scorched-in
hole where the Fenice ought to have been—and a pair of
red pumps she persisted in calling ruby slippers. The O'
declared, "As if nobody would know what red shoes meant
in Venice."

And of course she'd ordered a fireworks display on
Pennsylvania Avenue, to be viewed by the guests from the
top floor windows—the Capitol Page School, where Rain
had started his career. It was, remember, La Notte di San
Lorenzo. Also a "reception line" of life-size cardboard effi-
gies of all the Presidents and First Ladies. (Barb and Doug
had their pictures taken with the Fillmores.) And then, at
around ten o'clock, her tambourine dance, in which she
passed the basket, accepting nothing but the new Ben
Franklins. (She'd asked O'Maurigan, "You do not find it
vulgar?" "I think, Vana, adapting somewhat the words
uttered by Daniel Webster about John Jay, our first Chief
Justice, that when the ermine falls across your very shoulders, as oft it has, it touches nothing less spotless than
itself." "You are too kind. Yes, I must begin to do things for
Washington, if I am to return in triumph as Jackie. I must
not let that awful Bina Sella di Monteluce in London—how
do you say it—steal all my thunderbolts?" "Something like
that." "*Sì*—but of course thunderbolts are for Jupiter, *non è
vero?* I must not let her steal my—what?" "Why don't we
call them 'routines'?" Odette proposed. "*Ben detto, cara—
my routines!*")

Talk . . . talk . . . talk . . . talk. A couple of hundred dialogue balloons attached to pointing fingers. The strangest
thing in the whole evening was that since people here are forever quoting one another in desperate hopes of keeping in the

swim, seldom can you tell who's saying what without actually taking particular note of the face, and with everybody in masks, the true condition of social discourse became paradoxically more apparent. Some voices and manners—like Max Harrington's—were unmistakable; the rest . . .

"Some time early in the last century," Max was saying, "during Melville's lifetime, Winslow Homer's, and simultaneous to the invention of steam power, the ship of state began to be run by the new power professionals. But being new, and sentimental, the Republic, loath to forgo its symbols—I won't belabor the point, which is terribly simple. The American ship of state, manned to the last jibsail by these actors testing the wind of popular opinion and directing the course of human events, is of course *run* on *steam*, on a fairly straight course and a relatively even keel. But the men in the *engine room*, who spend their lives *regulating* the *steam*, don't get elected—they wouldn't know how—and don't pretend to stand for anything. Literally: they *will not stand for* such shenanigans. So the actor-sailors don't, by and large, indulge in them. When I read something like, 'The key to the American Progressive tradition has been the view that government's highest purpose is to strengthen the capacities of individuals to achieve self-reliance and to nurture the country's rich networks of civic institutions that are independent of both the state and the marketplace,' I just fall down on the floor and laugh. When I get up, I go to work *regulating* the *steam*."

"Or the helium reserves," I submitted.

"Well, I *do* take the long view. This whole cycle—and this election is eleventh in the cycle and the end of it—started in '52. Eisenhower *had* to run, and win: a victorious general in what had quite obviously become the world-imperial office—if only so that *lunatic* MacArthur didn't.

"The country *loved* MacArthur, and there weren't enough Republicans of sufficient conscience to forbear taking the

White House from Truman—*not loved* by the people in '52. Stevenson was a vain and idle character right out of Molière. The Misanthrope. And I'll tell you something else. A Nixon victory in '60 would have permitted an *honest* campaign in '64."

"The election of 1960 *was* a fraud!" the Alice Roosevelt Longworth mask declared.

"It was," Max gravely concurred, "and the arrogance of the mafiosi toward Camelot—they *always* collect, and they were owed not just by the Kennedys, but by the nation, for the invasion of Sicily. There *is*, you know, such a thing as *arete*."

"So you believe the Mafia did Dallas."

"Who do *you* think did," Alice Roosevelt Longworth crowed, "*Debbie?*"

"*Yes*," Max grinned, "the Mafia did Dallas. Johnson was relieved it wasn't Khrushchev and said, 'Well, Ah kinda liked the cocksucker—but Ah sure hate the sum'bitch brother.'

"So Nixon finally got it, but he was by then *so* nuts that the office was trashed. Whatever else you can say about *this* sum'bitch, he has revived, at least for *audition* purposes, a notion of the presidency we thought was gone forever. Course they may *kill* him for it."

More dialogue balloons drifted by—people talking through their assholes (bubble rings?) as if their assholes were lorgnettes improving their vision.

". . . And actually, it doesn't take this new book to demonstrate that the Krauts haven't a leg to stand on vis-à-vis what is still and ever shall be the central event of the twentieth century."

"I suppose that must be true, considering the fact that Dietrich gave both hers, and everything between them, to the service of the Free French."

". . . And I do not mean to align myself with the likes of that insane army of chronic litigants who flood the pro se division of the U.S. District Court for the District of Columbia with their daily grievances, filing early and often in the deluded hope that they will eventually strike gold."

"They won't kill him. He may, much like his idol, fuck bimbos, but, unlike him, he fucks ones unconnected to the mob."

"True—there hasn't been a bimbo in Arkansas connected to the mob since the days of Owney Madden."

"... The *New York Times*? I'm sorry, but I cannot take quite seriously a newspaper that does not run an astrology column."

"... And he's a lot smarter than you think. Yes, it *seems* he only says what they want to hear—the *trick* is he *lets* it seem that way. It's *reverse psychology*. The more they *think* he is saying what they want to hear, the more *anything* he says will seem to be to them—*since they don't know*—what they want to hear."

"Nobody realizes it, but Bosnia could at any moment explode again over the question of Herzegovina."

"The Europeans do not think of the Balkans as Europe. No European any longer scourges himself, smears himself with ashes, cuts out his tongue, breaks people on the wheel, or impales them—and in the Balkans they all still do."

"They do all *that* in eastern Tennessee too."

"The Balkans may yet prove important in terms of trade."

"Balkan *trade*? My dear, talk of *criteria*!"

"Really, there is no talking to these people."

"Well, *I* fail to see how either the national interest or the cause of humanity can be served by our intervening in a civil war raging like a venereal disease in the puckered bunghole of Europe! Let me tell you this—everything you need to know about the Balkans you can read in the Carnegie Endowment's *Report of the International Commission to Inquire into the Cause and Conduct of the Balkan Wars*. 'Houses and whole villages reduced to ashes, unarmed and innocent populations massacred *en masse*.' Et cetera. It was published in 1914."

"The space age turned out to be a crock of shit; the information age will too. You know what *I* call the Internet? The garbage pail of the American garbage mind! Call me Ned Lud, but mark my words, the Internet is destroying the workforce brain!"

"I recently read, 'Prolix documentation of the limits of language is a homosexual tic.' That true?"

"*Georgetown*. Real-estate flyers in 1800," I heard Dick Fauquier bawl under an Ezra Pound mask, "proclaimed, 'The elevated heights surrounding the town afford situations for gentlemen's seats.' *Gentlemen!* Lard-ass *poltroons*—then as now—to whom the placement of knives and forks at the dining table was relatively recent news. To any *Virginian*, they were *hardly* gentlemen. And in our own time? *Never* has that pretentious little *faubourg* been infested with such a variety of poorly dressed and badly behaved mortals as Georgetown in the sixties, during that pigshit Populuxe pornocracy 'Camelot,' with its 'Saturday Night on Saturn' sensibility and its lounge-lizard ethics.

"Badly behaved jacked-up civilians posing as flag ranks in mufti styled up as important agents of the world's destiny. Nothing but utterly commonplace garden-weed *grunts* of a very intense and *muddy* water. And now, today, as we speak, there are *deliberations* going on at Georgetown University at something called the Kennedy Institute of Ethics. *Kennedy* . . . *ethics!* I want to *scream*!

"And as for the election, the *only* way the Republicans can *possibly* take it, excuse me, is with a more *two-fisted* approach."

"Oh, dear."

"'Well, I *heard*,'" the Mamie Eisenhower mask declared, "they want him to go on at the convention as the Knight of the Doleful Countenance and sing 'The Impossible Dream.'"

"I wish the UFOs would land," Alice Roosevelt Longworth declared. "It would make Washington fun—which it never is unless there's a war on. Then and only then does it come into its own."

"I agree," said Ezra Pound. "And in the meantime, according to Alan Simpson, all *they* think we do is cheat and steal and whore around and feather our own nests and take care of ourselves and not them.

"*Take care of them?* You see the monster the liberals have created? *That*'s where Max Harrington is right and the CEOs are superior governors. 'Yes,' they say, 'we cheat and steal and whore around, *but so do you*, and we don't mind and we don't preach. We furnish *product.*' In the immortal words of the mayor of Indianapolis, 'You can get whatever you want on a hamburger from Wendy's, but you can't get it from government.'"

"Surely you can't get *whatever* you want," protested a female voice behind a Nancy Reagan mask.

"*You* can't, but the mayor had a point. The corporations have mastered the art of advertising to train *them* to want *only* what they can *get* on a Wendy's hamburger. The *pursuit* of happiness."

"Not happiness. But when I read a supposedly serious author like Ronald Dworkin to the effect that 'there is little evidence that citizens who take an active interest in politics could not without the blandishments of political advertising discover the statements and positions of serious candidates'— by which he says he means 'any candidate who would have any significant chance of winning if every voter knew his views in great detail'—

"What does such a statement—what does such a *pontificator* take his reader for, a fool? *No* candidate who has *any* significant chance of winning *knows his own views* himself. He can *only* know what he is going to *aver.* And that is that."

"In the very near future, events that rivet people's attention on the international stage will have become entirely regulated and predictable subject to LSD-sponsored trips of every wild kind—LSD being what I call Losers in the State Department. Talk about hallucinogenic! That is the aim: to make

New Age is what will save America—advertising a pure ecology and a renovated national psyche—so much healthier than
the reincarnated Civil War battles popular in this region."

"Excuse me, they are *not* re*incarnated;* they are purely *spectral*—nevertheless they heal. You don't even have to go to the
sites, though they are nice for picnics—which is what happened
in the actual conflict: people went out and had picnics and
watched the battles—Bull Run, for example, just a stone's
throw from D.C. And re-enactments are both so much more
exciting *and* so much more *elevating* than *politics*—all these
dreary Republicans and Democrats . . . who don't even *dress*
differently."

"Neither do Serbs and Croats. Neither, despite their
hvratski—that's alphabet—being rendered in two entirely different sets of characters, do they sound different over the
telephone."

"It isn't," the Ezra Pound mask declared, "as simple as
that. If you want to know why the Balkans make incessant war,
it's because of the *bards*—the last oral tradition in Europe.
They *depend,* as surely as Homer, on war—and of course
Homer was a multitude of careerists singing for their supper.
Only in the Alexandrian period, when epics were written *down,*
did war stop."

"Well, that *is* an ingenious explanation," the Mary Todd
Lincoln mask declared. "And it makes *Gone with the Wind*
more important than ever."

"Oh," a Columbine mask declared, "Ah jus' *adore* stories
'baht the Woah of Northrun Aggression—all those gleaming
sabers and yellow *sashes* our men wo-ah. Yellow sashes soaked in
red blood—I declare, it's enough to make you weep foah a
finah time!"

"The woman is mad, obviously," somebody whispered
after a long pause.

"The Madwoman of Shiloh," another quipped.

"In the Balkans," Ezra Pound chortled, "the bards in the

the international stage—housed at the UN—an entertainment mall like Broadway—a version of what the Broadway stage has become: sound and light—

"Smoke and mirrors—plus hedge funds, baselines, and Muzak."

"I suppose," a voice said, "people will stop going anywhere further than their computers to further their ends."

"Yes, the information age. Binary systems: all truth an infinite series of variations on the given and its opposite—but only if you reach *out* through the Internet, not by forsaking the daylight kingdoms of the mind to go down into the sunless seas of the communal cyberpsyche in these so-called *search* excursions that are like nothing so much as the morbid compulsion for *caving* that has lately—"

"Surfaced?"

"It reminds me of the hours and hours and days and weeks we spent at policy in my day," the baritone Mamie Eisenhower mask declared. "So, you see, I begin to understand these *delving* needs."

"Sure," an Adlai Stevenson mask hissed to one side, "the way science is always *beginning to understand* the human brain."

"Oh, yes, down *we* went, into the sinkholes of international intrigue, breathing as it were special mixtures of gases —information and disinformation sucked up by our Central Intelligence Agency sump pump providers—weeklong investigative and interpretive expeditions, often involving our being turned as it were upside down and thrust underwater, or subjected to crawls through long twisty passages lined with jagged thin-skin-shredding protrusions of all-too-human value judgment—from which we would emerge in the wee hours, having slept in our clothes or not at all, and having no more of that world's entire truth that was revealed in the narrow cones of light cut by the tiny lamps of our poor minds—with a nearly depraved craving for doughnuts."

"I think the double religion of *television* and the California

New Age is what will save America—advertising a pure ecology and a renovated national psyche—so much healthier than the reincarnated Civil War battles popular in this region."

"Excuse me, they are *not* re*incarnated;* they are purely *spectral*—nevertheless they heal. You don't even have to go to the *sites,* though they are nice for picnics—which is what happened in the actual conflict: people went out and had picnics and watched the battles—Bull Run, for example, just a stone's throw from D.C. And re-enactments are both so much more exciting *and* so much more *elevating* than *politics*—all these dreary Republicans and Democrats . . . who don't even *dress* differently."

"Neither do Serbs and Croats. Neither, despite their *hvratski*—that's alphabet—being rendered in two entirely different sets of characters, do they sound different over the telephone."

"It isn't," the Ezra Pound mask declared, "as simple as that. If you want to know why the Balkans make incessant war, it's because of the *bards*—the last oral tradition in Europe. They *depend,* as surely as Homer, on war—and of course Homer was a multitude of careerists singing for their supper. *Only* in the Alexandrian period, when epics were written *down,* did war stop."

"Well, that *is* an ingenious explanation," the Mary Todd Lincoln mask declared. "And it makes *Gone with the Wind* more important than ever."

"Oh," a Columbine mask declared, "Ah jus' *adore* stories 'baht the Woah of Northrun Aggression—all those gleaming *sabers* and yellow *sashes* our men wo-ah. Yellow sashes soaked in red blood—I declare, it's enough to make you weep foah a finah time!"

"The woman is mad, obviously," somebody whispered after a long pause.

"The Madwoman of Shiloh," another quipped.

"In the Balkans," Ezra Pound chortled, "the bards in the

tavernas are still re-enacting the Battle of Kosovo for the price of a slivovitz!"

"Well, my minister—*he's* a channeler and Web re-enactor—says he understands the Yugoslav wars as he never did Vietnam. He says, as in the South, devastation must be endured so that a new nation may be sown in the very horror of the mass graves."

"Really. Do you suppose if we gave the Balkans computers, they would get interested in re-enactments, and *channeling*—sort of like *bumper cars*—and stop doing the real thing?

"Well, I've got my *own* scheme to go on *Larry King* with—I call it the Great Palindrome. Do you realize 1991 was a palindrome year—and so is 2002, the year of both the Balanced Budget and the Tribulation? That's twelve years.

"The first six—which began with the Gulf War—will last until January 1997, the second Clinton inauguration—after which, for the next six years, *history will run backward*, until the second and *final conflagration*—Armageddon—will, as so often predicted, take place in the Middle East . . . or on the plains of Kashmir . . . somewhere like that."

"Whoever it was said whatever they said about history's tragedy repeatin' itself as farce would be right home here, and I don't see the harm in it."

"I agree—farce is *healthier entertainment* than war: it's *decaffeinated.*"

". . . And if you want to call me a fascist, well right then, go ahead, but *somebody* or *something* has *got* to unite, purify, and energize, if not the nation, then surely *my* ethnic class, the White Anglo-Saxon Protestant, that has indeed been put under a strain the like of few in history. Beset by internal divisions, the fear of decadence, *and* tumultuous social change. *There*, I *said* it!"

". . . that the computer and modems downsize the globe, enabling adepts to vault over walls of secrecy and control erected by governments . . ."

"You *do* know, don't you, the three ways computers are the same as men? One, they'll do whatever you tell them to, if you only just turn them on and push the right buttons; two, the best part of having them plugged in is the games you can play with them; and three, big power surges knock them out for the night."

". . . and like today's cavers, we were unique in that as we progressed we destroyed with our every breath the very environment that gave us employment—significance, if you will, or at any rate *use*—and now our like has been replaced, by the heroes you read about in spy novels who wangle a few precious computation minutes on a Cray supercomputer, jealously guarded behind windowless walls at the stone heart of the CIA or the National Security Agency. Do you know what the government operating system is called? It is called UNIX—and it is it and not I that does remember everything. *Eunuchs,* as in the rule of same in Babylon!"

"So, do you think the Republicans will get Clinton the same way the Dems got Nixon?"

"Nothing in D.C. happens the same way twice."

"In actual fact, nothing in D.C. happens the same way *once.*"

"Meanwhile, you might look up at your streetlights next time you're out wandering in this city of bloat, wreck, and shadow. If you see a small white box attached to the top of a lamp, imagine millions of bytes of information coursing out into my machine like bees to a hive. That's Ricochet."

"*Ricochet?* So you have joined a *militia*?"

"Very funny."

"I do not intend it to be funny. The militian issue is a crucial one of our time, and the trial of Timothy McVeigh *the* trial of century's end. I shall not be able to keep away from it; I shall become as obsessed, I foresee, as others were by that circus in Los Angeles. And I *ask* you—*is* the vexed question of whether or not some illiterate uppity cokehead nigger *did* or did *not* off his white cokehead slut wife and an uninvolved passerby of the Jewish persuasion in some overpriced neighborhood of that hellhole long overdue for dissolution into the Pacific Ocean to be compared *in any significant way* with the *tragedy* of this poor boy *rebuffed* by the country he loved not wisely if too well and driven by desperate voices to an act of high symbolic holocaust?

"Well, though I cannot see your faces, I can tell by your silence that I am safer with the other topics, so back to them.

"There are systems that satisfy your needs, and then there are those like Ricochet that satisfy your *desires*—thin-client architecture systems with built-in keyboard *scanners*, incredible 3-D arcade-quality *graphics*—the three Ds are for dark, damp, and *digital*. And *even a wireless mouse!*"

"Plato said in *The Republic* that any man given the power to be invisible would not be able to resist doing evil."

"We persist in thinking Plato's *Republic* is a wise document, many if not all of whose precepts we ought to consider when we consider government. But its arguments proceed from *deduction*, and if Freud proved *anything* it's that *anything* can be *deduced*. Logic is the smokescreen of thought, not its generative principle. I suppose the more women we let in, the more logic will be snuffed, until not even lip service to it will seem necessary. We can then proceed to government by *sortilege*, by *incantation*."

"Hitler did all that—and what I find naive is the belief that today's power holders cannot rely on religion, tradition, and obedience to solidify their rule—"

"That modernity demands rational reasons behind its rules?"

"Exactly—such variables as anarchic longings and romantic appeals to popular will may be called *dangerous*, but don't call them *irrelevant*. Combine liberalism with modernism and you are left with the overthrow of authority and the endless search for its substitute."

"You don't need to *search* for the *substitute*, all you *need* is the right *substitute* for the *search*."

". . . And I keep wondering, What if Habermas is *right*?"

"Urban America *is* a ticking social time bomb."

"The *tree* of the Republic is so distressed it has begun to *girdle itself*, circling itself with its own roots, and tightening . . . tightening the circle inextricably, until, inevitably . . ."

". . . *Moreover*, it is no mystery that only a decade *after* the publication of the book, construction began—in the middle of a *civil war*—on a *great white dome*."

"Modeled, we're always told, on the magnolia."

"*Nonsense*. A great white *hump* rising out of a *sea* of turmoil—it *couldn't* have been clearer!"

"Interesting. Do you suppose Melville was pleased?"

I was standing by one of the long windows looking out at the illuminated Capitol and the Washington Monument and the planes landing at National Airport as the sun set over the Potomac. Max Harrington came into view and collared me about Rain. I turned my back to the view of the Capitol dome while Max ranted on behind me.

"The senator in his goodness has created a monster who thinks he can actually represent an *issue*. He's undoubtedly on some drug. 'O full of all subtlety and all mischief is the child of the devil'—Acts 13:10. If he continues in the face of the senator's debility, well, he'll have to be *dealt with*."

I couldn't help shivering, longing to be away from all of it—the time, the place—and as if to speed me on my way, my D Street neighbor John walked up, in his angel costume, his halo a little bent from dancing, and handed me a small tape recorder.

"Here, I saw this at the foot of the sycamore as I was going out. I think it may be something you'll want to listen to. I'm afraid I have already."

I switched it on. The voice was Rex Vavasour's.

"... Then Bobby cut a deal with Mary Hoo-er. 'You get rid of the Kingfish, and you leave the weepin', wailin' niggers to *me*. I'll win easy in November and you're safe—that's my blood oath.' Well, Mary said, 'Fuck *him*! I'll get rid of the Kingfish all right, and take care of that lying little Mick scumbag next!' That *Mary*! People who said she was a sly old fox got it *all wrong*—

"Mary was exactly what she looked like: she was that ole *hedgehog* who knew *that one big thing*—and kept it, along with Dillinger's—right handy in her desk drawer to take out and blow on and *use*."

I saw Max go pale as others' voices intruded.

"... people whose views on international relations have been forged by the configurations and conflicts of an earlier time."

"But—whose *haven't*?"

"... yet another Washington book—urgent and soggy, like amphetamine and gin used to be in August; gobbets of interesting *disjecta membra* dish adrift in a tumbling onrush of breathless gossip. No distinction between real killers and those who come only to watch."

"That must be me," a Venetian man-in-the-moon mask declared. "I don't advocate anything—I just came down for the ball."

Suddenly Rain and the senator came up the grand staircase together, arm in arm, in plain dress. Galt walked right up to Odette, who held her ground. Looking around at the hall he declared,

"The joy of woman is the Death of her most best beloved
Who dies for love of her
In torments of fierce jealousy and pangs of adoration.
But an honest joy does itself destroy for a harlot coy.
It is an easy thing to triumph in the summers' sun.

It is an easy thing to rejoice in the tents of prosperity.
The man who permits you to injure him deserves your
    vengeance:
He will also receive it: go Spectre, obey my most secret
    desire
Which thou knowest without my speaking. Go to these
    Fiends of Righteousness
Tell them to obey their humanities and not pretend
    Holiness
When they are murderers."

"You must look after Rain now, Jack," Odette declared, with perfect composure.

Skipping the conga line (so *fifties*, so retro, like D.C.) I joined Odette, observing from the gallery, doing a kind of *"Per pietà"* over the masquerade—outlining the end of her D.C. stay in terms of a classic Venetian Italian commedia scenario.

O.J. took the stage ("Aretha is not going to have the whole of the evening to herself"). He first recited a passage from the ship diary of Niccolò Stolfo—see above—then, with Delmarva at the piano, sang "Beautiful Dreamer" in a most dulcet tenor, creating a really haunting Al Hibbler effect in the refrain "sounds of the real world." Vana was so charmed by said sound, she asked for an encore—whereupon he played his double-ace full house: from Al Hibbler to a sort of souped-up Johnnie Ray, ripping right into "La vita è una cosa tremenda" from *Livia Serpieri*, streaming real tears from blue-black eyes on "di morire all'alba," and from there, without pause, into "Vesti la giubba." It drove the astounded audience—some of whom remembered him from the Cosmos Club—bananas. "Ain't nuthin'," he shrugged to the *Washington Post* style reporter. "Jes' learnt by playin' de *nose trumpet* and then puttin' woids t'it."

Whereupon he encored with Turiddu's passage of desperate jocularity that begins *"Oh! Nulla! È il vino che m'ha suggerito,"* and swung into the finale—*"Per me pregate Iddio!"*

Vana immediately promised him a career—would he come to Italy? "I happen to have my passport with me, ma'am."

Rain bolted: I thought, this is it, he's going berserk. Galt looked completely helpless. To calm Rain down, Ornette ran after him, stopping him on the grand staircase, handing over his passport, saying, "You go—you be me. Make the bitch spend a nickel more for an Indian." Vana was aghast: it was Phil's Indian joke come to nightmare life.

Suddenly the Feds—Secret Service—materialized. Rain, like a rabbit, disappeared down the stairs and into one of the corridors, Ornette looking after him, intoning, "La commedia è finita." As the SS gave chase, he declared, "That boy knows every tunnel in the place; they won't get him." He then pulled me aside. "It is said: Beware the flood of Rain in Washington's low, lying areas, as when you go to find him, find him you will, in the Underground in Dupont Circle." Then he turned to Delmarva.

"Bye, bye, Miss Fly. I am off—but not like that Candy-Ass, expectin' the best of all possible worlds."

DELMARVA: You gonna send for your things?

"Sister Fly, I plan to get me all new things. I am goin' to a whole new fishbowl—to lunch at a place called Biffi Scala. Bye, bye shoo-fly pie in the sixth floor cafeteria of the LC and to all the nasty growlin' from that Republican Club across the street how if POTUS gets re-elected they goin' *impeach* him—which is they gonna stand him up in that well in the House of Representatives and *pelt him to death* wit' the state fruit of Georgia, wit' that ole Newt leadin' the attack like the barker on the midway what he is!

"So, I am goin' to the levee, but not in no Chevvy—I have seen the Porsche the diva drives, and I'm goin' in *it*, in the *back seat*, woman, to see the worst world *evuh*, and there to attract a lot of *expensive attention*.

"I do not know if in fact that old Greek was right: if with a long enough pole you can move the world—but I *do* know, from watchin' Olympic sport, that with a long enough one you can sho'nuff *pole-vault* out of where you is *at*. So, I done made my vow to the Lord—" he did a little shuffle step to the side—"I *shall* go, to see what the end will be. I may be sendin' you a message of solidarity from the mayor of Venice—or the president of Italy—a lot classier than one from Muammar Gadhafi, yes?

"Believe me, I am fearlessly determined on a valorous future, and something of a realization of life—according to the four out of seven principles of Kwanzaa that I particularly espouse, namely Kujichaguila, Nia, Kuumba, and Imani. Do you watch after this wide wonderful country for me, and rest assured that when I return in triumph to tell my story, you will feature prominently in it. In fact my idea is we wind up as a *pair* in the Great Blacks in Wax Museum in Baltimore.

"Meanwhile, driven hole-high by fate onto the putting green, I leave you to represent the principles Umoja, Ujima, and Ujamaa at the African-American Civil War Memorial Freedom Foundation parade down the Mall on September eighth. Can you do that?"

"Aren't I a woman?" Delmarva rejoined.

He then turned to me and lifted the interdict against reporting him. Citing Paul Robeson, Marian Anderson, and Leontyne Price, he declared his intention to combine their qualities.

As the fireworks commenced I hailed a cab and headed one more time north by northwest. Thus did I finally encounter the totality of my past life at the Underground's Conventions Party.

While a thunderstorm raged outdoors, indoors videos flashed and hot ice machines spewed fog. Tacky effects, but they brought me back to myself. The "theme" of the evening ran from "voting booths"—curtained-off sex areas—to a section marked "The Hill."

At the "Conventions" spotlights played on the floor at random, looking more like searchlights from the ground *up*, as if to spot bombers or black helicopters. Behind a black curtain the sex arena—called "The Buddy Voting Booth," under which the legs of the contestants were showing—some in pants, some in bare legs; some in shoes, some barefoot.

(I remembered telling Gennaio, "I was always the match that lit the long slow fuse that exploded the room into the orgy . . ." Whereupon I was blown out, as it were. It probably saved my life.)

Some DJ with a sense of—humor? something—had just finished spinning Lou Reed's "Take a Walk on the Wild Side" and was into the Ramones' "53rd and 3rd" until a voice screamed, "*Erase* that retro shit! Play Tribe 8—play *Pansy Division!*" I noticed three drag nurses with big nametags—Norvir, Crixivan, and Viracept—walking about wagging fingers and passing out condoms to a section called "Page School," where boys were taking "chances" on "getting into" the "Senate Cloakroom," a dark area I could just about make out as decorated to represent the real thing.

Then the video screen lit up, and in its glow I saw Rain, standing at the bar, in agitated conversation with the bartender. I approached.

The bartender appealed to me—that is, he sought my help.

"This kid keeps comin' in here and pleading for me to put on *Viet Man*. I tell him it isn't on video—it isn't in any catalogue. He tells me that's because the CIA got on to it—so what am *I* supposed to do about *that*? I tell him I'll put on *Don't Ask, Don't Tell*, it's hot—and he starts screaming to me and crying about his lost twin brother. This kid is fuckin' *crazy*."

Rain suddenly turned cool—as in collected—and countered the bartender. "Are you down from New York? You have that glamorous Deca-diamond-cut Splash bartender look that makes the talent in this tank town look like flabby femmes at a circle jerk."

He downed his double-something. "Firewater to the Navajo!"

"I thought you were a Shoshone," I challenged.

"I was—now I'm a Comanche. A Comanche is a Navajo with *low hangers*! You're smart; you're about to get your diploma."

(There was that particular empty space on my Sagaponack bedroom wall.)

"He is my twin—Joshua. The senator only knew the half of it. Our father—who if he's in heaven, has by now turned it into the same kind of hell he made Tangier—he had that special talent—was one of your buddy Max Harrington's reprobate crew from college days who committed murder on board—a gay knock—and they hid him on Tangier, where he went straight—ha, ha—married, went to seed, and became the drunken father of twin boys.

"Joshua showed up when I was in Page School and tried to get me to come away with him. Said we could make a great career in the *twin* craze that was sweeping gay porn. We went to New York. The New York School made a quickie which was shown at the Big Top, with a 'reception' in which we did a live sex—no problem, we'd done it as kids all the time—backstage behind the screen while our images flickered on the screen. We repeated it all at the Gaiety, but a mafioso booked Joshua for the overnight and abducted him. When I went looking for him, they broke my leg.

"I went a little crazy and the senator was sent for and took me back. Funny about being a twin—it stays with you. Last month, when he went off his rocker and lost Mrs. MacGown, he came to me in tears and told me that now we would be the two Witnesses of the End Time in Revelations. But I've had enough of twinship.

"Once the senator took me out into Chako Canyon and made me take off all my clothes, and he laid me on a flat rock at the center of a wheel of rock-paved paths, and he held a hunting knife in the air over me and prayed—"

(Isaac on Mount Moriah. Miss Faith liked to say, "Y'could *pray* over it . . .")

"—and the angel came, as it did to Abraham, and ordered the senator to spare my life."

"Which is more than you and your twin brother did for your father. On Tangier Island. You're not a Shoshone or any other kind of Indian—have never so much as set foot on a reservation."

"Figured that out all by yourself, huh? Well, he was evil. Joshua held his head back and I slit his throat. Then Joshua went to work, gutted him, took out his fake teeth—just like he always used to boast of doing whenever he ate pussy. I remember when he was done he looked down and said, 'That was the ugliest fuckin' face on a human being—not that that mother-fucker *was* human. More like the face on a grouper. Just right for chompin' tuna tail. He *couldn't've* sired us: we're much too *fine* looking.'

"Then he threw the corpse into the Chesapeake and swabbed down the decks with Lysol. Those boat police would find the cleanest boat on Tangier when they came looking—only they didn't. Instead Max Harrington came by with some of his crew. Then Joshua ran away, and . . . well, you know the rest."

(I had the feeling there was a whole lot more.)

The drink had perked him up considerably.

"In Washington, *I hold the cards.* One single revelation of one single indiscretion by a member of the Senate and the mark gets a one-way ticket to K Street—in a camp chair under an umbrella on Fourteenth, selling *pencils* in the shape of rolled Ben Franklins."

THE BARTENDER: This one really is a charmer, isn't he.

I saw Rain's eyes shift again, as if to an accomplice.

"I know what you like to do; you like to watch."

In fact, he had a point, a metaphysical point, and though,

as Oscar Wilde points out, a metaphysical speculation has no relation to the facts of life as we know them, it has every relation to the facts of life as we do not. But although I derive some satisfaction from having been given the job of *watching out for* Phil, and the plovers—I didn't *like* watching (the party I hadn't been invited to had crashed anyway, without me; friends had died long before their time), but *I'd just had to*. And now I was like the three ETs at the bar in *I Married a Monster from Outer Space*. (They weren't the "real" guys, remember? The real husbands were hung on hangers in a closet back in the mother ship.)

He continued on the Conspiracy. The cover-up was never completely successful—he knows who killed JFK's former mistress Mary Meyer on the C&O towpath in 1965 and why James Jesus Angleton went to Mexico in 1970 to snatch Winston Scott's diaries. Also, the true secrets of Area 51 near Groom Lake high in the Sierra Nevada.

"I found myself positioned right at the nexus of the governmental, industrial, and service sectors of the eighties boom economy; how could I know it would be rent asunder?"

Whereupon he passed out. The bartender handed me a card. On it were the instructions: "When I pass out call this number. They'll come and get me—but you better leave me upstairs on the sidewalk. If they come down here, they'll torch the place."

I called the number. A voice asked me to have Rain *delivered* to Lafayette Park. I got him upstairs and into a cab.

He woke in the taxi. "If you turn me over to them, you'll never hear of me again. This is one flap too many for them."

"If I'm willing to walk away with your story, you should trust me. Anyway, I have an ace in the hole."

I asked the cab to drop us at the Hay-Adams, where they remembered me from the breakfast with Max: very D.C. I dialed the number a second time, told the SS relayer to check with Sundance, then bring the senator across the street from the White House.

In minutes—much faster than 911—the senator arrived with them. As he enfolded the sobbing Rain, I thought *covering cherub*, and then of the Father in Balanchine's *Prodigal Son*, gathering Eddie Villella up into his arms: always made me cry. But more, much more, of a redheaded fireman whose name I couldn't remember either, who, in the unlikely event he is still alive, would have white hair like that of Galt, who turned to me and, in all his senatorial splendor, proclaimed:

"Go tell them this: overthrow their cup.
Their bread, their altar table, their incense and their oath.
Their marriage and their baptism, their burial & consecration:
I have tried to make friends by corporeal gifts but have only
Made enemies. I never made friends but by spiritual gifts;
By severe contentions of friendship & burning fire of
 thought.
He who would see the Divinity must see him in his Children."

Walking out and past the Lafayette Park of *Advise and Consent*, I looked across at the White House. "The intoxicating power of the building," I'd read, "is such that once you are in it, you never want to be left outside again."

I'd been in it twice; I never wanted to see even a picture of the place again in all my life.

We took off at last from National Airport. Washington gleamed below serenely, like Rex V.'s model. The cabin was a situation room after a crime, where the pieces are put together. Odette had taken off the Dior—which lay draped in tissue paper over a seat—and climbed into a pair of full-form khakis.

O'Maurigan spoke. "'I should not have trusted a page,' the senator says in *Democracy*. 'Nothing is secret here long.' Of course that here is not there. The Trylon and the Perisphere?"

"Yes, as clear as—"

"An infant memory. Clearly you were taken out to Flushing Meadow. And there would have been planes landing too —at North Beach Municipal Airport, before it was La Guardia—where we're headed. So there was here—for a time: a rescue time."

(Maybe it was that fireman with the red hair took me.)

"Here, or there," Odette declared, "I don't care. Like Maud at the end of *Democracy*, I must escape to Egypt."

"The Senate building," the O' said, "is a replica of the Great Library of Alexandria, and the Washington Monument an obelisk."

"A *blank* obelisk. Anyway, it's Lady Bunny's turn: we really should not be in the same town at the same time doing scenes. I spied her and her aggressive aides-de-camp barging through the gate at National Airport—itself an indicator: our crowd was always content to descend at the bus station—and you didn't need X-ray vision to clock the big-hair volume rods in their equipage.

"Yes, I shall rerun Bella Darvi as the Woman of Babylon in *The Egyptian* and, slathered in *eau de Nil*, visit the Temple of Dendur at the Metropolitan Museum, then go and sit in front of Cleopatra's Needle—a real obelisk. And if I ever need to think of a pyramid, I shall get Delancey to show me his number ones. Yes, I shall relish my chair days—I understand just what Bess Truman meant when she said she was glad to get back to Independence and out of her girdle! Like Scheherazade telling her tales and lifting the cup to her lips from time to time, I shall tell my tales of those who have died for love . . . or hatred."

Then to me: "I cherish your story, dear, as you well know, but that boy is the very idea of timeless, trackless wilderness itself. And the *hold* he seemed to have on you—well, it flicked me on the raw, so it did, as the rozzers used to put it in the 'Dilly."

O'M said, apropos leaving D.C., "It's certainly for the good. Whether or not it is for all time remains to be seen, but it is a good time to get out, just before Christmas in August, which must be *the* most horrific event of the whole Washington year. And just as the nine hundredth and last Book Bag quiz in the *Washington Post* has been answered." (That *number* again. I don't even know what it *means*.)

"For as has been said, there's nothing worse than being killed away from home by strangers."

Eleven / Terminal

The mobile, with dialogue balloons attached, lay on the floor like some elaborate kite, or the AIDS quilt, or a picture section, each balloon connected to a syntactical string, as if to a finger, by another variation of the verb "said," or like some dusty crystal droplet on the old chandelier in Max Harrington's mother's disused Kalorama ballroom. How to get the thing aloft? *Oh, just pull it.*

The debriefing, as told, took place just prior to Phil's return, after which I declared I never wanted to hear about D.C. again—as, sitting out back under the horse chestnut tree, we looked down to the pond, on which Vinny and Matt, two boys (to me), drifted along face-to-face and laughing in an old rowboat.

"Companions," O'Maurigan declared, "out of some utterly summer-idyllic, painterly American story."

I was checking the printout. "Not a book exactly, is it—not quite the hidden narrative of our time. The five-sided Chinese box full of other Chinese boxes, the circus clown car over the trapdoor—speaking of which . . ."

I reached over and picked up the *New York Times*, revealing the headline:

MAY-DECEMBER RITE ROCKS CAPITOL CRADLE

SENATOR WEDS FORMER PAGE IN GAY
MAY-DECEMBER SENSATION

Galt had become a major gay hero. The *Advocate* had been set to out him, but when instead of sending Rain back to the flight deck at St. Elizabeth's he saw the light of God's gay truth and proposed, it took up the story from the *Washington Post* and ran with it, until every gay rag in the country was forced to follow suit with front-page features on the nuptials.

"A la *June Bride*," Odette cracked, taking up the paper and busily scanning the story as if it were all fresh news to her, "without the complications. Too bad, it's the complications that make the picture. Also *very* like *Louisiana Purchase*—one of your mother's early tryouts, dear—with Irene Bordoni and Vera Zorina, second-act dream ballet by Balanchine. And don't miss this: it says the bride has been recently confirmed—or reconfirmed—in the Metropolitan Church of Something Spiritual."

The wedding took place at the reflecting pool beneath the columns in the Arboretum, and the reception in the Bishop's Garden of the National Cathedral, around the statue of the Prodigal Son. (I pictured the curious altar boys spectating from the vestry.)

O'Maurigan said, "You know, I find it odd that in this story the number eleven appears again and again."

"Even in K Street," Odette murmured from behind the *Times*, "the eleventh letter of the alphabet."

"Fascinating," I offered.

"In addition," she continued, putting the paper down, "eleven, besides being the number to date of the discovered black holes in the universe, of the states in the old Confederacy, and of the number of places on the Most Endangered List of the American Historical Preservation Society—is half the number of the old Capitol columns in the Arboretum.

"New York is the eleventh state in the order of ratification of the Constitution, and there have been eleven Presidents, starting with Roosevelt and the war. There are eleven caves from which the Dead Sea Scrolls have been dug, and there were, as I recall, in the old days, exactly eleven Irish bars between Forty-second and Eighth and the Greyhound bus terminal on the one side of the avenue at Fiftieth, and Madison Square Garden on the other: Dublin House, O'Donnell's, Kieran and Dineen's, Larry's, the Eagle, Gilhuley's, Pete Moran's, Morahan's, McGreevy's, Micky Walker's, and the Ringside."

(There's an Eagle in D.C. now, on New York Avenue. Leather and denim. I never went—not for want of costume, but because I kept thinking of Ganymede being carried away by Zeus in that form, as I'd been at a similarly tender age by the American eagle in what had seemed a magic carpet ride into the World of the Future as predicted by General Motors at the New York World's Fair of 1939, but had turned into something—but you knew that.)

"There are," I declared, "eleven hundred marines in residence at the barracks on Eighth and I streets, SE."

"Well, there you are."

o'm: Richard Feynman once said that there are about one hundred billion—that's ten to the power of eleven—stars in a galaxy.

"Eleven, in Shoshone," I ventured, "is *She-maie-ro-se-maie-to-a-gan.*"

"But," Odette continued after a long pause and a long look down to the pond, "I also like the number four—it says it all. If you consider the story's four main characters—"

o'm: We three.

odette: Yes, and one other.

o'm (to me): I have a notion he means we three and God.

odette: Or the Omniscient Narrator.

"This story," I protested, "hasn't got an omniscient narrator . . . has it?"

ODETTE: Of *course* this story has an Omniscient Narrator. Doing a fan dance, maybe, but omniscient nevertheless.

"Also, I find it fascinating that four is the maximum number of points of energy that can be located on a sphere such that each spot is the same difference traveling on the surface of the sphere from every other spot."

She then remarked that if their flight back had gone down, Rain would diabolically survive as the talking black box.

"*Vergangenheitsbewaltigung*. Remonstrance."

"*Vergangenheitsbewaltigung*-ho!" (O'Maurigan).

"*Vergangenheitsbewaltigung*-hoyotoho!" (Odette).

"It is," O'Maurigan continued, "a sometimes depressing, sometimes elating, but always intractable fact, that to the very degree that one becomes involved in the affairs of the world, one perforce confesses that one has no life of one's own to speak of."

"What about show business?" I demanded.

"Apart from the great fact that there's no business like it? Well, at the very least it can be said that it tries to encourage people to look to themselves in ways politicians dare not."

"So Rain got on the front page above the fold," I pressed him. "Does this mean the story has a happy ending? Do they live happily ever after, or is it the opposite?"

ODETTE: The opposite, dear, of they lived happily ever after is he dropped dead on the spot.

O'M: I don't call that the opposite. "He dropped dead on the spot" is more usually followed by "She lived on and had a ball." Unless, of course, she'd booked a seat on flight 800 to Paris.

ODETTE (to me): Your mother, dear, is terribly affected by that possible sabotage, for how she does resemble the old aircraft— over sixteen thousand flights, with a typical number of cracks in the front end, found and repaired again and again. Plenty of redundant structure responsible for carrying any number of passengers. Given her reputation, more likely to be shot out of the sky rather than come unstuck in takeoff.

"But if," O'Maurigan suggested, "the conflagration was the result of a loose spark from the faulty scavenge pump?"

"Well . . ."

"What *do* you believe is true," I asked O'Maurigan. "Is anything?"

"Everything between the lines. The notes in the spaces, put there by the close reader to complete the tune: that's true. Put another way, solids and spaces are of equal importance. Forces of action and reaction, expansion and contraction, where all is risk."

(I had asked Gennaio, in session, why at the words "the President maximally exposed" I'd gotten an erection, right there in the White House. "Because you're getting healthy. It would depress most people—attempting to stuff the spontaneous aggression such a statement prompts. If the sacred king is exposed, one must either fuck him or kill him. All the apostles who wanted to kill the Redeemer fled; Judas, who wanted to fuck him, sold him, in a stifled symbolic gesture that led directly to his suicide.")

"I think," Odette said, "the soap opera of Columbia the Gem of the Ocean ought to be entitled, like a recent treatise on soap opera I've come across, *No End to Her*—for it, like them, with its denial of closure forces us to honor a female perspective."

O'M: A transvestite perspective—

ODETTE: Same difference.

O'M: —thus escaping the linear narrative of traditional male genres.

(At long last, I thought, a working definition of "same difference.")

"But tell me this," I persisted. "What of the inherent tensions between realism and analogy, authenticity and art?"

"Fuck 'em," the O' declared. "I will allow that like the little scenes in the latter part of the *Aeneid*, some of the conversations in your account come across as perfunctory. But, as David Markson suggests, this is perhaps precisely what Virgil had in mind."

The party: Vinny and Matt had engineered the whole thing—caterers, etc. Then they left together to go to pick Phil up at the airport, leaving us, the Three Fates, with the knitting. Then Phil was back, with presents for everybody (including a model of the Temple of Concord in Agrigento in pink porphyry that created a sensation and got us talking again about the awful white of the classical-temple buildings in D.C.) and stories of Vana and Ornette (dubbed *Il Tutsone*) together in Rome that have rocked Italy—including a rumor that they have been booked together in *Cavalleria* and *Pagliacci* at La Scala. ("More likely," Odette snapped, "she'll get the poor Jackie librettist to include something unveiled about Malcolm X.")

I was back home, in the kitchen, with Vinny and Matt and the caterers. Odette and O'Maurigan had gone to the train station to pick up guests from the city and I could hear the locals under the horse chestnut tree, quacking over the cocktails.

"So Delancey is writing a new book; are we in it?"

"If we're not, we will have been."

"I do hope we are. I've never gotten past the third or fourth cut of anything—unless you count survival itself. What is the relation of this book to the pieces in the *Star*?"

"Odette says they are the pot of tea and this will be the sediment—the leaves; you know how she loves to do tea leaves."

"And we're in it; I like that. If you can't be a character in fiction, I always say, then be a footnote in history."

"Do you really prefer fiction?"

"Oh yes, I do. I don't mind these memoirs—there is some

value in reporting what went on, more or less; but to create a situation in which the *only reality* is the one you make happen on a page? Darling, who can doubt the moral superiority of that?"

"Delancey says his book is like a big crowded crosstown bus—in which he can't get anybody to move to the back."

"I *love* the back of the bus—when there are seats."

"They say the back of the plane is much safer. Do you think they really tried to blow up the President's plane?"

"I haven't any idea—but then I've succeeded pretty much in this administration in giving up on the idealization connected with the unconditional meaning of truth terms. I'm hoping it'll be a beach read."

Vana called to wish us a happy anniversary. Ornette, it seemed, was already creating a sensation, just walking the streets of Milan, chattering away in Italian, decked out in Versace.

"Be careful you don't lose him to that tailor."

"Gianni only likes dancers, not singers—but *caro*, I have found a *winner*—he will be the Otello of the new century!"

(O.J. Thello indeed.)

"And you will of course return as Desdemona."

"Oh, *caro*, if I thought such a thing were even *possible*—"

"You would confess your scarlet sins and go back to church."

"Don't be crude—I am often seen in churches."

"Actually, I think it's a divine idea—about Ornette, I mean."

"Well, if you do, then *you* must go back to church with Filippo—to make many, many novenas, because I *have* been thinking of *Francesca da Rimini*. The boy would create a *revolution*, and I—didn't you once tell me your church was named for the Santuzza?"

"It was Saint Rosalie's—it's been renamed Our Lady of Mercy." (Phil had been outraged. "Povera Santuzza!" he kept saying, and refused ever to go into the renamed church to light a candle for anything, traveling all the way to Holy Trinity in East Hampton in all weathers to attend to his private devotions—upon which, needless to say, I never intruded my curiosity.)

As ice cream, cookies, and coffee were served, Vinny and Matt left together for the Swamp to dance. A little idle speculation was indulged in—along with the gooey Godiva chocolates—as to would they dance wildly, do drugs, or seek out additional partners.

"Not the type—they're a pair of healthy halfbacks."

"Who between them, you mean, make up the one beast?"

"Oh, stop with the metaphors from football; what are you, lesbians? Anyway, there are no more halfbacks, they're called 'wide receivers' now. My, these cookies are divine—what are they?"

"Phil makes them—he calls them *ossi di morti*."

"Charming."

"Sicilians understand death in life, it's true."

"What those two boys *are* is a couple of *throwbacks*—to the *William Higgins Class Reunion*."

"Oh, my *dear*, do you go to class reunions?"

"We're having one now, talking of death in life. I was just remembering something Odette said, right at this table four years ago, about Clinton—something about starched napkins."

"It was a starched handkerchief, as I recall."

(I was collecting the soiled napery; all our linen is Irish, from Brown Thomas, in Dublin.)

"Some conversations cast long shadows, don't they."

"Well, I don't care how center Clinton's gone—somebody will feed the poor—if it means we don't have to listen to any more of that liberal crap. The Rosenbergs were innocent... welfare works... the police are unregenerate fascists... the girl can't help it. Really, I don't understand people's behavior anymore at all."

"Matthew Arnold said that behavior is not intelligible, does not account for itself to the mind and show the reason for its existing, unless it is beautiful."

"Republicans still believe something like that."

"As if anybody at this table ever voted, or ever will vote, for a Republican."

"I don't know—with all those terrible stories . . ."

"Now really, does he *look* like a murderer?"

"Well . . . *yes*."

"Lindsay. Everybody voted for Lindsay."

"Delancey is voting for the President."

"Excuse me, he is voting—and *pining*—for the *Vice* President!"

(My secret love no secret anymore. Not since Carol Burnett sang "I Made a Fool of Myself Over John Foster Dulles" had there been such merriment as over my being smitten with the VP, reaching fever pitch at the "sister's deathbed" speech at the Democratic Convention in Chicago. I'd been at a few sisters' deathbeds, and when the camera panned to an *actual family*, I lost it.)

"Isn't one of those boys called Matthew—talking of beautiful existence?"

"Moreover, he can—Clinton—play golf and tennis and polo probably, and sing a solo, and row—all on Martha's Vineyard."

"Well, if you ask me, it's been an all-too-dismal campaign, exacerbating the issue of the multifaceted sickness in the nation's civic culture, the government's paralysis produced by the national debt, the atomization and the isolation of individuals produced by the entertainment-driven media, all increasing the fragmentation of what used to be a shared body of information."

"A reasonable response in terms of the present situation, but does it reflect the future?"

"Nothing reflects the future!"

"Don't quibble semantics—you know what I mean."

"Nabokov calls the future the obsolete in reverse—I think that's kicky."

"I was myself once a shared body of information."

"The obsolete in reverse—that's me, darling, backing the Oldsmobile out of the parking lot at Barefoot Contessa."

After dinner we watched the latest rage on cable TV— *S.P.Q.R.*, featuring Anastasia ("the high priestess of D.C. cult camp," according to the *Times*) as Aphrodite, an Athenian courtesan in Rome during the late Republic, supine on a *Quo Vadis* couch, underneath a banner emblazoned "Regnabo, Regno, Regnavi, Sum Sine Regno" ("I shall reign, I reign, I have reigned, I am without reign"), dishing the political conventions ("Caesar, Pompey, what does it matter, they're all crooks"). Max had put it on, of course, and Bam-Bam was absolutely brilliant. With no writer credit (obviously Max's own work), it had a real "Are You There" quality. I thought, Sidney Blumenthal would have to go to some lengths to best it.

Then came the late news, with footage of Clinton's Radio City Music Hall fiftieth birthday and more on the senator's wedding to Rain, flashing back to his July 4 oration at Union Station.

"I must say he's well-spoken for a senator."

"I'm so glad, but couldn't we have some live entertainment? Get Delancey to sing 'Lazy Afternoon.' 'Lazy Afternoon' is the 'Pie Jesu' and the 'In Paradisum' of the Requiem for Gay Life. 'A big pink cloud drifts over the hill' is quite nearly as unspeakably beautiful as the French choir of alto and soprano angels."

"The senator reminds me—I want Phil to tell his Indian joke!"

"Aw, what—again?"

"Please, Filippo!"

I stepped out the back door to look at the moon, gone from gibbous to full. Inside, for live entertainment, Phil was doing his Indian joke. I can't do it—but it's about an Italian immigrant and an Indian chief and a "Weigh Your Fortune" scale they both get on while waiting for trains in Grand Central Station. The punch line is, "You weigh a hundred and fifty pounds, you're still a guinea, and you just missed your train." Phil tells it perfectly each time, and everybody screams with laughter, which never ceases to surprise and delight him. All of which was happening just then.

I began to feel feverish. Walking back inside, I began writing a note to leave on the kitchen table—something I used to do years ago under different circumstances, when indisposed of a midnight—when Odette came in.

"Going up to bed? Me too—they can't really talk about us with us sitting there."

"I guess not—this isn't Washington, is it."

"No—and have you ever been so glad about anything, ever?"

"Have you got something to read?"

"I thought I'd try that *Sandman* comic you brought back."

Sitting up, I liked hearing the guests out in the garden, under the horse chestnut tree. I thought of the Sandman and began to conceive of myself as a character—an *aging* one— vainly talking back to the creator, a child.

And out the window the horse chestnut canopied the talkers.

"Is he really all right? Delancey's never gone to bed early in his life."

"Until a minute ago" (O'Maurigan).

"Mrs. O'Doyle will look in on him to make sure he is. I *love* that Indian joke."

"Do you *really* think he'll keep his promises?"

"Clinton? He might."

"What with all one's protectors either fled or dead."

"As a matter of fact," the first speaker broke in, "with somebody like Clinton, it's better if he *doesn't* keep his promises—it indicates there's a fair chance he won't carry out his threats, either—and that's much to be desired."

"In any case, it's important to exercise one's right to vote, but the very possibility of choice depends on a residual domain or agency that can remain free only to the extent that it remains unexamined. Did you know that?"

"As if a girl in an emergency *has* any choice other than the first unlocked door."

I remembered the virtues bestowed upon confirmation. I heard myself going over them with Odette:

"There were virtues . . . and then fruits. Charity, joy, peace, patience . . ."

"Yes, dear, and I don't know if it's ever been pointed out, but if the Proustian madeleine is the Eucharist—and it is, without question, as surely as strawberry tarts are cunts—then that moment outside the Guermantes mansion—the uneven pavement turn—is certainly confirmation. We can tell for sure, you see, because it does *hark back*—"

"To Venice."

"To Venice, yes, but to the *baptistery* in San Marco. Confirmation, remember, is precisely the sacrament that *enables* that which baptism merely *entitles*."

"I never was confirmed; I only memorized the list of virtues."

"In which you require no instruction. As to the sacrament, we can correct the oversight when Vana's Martini becomes Pope."

The first of the twelve fruits, I remembered, was Charity. There she stands on the Civil War monument, in D.C.—at the intersection of Indiana and Pennsylvania Avenues—shielding a little boy under her cloak, with the legend "And the greatest of these is Charity." ("Well, dear," Odette said, "what with Faith broken and Hopes dashed on both—on *all*—sides, what else could they carve into the stone?

"The fact is, all the virtues are unstable. Faith presents itself only on those rare occasions in life when your ego is intact; Hope is, like all middle states or middle children, the most calculating—as has been said, it is the seeming encouragement of a faith the facts have never warranted, and would be offensive to the logic that is sometimes the only faith one has . . . except that outcomes are so nearly never the result of logic—and Charity is, after all, what they give you with anything they've got left over, or your last bargaining chip.")

"There's that mall," the first speaker was saying, "in Bridgehampton I've never been to. I should—it would make more sense than my driving the pickup to Two Mile Hollow every evening as I do, and sitting on that bench anent the fuck-pit dunes."

"Do you go there?"

"Yes, I do. I like to watch—from a distance."

"'In a far recess of summer/Monks are playing soccer.'"

"There *are* no more far recesses of summer!"

"Nor trips around the world, eh, lickety-split?"

"Be that as it may—from my perch surveying the scattered wrack of ages, I make out easily the parts most visible as they lie there on their beam ends in the dune hollows—their agile fingers scampering up and down intrepid masts like—yes, testosterone is as potent as crabgrass, and the goings on back there range all the way from a long, slow slide into a narcissistic swamp to compelling dramas—which when they aren't suggesting Butoh, suggest a dialogue with some supernatural force guided by pre-established cultural patterns dictating the whole compound misdemeanor—or installation—as decrepit old men's lives circle the bowl.

"And as I sit there with the planes of my face exposed to the slanting rays of the setting sun, their aspect unmitigated by any cunning rearrangement of light source, I resemble some brush arbor circuit revivalist who's been hanging over hell all night like a fly in a spider's web watching the devil cooking cabbage."

(I thought, *That's* what I was doing all those months. "Oh, for the days when we were good," Miss Faith used to cry out in her down moods, "when 'the rail' meant *communion* and not *brass,* and we knelt at it to the strains of 'Panis angelicus,' didn't collapse to it in hysterics off the barstool to the wail of 'I Will Survive'!")

"Squat on a seeker's bench—gazing out at the Atlantic for salvation. As the poet says, '*Confundiéndome entre las arenas/siendo empujado por oleas de gente.*'

"I used to say—with Zola—that I came into this world *to live out loud*—but the only thing I ever got to do out loud was cry, and one day I said to myself, 'Unless life is all crying, I must rethink my strategy.' But now I ask, who was kidding who? After all, if life is what you make of it, then death is takeout."

"Nonsense, woman. If you put your mind to it you could regain all your former clout—and *use* it in the campaign. But you must stop tormenting yourself among the bladder wrack at Two Mile Hollow. Take another leaf from Matthew Arnold's book; go over to Water Mill and watch the Buddhist monks do their sand paintings. When they are through, they throw the colored sand into the Atlantic—to purify it."

"How sweet."

"Clemency. I certainly approve of that—especially now in August—whether the Rosenbergs were guilty or not. There's a reason why the old rabbis taught that from the beginning of Av we diminish happiness."

"But why do sinners' ways prosper?"

"Why do fools fall in love? Well, at any rate, our heyday, like the New York City Ballet, is finished—*over.*"

"Are you feeling bad about being old, dear, or are you feeling old about being bad?"

"*June*, stop *tormenting* Auntie! *Really*—the *crust!*"

"Oh, let him go on—if it's the truth you like. The fact is, I'd have much earlier taken a leaf from Delancey's book and gone home to bed, but that I've come to fear my dreams. Only last night I awoke from a ghastly one of beating chicken breasts with the flat of a cleaver, and the chicken breasts were *whimpering*. I needn't pay a head shrinker to tell me the meaning of *that*!"

"*I* remember that at confirmation you took another name—like when you came out, remember—your camp name?"

"Sweet of you to change the subject to adolescent rites of passage and new names—but it's too late. Happily, we have Delancey and Phil—neither has cause to fear his worst dream, since their best has come true—as our friends and *elected representatives* to the court—or, rather, the *Congress*—of Love."

"The senator Phil and Delancey his page?"

"Precisely—and now, darlings, I really must be toddling home to Toad Hall and beddy-bye."

Whereupon, cast as the page—the way in Spanish the role you take in a play is called the *papel*—I enacted my dream of Washington, for which I didn't exactly beseech the Sandman. (Everybody by now knows you ought to be careful of what you ask for—you might get it. What they don't know is to be attentive not of what you *don't* ask for, but of asking would it be all right if you didn't get *this*.)

The map—me in the tree, at the Navy Yard climbing toward the Mall, seat of memory. In that seat I remember the brothers talking at Lincoln Hall, and then from below, resembling a little voices under the horse chestnut, voices of D.C.

ODETTE: And now we see Columbia as Lola Montez, on display in the menagerie on the Midway.

A VOICE: The *tree* of the Republic is so distressed it has begun to *girdle itself*—circling itself with its own roots, and tightening . . . tightening the circle inextricably. Inevitably . . .

I reach the Mall and look toward the Capitol, the great white humpbacked whale, over which hovers the illusory image of the Speaker, an unlikely, if putative, Ahab, in Wellington costume. I hear Dick Fauquier say, "The optics of the toy—you see what's not there. You see the Speaker of the House dressed for battle—but he is not there. He is sitting on the floor of the Rotunda, working on his tactics speech. But you can hear him over the PA." I do.

"The dilemma we have at the moment is the *regular order* is *not allowed* because we have a procedure on this bill *to fill the tree*, which prevents *a second-degree amendment* at some point *to get back into consideration of it.*"

Voices gather around the tree. "Fill the tree—fill the tree!" Then a word changes: "*Fell* the tree—fell the tree! Root and branch, way to go—what a camp: *fellatio!*" The drag queen from *The Delancey Retort* approaches with the axe. I scramble further out on a limb. I hear somebody say, "He's gone out on a limb for this assignment!" and at that point the limb I'm on breaks and I go crashing down to the Mall, where the show is in progress at the Silly Theater next to the Monument.

I hear my voice from the debriefing—suddenly I'm like George Burns watching myself on television. "I decided that D.C. looked like Venice—the Washington Monument was the Campanile, the Jefferson Memorial the Redentore—and there was the Ferris wheel, indeed powered like a mill wheel, by the Potomac, onto which, like into a chariot, I'd been invited for a spin, to check the overview from the high places of power."

Up the Potomac comes a paddle steamer called the *De Witt Clinton*. (For me "Clinton" was another movie theater in the old neighborhood, the one I sold candy in, underage, after school, where I first saw Stanwyck, in a comeback double feature of *Double Indemnity* and *Ball of Fire*, and where I got framed for holding burglar's tools and sent up the river.)

MAX'S VOICE: Clinton? No party man at all, of course—rather a startling piece of loose cannon, a force no party can count on—except one of a night's duration in a backroom—a confidence man on his own showboat.

On the boat in the card room, Harry Truman is playing the piano just like he did in that whorehouse in Kansas City.

A REVELER BEHIND A REX VAVASOUR MASK: Oh, it was a longer voyage than any sailor ever sailed from May to December that our haberdashing Harry took from those Prendergast Kansas City cathouse parlors to the pinnacle of power and his dealings with the striped-pants boys and other fauna of Washington.

On deck Madison De Witt is dealing the Tarot of Washington, in the manner of Melville's Confidence Man. Next to him sits Hillary Clinton, in costume as Dolley Madison. Hillbilly Goatboy, in Jefferson costume, approaches to gloat on the coming campaign.

"Me as POTUS, you as Veep, it's gonna be a knockout!"

"Yes, you have the mark of a true killer."

"Surely you mean champion?"

"Not to *me* you're no champion; but you're an *improbable* person—we have that in common."

"The people love me—I've proved it."

"In the state of being in love, in hypnosis, in psychoanalysis, and in the choice of leader, a kind of projection of the superego takes place. Whereas in superego formation an object relation is abandoned and replaced by an ego alteration, here an object relation begins by an object taking over regressively the function of a part of the ego. This is clearly seen in persecutory delusions, in ideas of reference, and on every election day."

Then Madison turns to me.

"They told me you came looking for the boy you were."

"You could say that."

"And found only reform-school material."

"That's what I was."

(O'MAURIGAN: You weren't Owney Madden; you were a Ganymede, carried away by the American eagle.)

"But is it what you want to be—to have been?"

"History can't be rewritten."

"Then why are we here—what is the theater for? I am essential to the theater. In it I toil not, neither do I spin, but I can—and do—*arrange* and *dispose* . . . and *in*dispose—isn't that so, Doll."

HILLARY/DOLLEY (a little despondently): Yes, Madison.

"Such a boy I would get for you that never needed reform. Do not smile, for as whooping cough and measles are juvenile diseases, yet some juveniles never have them, so there are boys equally free from juvenile vices. A boy with a sound mind in a sound body—such is the boy I would get you. If hitherto, sir, you have struck upon a peculiarly bad vein of boys, so much more the hope now of hitting a good one."

The boat is taking off for the Democratic National Convention. I'll catch up with it later: right now I have to get to rehearsal for *The Delancey Retort* at the Edge.

I enter the stage door to find that the day's shoot has been changed to *The Man Who Came to Dinner with the President*, starring O'Maurigan as Sheridan Whiteside, Odette as Lorraine Sheldon, and me as the small reporter. I panic: I don't *know* the part. O.J. and Gore are rehearsing a duet, "Beautiful Dreamer."

Anyway, the stage-door attendant (in the movies he's always called Pop: Guess who? Phil) is deep in conversation as I pass with another redhead. Owney Madden. Pop tells me, "Message here for you." He hands me the envelope. I open it. "The 1st case is short; the 2nd and 3rd are cases where any interruption might occasion errors difficult to be corrected.

The lead is indisposed; you're on tonight. So arranged August 11, 1996."

"Yeah," says Pop, "you gotta go on. They got a fire over at the White House. The mob started it. They want you to keep the people happy."

"I'm too *young* for Sheridan Whiteside!"

Hildegarde Dorsay sashays past, followed by O.J., Delmarva Fly. "Nonsense, chile," chides the Black Pearl of the Chesapeake, "it's a *benefit*! Get yo'self intuh that wig and beard and *pa-foahm*!"

I go out onstage, wigged and bearded, saying, "Here goes nothing." I spy a banana peel, but instead of avoiding it, walk right into it, slip, fall, and break a leg: feeling relieved. I say to myself: *I remember this—this is in the part.* I'm carried back into the wings, where Miss Faith and Miss Hope put a splint on my leg, while Miss Charity lights Owney Madden's cigarette.

Then, as Pop's voice intones *"in bocca di lupo,"* I start praying: *"San' Antonio della barba bianca, 'fa mi trovare ciò che mi manca."* I am carried quickly back onstage where Sheridan Whiteside's Christmas radio broadcast is set up as in the play. Odette sweeps in as Lorraine Sheldon.

Hildegarde Dorsay, O.J., and Delmarva Fly are trying to coax Odette into the mummy case—with the face of Eleanor Roosevelt where the face of Nephtys belongs—echoing her remarks upon leaving D.C. "Yes," Hildegarde mimics, "Ah shall rerun Bella Darvi as the Woman of Babylon in *The Egyptian* and, slathered in *eau de Nil*, visit the Temple of Dendur at the Metropolitan Museum, then go and sit in front of Cleopatra's Needle—a real obelisk. And if I ever need to think of a pyramid . . ."

"*You* get in, dear," Odette whispers to Hildegarde. "Ancient Egypt is so very *you*!"

Hildegarde, inside the mummy case, crosses her arms and looks to heaven, then addresses O.J.: "Ah don't know, chile—it's *numi* to be the heroine in the opera—and a credit to the race—but you know the profession is like politics: it can absolutely *entomb* you. You'll never more be a blackbird on the wing."

O.J. and Delmarva slam the mummy case shut. Eleanor Roosevelt's face on the mummy case orders them, in a kind but peremptory white-1930s patrician way, "Thank you, Delmarva. Now, James, will you kindly bring the car around? I have a coffee appointment with dear Hillary at the White House."

"There's a fire at the White House, ma'am," O.J. cautioned.

"I know, James—set by the British—they never stop trying—and Dolley and Bess and Hillary and I are the ones to put it out! Franklin and Mr. Truman and all the men are all gone to the convention—but I believe there's fire there too. Franklin is sure it's the fascist underground. I must say it's on days like this when I agree with Bess—it *would* be wonderful to just go home, take off one's girdle, and watch the rest of the world go by!"

"Well, ma'am," O.J. then said, "I will take you on this one last ride—in consideration of what you did for Miss Marian Anderson down there at the Lincoln Memorial—but after that I am off to the airport to catch the shuttle to New York and then the night flight to Rome, for I am to become an opera star."

"That is very enterprising of you, James. Many Americans have done well in Europe—and I believe you will set a better example in Italy than some, such as Ezra Pound and Clare Boothe Luce. So, when you leave me at the White House, walk right over to McPherson Square and board the Blue Line for National Airport—and be careful, James, not to board the Orange Line, or you will wind up in Vienna—although I believe some Americans have become opera stars there as well."

Fade out/fade in. Having closed the first half, I, a showbiz celeb, am on call at the convention. "But what will I *do*?" I wail. "Do your new one-man show," Pop/Phil says. "I have no new one-man show." "Then whaddya been doin' all this time I been in Sicily? And wear your Egyptian cotton white shirt, OK? The label says here it's made in America by a labor force of skilled textile workers."

At the convention: Max Harrington is standing by a wagon selling balloons and blowing them up from tanks marked "Helium reserves." As each balloon inflates, the sound of fast-forward dialogue is heard, and on each balloon a sentence appears.

There's a backroom. Hillary is jumping up on the round table, under the orange neon light, shouting, "It's *show time*! *I* am *FLOTUS, wife* of *POTUS*!" She jumps down to light Owney Madden's cigarette. Madison De Witt is glimpsed in the corner, advising Chelsea. "My dear, do you see that man over there? That's a *delegate*."

Hillary starts singing "I'm just a little girl from Little Rock." Chelsea Clinton runs in, followed by a chorus of Chelsea Girls, in tight-fitting sequined fifties fishtail dresses . . . thoroughly 1956. Madison De Witt enters. He pulls Hillary off the table and slaps her face. "From now on, you belong entirely to me, do you understand?" "Yes, Madison," she sobs. "That I should want you at all," he growls, "suddenly strikes me as the height of improbability."

Chelsea Clinton starts crying. As Madison leaves Hillary, and approaches, she jumps up on the table behind Holly Woodlawn and starts singing in German: "Vorüber—ach, vorüber" (the opening of Schubert's "Death and the Maiden"). Madison reaches up to the terrified child and sings, seductively, "Gibt deine Hand." The Chelsea Girls all start shrieking, "*Stop*—in the n*aaa*me of love!"

Owney Madden steps in. He slaps Madison across the face several times. All the girls surround him, vying to light his cigarette. I am approached by Billy Blythe. "This is thuh backroom, i'n't it?" "Yes, that's right. You've made it so far. I take it Dorothy Dean and Mr. Miss Fierce Thing let you in." "Yes. Ah

sort of had tuh agree tuh two of Miss Dean's demands." "Oh?"
"Yes, Ah had tuh promise tuh let her read from Kant's *Critique
of Pure Reason* at thuh Inauguration. That wasn't hard at all."
"And secondly?" "Well, Ah had tuh agree tuh *come up and
see her.* Tonight . . . upstairs—later, she said, after *The Velvet
Underpants.*"

Enter Dorothy Dean, in her little black Yves St. Laurent,
carrying her golliwog doll. She snorts at POTUS.

"Y-y-you *are* a *Rhodes* scholar, *aren't* you?"

"Yes man, Ah am."

"Y-y-*yes.* Y-you remind me of a cross between Kris
Kristofferson and Clint Eastwood—two *real* men. Y-yes, a real
man in this den of liberal fairies! D' y-you *drink*?"

"Uh—no, ma'am, I don't."

"Th-then I may not be able to have *anything* to *do* with
you. Nevertheless, come with me *now* to the backroom. It is
there, under the orange neon lights, that the *real* deals are
made."

Owney Madden walks over to Hillbilly Goatboy with an
unlit cigarette in his mouth. Hillbilly Goatboy lights it.

Bill as Gaylord Ravenal sings, "I drift along with my
fancy." Then, interrupted by Owney Madden, who points to
Madison De Witt lurking against a jetty with Chelsea, he
marches over, decks him, and, after going through his pockets,
rolls him into the canal.

"He's showing character!" a voice proclaims; "he's protecting his own!" The Chelsea Girls kick in with "Fish gotta
swim, birds gotta fly/They're gonna give the job to this
guy/Can't help lovin' his badass line." Al Gore appears and
quotes from *Earth in the Balance:* "Aficionados of the sym-
phony recognize a crescendo as the point of maximum instability of a piece of music, coming just at the point where the
music flows into a new equilibrium with resolution and harmony." Chelsea runs off up the showboat gangplank. Bill and
Hillary lift off into "Only Make Believe" and moments later

Chelsea reappears, with her devoted girls, now in nineties teen casual drag: they break into "Stand By Your Man."

The Ezra Pound Mask takes center stage. "It's time this whole charade was unmasked for what it is—a Venetian comedy—and this place for what it is—*Venice!* And this celebration for what it is—the *Redentore!*"

The Redentore because it is in dreaming, as Fritz Perls pointed out, that on the gestalt level everybody and everything in the dream is you (and yours). So in itself the Redentore dream illustrates, according to Gennaio, what force trauma has in shaping dreaming—even forty years on—and what dreaming itself does to the traumatized mind.

Odette, unmasked as a man by Ezra Pound, takes a mike, steps into a spotlight, and, taking off her wig and eyelashes, sings:

> "The party's over—
>   It's time to haul it away—
>   You get to bay at the moon,
>   They've hustled the goon away."

A dog act runs onstage, howling. Odette continues,

> "You pranced and screamed through the night
>   It seemed like your right
>   Peeing all over them."

Somebody yells, "Thank you, Miss O'Doyle, we'll be in touch with your agent. Next time could you maybe do it on a tightrope?"

Suddenly *I* am being called to the stage. It occurs to me that it doesn't matter what I do—because a celebration is cooking up as the roll of the states is called, and delegates start marching down to the Mall along all the state-named avenues of D.C. at the same time that all the gondolas are converging at the Jefferson Memorial: the Redentore is coming; the plague will be lifted.

I might as well just sing "America, I Love You" . . . which in gay voice I begin to do.

> "Americaaaa—I love you
> You're like a sweetheart of mine
> From ocean to ocean—"

The Redeemer of the Democratic Party—William Jefferson Blythe Clinton himself—is being lifted onto a donkey wearing a stars-and-stripes tall hat, and palm fronds are being strewn in their path as they progress downstage.

I feel like a combination of the Evangelist in the St. Matthew Passion and the MC of the Night of a Thousand Gowns. Al Gore makes his long-awaited entrance on the swan boat. Bill embraces him in manly fashion. They exchange a very long soul kiss and then beckon to yours truly. Phil runs in handing out tickets: "Admit One Delancey to the White House in the Company of Bill and Al."

Al/Lohengrin comes downstage. "Soon we will learn to recognize how crescendos in human affairs frequently signal the beginning of systemic, chaotic change from one form of equilibrium to another. The relationship between human civilization and the earth is now in a state that theorists of change describe as disequilibrium. At the birth of the nuclear age, Einstein said, 'Everything has changed but our way of thinking.' At the birth of the environmental age—"

Hillary/Columbia calls from her perch, "But do you *sing*?"

POTUS arrives downstage left, Bible in hand, and kneels, solemnly intoning: "Ah-William-Jeffuhsun-Billy-Blythe-*De*-Witt-Clint'n do solumly *sway-uh* t'execute thuh office uv President of the Star-Spangled Land of the Free To-nayht Show, Home of the—"

The chorus of drag queens intones, "Home of the Braves . . . home of the Red Sox . . . and hoooome of the Booooston Beguine." Chelsea runs down and kneels next to her father, singing, in a voice prettier than Margaret Truman's, "O mio babbino caro."

Fireworks bursting everywhere: the Redeemer is come. Hillary, in an Ozark Minnie Pearl voice, weighs in with "Square Dance, the Washington Square Dance . . . No round heels because the Washington Square Dance is square!" I reprise "America, I Love You."

A boy in the guise of Sebastian from Titian's *St. Mark in Glory with the Saints* runs up to me, in his underpants, imploring, "I am the son of Niccolò Stolfo—call me Nico. Take me to America, *signore;* I protect you from the plague!" "I'll take you if you change your name to Rico." "For love, *signore*, you may call me Rico!"

I open my Leo Lerman cape and, like the covering cherub, envelop him. As we start to leave, Odette approaches, singing, "Take off your makeup, the party's over . . . it's all over, my friends." I take off my makeup; I'm me now.

I woke to see Phil—the real one—outlined in the moonlight, standing in the window. As it used to say in novels, he then threw off his robe and slipped into bed.

The day after the first debate (October 7) the headline in the *Washington Post* read "Clinton, Dole Stress Differences." This was a *campaign?*

"Oh, well" (Odette again), "no more the high melodramas of our youth, in life or in politics. It's a new age."

So I went down to the one-room schoolhouse to vote; I felt a little bit like it was a straw poll for a straw man—a fascinating one in many ways, but not . . . well, let me just say that I kept looking at the picture on the *right* side of the campaign button.

Added to which, the walk down Sagg Main Street is always a bit of a spiritual obstacle course for a sensitive soul susceptible to nostalgia. Sagaponack is a small village *so* preserved that many persistent, abiding, self-regarding apparitions of former times intrude. Vintage cars, old barns, the schoolhouse (you could imagine Our Lady of Sagaponack appearing on the roof announcing her satisfaction at the Conversion of Russia, her displeasure at the wretched excesses of mall civilization impinging on Sagaponack from just north of the Montauk Highway, giving explicit orders for the restoration of St. Rosalie to Bridgehampton).

Too many apparitions of the dead in sunlight. Refugees from the weekly "Recovered Past" photo-identification contests in the *East Hampton Star*, and in particular of Truman (Capote, not Harry) staggering up and down Sagg Main Street in a blackout. (I'm afraid of that apparition. I shouldn't be; Truman was invariably nice to me, whether we ran into one another at the Swamp in the middle of the night or in broad daylight on the way down to the beach.)

Anyway, I voted for the face on the right side of the campaign button—POTUS's covering cherub. And maybe I voted for the covered one on behalf of all those boys from shit's creek I have known who did get sucked into that mire of arrogance, ugliness, and mendacity, only then to be told *get lost* (they did). And maybe because my heart was no longer really in it even for them, I just put my vote—again—where my heart still ought to have been.

And so it's come full circle, joining the list of other circles: The snow-scene crystal paperweight. The wheels within wheels: The Ferris Wheel of Fortune. The wheel of life, and its axis with jazz and cocktails. The stereopticon prison of D.C.

Rain's motorcycle's wheels. Rex Vavasour's perfect circle, zero.
The Metro's wheels. Roulette wheels. D.C.'s circles (remembering that White House circles are really, appropriately,
ellipses: "This whole powerful understanding of the world,"
Feynman said, "begins with the proof of elliptical orbits."
Thus while running around in circles always means getting
nowhere, *orbiting in an ellipse* is indicative of the plan of the
Cosmos or of the mind of God.)

The wheels on the little half-moon-shaped clown car that
stops over the trapdoor and lets out all the clowns—the senator's ten thousand men, astonishing the populace every time.
Dealers' wheels.

The *belew* moon. Vana's open umbrella twirling. The base
of the cone, the circumference of the cylinder, and the innumerable array of wheels that constitute the sphere—the cylinder, the sphere, and the cone being the three forms which are
said by artists to underlie all nature. All the pizzas POTUS
sent out for during the budget crisis. All the balloons with all
the dialogue in them (exhausting the helium reserves).

All the bubble butts on all the little hookers in the Beltway; all the decrepit old men's lives circling the bowl. Each of
the 139 pearls in Jackie's faux-pearl necklace. The circle of the
columns of the original Capitol in the Arboretum. The mechanisms on the Senator's old pocket watch. The nothing that
really changed.

(Or as Odette so memorably summed up my evaluation
and Homeric prophetic attributes of the events of that memorable season, in terms of the excoriating national melodrama
that ensued: *much that would come to pass did so.*)

Then just yesterday I was watching television news in the
aftermath of a spectacular foiled bank robbery in North Hollywood, and this woman comes on. She's a little overweight, a little anxious; she wasn't there the day before for the shootout,
but she might have been (like she might have been a tourist at
the Capitol on the day that Washington, if you believe Rain,

was almost hit by sarin terrorists). And she said to the news cameras, "Everybody's talking about moving away, but where are you going to move—Beverly Hills? This could happen anywhere. So you go to the bank, and you take out your money, and you spend it . . . and that's life."

That's life . . . in America.

A NOTE ON THE TYPE

This book was set in Janson, a redrawing of type cast from matrices long thought to have been made by the Dutchman Anton Janson, who was a practicing type-founder in Leipzig during the years 1668 to 1687. However, it has been conclusively demonstrated that these types are actually the work of Nicholas Kis (1650–1702), a Hungarian, who most probably learned his trade from the master Dutch typefounder Dirk Voskens. The type is an excellent example of the influential and sturdy Dutch types that prevailed in England up to the time William Caslon developed his own incomparable designs from them.

Composed by NK Graphics,
Keene, New Hampshire
Printed and bound by R. R. Donnelley & Sons,
Harrisonburg, Virginia
Typography and binding design by
Dorothy S. Baker